AMERICAN
MAZE

AMERICAN MAZE

Only One Way Out

CB

Ralph Peduto

Author's photo by Dina Scoppettone.
Cover design by Markos-Cory Moreno.
Interior design by DreamWriter (*Dreamwriterservices.com*)

ISBN 978-0-9841140-4-7

Printed in the United States of America

RIVER SANCTUARY PUBLISHING
P.O Box 1561
Felton, CA 95018
www.riversanctuarypublishing.com
Dedicated to the awakening of the New Earth

Counting the cars on the New Jersey Turnpike:

They've all come to look for America.

—Paul Simon, *America*

~1~

HELL HATH NO FURY

The night was clear, the moon full, and the dissonant symphony of squeaking bedsprings could be heard as Cal and Angela played their mattress duet.

The stately doors, her soft inner thighs, between which lies the mouth to that cavernous labyrinth wherein are held all of life's great mysteries, were now flung open wide for Cal to contemplate, explore, and penetrate. Her warm, moist sleeve held firm his thick, pulsating member. They were coupled at a place sight unseen.

Angela moaned. Her soft refrain blended with the steam-heated apartment's hissing radiator, then joined with the breeze that stole in between sash and sill, past billowing curtains before finally escaping with it out into the cool, black November night that enveloped the tall, mute, naked, deciduous trees standing guard over this street in the Marion section of Jersey City, silent sentinels deaf to the sounds of coitus.

A pair of headlights appeared on Broadway, then turned down Corbin Avenue exposing the bare branches of the young oaks that reached unsuccessfully for the late fall's early morning sky. The eerie silence of this sleepy neighborhood had been invaded. The source of the headlights was a slow-moving, brand new, 1963 black Chrysler LeBaron. It crunched to a stop, crushing a mound of dead leaves and dried twigs piled high alongside the curb in front of the well-maintained apartment building where Angela lived.

The man in the Chrysler turned the ignition key; the soft hum of the powerful engine died.

Angela stopped cooing.

A lone, great-coated figure emerged from the LeBaron. He swung the huge door; it caught with a solid clasp.

She changed her gaze from ceiling to window.

"What's wrong?" said Cal.

A look of apprehension crossed her brow. She did not answer.

Outside on the sidewalk, the man looked up to the slightly ajar second floor window; a glint of pleasure sparkled within his eye.

"Cal, I think that's my old man's car. He's supposed to drop by for a visit."

"It's twelve-thirty. Your dad's visiting?"

Angela, clutching at concepts, said, "Yeah, he wanted to discuss some business with me. He's like that. You know him!"

"Relax, he's probably still down at the club."

With that, Cal pulled her close, and once again they resumed their lover's rock 'n' roll.

But out on the street, at the front door, the man now fumbling through his key purse searched, selected, and separated from the rest the proper key; now, with a deft motion, he plunged it deep into the keyhole's well. The key, at the man's command, negotiated the tumblers within. He twisted it to the right. The foyer door opened wide before him.

Angela jumped up, "That's him! You've got to go!"

Cal reached for the box of Kleenex, pulled one out, wrapped it around his pecker, yanked off his condom, and handed it to her. Angela, at first unsure what to do with this gift, crumpled it into yesterday's newspaper and tossed it into the empty tin wastebasket where it hit with an echo, bounced, rattled, rolled, and settled.

Cal pulled on his BVD briefs, gathered up his clothing, and headed for the door.

"Not that way!"

Cal looked around the room, "What're ya talkin' about? That's the only way!"

"The window; you've got to use the window!"

"What window?"

She pointed to the slightly open window with its curtain gently floating in the breeze. "That window."

"But Angel, baby, we're talkin' two floors here."

"Cal, sweetie, through the window you've got a chance. Use the door and you're a dead man."

"The window... What a great idea! Why didn't I think of that?" He threw his clothes out of it.

"Now you," she said.

He scrambled out the open window and remained suspended on the sill by his elbows.

"Oh Cal, you look so cavalier hanging there."

He surveyed the girl within and the solid, dormant lawn below. She grabbed him around his neck. "One last kiss, my stud."

"You just might be right," he said.

They kissed. He let go.

A key went into the door. It opened two inches before being stopped by a chain—a knock.

Angela, tidying up the room, said, "Who's there?"

"Who da hell d'ya think?" was the deep-voiced reply.

Now straightening up the bed, she said, "Soapy?"

"No, Mother Goose."

Punching up the pillows, she said, "Here I come darling."

Naked, she opened the door.

There framed in the doorway stood Soapy, the driver of the Chrysler. He was six feet tall, twenty-five years young, and 195 pounds of pure muscle, making him two inches taller, thirty pounds heavier, and four years older than Cal. His six foot frame blocked out the vestibule light. He removed his hat. The light shone on Angela's lovely face. She stood five feet four with black hair and soft gray eyes, her skin radiating with the inner peace that comes with the orgasmic territory. She wavered in and out of the light, a feather in the breeze. Soapy threw his hat across the room; it landed on the bed. He picked her up and sauntered over to his hat. He dropped her; the bedsprings gave out that old familiar refrain. Now, when Soapy took off his greatcoat, Angela came to his assistance. She undid his belt, pulled down his zipper, and reached in for his key, the only one that could truly unlock the vast pleasure rooms deep within.

Meanwhile, among the bushes, Cal was scuffling around in stocking feet gathering up his clothing.

He hobbled toward the sidewalk, dressing along the way.

On the sidewalk, he pulled on his shirt. Bending down to tie his shoelace, he noticed the Chrysler parked right in front of him. He looked from car to open second floor window just in time to see it closing. "Why that no good ... Her father, huh?"

Casually, he meandered over to the LeBaron and bent down as if tying his other shoelace.

Another sound was now added to the night music: the hissing of thirty-six pounds per square inch of trapped air escaping into the dark. The rear, right, curbside tire of Soapy's LeBaron went flat.

Beaming with satisfaction on a job well done, Cal gave one last look up to the softly lit window before jive-stepping down Corbin Avenue toward Broadway.

***

The Rag Doll Nightclub was a lounge lizard's paradise located in the wild anything-goes section of Union City. The ceiling of the barroom, covered with mirrors, reflected the entire scene below, which consisted of a huge racetrack-shaped bar with padded-back stools and two go-go cages, one at each turn in the bar. Between these two cages was a small bandstand big enough to hold a small, four-piece swing combo, electric keyboard and all. A tiny dance floor was situated in the rear of the room where the weekend sharpies would hide and nurse their one-drink minimum while trying to score on the local babes who would come from all the surrounding neighborhoods to drink and dance the weekends away.

There was no band playing tonight, and the only people dancing were a middle-aged couple moving loosely to a very loud jukebox.

A phone started ringing over the loud music. Rayf the bartender picked it up and said, "Hello, Rag Doll."

The metallic sound of Cal's voice responded, "Rayf, I'm in a slight jam. You gotta come over and pick me up. I'm at the public phone booth on Tonnelle and Broadway."

"Hey Cal, what the hell's a matter with you? I'm tendin' bar, man. Like I'm workin', dig?"

"Hey, I called you for help, not for a lecture, man."

"What happened this time?"

"Pick me up and I'll tell ya." Cal hung up.

"That crazy sonovabitch," said Rayf to himself.

He threw his bar rag onto the bar and called out to the owner-bartender, "Jimmy, be back in a half-hour. Gotta pick up my mother."

"Yeah, I got your mother," yelled Jimmy-the-wise over the jukebox's din.

Rayf got into his 1956 two-door, hardtop, gray-primed Chevrolet and pulled out of the empty Rag Doll parking lot. On any weekend night this lot would be jam packed with lounge lizards' cars, but this being a Tuesday night there were only three cars parked in the back.

He drove down the Secaucus Road hill and took a left, heading south on Tonnelle Avenue.

Tonnelle Avenue runs north to south. It is the main, pot-holed, industrial artery that connects the George Washington Bridge at its most northern end to the Holland Tunnel at its southernmost end with the Lincoln Tunnel, smack dab in the middle. Rayf was heading south on this four-lane road that carried big rigs, straight jobs, oil tankers, steel-hauling flatbeds, and every other kind of vehicle that lugged supplies meant to stoke the great fires of industry and commerce. What Union City did for lounge lizards, Tonnelle Avenue did for hijackers.

Hijacking was spoken about as casually as the weather on the Third Street corner where Rayf and Cal hung out. And every so often a big rig with its doors flapping in the breeze, as empty as the center of a donut, would turn up parked right around the corner under the brand new New Jersey Turnpike extension.

A network of informers kept the hijackers posted. The informers—sometimes drivers, sometimes freight handlers, checkers, or shop stewards—would drop a dime whenever precious cargo was set to roll. The mob took care of the rest.

The driver of the rig would either relinquish his load or his life. Some gave both.

On the way down Tonnelle Avenue, Rayf pulled into the White Manor hamburger joint, a White Castle imitator. The all-white porcelain building resembled a castle and sold square, silver-dollar-sized hamburgers with onions and pickles. These sold for 12 cents per. You ate them by the dozen and dealt with the heartburn later. They also served coffee and were open twenty-four hours a day.

As always, when Rayf pulled into the White Manor parking lot, the smell of greasy little hamburgers conjured up memories of better times. *Many a summer night was spent here beneath these same fluorescent lamps, listening to doo-wop instead of this Motown, folk, and beach jive that they try to pass off for rock 'n' roll today,* thought Rayf. He clicked off the radio, got out of the car, and walked across the black-topped lot towards the building.

He and Cal used to hang out here back in '59, only four short years ago. Back then the carhops would service the cars on roller skates, their ultra-short skirts whetting many a youthful male appetite. That was the summer when Rayf finally graduated from a turbulent, five-year high school hitch and the year Cal was thrown out of Saint Joe's Prep, a Jesuit high school for the gifted and promising. One year later and Cal would be working for the mob—his gift was for numbers and his position within the mob looked promising.

Within that one year, Cal had worked himself up from lowly number runner to one of the top sports bookies in the city. But those summer nights were history as Rayf stepped into the blinding, greenish-white, fluorescent-illuminated interior of the all-white, castle-shaped building.

The counter resembled a huge, white Formica horseshoe.

As he waited for the waitress, he thought, *Nothing remains of those innocent days.*

He looked around. The place was empty. He was the only one in the joint. The waitress, taking her time, came out from the back room. *She has a body that won't quit and a set of tits to match*, he thought as he looked her over from head to toe. He was wrong, he conceded, some things never do change. She smiled. Her teeth looked like a picket fence with a couple of slats gone missing—here a gap, there a gap, so on and so forth. But what a bod! He smiled back. Her nameplate read Terry and that's what he called her when he ordered two containers of regular coffee to go.

She gave another smile and plenty of cleavage. She turned around, bent down, and when she did her short, tight, white skirt made the outline of her ass look like a heart.

She's sweet enough for a buck tip, he thought.

Yeah, he said to himself, *yeah, that's what I'll slip 'er—for the moment that is.*

When he got up to leave with the bag of coffees in his hand, he looked back—and sure enough there came the cutest wink this side of downtown. She stuffed the buck into her bra.

Rayf winked back and said, "When you get off work tonight, meet me at the Rag Doll in Union City. I tend bar there; drinks are on me."

She smiled that smile and said, "I'll be up around two."

He felt great now as he took the six, half-moon shaped concrete steps from faux castle to parking lot two at a time and ran back towards his gray car. Here was a brawd that he would love to jab.

Now when he started up that '56 Chevy and turned on the radio, he thought, *Motown is the sweetest music that rock 'n' roll has ever produced.* He pulled out of the lot and continued towards his stranded friend. And when he thought about Cal, he was glad that he had never succumbed to the lure of the mob.

***

Cal was sitting on a vacant storefront windowsill awaiting the arrival of his friend when he saw Soapy's black Chrysler make the turn out of Corbin Avenue and head up the Broadway hill.

Cal jumped to his feet, put his thumb out, and hailed a ride. Soapy stopped the car near Cal, pulled down the electric window on the passenger's side, and yelled, "You ready to turn in your book?"

"Nope," said Cal.

"Then why the hell're ya stoppin' me for?"

"'Cause I wanna see if ya mother needs a spare. Ya got one, don't ya?"

"No. But my spare's flat. You wanna blow it up?"

"I'll blow up you and this whole friggin' car," said Cal. "That's what I'll blow up."

"Ya know, if you were not also employed by da man I am afraid dat I'd be forced to take ya out," said a very calm Soapy.

"Why don't ya hit the fuckin' road," yelled a beet-red Cal.

"Just get ya book ready, toughy," said Soapy as he eased his big, black boat down Tonnelle Avenue toward the circle that swings north to Union City, west to Newark, or east towards downtown and the Holland Tunnel.

Cal punched the phone booth. He hurt his right hand.

As Rayf approached the black underbelly of the Pulaski Skyway that stood dumb and somber above the Tonnelle Avenue Circle, he saw Soapy's big black bomb on the opposite side round the curve and veer off eastward towards the Holland Tunnel and downtown.

Four blocks later and he could now see Cal on the other side of the street pacing up and down near the phone booth. Cal was favoring his sore right hand.

"You call for a taxi?" he shouted.

"Ya know I almost got killed thanks to you," yelled Cal as he ran across the street to the gray car.

"What the hell did I do?" said Rayf.

"Ya took your damn sweet time, that's what ya did," said Cal as he jumped into the passenger's seat.

"From now on call a cab, ingrate. Here's your coffee." Cal took the container and with that Rayf peeled out, hooked a U-ey, and headed back in the same direction that Soapy drove off in.

They didn't speak until a half mile past the circle.

"That dirty crumb is messin' with my chick," said Cal.

"Who's messin' with which chick?"

"Soapy's messin' with my Angela."

"Angela?!" said Rayf as he swerved to avoid a pothole. One blast of air horn—he hit the pothole. Cal's head snapped back and forth.

"What the hell're ya tryin' to do, give me whiplash or what? G'head I could use the bucks. Look at this, man. I scalded my balls. Thanks for nuthin', speedo."

"You messin' with Petey's daughter?"

"I ain't messin' with her. We're in love. It's Soapy that's messin' with my chick," said Cal.

"You keep messin' with her and you'll be lucky to have nuts to spill coffee on. I think you are out of your friggin' mind."

"Big deal. Petey. He shits just like me and you."

"We're not talkin' about regularity, man. We're talkin' arm length."

"So he's got connections, so what?"

"So you're crazy. That's what."

"Ya know what your problem is, Rayf?"

"Problem? I got a problem?! I think you're the one with the problem," now half to himself, "Petey. You don't mess around, do ya?"

"What's the difference between me and him!? G'head, tell me."

"Well for openers you're a two-bit sports bookie and he controls you and the city. Should I go on?"

"Not necessary. Anyone ever tell ya that you are very entertaining?"

"Fer crissakes! You turn your book into him. And yes, many a brawd up in Union City has told me that very same fact."

"Union City! Gimme a break, will ya. Them chicks up there got about as much class as the ladies room you got in that joint."

"What do you know about the ladies room?"

"I checked it out, okay? Come on, get me up there. I need a drink."

As they drove past the White Manor on their right, Rayf saw Terry doing her counter thing.

"So you're humpin' the boss's daughter! Will wonders ever cease?"

"Not if I can help it," said Cal.

***

Capo Pietro "Petey" d'Alloro was forty-five years old and already in charge of Jersey City. He operated out of store fronts and from behind candy store offices within the village, as the Italian section of downtown was affectionately dubbed by the immigrants who had gathered there many years before—strangers in a strange land.

Pietro was a second generation Sicilian-American and a made man in *L'onorata societa* and, like his father before him, had gained the respect of the poor and downtrodden.

His father, Giovanni, emigrated from the village of Monteleone, a town in Sicily which consisted of a hodgepodge of hovels with mules hitched to posts out front. Gio arrived in America in 1907, a poor seventeen-year-old country boy, with his life's possessions in a carpet bag, a letter of introduction to other *amici* within the "society of friends," and a strong will to succeed at the American dream.

Once in America, Giovanni worked hard at cultivating other influential friends in the industrialized new world of New Jersey.

He quickly learned the ways of the industrial jungle and with sharp wit and faster hand increased his power base by protecting many *pisani* from cruel sweatshop operators and the long arm of the strange new-world law. At the same time, he exacted tribute from legitimate businesses by enforcing the decrees of various underworld bosses.

He eventually learned the trades of the mob well enough to strike out on his own with a merchant insurance business. He offered one policy: pay or pray.

He had help in building his business. It came from the American press. Their tales of Italian thugs and hoods preceded Giovanni, making all potential clients virtual pushovers.

And so it was in this manner that he increased his sphere of influence, thereby gaining the respect of family, friend, and foe—a respect rooted in fear, *farsi rispettare.*

In 1938, Giovanni died of pneumonia while serving time in Rahway State Prison for breaking the newly drafted federal law of taxed income. He was forty eight at the time of his death and capo of a Jersey City, New Jersey *cosche.* He left behind a wife and two children, a boy and a girl. His son, Pietro, was only twenty years old at the time of his father's death and by forty five was *pezzi da novanta,* the big shot boss of a New Jersey *consorteria,* a loosely formed alliance of crime families known as *cosca.* Giovanni's daughter, Camille, would eventually become a nun. And it was whispered in almost imperceptible tones by the grandmothers in black who shopped the old bushel boulevard of the village, that Sister Camille was paying for her father's and her brother's sins with prayer.

The sin that these bosses understood very well needed no translation; it was oppression. This they understood no matter what the tongue. These *capi Mafiosi* were accustomed to foreign oppressors taking over their island nation and raping their women. They learned the speech that takes place behind the eyes. A telepathic bond was formed as it is with all oppressed people—even here in America, when the Irish cop on the village beat would swipe an apple or demand a free choice cut of beef for his family's table, these people would take a mental note of this callousness and bite their tongues. They knew that their day would come as it always does to those who wait. For when the fat get fatter, the lean get keener.

But it was during prohibition that capo Pietro's father, Gio, became a real contender. For that was when the people called for booze, which he supplied, and in so doing found many corruptible friends in very high positions. The mafia has always dealt with the lowest common denominator, the small man. When the small man has no one else to turn to, there will always be the bosses who will be there to listen, for a price.

And like his father before him, capo Pietro was listening on this very night as he held court behind Miranda's Coffee Shop on Third Street when Soapy's Chrysler pulled up, parking tight to the curb. It glistened beneath the street lamp where stood ten young men ranging in ages from eighteen to twenty five. Some were talking softly, some pitching pennies, and some watching Soapy as he folded out of the bowels of his black beauty, pulled out a clean white handkerchief, and wiped a speck of dust from the hood of his dream car. Speaking to all ten guys at once he said, "Keep your asses offa da car or I'll have ya simonizing it till ya arms fall off, ya hear?"

Punky, the smallest of the group of ten, cupped his hands over his mouth and with a deep guttural burst shouted, "Eat shit, Soapy!"

Soapy immediately took off after the fleet-footed Punky, who shot up Third Street and cornered Colgate Street before Soapy could even get up the slightest speed. Soft Italian feather-weights were no match for high-topped sneakers. One was meant for style, the other for traction. The remaining nine guys let go with Bronx cheers to Soapy while egging on Punky.

Soapy, winded after ten yards, stopped, turned around, dusted off his greatcoat, and adjusting himself by the lapels said, "And that goes for da rest uh ya mush heads."

Several outbursts of "Up yours'" and "Fuck you" followed Soapy as he walked down the alleyway towards capo Pietro's office, stopping abruptly when he knocked on the door.

The door opened, giving off a crack of light; Soapy whispered, "It's me." The slash of light from the opening door grew wider, painting his frame and causing his dark silhouette to give off a long shadow that fell amid the warm yellowish bath of light onto the cold, two a.m., concrete alley side-walk. He stepped in. The shaft of light vanished with him, closing out the world from the innermost folds of the boss's den and Soapy within.

Six men were standing around the room as Soapy entered. All six men nodded to him as he quietly entered, joining the group.

On his right was Ski, the one they called Counselor. He was a kind enough looking man of Polish descent with a high forehead, who looked more like an English professor in his suit and tie than a killer who would strike at the drop of a hat and think more of the dust on the brim of that hat than the man on the ground. Next to him was Smiles, the manic-depressive of the group. Smiles, it should be noted, would wear his crocodile-like, wise-guy grin to his death, which would occur on June 2nd, 1967, when he would be gunned down outside a union shape-up hall.

Next to him was Dum-Dum. To say that Dum-Dum was the illiterate of the group was true enough, but to say that he was without creativity would be false. He had developed a use for the two-by-four that would have never crossed the mind of any sane carpenter. And there, on Petey's right, was Lefty, the German kid who grew up with him and just so happened to be left handed. He was Petey's go-fer. Seated at the table littered with comic books was the Ice Man. The Ice Man was a comic book aficionado and got his nickname from his father who, in the old days, ran an ice business. Ice Man Jr. was still very handy with an ice pick. And last but not least was Ali Baba who, like Ski, always wore a suit and tie. Ali Baba, guarding the door, was a half breed—his mom Irish, his dad Sicilian. Physically he took after his father, big and swarthy. He looked, to the boys, like a 1930s Hollywood version of an Arab, hence his nickname. It was rumored that at sixteen years of age he found both his parents dead on their kitchen floor, two weeks apart, first mom then dad. Some people attribute this to his choice of occupation. And many a psychiatrist will ponder this last fact. But whatever the excuse, he certainly was not playing with a full deck and came with a very impressive list of hits to his credit. "Ali Baba," as they said on the corner, "is one mean cat."

So this, then, was Petey's group, a room full of goons of mixed nationalities. To say Petey was un-American would be unfair. His ranks were comprised of an all-American mix. Dregs, true, but Americans nonetheless. He even employed number runners from the predominately black neighborhood of Greenville to add to his ever expanding book. After all, this was America and Petey was an equal opportunity employer.

All of the men were giving their undivided attention to the court proceedings that were taking place within the neat, makeshift office.

Behind the large desk sat Pietro d'Alloro, studying the man who stood before him. John Cangi, a confirmed junkie, was squirming and trying to keep his cool while under the leader's gaze. Cangi had center stage.

"I'm tellin' ya Pete, I'm clean. I ain't done no drugs in six weeks. So help me. I swear on my mother's grave," said Cangi while scratching at his arms, neck, and stomach.

"Cangi, I'm going to tell you this once, and that should be enough, right?"

"Right, Pete."

"Mister d'Alloro to you, shithead," said the giant Ali Baba.

"Sorry, Mister d'Alloro."

"I do not want my neighborhood poisoned by you and your shit. Do you understand?"

"Yes, Mister d'Alloro."

After a very long pause the capo resumed, "This question I must ask you. Do you know the consequences if any dope ever turns up in this neighborhood with your name attached to it?"

"Yes sir, I think I do."

Capo Pietro was allowed to do business in this city. He paid the officials for his crime franchise. There was only one provision in his contract—no drugs allowed in the neighborhood. Drugs would only draw angry complaints to the police. And it was this police activity, along with the accompanying publicity, that neither crook nor politician wanted or needed.

Capo Pietro's eyes now burned a deep red as he stared for what seemed to Cangi an eternity. Then he spoke. "I don't want to ever see you down here for the rest of your life." He paused. No one in the room dared breathe as he prepared his finish, saying very softly, "Now leave."

In a rush, Cangi bowed to capo Pietro backing up all the way to the door that Ali Baba and Dum-Dum protected. He bumped into the large men and recoiled in fear only to see the smiling face of Ali Baba leaning down to greet him eye to eye, "What's a matta, scaredy cat junkie? Afraid ta go bye-bye?"

The men in the room laughed.

Ali Baba threw Cangi out into the alley, "Go ta da Ricans where ya belong, fleabag."

Cangi picked himself up and ran down the alley past the jeering ten hanging the night away.

"Close the door," said Ski the counselor. Ali Baba complied.

"Soapy," said Petey, "you squared up yet?"

Soapy, dropping off several envelopes said, "Not yet, Petey. I still got Cal's slips to pick up and then I'm square."

"Good man. Now go take care of your business."

"Yes sir," said Soapy, turning to leave.

He took a few steps before the boss spoke once again, "Oh, and, uh Soap…"

Soapy stopped dead in his tracks, did an about-face and said, "Yeah, Pete?"

"And stay away from the girls."

Fumbling with hat in hand, he looked around the room wondering if capo Pietro was hip to his shenanigans. *Best to play along*, he thought, blurting out, "Right, Petey! Right. No girls."

Again there was laughter and then the leader said, "That'll be the day." Searching for the joke, Soapy faked a laugh, bowed, and ducked out of the office, leaving behind him capo Pietro, his counselor, and soldiers all in a fit of laughter.

***

Back at the Rag Doll Nightclub, Rayf poured drinks for the middle-aged couple down near the dance floor. Cal, in the meantime, was up front nursing his ego by putting the make on Franny, one of the cute little bar girls who frequented the place all week long. Cal's concept was simple; he would immerse himself in this new girl in order to forget Angela. They were drinking scotch on the rocks.

Cal called out to Rayf, "Yo Rayf, me and Franny over here are gonna go and catch that band at Rondo's. When the hell're you guys gonna get a band in here on weeknights, huh? Christ I don't even know why I come in here during the week."

"Bitch and moan. Is that all you ever do?" said Rayf.

"Me and my girl Franny over here are cruisin' for some action. Ain't that right, sweetheart? Tell 'im."

"Yeah," said the gum chewing Franny.

"See, what'd I tell ya! Here, do me a favor. Give this envelope to Soapy when he comes in. I can't wait all night for that jerk." He handed the envelope to Rayf.

"Anything else, Mister Big Shit?"

"Yeah. And don't lose it," said Cal as he walked out of the nightclub with his latest flame.

Rayf stashed the envelope near the cash register and then turned to take care of the couple down at the other end of the bar.

Several minutes passed before Soapy entered the nightclub.

"Yo, Rayf. Where's jerk-off?"

"Who's that, Soap?"

"Your asshole buddy, dat's who," said Soapy taking a stool.

"You drinkin'?"

"Scotch on da rocks, Dewar's. Well where is he?"

"Who the hell is *he*, flat face?"

"Cal, dat's who."

Rayf, pouring the shot, said "Cal! Why didn't you say that in the first place?"

"Ya knew damn well who I was lookin' for. He leave anything fer me?"

"Come to think of it he did," said Rayf. He slid the envelope down the smooth-topped mahogany bar. "Here."

Soapy stashed the envelope inside his suit jacket, drained his glass, and pulled out a pack of matches to light his cigarette.

Waiting for Rayf's return, he entertained himself by playing with the book of matches. And when the bartender finally did return he said, "Fill 'er up." And while Rayf was pouring, Soapy continued with, "Hey Rayf, you ever been to Florida?"

"Nope."

"Man, I just got back from dere. Hey, if ya ever get down dere maybe ya could work in a joint like dis." He threw the book of matches at Rayf.

Rayf caught the matchbook, studied it, and said, "What's this?"

"What's it look like? It's da Pink Flamingo. Can'tcha read, man?"

Rayf turned the matchbook and looked at the slick cover. There was a picture of a pink flamingo emblazoned on a red background with the words Pink Flamingo in bamboo-style typeface.

"Dat's da kinda joint dat you belong in, man. You got class. No kiddin', man. You'd do good down dere, so help me."

"Thanks but I'm happy right where I am."

"No offense, but if ya ever change ya mind just tell Johnny who owns da Flamingo dat Soapy sent ya, and ya'll be in like J.F.K., so help me. I just got back from dere—had to fly in on business. What a joint Miami is—brawds, sun. Oh, man. Well, anyway, I gotta get goin'. Gotta turn dese slips in t'da man."

Rayf pocketed the packet of matches.

Soapy downed his drink and tore into the envelope. His face froze. "What da hell is dis?" said Soapy, removing a Trojan condom from amid Cal's slips.

"Looks like a scum bag to me," said Rayf ringing up Soapy's ten dollar bill.

***

Thursday of the same week found Rayf parking his gray-primed Chevy on Third Street, just across from capo Pietro's office, which was located directly behind Miranda's coffee shop. He parked the car, got out, and walked up towards the corner of Third and Bushwick.

The neighborhood, like so many other inner-city neighborhoods of the day, had fallen into disrepair. Many of the first generation Italian-Americans who were born in this area had since moved to the suburbs, a recent social experiment made possible by the car and the modern highway system.

The vitality and growth of this once busy neighborhood, of which Third and Bushwick Streets were at its heart, had given way to stagnation and decay. But to give it up, for some, would be like asking a child to give up its favorite tattered blanket. True, it may be old and useless, but the rich storehouse of memories that it evoked was enough to draw them back to stand on this corner to continue to while their lives away.

It was one o'clock in the afternoon, and for Rayf, the day was about to begin.

There were already four guys holding up the corner when Rayf approached at a snail's pace. He stopped, checked out his reflection in a vacant storefront window, combed his hair, and resumed with his leisurely stroll up to the corner.

Cal was also closing in from the Bushwick Street side.

Doctor Benny, an ex-M.P. and not really a doctor at all, was giving a dissertation from an article he had just read in the New York Daily News on LSD, the still-legal and first synthetic psychedelic drug of California fame.

These guys took their news with a grain of salt and a lot of humor. As with all other neo-feudalistic societies around the globe, they received their news and information from the more established sources, the profit-motivated media. It was the rare few who received parental editorials. And even in these rare cases, the words and experiences of their parents, though painted with plenty of personal passion, were still all lumped together with the rest of the stories being pumped out by the big business presses; therefore, they were considered by the distrustful eyes of these kids to be nothing more than attacks aimed at crippling their individuality.

Consequently, due to this view of the world picture, their conversations took on the breadth and depth of a supermarket tabloid, more hype than substance. Doctor Benny spoke to a skeptical audience.

Dr. Benny, who had served in the Army, was part intellectual and part sadist. In his youth he had performed many an operation on quite a few unwilling cats and dogs, hence his nick-name Doctor. He received an honorable discharge from the Army because, as the guys believed, he had had two years to get close to, and fondle, an arsenal of weapons. Now he was back, more worldly, but still on the same corner with the same guys.

These gatherings took place religiously every day, rain or shine, without fail, on the corner where the boys spoke in true Hollywood tough-guy fashion as per movie macho pitch men like George Raft, Edward G. Robinson, and Humphrey Bogart.

Dr. Benny at this very moment was talking in this side-of-the-mouth fashion to the three half-interested corner pillars—Punky, the little tow-headed guy known for his ball-breaking attitude; Chubby, the medium-built guy, who might have lost his baby-fat but not the nickname; and Anthony, the weekend ladies' man of the corner.

Rayf and Cal arrived at precisely the same time. They melted into the group just in time to hear Doctor Benny say, "And a lot of people who take the stuff get what you call flashbacks, where they actually see buildin's meltin' and all ..."

"Sounds cool to me," said the just-arriving Cal.

"What's that, Doc?" said Rayf.

"LSD trippin'," said Dr. Benny. "People who have taken the stuff have seen some weird things. Like they hear dogs talkin' and all."

"Bullshit," said Rayf. "What do you know about LSD? You were an M.P."

"More than you, draft dodger."

"The only draft I'm dodgin' is the wind from your mouth," said Rayf.

"Score one for the Rayf!" said Chubby.

"Gimme a smoke," said Punky to Cal.

"Get yer own," said Cal.

"Cheap son of a bitch."

"Look who's talkin'," said Cal, "You smoke? Then get a job and buy 'em."

Punky growled at Cal and then said, "You got a smoke, Rayf?"

"Yeah, but they got plutonium in 'em."

"What's dat?" asked Punky.

"You smoke 'em, you don't have flashbacks, you become one," said Rayf.

"Fuck you, too," said Punky.

"Ya know, Cal," said Doctor Benny, "it might sound like fun, but that stuff could really mess up your brain fer permanent, man—like you could go totally nuts."

"You mean like you?" said Rayf.

"I don't even know why I talk to you guys."

"You ever take any, Doc?" said Anthony while adjusting his immaculately combed hair.

"No, but I dragged a lot of jerks into the medics who did. They were out of their friggin' minds, man," said the former M.P.

"You could've fooled me, Doc," said Rayf. "The way you act I would've sworn you took it regularly."

"Fuck off, Rayf," said Doctor Benny.

Cal, pulling out a deck of cards said, "How's about a little three-card ante?"

"Count me in," said Rayf.

"Me too," said Punky.

"Me three," said Anthony.

"You're number four," said Chubby to Anthony.

"I was just carryin' on with the one-two-three thing."

"Yeah, yeah," said Chubby, "I got your thing."

"Fuck you, Chub," said Anthony as they gathered to play.

They all moved over to a stoop in front of a deserted storefront doorway to shuffle away a few hours.

"I'll play chickee," said Dr. Benny. He walked back to the corner to watch for cops.

Dr. Benny, unlike the rest of the boys, was not afraid of work. To him work was something one did for a living and not something to be feared. To the rest it was a curse. But gambling, on the other hand, was a different matter entirely, especially when it came to the game they called three-card ante.

Three-card ante was a form of poker that was played with only three cards. And, same as the boys, it was a fast one-two-three type of card game that called not for skill but bravado, pure luck, and lots of bluffing.

First, the ante, which on this day was five cents; then the dealing of the three cards, one at a time, to all players; then the betting.

It played just like poker—flushes, straights, pairs, and so on. But with only three cards and no drawing, a pair would be a good hand and, in many cases, the holder of a picture-card-high hand could bluff his way to winning the pot.

"OK," said Cal, kneeling down, "nickel up." He shuffled the cards.

"Who's got change of a buck?' asked Punky.

No one answered. "I'm off five cents." He pulled a nickel slightly out of the pot to show his indebtedness.

"Everybody in?" said Cal. "Cards comin' about." He dealt swiftly.

Once all fifteen cards were dealt, he said to the first man on his left, "It's up to you, Ant'ny."

"Why I gotta go first?" said Anthony.

"'Cause you're first," said Chubby, who was last.

"Then I pass."

"Cost ya a dime," said Rayf, next in the circle, as he threw in a quarter and pulled back fifteen cents.

"Call ya," said Punky, now pulling another dime from the pot.

"See your dime, and up you ten," said Chubby, the last man before the dealer.

"Wait up," said Cal. "Let me check dis out." He studied his cards and the faces of the players. "Eat shit," he said as he folded his hand.

"Cost you twenty, Ant'ny," said Rayf.

"Check... out." Anthony threw in his hand.

Cal picked up the discards.

"Call," said Rayf, throwing in his dime.

"Then I'll see your dime and raise ya ten more," said Punky to Chubby while throwing in his dollar bill and taking back sixty-five cents.

"I got your raise," said Chubby, "Right between my legs."

"Ya in or ya out?" said Punky.

"I know you ain't got shit," said Chubby.

"You know so much? Then pay to see," said Punky.

After some serious deliberation Chubby said, "Fuck you," he threw his hand in.

Cal picked up the three discards without looking at them and folded them back into the deck.

"Rayf," said Cal, "it's just you and him."

Rayf looked over at the little blond weasel and then back down to his cards and said, "I'll see your dime and raise you a quarter."

"Hey, what is this?" said Punky. "Once ya check, ya can't raise."

"Who checked?" said Rayf.

"Then ya can't bet a quarter after there's been two raises."

"Where'd you get that from?" said Rayf.

"That's the rules," said Punky.

"Bullshit," said Cal, "Cost you a quarter, Punks."

"You're a jerk-off, know that Rayf?" said Punky as he flung his cards up against the plate glass window.

"Don't throw the fuckin' cards," said Cal, who was now slapping Punky behind the head.

"Fuck you, your cards, and your lousy friend over there," said Punky.

"Who you callin' lousy?" said Rayf, cuffing Punky behind the head.

"Fuck you, Rayf," said Punky. "I ain't donatin' no more money to you assholes." He steamed away to join Dr. Benny, holding up the street corner.

Cal retrieved the cards and said as he handed them to Anthony, "Your deal, Ant."

"Hey," said Rayf, while scooping up the pot, "I win today, I buy everybody a cup of coffee at Miranda's."

"Oh, watch out guys," said Chubby, "We got us a big spender, over here."

"Everybody that is, except Chubby," said Rayf.

The game went on like this for three more hours. New guys came along and old guys left. Some won and some lost. But this was how it went; if you sat in to win, you also took a chance on losing, too.

***

For Cal, the following eight days went by pretty much without a hitch. Football teams won, football teams lost, bets were made, and some people won, but mostly people lost. Cal's book was building steadily; he was an up-and-comer, a mathematical wiz. He could lay odds with the best of them, and nine times out of ten he'd be right on the money. But sometimes it is that one bet out of ten that breaks the bank.

That bank-breaking wager came in late that Friday afternoon, the day of the week when all the neighborhood dudes would get out their tailor-mades to hang around the corner until night fell, waiting for the choice pickings up there in Union City. All bets were in, nothing could go wrong. Nothing that is, until Angela pulled up to the stop sign on Third and Bushwick in her brand new, baby-blue 1963 Corvette.

All the sharpies on the corner looked at Angela with quiet longing. They looked but they dared not touch until she herself peeled one of them from the deck. Punky shinnied up the street sign pole to get a better look into the Vette. Angela was wearing her shortest and tightest skirt, hiked up just enough to show a trace of black and white polka-dot panties, which barely covered that spot that many a man would die for. Punky let out a soft, wolfish, "Oooooh."

But from up there on that pole he could not see her eyes, those gray eyes that flashed to Cal a silent order for him to meet her at their secret rendezvous. The second look flashed, now!

As she pulled away, Punky slid down the pole and said, "Oh man, I saw her pussy. I swear!"

"OK, what color hair she got if you saw it?" said Chubby.

"It looked like it was uh ... uh, black and white. Yeah, that's what it looked like."

"I got your black and white," said Chubby, tugging at his own crotch.

"Fuck you, Chubby," said Punky. And the chase was on. But this time Chubby also had on his high-tops, and now they could hear Punky crying "Uncle!" a block-and-a-half away.

Cal was slowly moving into gate position. He was looking for his exit cue when Anthony spoke up, "Hey Cal, did I see Angie give you the high-sign or what?"

"You need glasses, hair brain," said Cal.

"Hey guys, who's got the e-gal vision on this corner? Tell mister numbers over here," said Anthony.

"He's got it," said Joey, another one of the hanger-outers.

"That's right," said Dr. Benny. "That cat'd spot a tomato ten blocks away and tell ya the color of her eyes, I swear it."

"Then why don't you let him take a look up your ass and see when the next train's comin' in," said Cal to Dr. Benny, as he turned and walked away to keep his rendezvous with Angela, four blocks away.

***

Their secret meeting place was underneath the brand new New Jersey Turnpike extension. Which stood one-hundred feet above the old P.S. No. 5 schoolyard; the schoolyard backed up to the old railroad tracks that lay up on a small hill that was just below the granite cliffs on which stood the neighborhoods of the Jersey City Heights and beyond that Marion, the section of the city where Angela kept her apartment.

From up there on those granite cliffs one could see all of downtown, the top of the Turnpike, the Hudson River where stood the Statue Of Liberty, and the Isle of Manhattan that she faced—and at this very moment, Angela's baby-blue Corvette.

She was parked where Third Street dead-ends, way back near the hill. Cal was approaching the car from the railroad tracks. He skipped down the hill in a cloud of dust and crept up on the driver's side. Angela was busy polishing her nails when Cal popped his face into the open window and startled her. She spilled some of the hot-pink nail polish onto her light-tan, leather upholstered seats.

"God damn it Cal! Look at what you made me do! You and your fooling around. Christ, you scared the shit out of me."

"Hey, you knew I was comin'."

"That's just what I wanted to talk to you about. Get in here." Cal got in the passenger's side, sat down comfortably, and said, "Wha'd'ya mean, that's what you want to talk about?"

"Your comin', that's what."

"What're ya talkin' about? I no follow."

"God damn it Cal, do I have to spell it out for you?"

"Look, I ain't that dumb—how's about a hint?"

"I'm pregnant. OK? And you're the father. So there!"

"I'm what?"

"I just came back from the doctor and he told me I'm pregnant. Six weeks gone."

Angela broke into tears. Cal sat there dumbfounded. After several seconds he said, "What're you gonna do about it?"

Through sobs she said, "What do you mean?"

"You know, like get it fixed."

'You mean like an abortion?"

"Yeah."

"How could you ..."

"Well, I think it'd be the best thing to do for all concerned. Don't ya think?"

"I'm in trouble Cal, don't play around, OK?"

"I'm not playin' around. I mean it!"

"Cal, I've got news for you. We're getting married. You did it and you're going to face up to your responsibilities. Do you hear me?"

"You're only nineteen. Ya got your whole life ahead of ya."

"I *had* my whole life ahead of me."

After a pause Cal said, "Angela, not to be rude or anything like that, but how do we know for sure that it's like, my baby?"

"What are you insinuating? That I'm a run-around?"

"No. But I always protect myself. You know that."

She responded without dropping a beat, "I pin-pricked the bag."

"You what!?"

"You heard me."

"Then baby, it's your fault and not mine."

"Is that right, wiseguy? Who do you think my father's going to believe, me or you?"

"Ya wouldn't do this to me, would ya?"

"You just watch me, buddy. You just watch me."

"What about Soapy?"

Her head spun around with the speed of a snake and he could have sworn that he saw a trace of red in her eyes when she said slowly and quietly, "What about Soapy?"

"I don't know, aren't you seeing him, too?"

"No I am not," very civil now, "What ever gave you that idea?"

"Well, I just kinda put two and two together, that's all."

"Well, you figured wrong."

For the longest time Cal felt like a total fool. He couldn't get comfortable no matter which way he sat. He wanted to compliment her on her underwear but that would be like giving a match to a woman on fire.

He thought and thought. He thought so hard that he actually felt a headache coming on. Angela sat there with her back towards the mountain and faced Cal, who squirmed and squirmed until he could take no more and then he said, "Well, if that's all ya got to say, then I guess I'll be leaving."

Again, he could have sworn he saw fire in her eyes and knew it was coming out of her mouth when she said, "So you guess that you'll be leaving!? Just like that? Huh? Well let me tell you something, young Turk: your ass'll be grass if you walk out of this car. Do you hear me?"

"Ya threatening me now?"

"You are God damned right I'm threatening you. You leave this car without telling me that you'll marry me, and I'll tell my father. And of course you know the rest, Mister Missing Man."

She had hit a nerve deep in his psyche. But why was it that he wasn't the least bit frightened? Why wasn't he shitting in his pants like he thought he should be? All he could say after he stepped out of the car, gently closed the door, and leaned into the open window was, "See what Soapy has to say."

He turned and walked away from the dead-end street, away from the mountain, and back towards the corner and the boys who were getting ready to tear up the town tonight. But somehow he knew he wouldn't be having any fun that night. And he wondered, as he walked very slowly down the middle of Third Street, if he'd ever have any fun ever again.

The roar of the Vette peeling rubber and heading straight at him ended this mental state of affairs, and he ran as never before. She was closing in on him fast. He jumped the curb and ducked into a warehouse doorway. She followed, and creamed her right front fender into the doorway wall. The sound of tearing fiberglass, broken headlights, and peeling rubber was all he heard. An instant later she was two blocks gone.

He felt himself up to make sure nothing was broken or smashed. He was all there. Next he looked after her to make sure she wasn't circling back. She wasn't. He resumed breathing and started walking. But this time he wasn't heading for the corner; no, this time he was heading for his pad. This was a situation that needed lots of thought and the boys on the corner would be of no use to him now.

On the walk home he thought, "Hell hath no fury like the wrath of a female bettor, welshed." He knew he'd have to think of something, and he knew he'd have to think of it fast if he had any intention of ever seeing twenty-two.

~ 2 ~

FIGHT OR FLIGHT

The heart of the master is strong. He must provide for the many. It is his duty. They are weak and depend on him for direction and sustenance. He was the one chosen by fate to lead. They, by fate, were chosen to follow. These were the thoughts of capo Pietro as he ate alone in the large dining room of his twelve-room villa in North Arlington, New Jersey, far enough away from his business dealings to don the cloak of respectability, yet close enough to respond within minutes.

His elderly maid, dressed in black, brought him his plate of lasagna and took away the empty cup of minestrone. She was off to prepare the salad.

In the meantime, Angela's dented baby-blue Corvette pulled up outside the gates of her father's estate and drove deliberately over the warning device, which caused her father to stop eating mid-bite. Mouth wide, lasagna-laden fork suspended in mid air, he looked at his butler and gave a nod. Off went the man to check on the arriving guest. He resumed eating his dinner.

Several mouthfuls later he heard the front door swing open. He listened to the footsteps and recognized them to be those of his daughter. He lay down his fork, and with lap napkin dabbed his mouth to greet his one and only.

Angela approached the dining room, stopped beneath the alcove, and looked at her father for an eye-fluttering moment before she bowed her head in shame.

Her straight black hair hung down over the shoulders of her beige, short-skirted topcoat. Her high heels added two inches to her petite five-foot-four frame.

The butler approached to take her coat. She shrugged him off.

Capo Pietro dismissed the help with the wave of a hand.

He studied his daughter standing there before him in that big house. How small, how delicate she looked—*almost like a lost child*, he thought, with her head hanging down, chin on chest.

He slid his chair back and started walking towards her. The echo of his footsteps resounded off the dining room walls. With a curled index finger he raised her chin. Their eyes met. He thought, as he looked deep into those gray orbs, that they had never looked sadder.

Her sadness brought back the memory of her mother, his beloved wife. She had had the same look on her face when she gave him the terrible news that the doctor gave her on that day so long ago; the news that she had only six months to live.

Angela was only seven years old when her mother died of cancer. He attired the child in her white communion dress for her mother's funeral, much to the chagrin of the grandmothers in black. They had insisted that she, like them, wear black, for this was a day of mourning and black showed respect for the dead. But he ruled and his wish would be carried out, that his daughter should not remember her mother in black for death, but in white for life. For she had a long and wonderful life before her, and he would make sure that she got whatever it was that she wanted.

He asked softly, "What's wrong, sweetheart?" She sobbed. A tear fell from her eye. "Is it the apartment?" he asked with hope. "It can all be fixed, honey. What is it?"

She struggled to get the words out, words that were blocked deep within by shame, sadness, sorrow, guilt, and dishonor. Struggling in this manner the words finally made it up from somewhere deep down inside, around all of those thorns and up to her sweet, red lips where in a whisper they were released. "Daddy, I'm ... I'm pregnant."

For a brief moment relief flooded the father's chest. His worst imaginings had not materialized, but then the cloud of parental concern crossed over his heart, "Are you sure?"

Through sobs, she said, "Yes father, I'm sure."

He did not have to ask the next question; it was implied in his silence. She waited, then meekly said, "Cal."

His big hands held her at the shoulders. He brought her in slowly for a bear-sized hug. He patted her back while speaking reassuringly. "There, there. Everything is going to be all right. Papa will take care of everything; nothing to fear."

With that, Angela broke into tears.

***

It was Sunday, November 17th. WNEW-AM was playing a medley of songs from "The Chairman of the Board," a title bestowed on Francis Albert "Frank" Sinatra by William B. Williams, the WNEW-AM weekday DJ. Soapy, who was polishing his black Mariah, leaned into the open door of the car and turned up the volume on the radio. The dulcet strains of Frankie floated out over this unusually warm November afternoon.

To say these guys were Sinatra fans would be putting it mildly. Frankie was born and raised in Hoboken—not five miles from this very corner, making him one of their very own. They didn't see themselves as fans. They thought of him more like family.

Soapy stopped polishing and with the style of a barroom singer crooned along with Francis Albert, "Set 'em up Joe ..."

Now Punky, Chubby, Joey, and Anthony joined in, all five off-key admirers warbling along.

It was a good time for them. They had no problems. This was their world. Occasionally, rumors came in from beyond the neighborhood of other worlds, other lands, but these they discarded. For their world consisted of making enough money to get them from Friday to Monday and through the weekend with good-time memories to relish from Monday to Friday.

And as they swayed and sang along with Frankie over WNEW-AM, they, each and every one, were rehashing some wonderful weekend dream, a weekend that was drawing rapidly to an end. All of them that is, except Cal.

Cal, at this very moment, was in his own apartment, one block away on Bushwick between First and Second Streets, still living the weekend. His life was somewhat different than the rest of the pack. His weekend ran from Monday to Monday.

When the music segued to the sad, yet hopeful sounds of Sinatra singing "Try A Little Tenderness," Cal rolled over the naked body of Franny lying there in his bed, pulled out a Camel, and lit it up while listening to his radio.

He put his hand behind his head and watched the cigarette smoke as it rose up in thick little rivers, only to fade off and vanish into thin air. He listened, smoked slowly, and felt the warm flesh of his latest girl by his side.

"A penny for your thoughts," said Franny.

Cal looked over at her. She was frail and lovely; *maybe just a little too thin*, he thought, as he looked down and saw the bones protruding from her pelvis beneath her soft, flat belly, just below her honey-dew sized tits with those tiny, cherry nipples. He doused his cigarette in the melted ice of the squat crystal glass tumbler and rolled over on his side to face her. He had a sudden urge for fruit salad.

"I'm talking to you," she said.

"What?" said Cal, coming out of his dessert day dream.

"A penny for your thoughts, I said."

"Oh."

And with that utterance, he grabbed her hand and placed it gently on his baton. By the look in her eyes, he knew she knew the answer.

He touched her legs. They sprang open for him.

Sinatra was now up to the part in the song where he sings that while she's waiting you should try a little tenderness.

The boys on the corner, lost in their reverie, sang right along with old Francis, a reverie that was soon to be broken when Ali Baba tapped Soapy on the shoulder just as Sinatra started singing "The Second Time Around."

"Man wants ta talk ta ya," mumbled Ali Baba to Soapy. Soapy nodded. Ali Baba walked off. Soapy reached into his car, pulled the keys out of the ignition, and cut Francis Albert off in mid phrase.

Punky, caught in the middle of a nightclub singing stance, yelled, "What the hell are ya doin', Soap? It was just gettin' good."

"Gotta go, flakos," said Soapy as he left the corner of Bushwick and started walking down Third Street. He walked a ways, stopped, turned around, and yelled back proudly, "Duty calls."

"Ah shit," said Joey, the quiet kid. "He was just gettin' into the groove, man."

"Yeah," said a disappointed Anthony.

"Hey," said Punky, "ya think he's ever gonna get back with Nancy?"

"Who, Frankie?" asked Anthony.

"Yeah."

"Never happen," said Chubby. "Not after all a dem Hollywood brawds."

"But I mean, listen to the lyrics," said Punky. "Remember the part in the song where he sings that it's better with two feet on the ground and the second time around and all?"

"Yeah, what about it?" asked Chubby.

"Sounds like he's talkin' directly to Nancy if ya ask me," said Punky.

"Who's askin' ya?" said Chubby.

"Fuck you, Chub," said Punky.

This is the way their talk went—on and on. It segued into all sorts of fantasies from girls to money, then back again. For this was how they passed their days, and this, their talk, was the currency that was used on the corner where they spent their lives.

Now Rayf, on the other hand, was singing a different tune. He had his radio dial set to WINS-AM, or as the jingle would sing at the end of each rock 'n' roll record, "Ten Ten WINS, New York." "Walk Like A Man" was playing.

He was at the stove cooking ham and eggs. He wore boxer shorts and socks. The radio was up full volume and the pad was being rocked by the electronic voices of Frankie Valli and the Four Seasons. He sang along with them at the top of his voice.

Rayf rented the top floor apartment of a two-story walk up. The house, on Liberty Avenue in the Jersey City Heights section of the city, was equidistant from the Rag Doll Nightclub and the downtown Third Street corner, five miles in either direction. It was situated at the top of a hill on the western slope of the city. The kitchen windows offered a panoramic view of the Jersey meadowlands. To the left, in the distance was a spur of the Hackensack River. Straight ahead, out near Secaucus, cutting through that mountain in the near-distance, was the New Jersey Turnpike. And in the foreground, running in the same direction as the Turnpike—left to right—was Tonnelle Avenue. In the yard stood a giant oak tree that was taller than the house by half. And stretching from it to the house was a clothesline on which Rayf had hung a solid, softball-sized, bell-shaped birdseed sculpture by Hartz Mountain, a gift on the line to the song birds who chirped along with him as he sang his rock 'n' roll concertos.

He called out over his left shoulder into the bedroom, "Hey Terry, how do ya like yer eggs?"

From off in the other room Terry said, "I hate eggs."

More to himself, "So I'll eat 'em myself."

Terry, the girl from the White Manor, walked out of the bedroom wearing one of Rayf's shirts.

He turned to her and saw those healthy legs sticking out from under his all-cotton Arrow dress shirt. He stopped cooking, turned off the stove under the greasy skillet, and walked over to her.

She smiled that smile. He put his hand up under her skirt-like shirt and started massaging her soft, hairy mound. "I guess breakfast can wait," he said.

They kissed and danced back into the bedroom which consisted of a bed without sheets under a window without curtains.

She unbuttoned the only thing she had on, his shirt, and fell back onto the bed with knees bent and legs open. With her index finger near her entry point, she curled him in. In he went boxer shorts, socks, and all.

This was how Rayf spent most of his days, for the bartender usually has choice of the house, and breakfast doesn't start until after noon.

The "Ten Ten WINS, New York" D.J. announced, "A blast from the past." Buddy Knox started singing "Party Doll." Up went the volume as the two lovers rocked the day away.

***

Soapy, in the meantime, was seated at the front end of the eight-stool counter in Miranda's coffee shop waiting on Pete, who was in the back room finishing up some other business. Soapy watched as Miranda—the five-foot tall, 200-pound woman in the colorful apron over the floral patterned housecoat—performed her busywork.

Miranda's was situated diagonally across the street from P.S. No. 5 and served as a sugar-rush stop for the mob of kids that flooded in and out of the place all day long. In the front section of the store she sold candy, cigarettes, and soda, the last of which caused her much pain and distress; for it was here that she fought the constant battle of keeping the soda caps from rusting the necks of the bottles. This she saw not only as her job but her very reason for living.

The coffee shop was set off from the front section by an alcove.

Besides there being a counter in the coffee shop area, there were two tables, one on each side of the small room, separated from one another by a jukebox that was pressed against the interior alley wall; the same alley that led into capo Pietro's office located in Miranda's back room. She rented to Pietro so, in effect, had nothing at all to do with his business.

The back room office had one more entrance, and it opened directly into the rear of the coffee shop, eight stools away from where Soapy now sat sideways on the spin-stool with his back to that door. He was sipping his coffee and watching Miranda with the cherry pepper-like nose at the soda case in front of the huge plate glass window that opened onto Third Street just beyond.

Miranda, with a wart on her chin that sprouted several black hairs and a mouth that sported only one upper front tooth, was cursing, "Doze little sumunabitches." They were forever knocking her bottles over into the icy cold water; into that same chilly water that turned her fat little white hands a puffy shade of bright red-orange. She wore her gray-brown hair fashioned tightly into a bun. As he watched and waited, Soapy thought it made her big face, look even bigger and bolder.

He would wait on Petey. What else did he have to do? Here sat a professional waiter. He could wait for days if necessary. On one job, he remembered waiting in the back of a van for four days outside Tony The Toad's apartment building. It is rumored that Tony The Toad now lends his support to one of the many concrete columns that hold up the brand new New Jersey Turnpike extension that towers one hundred feet above the old P.S. No. 5 schoolyard just down the street.

Soapy stirred his coffee in a very in a genteel way with his ringed pinky waving in the breeze. He liked his coffee sweet.

Meanwhile, in the back room office sat the usual group of six men. Ski and Smiles were playing cards. Lefty and Dum-Dum were whispering about something to each other. The Ice Man was reading a comic book, and Ali Baba was cleaning his nails with a knife.

Capo Pietro was on the phone. He spoke softly, "Yes. Yes. OK, very good." Conversation over, he hung up, sat back, breathed deeply, and told everyone to leave. Everyone that is, except Ali Baba.

The door leading into Miranda's opened. Out walked the five hoods. Soapy turned and watched them walk out. The Ice Man yelled, "Hey Miranda, how's 'bout a cup a dat mud?"

She yelled back, "Get it yourself. I'm a up to my elbows inna ice water. Dem little sumunabitches."

Ski and Smiles sat down at one of the two coffee shop tables near the jukebox, while Lefty and Dum-Dum sauntered quietly towards the open Third Street door. Near the soda case, Dum-Dum goosed Miranda. She jumped up and splashed the two with a cupped handful of ice cold water; they ducked and ran out of the place as kids would, laughing all the way.

The office door closed. Inside, the boss said to Ali Baba, "Get him in here."

The office door opened once again and once again Soapy turned to face it. This time Ali Baba stuck his head out and called, "Soapy, let's go."

Soapy stood up, walked towards the office door, and gave Ski and Smiles, who were sitting at the table, a look as if to say: "See, I'm important too!" They paid him no mind but continued with their conversation. The Ice Man took Soapy's place at the counter and watched Miranda as she wiped her cold hands on her apron before walking behind the candy counter to continue with her busywork.

Soapy closed the door behind him.

***

Later that day, around dusk, many worlds away, Henry Duncan wasn't thinking about Vietnam or "dem crazy white people" as he referred to them; the ones who climbed up water towers and sniped unsuspecting pedestrians for sport, as was the current fad presently sweeping the nation. He wasn't even thinking about those white college protesters or his job as stable boy here at Yonkers' Raceway, which he was just about to quit. He had other people on his mind as he said his goodbyes to the other stable boy, Lucius Taylor.

"Well," said Henry, while clasping Lucius's big rough hand, "Ah guess ah'll be catchin' ya next season, Lucius."

"Don't go, Henry. Come on over ta Roosevelt wid me, man. It ain't safe down dere."

"Hell, all's ah's gotta do is git pass da Klan, man. Den ah'll be home free. Ah'll be OK. Dontcha worry 'bout me, bro."

"You got 'nuff cash?"

"Nuff."

"How much?" Lucius asked.

"Twel'-fitty, last time ah counted."

"Sheet, man! Dat ain't even nuff to git ya trew Jersey, man. Best not go, Henry."

Henry slapped his beat up 1940 Ford Deluxe Fordor sedan and said, "Sheet, me and ma Fode ain't 'fraid a no whiteys. We'll make it wit' plenty ta spare, lord willin'. See ya, Lu."

Lucius ran to the stable, pulled a horse blanket from off the half open stable door, ran back to the Ford, and stuffed it into the back seat. He then pulled out a pint of sneaky pete from his back pocket. "Here, Henry. Da blanket should keep ya warm. Lord knows you ain't got no heater in dat dere contraption. An' look man, ah ain't got no money, bro, but at least dis here wine'll help numb ya when ya need numbin'."

"Thanks. Lucius," said Henry taking the bottle. "Ah be seein' ya, bro."

Concealing the tear in his eye, Henry opened the old Ford door, got in, slammed it shut. started the car up, and waved good-bye. Lucius Taylor was left standing in a cloud of smoke and dust.

***

The night was clear, the moon was new, and the Chrysler LeBaron was parked across the street from Cal's apartment house on Bushwick Street, which was just around the corner and two blocks away from Miranda's Coffee Shop.

Cal lived on the top floor of a three-story walk-up. The six railroad rooms, called such because they were laid out the same as Pullman cars, one after the other, had since been divided from the original six rooms into two, three-room apartments. He now lived in the front three rooms, one of which looked out over Bushel Boulevard, a nickname given to Bushwick Street back when the street used to teem with open air markets that sold farm-fresh produce.

Cal could remember climbing up to the rooftops to look down at that passing Bushel Boulevard parade, which consisted of men in dirty white aprons hawking their wares to women who would haggle over the prices while their children would chomp Italian ice. And mixed in that crowd was the legless colored man in a worn and frayed WWI Army uniform, pedaling down the street on a skate-wheeled platform with wooden blocks tied to his hands, while playing a kazoo that was strung around his neck with a piece of stiff wire. You threw your coins into his tambourine where they rattled around jingling your musical contribution. And then there was the wino they called Bottle John who would sing very sad Italian opera ballads while weaving through the throng and waving his jug of ruby red vino in his right hand. The language may have eluded Cal, but the true meaning of the soul-sad songs didn't escape him—"Mama" was the message. And then, of course, there was the ever present cop on horseback tipping his hat to a lovely signorina.

Days come, days go, and the Bushel Boulevard road show, like all other shows, eventually folded its tent and dispersed. Now there were better deals to be had down at the local A & P.

By '63 Bushel Boulevard was in dire straits. Most of the original stores and shops that had thrived there had since closed their doors and were now either boarded up or torn down completely, leaving empty spaces where buildings once stood. But other businesses had come to take their places. One of these newer stores was Jig's, a recently opened dive of a bar directly across the street from Cal's apartment house where winos now gathered to drink rot gut whiskey while spitting onto the dirty sawdust floor. And two stories directly beneath Cal's pad, at street level, was a storefront that once housed Debacos Pastry Shop, an establishment that used to add the sweet smell of Italian pastries to the fragrant aromas of the marketplace. Debaco's had since been converted into a second-hand store that now sold broken down things to destitute people. The only thing that remained of the old days was Harry's Fish Market diagonally to the left and across the street from Cal's. Harry was a stern taskmaster and modern businessman who knew how to grow with the times. He employed mostly black laborers.

Besides Harry's unbiased attitude and longevity, he also had the distinction of having his one and only son, Nicky Dee, become the first suicide-attempt statistic recorded for the brand new New Jersey Turnpike extension. Nicky Dee was nineteen at the time of his jump, long beyond the age of reasoning. So one would think that Nicky should have known better than to test a law that had taken man thousands of years to postulate, the Law of Universal Gravitation that Sir Isaac Newton expounded upon in 1687. One would also think that two hundred and seventy-six years would be time enough for that fact to sink into Nicky's gray matter. Not the case. The thing old Isaac didn't take into account back then was falling bodies with broken hearts. Nicky's girlfriend Donna left him for another guy.

Suddenly, one discovers that Nicky Dee was not ignorant of the Law; as a matter of fact, just the opposite held true. One finds that he used the Law as a tool devised for his own destruction. A messy and inconsiderate method, granted, but Nicky, it should also be noted, was myopic. He landed in a very deep and muddy construction ditch. His suicide attempt failed.

So instead of dying, he joined the folklore of the neighborhood: a twisted little man with a crooked smile who hobbled up and down Bushwick Street on two canes, supporting a broken spine.

It was ten o'clock when Cal and his new girl, Franny, finally arrived at the front door of his humble Bushwick Street abode. It was Sunday night and this section of Bushwick Street was deserted except for Nicky Dee who was just now hobbling past. Nicky nodded hello to Cal and winked regarding the new girl.

Soapy also noticed the pretty little babe with Cal—one he'd love to get his hands on. But because of her and Nicky, they would have to wait until Cal was safely inside his apartment before they made their move.

Cal, through the corner of his eye, caught the movement of Soapy and also noticed that Ali Baba was sitting shotgun in the LeBaron. He saw them there, true, but thought nothing of it, for this was their neighborhood, too.

Cal swung open the unlocked street door. The musty smell of mildew greeted his olfactory. A bare, sixty watt light bulb lit the dingy hallway. With Franny in front of him, and holding her about the hips, they climbed the dimly lit dilapidated staircase. Her lose fitting dress could not conceal her lovely buttocks.

Soapy waited until Nicky Dee hobbled out of sight. And when he saw the lights go on in Cal's third floor front room, he gave Ali Baba a grunt. The two men stepped out of the car, closed the doors, and walked across the street.

Cal was in a lover's clinch: kissing her face, neck and cleavage, when all of a sudden the apartment door was kicked open. And standing there was Ali Baba with Soapy just behind him.

"Your number's up Cal, let's go," said Ali Baba with a frozen smile.

Cal, like a man trying to shake off a bad dream, looked from Franny to the thugs.

"Let's go kid, we just wanna talk to ya," said Soapy.

"About what?"

"Business," said Ali Baba.

"I got no business with you two."

"I'd rather we do dis quietly," said Soapy.

"I'd rather we don't do this at all," said Cal.

Ali Baba was now closing in on Cal.

Cal knew it was now or never as he moved behind the girl and threw her at the giant. Ali Baba caught Franny as if he were catching a fly. He threw her down onto the hard, linoleum-covered floor. Cal ran past Ali Baba and kicked Soapy in the nuts. Soapy went down with an awful thud and, as he fell, his key purse dropped from his pocket.

The slow-moving Ali Baba picked up a chair and threw it at Cal, who had just skidded through the open door and was now running down the stairs.

The chair shattered. Ali Baba, looking for something else to throw, picked up the key purse and charged to the stairwell. He threw it at Cal, who had just reached the second-floor landing. Cal turned and saw the speeding projectile heading right for his head; he ducked and caught it in full stride.

By the time he had hit the bottom landing he knew he had the keys to Soapy's car in his hand. And when he flew out of his apartment house, he headed straight for Soapy's car, pulling out the car keys as he ran.

He opened the driver's door of the LeBaron easily enough; now he fished around for the ignition key. He tried one, two keys. Now he saw Ali Baba charging out of the front door; *he looks like a rhino in hot pursuit*, thought Cal. He tried the third key. It worked.

Ali Baba was at the passenger's front fender when the engine roared to life. Cal hit the gas. Ali Baba went flying up and over the hood, then over the windshield; through his rearview mirror Cal could see Ali Baba roll down and over the back window, and then bounce over the rear left fender. *Ouch*, said Cal to himself as he fish-tailed up Bushwick Street, sped under the train trestle on Railroad Avenue, and then—as far as Ali Baba could see from laying there on the street—the Chrysler was out of sight.

At this very same moment, ten miles away, Ray Falcone was dancing with a bar stool in the empty Rag Doll Nightclub while Jimmy, seated behind the bar, was buried in the *Jersey Journal*, a broadsheet-formatted daily newspaper with the content quality of a tabloid. Two headlines caught his eye—one screamed, "189 Negros Sized in South Carolina Anti-Segregation Protest," and the other read, "Federal Government Orders All Geographic Sites Using the Offensive Term in Their Titles to be Replaced with the Word Negro." Jimmy snapped the big-sheeted newspaper with a flick of his wrists and folded it open to the sports section.

Rayf was singing and dancing to the Frank Sinatra tune, "Saturday Night Is The Loneliest Night Of The Week," with new lyrics created by Rayf especially for this evening: "Sunday night is the deadest night of the week. 'Cause that's the night when my bar stool and me, we go dancing seat to cheek ..."

He put the stool down, sat on it, and said, "Hey Jimmy, ever think of goin' dark on Sundays and Mondays?"

Jimmy, without looking up from his newspaper, said, "One big spender walks through that door and we're over the top. You gotta learn to be patient, kid. It's a virtue."

"Is that right?"

"That is right," said Jimmy as he turned the page.

Cal at this very moment was parking Soapy's '63 Chrysler in the Rag Doll parking lot. He pulled the black boat alongside Rayf's '56 gray Chevy and when he opened the huge door of the LeBaron, the overhead dome light exposed one .38 revolver with muzzle nuzzled into its seat. The look on his face told the story. His number, for some reason, was up. Soapy and Ali Baba were contracted to take him out.

He got out of the car and threw the gun up onto the Rag Doll roof. Inside, Rayf and Jimmy looked up past the mirrored ceiling to the sound of the thud.

"What's that?" asked Rayf.

"Reindeer. Wha' do I know?"

Cal came running into the bar.

"Rayf, gimme a dime."

Rayf flipped him a dime.

Cal ran to the phone booth, picked up the phone, and dialed.

In Angela's apartment, the phone rang. She looked at it and on the fourth ring picked it up. Slowly she raised the receiver to her ear. She did not speak, she just listened, then she heard Cal's voice on the other end.

"Angela, this is Cal."

"What do you want?"

"Soapy and Ali Baba are gunning for me. What's the scoop?" No answer.

"Angela? You hear me? Angela!"

Angela, now staring vacantly at the phone, hung it up. Cal heard the click. He banged the phone box twice and then rammed the phone into its cradle. With a slam he charged out of the folding glass doors of the wooden phone booth and stormed up to the bar.

"White Horse on the rocks," said Cal.

Rayf, pouring the drink, said "What's wrong?"

"Nothin'. Gimme a smoke."

Rayf pulled a smoke from Jimmy's pack and tossed it to him.

"How 'bout a match?"

"Ain't you got nothin' man?"

"Match me," said Cal, nervously.

Rayf flung a book of matches at Cal.

Cal struck the match and noticed the matchbook cover while slowly raising the lit match to the cigarette dangling from his lips. He stared at the matchbook, burning the name on its cover into his memory, Pink Flamingo, Miami Beach's Coolest Hot Spot, he slipped the matches into his shirt pocket.

"Well, what's up, man?" said Rayf.

"Nothin'," said Cal, deep in thought. Then with a forced laugh said, "Hey, I got a new car, man."

"Get out!?"

"No, really, I just bought it less then an hour ago."

"Whacha get?"

"A brand new Chrysler."

Jimmy looked up from his paper, then turned the page.

"A Chrysler? Where'd ya get the cash?" asked Rayf.

"I had twenty bucks on 714."

"Twenty? That's like, let's see … eleven thou. What a score, man!"

Jimmy peeked over the paper, then re-submerged.

"You got that right."

"Where is it?"

"Right outside; wanna go fer a spin?"

"I don't know." Looking to his boss, "Yo, Jim, Cal's gonna show me his new car. We're gonna go for a spin. He got a brand new Chrysler."

"What model is it?" Jimmy to Cal.

"LeBaron."

"Many happy miles, see ya in a few," said Jimmy.

Rayf grabbed his light-blue, waist-length windbreaker and jumped over the bar. Both guys left the joint.

Outside in the Rag Doll parking lot …

"Looks just like Soapy's," said Rayf.

"That's who I just bought it from."

"What are ya tryin', to get in good with Angela or somethin'?"

Cal stopped in his tracks, "Don't you ever mention that brawd to me again. You got that?"

"Angela. Angela. Angela. And fuck you and your car," said Rayf as he turned to go back towards the bar.

"Hey, I'm sorry, man. Forget it. I'm just a little pissed off at her right now. Come on."

Rayf jumped in.

Cal started up the black bomb, eased her out of the parking lot, and drove down the Secaucus Road hill towards Tonnelle Avenue.

At the bottom of the hill Cal took a right heading north on Tonnelle Avenue towards the Lincoln Tunnel. This stretch of Tonnelle Avenue held many memories for both men; it was motel row.

Cal gestured to the Sleep-Inn coming up on the right.

"I was in there last week with Mary Jane Hearty. Good stuff, man."

"What're you, one of those kiss and tell guys?"

"No. I just thought you'd be interested in that they upped the rate."

"No shit?"

"No shit. They're askin' twelve bucks on Fridays and Saturdays."

"What's wrong with usin' your pad?"

"Angela," said Cal.

"The Roundup's your best bet, man. They're still ten on weekends and eight dollars Monday through Thursday. Twelve dollars! Fuck that."

"And they're even askin' for proof."

"Of what, marriage?"

"Nah. Your driver's license. So I had ta show 'em hers. Mine's is still in the mail," said Cal as he broke out laughing.

"Just don't get caught speedin' with me in the car."

Now up ahead, on the right, at the Highway Three intersection, all stainless steel and glass, gleaming in the night, was the Big Top Diner. The boys would usually meet at the Big Top after all the action in Union City was over. They would go there to talk till dawn. They'd talk about the usual things—money, women, and gambling.

When Cal told Rayf that he had to make a phone call regarding a bet, nothing seemed out of the ordinary.

The big LeBaron glistened under the fluorescent lamps as Cal pulled into the huge parking lot.

"I'll be right back. Oh! You got a buck?" said Cal.

"Thought you had eleven grand?"

"I do. But it's all in big bills."

"I gotta get back to work," said Rayf while handing Cal the buck.

Cal charged up the steps, got change of the dollar, and jumped into the nearest phone both. He dropped a dime into the slot and dialed.

Nothing that happens can ever surprise a Union City bartender. Jimmy had seen priests from Bayonne soliciting hookers; junkies selling their wives; women selling themselves for a drink; tough guys biting the big one; and psychologists acting like ducks and quacking until he had to have them bounced out of the place. So when the phone rang and Cal said, "Hello, Jimmy this is Cal," he was not surprised to hear the rest.

"What is it Cal, car crash?"

"Worse. Rayf over here just got a bug up his ass."

"And?"

"He's talkin' crazy."

"What else is new?"

"Yeah, but I ain't never heard him like this before. He's talkin' Canada, draft dodgin', quittin' his job! I can't figure him out. So I say to him, 'Hey man, you're workin', you can't just walk out.' And he says, 'Fuck I can't. You just watch me.' So I say, 'But what about your job? You might lose it and what about leavin' poor ol' Jimmy up there all by himself?' And here's where he says, 'Fuck him.' That's what he says. What can I say, Jim!?"

Jimmy, without missing a beat said, "Tell 'im to have fun in Canada."

And then he hung up the phone. Walked over to the TV set and turned on the small, black-and-white under the bar and clicked around the dial until he found the Amos 'n' Andy show.

Cal walked out of the phone booth, out of the Big Top Diner, and down the steps over to the Chrysler where Rayf was leaning up against the right front fender.

Rayf called out, "Hey, ya know you got a dent in your right front fender over here and one on the hood, too?"

"Yeah that's why he gave me such a good deal," said Cal as he jumped into the driver's side and headed west towards the New Jersey Turnpike.

"Where we goin'?"

"I want to open 'er up on the Turnpike. You game?"

"Sure, a half-hour and that's it. I gotta get back to work.

"Relax, man. Hang on." He hit the gas.

***

The Yellow Cab pulled up in front of the Rag Doll, and out popped Soapy and Ali Baba. Soapy told the cabby to wait.

Jimmy was adjusting the picture on his TV set when Soapy and Ali Baba swung wide the door and very cautiously walked in.

Ali Baba stood by the door as Soapy approached the bar.

"Where are they?" said Soapy.

Jimmy still adjusting the set said, "Where's who?"

"Cal and Rayf."

"You just missed 'em."

The art of selective memory in the barkeep trade is legendary. So when Jimmy-the-legend heard Soapy ask, "Where'd dey go," he actually believed it when he replied, "Got me."

"Rayf's car is still out dere. Now, where are dey?" said Soapy.

Jimmy, from behind the bar walked over to Soapy, "You drinkin'?"

"Scotch straight up, Dewar's."

Jimmy looked towards Ali Baba.

"Make dat two," said Soapy.

Jimmy, while pouring the shots said, "They went in Cal's new car."

"Cal's new car?" said Soapy.

"Yeah. Brand new Chrysler LeBaron."

"Why dat no good son of a … Did he say where he got it?"

"Yeah, cracked 714 for a double saw." Placing the shot glasses on the bar he said, "Here ya go, two Dewar's."

"Why?" said Soapy to Ali Baba, "Why da hell'd ya have to trow my fuckin' keys at him fer Christ sakes? Doze two bastards are gonna wreck my fuckin' car."

Ali Baba lumbered over to the bar, picked up his drink and mumbled, "When I get my hands on doze two sonuvabitches, ya gonna see a double saw." He swallowed the shot in one gulp.

Jimmy by now had deduced the situation and took a mental note of it, but he never let it show on his face, for that is no place for a barkeep to wear his knowledge.

Just then the taxi driver walked in and up to the two men at the bar, "Should I, like, keep waitin' fer you two or what?"

Ali Baba looked from the cabby to Jimmy, then to Soapy he said, "Drink up." Then to the cabby, "Shut up and wait; we'll be right dere."

The cabby left.

"Did dey say where dey was goin'? When dey's comin' back?" asked Soapy.

"Nope."

"Any info at all?" said Ali Baba.

Jimmy looked at the giant and knew that for his own good, he had better throw these guys something, "Oh, yeah, yeah. Rayf quit."

"And you just now remember dis?!" said Ali Baba.

"He just now quit," said Jimmy. "Not a half-hour ago."

"Doze bastards," said Soapy.

"Take care of 'im," said Ali Baba, turning to leave.

Jimmy swallowed and expected the worst.

Soapy peeled off two twenties and threw them onto the bar, "Keep da change."

The two men walked out to the waiting cab.

Jimmy walked over to the register, rang up the forty dollars and said to himself: "See what I mean, two double saws. And all's it took was a little patience." As he closed the money drawer, he said "Like I said, it's a virtue."

He pulled up a barstool and turned up the TV volume just in time to hear the electronic voice of The Kingfish saying, "Holy Mack'e'l, Andy!"

***

The taxi pulled up underneath the street lamp on Third Street in front of Miranda's. Out stepped Soapy to pay the cabby. Ali Baba started walking down the alley past the shrine of perpetual hanger-outers; they watched him pass in silence, but not so with Soapy.

"Hey Soap, that your new car?" asked little Punky in his big, guttural voice.

"Don't fuck around, punks, I'm warnin' ya," the tone of Soapy's voice said it all. Not another wisecrack was heard.

Inside Pete's office walked first Ali Baba, then Soapy.

"Well?" said capo Pietro very quietly.

"He got away Petey," said Soapy.

"He what?"

"Yeah. Dat clown over dere trew my fuckin' keys at him and da rest is history. Da little sonuvabitch took off wit' my car. Him and his asshole buddy, Falcone."

"Where to?" said Pete, very calmly.

"I don't know." Now looking at Ali Baba, "All's I know is dat dey got my fuckin' car. Can ya believe dis?"

"Relax," said Pete, "Calm down."

Soapy took a deep breath. Ali Baba rolled his eyes, all this fussing over a car.

"Wha'da we do now, Petey?" asked a calmer Soapy.

"We wait."

"Whatever ya say, boss."

"Patience," said the boss.

The seven men in the room nodded in agreement. They'd wait.

***

The shiny black Chrysler moved through the night heading south on the New Jersey Turnpike. Here was a vehicle made for the night, made for speed, made for distance. This big car with eight blasting cylinders trying to break loose of the cam shaft that held them bound at one end and the spark plugs exploding in their faces thousands of times per minute on the other.

From inside the car it was silent running. It was as if by magic they passed hundreds of lesser cars, cars that were built to be beaten, cars that were built for the junk heap, cars that couldn't keep up with this big black Chrysler even if they gave it their all.

This LeBaron that ruled the road was not yet ready for the junkman's pile. Not just yet, anyway.

"Pull over," said Rayf.

"What for?"

"Pull the fuck over! I'm warnin' ya."

"OK. Next Howard Johnson, OK?"

Cal looked over at Rayf and thought to himself, *Maybe I shouldn't have told him.*

Rayfs' strong jaw was locked shut.

The orange and aqua blue Howard Johnson loomed up ahead. The Chrysler navigated the long slip of an entrance driveway and parked in a no-parking zone.

Rayf jumped out and headed for the bank of telephones inside.

Cal, leaving the keys in the ignition, swung out of the Chrysler and, at a safe distance, followed Rayf into the Howard Johnson.

Rayf opened the large, swinging door and felt the draft of warm air that carried with it the sweet smell of fresh-made coffee mixed with the scent of cheap perfume. At the cashier's counter he got some change, got into a phone booth, dialed the operator for long distance assistance, deposited the coins, and waited nervously for someone to answer.

Eighty miles away the phone rang off the hook.

Jimmy picked it up on the tenth ring.

"Y'ell-low, Rag Doll, Jimmy speaking."

Rayf's metallic voice answered, "Jimmy, I'm with a fuckin' nut …"

"Who is this?"

"Jimmy, it's me, Rayf. Can you hear me OK?"

"Yeah, g'head."

"Cal, he's on the lam or something. He even stole Soapy's fuckin' Chrysler. Can you believe this?"

"Yep."

"Look Jim, I'm gonna catch a bus or somethin'. I'll be in tomorrow night. I'm sorry about this, really."

"Rayf?!"

"Yeah, Jim."

"Want some advice, kid?"

'Yeah. Sure. Shoot."

"Keep going."

"What? How's the connection?"

"Fine. Like I said, I hear you just fine. Can you hear me?!"

"I think so."

"What'd I just say?"

"You just said to keep going."

"No question about it. Keep goin'. Ali Baba and Soapy were in here just a few minutes ago and by the looks of it, they're gonna bang ya both."

"Soapy? Ali Baba? Why? Did they say why?"

"I guess 'cause Cal stole the Soap's car. Look kid, I only report. I don't inquire, and by tellin' ya this much I'm already sticking my neck out, capisce?"

"Yeah," said Rayf weakly.

"Uh, one more thing."

"What's that, Jim?"

"Lose my phone number." And with that, Jimmy hung up.

Slowly Rayf hung up, turned around, and looked at Cal, who was now sitting on a large, over-stuffed, orange Naugahyde couch near the entrance.

Cal looked back at Rayf and gave a shrug that said, 'Whatcha gonna do?'

Rayf was boiling as he closed in on his friend who had just cast their fates to the winds.

~ 3 ~

THE NEW JERSEY TURNPIKE

The coffee was warm, dark, and bland. What the coffee lacked in taste and the room in warmth, the waitress more than made up for in friendliness.

There were four horseshoe-shaped counters in the dining room. Cal and Rayf sat at the bend in the one furthest from the entrance. It gave, according to Cal, a longer view of her comings and goings.

"She a beauty or what?"

"Yeah, yeah," said Rayf. "So let me get this straight. You knocked her up ..."

"No, no. I said she blamed me."

"But you were banging her, weren't you?"

"So what! You were probably the only one who wasn't. And anyway, I always used a rubber." Cal was now speaking into his cup, "I wouldn't trust those guys with your dick."

"Well, it wasn't my dick. And I'm payin' for it! Son of a bitch," said Rayf. He sipped the generic blend and wondered if he'd ever drink another cup as good as Miranda's ever again.

"So then Soapy and Ali Baba break into my pad and try 'n' drag me out. Just when I'm with ... Hey you shoulda seen this one Rayf, really," said Cal who was now forming a picture of her in the air with his hands. "She was so sweet and tender. Her name was Franny. Ya know who she looked a lot like? Betty Jane Mulrooney from Marion—you know the blond from ..."

"Yeah, you picked her up in my bar. Remember?"

"Right ... forgot."

"So then what happened?"

"So I get past 'em and ..."

"Steal their car and kidnap me."

"Hey, I didn't kidnap you. You're over 21."

"Well, for your information, Jimmy told me that they came lookin' for you, and I am now implicated. Thanks a lot, shithead."

"Relax. Look, it's almost December. And I hear it's like eighty and ninety degrees in Florida all year round."

"Is that where you intend on going?"

"We, Rayfie boy, we! *We* are going!"

"In a pig's ass we ..."

Just then the waitress approached and said, "More coffee, boys?" *She couldn't be more than eighteen*, thought Rayf.

"Yeah," said Cal. "Hey, hey! You wanna go to Florida with us?"

She stopped pouring and said, "Yeah sure, right?!"

"Hey, I'm not kiddin'. We got us a brand new Chrysler sittin' right out there, and we'd love to have you join us. Wha'd'ya say?"

She put the Silex down on the hotplate and studied the two guys.

Rayf sat there solemn; black hair, deep olive complexion with dark eyes. *Definitely Italian*, she thought. And by his build and height, which she figured to be five feet ten, she pegged him for a former high school football player. Cal on the other hand had dirty-blond, straight hair with deep blue eyes and a light complexion. But try as she might she couldn't guess this one's hyphenated nationality. The only thing she was sure about was his sport, and womanizing, as far as she knew, was not an Olympic event. Not just yet anyway. He gave her a wink.

"Well?" he said.

After a slight pause she said, "Well, I ... I'll have to think about it."

"What time you get off?"

"Twelve thirty."

"Hell," said Cal, looking at the big clock on the wall over the kitchen entrance, "that's like only an hour-and-a-half away. We'll wait for ya."

"Miami?" she asked.

"Yeah, where it's always summer."

She wrapped her arms around herself and looked deep within to her own dreams. "I've always wanted to go to Florida," she said softly to no one in particular.

"Now's your chance, Suzie," said Cal, as he gulped down the lukewarm, coffee.

"How'd you know my …" then looking down at her name tag, giggled and said, "Let me think about it."

Cal noticed a new bounce in her step as she walked back through the swinging kitchen doors. And he thought to himself, *Got that chick!*

He said to Rayf, "And you're worried!?"

"And you, my friend, are completely out of your fuckin' mind."

***

A pea-green, box-shaped, 1949 Plymouth pulled up in front of Angela's apartment building. Out stepped Soapy. He slammed the car door shut. It closed with a tinny rattle. He looked disapprovingly at the green box-shaped car as he walked over to the front stoop of the apartment house.

He skipped up the front steps and rang the bell for number 2A. The door buzzed. Soapy was admitted. He took the inside stairs two steps at a time. He knocked on the door.

"Who is it?" said Angela from behind the locked door.

"It's me," said Soapy, impatiently.

Angela opened the door, but turned her back when Soapy entered.

"Hey! What's wrong wit' you?"

"Nothing."

"Den why da cold shoulder?"

"I've got a headache tonight, Soapy, I'm sorry."

"Ta da!" he said, pulling out a tin from his greatcoat. "I got da aspirin. Not ta worry."

She sat on the bed, kneading her hands. Her thoughts were all a jumble. She knew too much, yet not enough.

"Soapy," she blurted out, "why are you after Cal?"

With one arm out and one arm still in his coat sleeve, he stopped. "How d'ya know? Your dad tell ya?"

"Kind of," she said meekly.

He finished removing his coat. "Hell if I know! Da man says 'jump,' I say how high? It's my job. I don't ask da man no questions. It's better dat way, no?"

"Yes," said Angela, straightening up with a smile. "Yes, Soap, it's better that way."

He took her hand. She stood up. Now he bent down to kiss her. At first she resisted, then slowly but surely she wrapped her arms around his neck

as he lifted her off her feet with his huge hands planted firmly on her buttocks. Now she wrapped her legs around his waist. A feeling of relief filled
her as her skirt pulled up and his tongue darted deep into her throat. *Ah,*
she thought to herself, *no one knows.*

He laid her down gently upon the bed and very carefully removed her
panties. With his entrance came a feeling of pleasure that untied the great
knot of her anxieties.

***

The 1963 Conoco pocket touraide map of the United States with its
smiling cartoon characters of friendly gas station attendants and happy
family groups shown touring across country were in sharp contrast to the
two real young men who were still sitting in the same place at the Howard
Johnson counter. Cal was tracing with his finger the route that they would
be taking to Florida on their just-bought map. This was an oil company map
and the primary business of oil companies was to sell gasoline in order to
fuel this map of dreams, hence the cartoon characters, making the price
of gasoline easier to consume.

"OK," said Cal, "We take the Turnpike south into Delaware where we
continue on US 13, which takes us to either the Chesapeake Bay Ferry or
the bridge at Garsonville, Maryland. Either way we go past Norfolk, Virginia. ... Norfolk! Norfolk! Hey! Ain't that where Beaks is supposed to be
stationed at?"

"Yeah, so?"

"So maybe we could stop by. Say hello. You know."

Rayf did not respond.

"Just a thought," said Cal. "Well, anyway. Then we take 58 East to Interstate 95 and 301 South to Jacksonville, from there on out we ride Highway
1, the coast route, all the way down into beautiful Miami Beach. And then
it is hot sands loaded with hot little muchachas just for little old me and
little old you, pardner."

"Let me see that map," said Rayf, tearing it away from Cal.

At this very same moment a chopped and raked maroon 1955 Hudson
Hornet Custom Hollywood coupe with dual glass-packed mufflers pulled
into the Howard Johnson parking lot. In the car were two skinny kids in
black leather motorcycle jackets. The passenger nodded towards the black
LeBaron. The Hudson Hornet parked next to it.

The driver turned off his headlights, but not the engine. The passenger got out. Now walking around the Chrysler as though he were viewing it on a used car lot, he kicked the tires and then looked into the driver's side window and saw up there, in the visor, the N.J. Turnpike toll ticket. He turned around, his greasy hair shining under the outdoor lights, and gave a crooked smile to the Hornet's driver.

Back at the counter Rayf pointed to Virginia on the map and said, "I used to know a family in Newport News, Virginia. My aunt married a guy from down there."

"Your aunt married a rebel?"

"Yeah. He was rebel and part Indian too."

"You mean, like Tonto? Get out!?"

"No, I'm serious."

"Then how come I never got to meet the cat?" said Cal.

"He got killed in a car crash," said Rayf. "One drink too many, only six months after they got hitched."

"Jesus!" said Cal. "There it is again, marriage and death. So I guess he's out."

"What d'ya mean?"

"We can't go and visit him in Virginia. Yo Suzie, you comin' wit' us or what?"

The waitress came over to give them a refill.

"Well, are ya goin'?"

"I thought it over and. ... yes. I'll go, but first you've got to take me home. I live just off the next exit near Camden. And I've got to pick up some things, 'K?"

"Camden!?" said Cal.

"Yeah, Camden. Why?"

Cal to Rayf, "I never met no one from Camden. How 'bout you?"

Rayf just looked at Suzie; she reminded him of someone, but who?

"Hey, I'll have you know we have the distinction of having the world's first drive-in picture show," said Suzie.

"Is that right?" said Cal.

"That's right. It celebrated its thirtieth anniversary last June."

The Roosevelt Drive-In Theater in Jersey City, where Rayf and Cal took their girls, also had a world record even though it opened twenty-two years after Camden's. The Jersey City drive-in was built atop one million tons of hexavalent chromium, the world's largest known illegal chromium dump. Hexavalent chromium would eventually be rated right up there with the top thirteen most dangerous carcinogens known to man. Toxic waste disposal goes Hollywood.

There were three producers of this toxic waste back there: Maxus Energy of Dallas, P.P.C. Industries of Pittsburgh, and the Allied-Signal Corporation of Morristown, New Jersey. Which one of these three little piggies did it remains a mystery right up to this day.

And since none of these three young people knew anything about this record at the time and probably wouldn't have cared even if they had, they all laughed when Cal said to Suzie regarding the Camden drive-in's record, "Guess you had lots of practice by now, huh?" They all laughed.

"All kidding aside, I've got to pick up a few things, 'K?"

"Sure, what the hell. We got all the time in the world. Ain't that right, Rayf?" Rayf did not respond.

"And mums the word. Don't tell anyone," she said, "'K?"

"Sure, whatever you say, Suzie."

Then it dawned upon Rayf, and he knew who she looked like. She looked like his dead uncle Zeke's niece, Lucy. Now it all came back to him, how his Uncle Zeke's widow, Aunt Joan, had tried to fix him up with her late husband's niece.

It was three years ago when he had just turned eighteen that his Aunt Joan had invited Lucy, the sweet seventeen-year-old Southern belle, up for a "come-see-New York" trip, " ... and, oh, by the way you must meet my nephew, Rayf, while you are here."

This meeting coincided with Rayf's fifteen-year-old sister's shotgun wedding. His sister got knocked up and had to get married in order to protect the family's reputation.

Rayf had met Uncle Zeke's niece at his sister's wedding reception; their passions flared. So off they went to the Mayfair Motel out near the Anheuser Busch Brewery plant.

After the tryst, he suited up once again in his tailor-mades, she in her dainty dress, and together they went back to enjoy what remained of the festivities—a wedding reception for a fifteen-year-old girl and a sixteen-year-old boy playing husband and wife to a house full of adult guests. Through forced smiles, the guests offered their congratulations that, to Rayf, looked and sounded a lot more like condolences.

He decided to keep all this to himself—for the time being anyway. When he studied Suzie, who was still talking to Cal, he was amazed at the resemblance between this girl and that sweet Southern belle, Lucy. Both had the same sparkling blue eyes and reddish-brown hair that hung down in ringlets over fair skin. In place of anger, new thoughts began to occur, thoughts that seemed natural and right. What the hell, maybe this was all meant to be: Suzie-Lucy, going through Virginia and all. And here he stopped cold. His eyes narrowed, revealing yet another thought forming in his already overactive imagination. Perhaps Cal had succeeded in conning him. So he fished around in there for some other, more practical thoughts, and he came up with memories of Angela, of Soapy and his LeBaron which Cal had stolen from him not three hours before, and of Petey and his boys who had long-term memories and even longer reaches—and it was this thought that brought him right back here to his senses.

Suzie was sashaying back towards the kitchen.

"Remember," said Rayf, "we get caught, you dragged me into this."

He said this, even though he knew that they'd have to take him out for just being with Cal. Like that time when Charlie Romano, a hard working family man, was rubbed out along with Sammy Needles just because he happened to be in the same car. Needles took one bullet to the back of the neck and another behind the ear while Charlie got it once through the temple. The bullet configurations spoke volumes: the former was a job, the latter a necessity.

"Yeah, yeah," said Cal. "Will you forget about those guys for Christ sakes? Look, she's comin' with us, man. We are about to start on the party of our lives."

Twelve-thirty a.m. rolled around when Suzie took her leave and waved for the guys to follow her. The door of the Howard Johnson swung open and out walked Suzie, Cal, and Rayf.

Cal couldn't contain his excitement, "Wait'll you see this bomb. It's big, black, and cool, man. Wait'll you see it. And the back seat?! Ooo la la!"

Suzie laughed. And in spite of himself, so did Rayf.

"Don't get the wrong idea," said Suzie to Cal.

"Who me? I'm a good boy," said Cal, imitating Lou Costello and thereby getting an even bigger laugh.

They were high on life and at least ten cups of coffee as they walked over to where the car was parked. They stopped.

"We parked it right here. Didn't we?" said Cal.

"Yeah," said Rayf. "Or ... maybe it was over here."

They walked over to the next row of cars, looking up and down the parking lot.

"It's got to ... Holy shit, it's gone!" said Cal as he turned white.

"Oh man, we're in deep shit now."

"Soapy's car ..." said Rayf.

"Well boys, where's the big, black bomb?"

"It's gone, Suzie. Some sonuvabitch stole it," said Cal.

"A likely story," said Suzie.

"Hey, where you going?" yelled Cal.

"I'm going home. Where do you think I'm going?" said Suzie, who was now walking back towards the warm glow of the Howard Johnson.

"What about us?"

"What *about* yous?" shouted Suzie as she pulled open the large glass door and disappeared inside.

"Nice friend she turned out to be," said Cal.

"What do we do now, wise guy?"

"Think. I need time ta think. What time is it?"

"Quarter to one in the friggin' morning."

"Hmm. Let's go inside. We need ta think."

"You had better come up with something."

"How much money did you say you had?"

"I didn't," said Rayf.

"Well, how much?"

"Twenty bucks. And you?"

"Five."

"And the eleven grand?"

"Let's see," said Cal, "that gives us twenty-five dollars total."

"I asked you about the eleven grand."

"I ... uh ..."

"You made that up, too. Didn't you?"

"We'll get out of this so help me. We'll get out of this. I promise."

Rayf pulled out the Conoco pocket touraide map from his back pocket and slapped Cal over the head with it. "You lying bastard, sonuvabitch."

Cal ran off towards the Howard Johnson, Rayf chasing in mad pursuit.

~ 4 ~

FREEDOM RIDIN'

With Yonkers behind him, Henry Duncan drove down the Westside Highway and escaped New York City through the Holland Tunnel. This spit him out into Hoboken and right onto the brand new New Jersey Turnpike extension that rose 100 feet above the old P.S. #5 schoolyard, directly over the same spot in the road where Nicky Dee took his now-infamous, neighborhood record-setting forward, backward, multi-twisted somersault. And within a quarter of a mile Henry would be just an apple's drop above that same downtown street corner where the boys were still hanging out into the wee hours of the morning.

By now Henry had six dollars and twenty-five cents left to his name. He had thirteen hundred miles to go.

He took a swig of cheap wine and turned up the radio.

The boys on the Third Street corner could not hear the Motown beat that filled Henry's ears to mix with his rapidly rising blood-alcohol level, which caused the road before him to sway, shimmer, and melt in the dark, northeastern night. They were too busy pitching pennies, talking, or combing their hair to pay any attention to the millions of cars that passed overhead day and night, night and day.

Henry opened his window, breathed in the cold, damp air through his wide nostrils, and figured he must still be somewhere in Jersey. He noticed—off in the distance, on his left, in the same direction as the Manhattan skyline—out there on a small island, all lit up in the night, butt-end facing him, the Statue of Liberty. But from this point in time he had no way of knowing about the museum that would eventually house a display within that statue's pedestal showing how hundreds of thousands of his African forbearers had arrived on these shores in chains, lying down on two-foot-high shelves piled six deep, like so many loaves of bread in an oven. Instead, all he could see was the New Jersey Turnpike ticket station up ahead. Determined to make the tollbooth and beyond, he clenched the steering wheel and drove on.

***

In the meantime, Rayf and Cal were learning the fine art of hitchhiking.

It was a cold Monday morning, and they had counted one hundred and twenty-five cars that had passed them by as they stood at the end of the long Howard Johnson exit ramp that headed south.

They had argued the first hour of the new day away and were now somewhat resigned to the fact that they could not look back but had to roll on.

It was here that the one hundred and twenty-sixth car materialized in the form of a plain black 1960 Chevrolet sedan.

The black Chevy pulled over in front of them. Rayf and Cal ran up to it.

Rayf looked in and saw a preacher man at the wheel, clerical collar and all. And in the passenger's seat sat a sweet, shy-looking girl, whom Rayf figured to be no more than sixteen.

"Where you headin?" yelled the preacher in a friendly tone.

"Florida," said Cal, boastfully.

"Hop in. I'll take you as far as Delaware."

"Cool," said Cal. Then under his breath to Rayf, "Man, we are on our way."

And as they piled into the back seat of the four-door sedan the preacher said, "Where you boys from?"

"Jersey City," said Cal.

And it was here that Rayf and Cal got their first lesson in the hitchhikers' protocol, the small-talk ritual; a ceremony not too dissimilar to the circle and sniff routine used by dogs. This verbal circle-sniff served two functions: one, it helped the hitchhiker "picker-upper" get better acquainted with the hitchhikers by finding out who they were, where they were going, when and even why they were going there, and what they were going to do when they arrived; two, it served as a form of entertainment.

"Why you headin' to Florida?" said the friendly preacher.

"To see the sun and the sand," said Cal.

"What sort of work you boys do?"

By time the preacher got around to the third "W," Cal was already winking to the lovely young girl whose face, lit by the courtesy light, reflected softly in the rear-view mirror. And when Cal did the talking, Rayf did the winking, and wondered about the girl: *Who is she? Is she his daughter? His girlfriend? Kinda young for that. Or is she just a member of his flock?* These questions he would never ask. *It wouldn't be cool*, thought Rayf as he jostled for a better view of the girl.

They played this game for a full ten minutes, never realizing that the preacher was on to them right from the start. As a matter of fact, it wasn't until he pulled over to the shoulder of the road did they realize that their ride was over, because that's when they heard that preacher man say, "All out, boys."

"What?" said Rayf. "This ain't Delaware."

"Out!" said the preacher dryly.

It only took a moment for them to understand. And then it dawned upon them with the blinding flash of an overhead dome-light that they had been caught making eyes at the picker-upper's girl.

And so they ambled out of the Chevy sedan and watched it roll off towards Delaware, without them.

And it was here that they learned the first law of hitchhiking: never get caught making eyes at a picker-upper's girl. Somebody might just be watching.

***

It was illegal to be hitchhiking on the New Jersey Turnpike, but this was another law that they were unaware of as they sat there on the dead, grassy slope alongside the four-lane straightaway with thumbs waving in the breeze.

Here they reminisced about which one did the preacher's girl really like better, and how preachers could even spoil wet dreams, and what was that preacher doing with such a "young chick?"

They stopped counting the cars that rushed past them ten and twelve at a clip, and they wondered deep down inside if they'd ever make it past Camden, never mind Florida.

It had been three hours since they left the Rag Doll, and they had only progressed ninety miles. Cal figured at this pace they'd make it to Miami sometime around Christmas—that is if they didn't starve first.

Time passed. They kept their thumbs out.

Eventually, they developed a system. While one would rest, the other would plead to the mass of oncoming traffic.

Henry drained the last drop of sneaky pete and threw the empty into the back seat. He had all the windows fully open. Even this couldn't keep him awake. He kept dozing off only to wake up an instant later to the sounds of blaring horns. The road ahead blurred and shimmered. And then, between heavy eyelashes, he saw the median strip coming right at him. Quickly he turned his wheel to the right, and in so doing cut across four lanes of Turnpike traffic in one clean swoop. Then he blacked out.

Rayf, who was hitching, saw the Ford heading right at them. He yelled to a bug-eyed Cal; together their short lives flashed before their eyes.

Henry's crumbling body knocked the car into neutral. His knee jammed into the brake pedal. The Ford screeched to a dead stop, missing them by ten feet. They ran up to it.

Rayf was the first one to reach the car. He stuck his head into the open passenger's window. There was no one at the wheel.

The engine was racing at full throttle.

Cal pulled open the rear door, jumped in, and yelled, "Florida, James."

Rayf saw the driver sprawled out on the floorboard. The guy's head was pressed to the gas pedal. Rayf pulled open the front door and yelled, "Cal, give me a hand."

Cal jumped over the front seat and together they dragged the unconscious driver over to the shoulder of the road where they laid him down on the slope of, dry, dead grass.

Rayf slapped his deep brown cheeks. Henry's bloodshot eyes popped open and the first words out of his mouth were, "Is you boys Freedom Riders or Kluxers?"

"We're hitchhikers," said Cal.

"You drive?" said Henry.

"Yeah," said Rayf.

"Good. Then dri' me home."

Rayf, who was now propping Henry up, said, "Where's home?"

"O-lando, Florida," said Henry. And then he passed out.

Cal grabbed Henry by the feet, Rayf held him under the arms, and together they hauled him feet first through the rear door.

"Where the hell's O-lando?" asked Rayf, grunting under the load.

"Got me. All's I know is it is in Florida. And that, my good man, is where we are heading," said Cal as he laid his end down and jumped over into the front seat. "Come on Rayf-o we are on our way-o to O-lando."

Rayf jumped out, slammed the rear door shut, and hopped into the shotgun seat.

Cal hit the gas and let off the clutch, peeling out amid a hail of dirt, dust, and gravel. They had their car and were on their way to Florida.

As they drove, they plied Henry with the small-talk ritual.

He told them, from underneath that horse blanket in the back seat that he was twenty-seven years old, worked as a stable hand in all the trotter racetracks up north, that he wanted to get home to see his family in Orlando for the holidays, and he just wanted to get there alive.

Rayf clicked on the radio and started tuning for some rock 'n' roll. Instead, he found Peter, Paul, and Mary singing "Blowin' In The Wind" by Bob Dylan.

During this period of the sixties there were four types of popular music fighting for the youth share of the market. There was moon, spoon, June rock 'n' roll, and white, beach-type rock. Both served as entertainment only. On the other end of the spectrum was Motown, pumping out black gold. This music was a combo of hard-driving Rhythm and Blues with lyrical and soul overtones that made it border on the gospel. It made people keep the beat whether they liked it or not. The fourth genre was white, folk music, of which Peter, Paul and Mary were at the top of the charts. This music sang about the pressing issues of the day with lyrics about a society heading for rough times. "Blowin' In The Wind" described the many changes that were going to take place within this society and asked questions no other commercial music genre ever dared to ask, like how long will it take before certain people will even be considered people?! And when will all wars be banned? And when will there be peace?

These songs sold serious messages wrapped around catchy melodies. It was pop music with a slant.

Rayf and Cal drove through southern New Jersey singing along with the radio while Henry, under the horse blanket on the back seat, was out like a light.

They were heading south.

Ah, thought Cal, breathing in the smell of musty upholstery, cheap wine, dusty horse blanket, hay, and previously eaten hay, *we're finally on our way*.

It was two a.m.

***

Rayf had been to the South twice before—the first time when he was three years old, with his mom. She took him to visit his dad who was stationed in Little Creek, Virginia during WWII. They rented an old shack on the beach that time. The second time was with his dad to pay their respects to his late uncle Zeke's family. That time he was ten years old.

The only two things he remembered from the first trip were sitting in a beached rowboat filled with ice. And the other, sitting in the middle of a table eating butter out of a bowl. His mom chastised him on both occasions.

He remembered more of the second trip.

As a matter of fact, it seemed the closer he got to the South, the more experiences he recalled. It was as if he had lived two entirely separate lives, one as a Yankee, the other as Johnny Reb.

The farthest south Cal had ever been was Long Branch, New Jersey.

Cal pulled over. Rayf got behind the wheel. Henry groaned from deep in the back. And within minutes, Cal was snoring.

Rayf was glad to be out of the elements and rolling.

He was only behind the wheel for a few minutes when he saw the road sign: Last Exit, Tollbooth Ahead, Prepare to Stop.

He shook Cal.

"Wake up you phony bastard."

"Wha'? Wha's a matter?" said Cal.

"You know when to sleep, huh?"

"What? What's wrong, man?"

"The tollbooth, that's what's wrong."

"So pay the guy and leave me alone," said Cal, as he rolled over to face his side window.

Rayf reached over into the back seat and shook Henry.

"Wot is it, man?" said Henry. "We dere yet?"

"You got any money?"

"Six or seven dollas, why?"

"'cause we gotta pay the man to get out of New Jersey, that's why."

"Den pay 'em. Make in out like it's yo car, 'K?" said Henry as he fell back to sleep.

So there it was, Rayf at the helm with one guy feigning sleep in the shotgun seat and the other in the back seat, one horse blanket to the wind.

He could have sworn he saw Cal peek as he pulled up to the tollbooth. "Hey, Cal!" yelled Rayf, as he handed the toll collector a five-dollar bill. I want you to know I know. You rat bastard. And this you ain't dreamin' pal."

Cal mumbled. And when the Ford pulled away from the tollbooth, he woke up.

"Enjoy your sleep?"

"Huh? Where are we?" said Cal, as the *Welcome to Delaware* sign slid by. "Geez, I musta been sleepin' fer a few hours, no?"

"Try like ten minutes."

"Ten minutes and we're in Delaware already. Amazing what a few minutes of sleep can do for ya."

"Especially when you do it at the right time."

"I don't know what you're talkin' about," said Cal, nestling down. Here he was breaking free of Petey and the neighborhood, and in a very short while he would be in Miami Beach living the good life.

He imagined himself on the beach with fancy drinks and even fancier babes. He settled down to sweet tropical dreams.

Rayf looked at the fuel gauge. "We're gonna be needin' gas."

"Don't worry about it," said Cal. "I'll figure something out."

"Now I'm really worried," said Rayf.

"Relax, will ya?" said the dreamer.

Man's got a clear head, said Rayf to himself

Rayf took a left and headed down the peninsula that was comprised of three states: Delaware, Maryland, and at its very tip, Virginia.

They dropped down past New Castle, Delaware and proceeded inland. They drove through towns named Odessa, Blackbird, Cheswold, Viola, and Dover, the capital, where the governor's house, prior to the Civil War, was once used as a station in the Underground Railroad. Now here they were, ignorant of this fact and traveling in the opposite direction.

And as they passed through these little towns with their strange sounding names that dotted the countryside, they began to fall under the traveler's illusion that all the people and places that they were passing were somehow different than what they had left behind. True, they were breaking free of the gravitational pull of their own neighborhood, but, unbeknownst to them, they were passing through a universe made up of many other neighborhoods where millions of other people just like themselves remained prisoners to their own trappings.

As they approached Chesapeake Heights, Maryland, which was just over the Delaware border, Rayf said, "My sister got married in Maryland."

"Why all the ways down here?" said Cal.

"Not down here, but in Maryland, up in Elkton near the Delaware border."

"Like I said, why all the ways down here?"

"It was like a shotgun wedding. And down here all you gotta do is get a marriage license and get married. No questions asked."

"Shotgun," muttered Cal.

"Yeah," said Rayf.

"I shudder to think that something that serious could be as simple as that. It turns my blood cold."

Rayf, with his eye still on the dark, winding, country highway with its clumps of trees silhouetted against the dark sky said, "Yeah, her husband's too."

"How's that?"

"He left her last year with two kids—disappeared."

"Just like that?"

"Yup."

"How old was he?"

"When he got hitched?"

"Both—when he got married and when he split."

"Sixteen when he married and nineteen when he ran off."

"And her?"

"Fifteen and eighteen."

"All those lives fucked up just for a jump in the sack."

"She wouldn't give up the kid; wanted to get married."

"Right here in good old Maryland?" said Cal.

"Yeah."

The trees started thinning out as they drove down the tri-state peninsula. On their left, the Atlantic Ocean; on their right, the Chesapeake Bay.

Rayf breathed deeply, and his sense memory conjured up a scene of a ten-year-old boy out on the great bay with his dad and some of Uncle Zeke's men folk, relatives fishing for croakers. Even though eleven years had passed since that time, he could still hear those croakers dying on the floorboards. They made sounds like a wooden rowboat creaking apart. Rayf wondered back then as he watched them squirming around down there if they weren't calling out to him, "Please throw us back into the water, boy. Please." He exhaled, and the memory vanished.

And now, he felt the magic of that great bay which the Algonquin people had used as their summer home and had called *Chesepioc* or Great Shellfish Bay—the same bay that Spanish explorers had first set sight on only thirty-three years after Columbus' maiden voyage to the new world and called the Bay of the Mother of God which was rapidly becoming an ecological disaster. Yet here it was still casting its spell, but this time on the unsuspecting Ray Falcone behind the wheel of Henry's 1940 Ford in the year 1963.

"It might all be tied together," said Rayf.

"What're ya talkin' about?" said a groggy Cal.

"Everything—your life, the stars, the earth, the water—everything."

"Just as long as me and Angela ain't. Everything else could be," said Cal, as he slid down into napville.

They drove on.

The Chesapeake is fed by over twenty-three rivers, only one of which Rayf and Cal knew by name, the Potomac—not from their geography lessons, but from history and George Washington fame. And yet that tributary is only a minor contributor to this 64,000-square-mile watershed that is, in all actuality, the lower Susquehanna river. It's a huge, winding snake of a river that emerges at the southern tip of Ostego Lake, a lake just outside of Copperstown, New York in Ostego County, a site settled by the father of James Fenimore Cooper, author of The Last of the Mohicans. The river was named after an Iroquoian-speaking American Indian tribe that resided along its banks and populated Pennsylvania, New York, and Maryland right up into the eighteenth century. But the last twenty souls of the Susquehanna, unlike J.F. Cooper's fictionalized account of the mythical Mohicans, were slaughtered by white settlers inflamed by accounts of an Indian war on the Pennsylvania frontier several hundred miles away in the year 1763, exactly two-hundred years before Rayf, Cal, and Henry's road journey.

But the guys in the Ford in the year 1963 were completely unaware of this fact or of the 444-mile-long river that still bears the name of the extinct Susquehanna, and which still flows strong and southward to join with the bay at Havre de Grace, Maryland.

From Havre de Grace it is a two-hundred-mile trip to the open Atlantic Ocean at Cape Charles, Virginia, where all of the sweet waters head for the briny deep and to where Rayf, Cal and Henry were fast approaching.

At Grasonville, Maryland Rayf had to make a lone decision—either take the toll bridge into Annapolis and drive down into Norfolk or save eight hours by taking the ferry at Cape Charles. He waved good-bye to the bridge. It was another two hours before they finally arrived at Cape Charles.

"Holy Christ!" said Rayf, slowing down. "Hey Cal, get a load of this."

Cal, wiping the sleep from his eyes, said, "What happened, an accident or something?"

"No. It's the line for the Chesapeake Bay Ferry, man. I should've taken the bridge."

"The bridge?"

"Two hours back. Shit!"

There were at least one hundred cars waiting ahead of them.

Rayf pulled onto the end of the line, shut down the car, and got out. All the vehicles had their engines off. It was very quiet.

His first impulse was to try and sneak ahead. But he did not want to become the first guy from the neighborhood lynched in old Virginie.

So instead, he lay down on the warm hood of the old Ford, looked up at the mid-November nighttime sky, and figured that eventually he'd come up with something. That is when he saw them.

He had never seen so many in his life. There were millions and millions of them. It was as if someone had dumped out tons and tons of extra stars into the heavens. He thought, *Hey, there's the Big Dipper and there's the Little Dipper*. Two constellations even city boys were familiar with. He wondered as he lay back on that warm hood if he had ever really looked into the nighttime sky before. He wasn't sure if he had. If he did, how come he had never seen this? He breathed deeply and noticed another phenomena: fresh air.

"Cal, get a load of these here stars!"

The door opened and out crawled Cal. He leaned his back against the right front fender, looked up at the sky, and said, "Holy shit, will you look at that!"

"The sky," said Rayf. "It's so clear down here. And smell that air."

Cal climbed onto the hood with Rayf and looked up to the black sky with its millions of stars. They were spellbound by the immense expanse above. The sky had become an inverted bowl of stars.

They watched. And since the line moved so seldom and so slowly, the two guys took turns in pulling the car up. While one would drive, the other would remain flat-out on the hood.

Cal tried to get Henry to come on out to see the stars. But Henry told him that he had already seen them and was happy right where he was.

One hour had passed. Now they were within range of an all-night diner. It was a huge, white building all lit up with flood lights on the outside and fluorescent lamps on the inside.

They decided to grab a cup of coffee and invited Henry. He declined, pulled himself out of the back seat, and volunteered to move the car while they went for their coffee. And no, he didn't touch the stuff. So off they went towards the big, white diner in the night.

They opened the door and stepped into the greenish-white fluorescent hum. There was a long, straight, Formica-covered counter that went on forever. It seated fifty people at a clip on low, backless, spinning stools. The place was jam packed, yet filled with the quiet of strangers breaking commercial bread.

There was no room at the counter, so they waited. When two places became available, they stepped up and took their seats.

The young black counterman took their coffee order and returned in a flash. The place was so busy that the help here was trained to run back and forth, not walk.

They were drinking their coffee when all of a sudden a ruckus broke out. Rayf looked down the long counter to his right and saw a white customer grabbing the black counterman by his white, uniformed shirt front.

Rayf looked around the room and noticed for the first time that all the customers were white and that no one was paying any attention to the scene taking place not eight stools from where they were seated.

The white man held a steak knife pressed to the black counterman's throat. He was threatening to kill him right here in front of all these people.

Cal's knee-jerk reaction was to jump up and go to the counterman's aid, but Rayf pulled him back down.

"What the hell are you doin', man?" whispered Cal. "That crazy son of a bitch is gonna kill that kid!"

"Look around you."

Cal did.

"And?"

"Notice, nobody in the entire place is lookin' at him!?"

"So?"

"So, we're in the South, man."

The two guys from Jersey City looked around the room and noticed that not one person had missed a mouthful during the entire fracas. Rayf and Cal drank their coffees, paid their bill, and stepped out quietly into the night.

Out front Rayf noticed a sign in the window, which read: Whites Only. He pointed it out to Cal.

Rayf looked at the sign and then up to the sky just to make sure they were still where he had left them. And sure enough, the stars were still there.

On the way back to the car, Rayf got to thinking about the meaning beneath Dylan's "Blowin' In The Wind" lyrics, where the singer asks: *"How many roads must a man walk down before they call him a man ..."* and *"How many times can a man turn his head and pretend he just doesn't see?"* Rayf wondered if these lyrics were what he had just experienced first hand.

He wet the tip of his finger and held it up to gauge the wind's speed and direction. There wasn't even a breeze.

When they got back to the car they told Henry about what they had just seen and he said, "Dat's da way it be down here, boys. Dat's da way it be." He crawled into the dark of the back seat.

They boarded the ferry as the sun started to lighten the nighttime sky.

It was 6:30 a.m. when the ferry shoved off amid clanking chains, churning screws, blasting horns, and raging diesels.

As they cut through the water and the day brightened, they could see something unusual taking place out there. Off the port side they could see construction barges and huge pillars sticking out of the bay. Now they could see man-made islands strung together by bridgework that would dive into an island, tunnel its way up to the next island, and once again resume as a bridge. This was the brand spanking new Chesapeake Bay Bridge-Tunnel, a 17.6 mile span that was being built to resist twenty foot waves from the open Atlantic. It was scheduled to open in 1964 and would thereby cut the commute across the bay from eighty-five minutes to only twenty.

And Rayf was glad, for he was sure that this new bridge would put that roadside ferry diner out of business. *This*, he thought, *is progress.*

On the car deck, they watched and waited for the Virginia mainland to appear out of the mist. The brisk, morning sea air gave them a hearty appetite.

"Cal, I ever tell ya about the time I came down here to visit my late Uncle Zeke's family?"

"No."

"I was like ten years old and we came down to pay our respects to Zeke's folks. Man, I'll never forget how they treated us."

"Who's this Uncle Zeke?" said Cal.

"The rebel guy that my Aunt Joan married?"

"Oh, yeah, yeah," said Cal, halfheartedly.

"Well, when we went down to visit them, they fed us like there was no tomorrow. The women cooked up piles of bacon, steak, and ham. They brought in platters of pancakes, and fried eggs by the tray. There were gallons of coffee and warm milk, tubs of sweet butter, pitchers of syrup, and stacks of toast. The women kept taking plates away and bringing new ones back. Man. And this was just breakfast," said Rayf.

The sea air made it so that they could almost see and smell all of that talked-about food, but their imaginations weren't strong enough for them to taste it.

"Stop talking about food for Christ sake. I'm starving," said Cal.

"Yeah," muttered Henry, "Me too."

"Man," Rayf, went on. "They just kept bringing it on. Man, you have got to experience Southern hospitality to believe it."

"Yeah," said Henry, "You got dat right!"

"I'm really starving," said Cal.

And it was decided since this ferry docked in Norfolk, Virginia—home of America's largest naval installation, the Norfolk Naval Station—and since their buddy from the neighborhood, Beaks, was stationed somewhere around here, they would stop in for a friendly visit, get a little bit to eat, borrow a few bucks, and maybe even gather up a change of clothing while they were at it. What's the use of having friends if you can't rely on them in times of need? Thus went their scheming as the Virginia mainland grew closer across the waves. The ferry docked in Norfolk.

They drove off.

After much turning, weaving, and driving all over the city they finally pulled into a gas station to ask the gas jockey which way to the navy base. He gave them proper directions, and they found their way to the gate in no time.

At the gate they encountered the Shore Patrolman on duty.

"Yo!" said Rayf. "Where's The Beaks at?"

"Excuse me, sir?" asked the ramrod Shore Patrolman

"You ain't gotta call me sir. Where's our friend, Beaks?" said Rayf.

Cal, in the passenger's seat, started giggling and through his laughter said, "Hey, you a friend of Dr. Benny's or what?"

They both laughed at this one, while Henry let out a loud snore.

"Now if you boys feel like jivin' someone, you best wait till I'm off duty, 'cause I kain't kick yo asses in this monkey suit, dig?"

"Relax, man," said Rayf. "We're just lookin' for an old buddy."

"What's his name?" asked the business-like SP, "I'll see if I can locate him."

"Beaks Cellini," said Rayf.

"Spell it."

"How d'ya spell his name?" said Rayf to Cal.

Cal leaned his face out of the driver's window and started spelling, "I think it starts with a 'ce' that sounds like the 'ch' in checkers ..."

"Just spell it," snapped the SP.

"... l, l," said Rayf.

Now both at the same time: "... i-n-i..."

The SP started searching through his book as Henry sat up rubbing his eyes and said, "We in O-lando yet?"

"Not yet Henry," said Rayf.

"There's a Cellini here all right. But no Beaks," said the SP.

"He meant Eddie; Eddie Cellini," said Cal.

"I'm showing an Edward Cellini."

"Yeah, that's him," said Cal. "Can we see him?"

"I'll check," said the SP.

He got on the phone.

Another car pulled up right behind them. With a military point, he said to the Ford, "Park over there till I get through." He then waved and saluted the other car onto the base.

"Big shit," said Cal. "How come he didn't salute us?"

Rayf pulled over into the area marked Visitor Parking.

Everyone in the neighborhood knew the reason why Edward "Beaks" Cellini joined the Navy. Even though he said it was "to beat the draft and not wind up fighting that new war over there in the jungles of Viet Nam"—which just so happened to be a small, yet recurring story on TV for the past two years—they knew the real reason was that he was cheap and wanted free dental work.

Beaks' thrift was legendary on the Third Street corner. Rayf and Cal wondered if they could even get a cup of coffee out of him, never mind a meal. For it was rumored that Beaks still had the first nickel his dad had given him on his first day of grammar school.

They waited for a half hour, and then they saw coming right toward them, bigger than life, their meal ticket. He was dressed in denim and looked trim. *His nose is still three times the size of the average nose*, thought Rayf.

They jumped out of the car and ran towards him.

The SP blew his whistle.

They stopped in their tracks.

The SP waved for them to come back outside the gate; they complied.

Beaks waved to the guard and walked up to his friends.

"What brings you down here?" he said.

"You," said Rayf.

"Man, you both look like shit!"

"We hit the road," said Cal. "And thought we'd give ya a call."

Beaks was eyeing his two old friends with the knowledge that can only come from a lifetime of experience.

"So you thought you'd give me a call!? Bullshit! What's up?"

"We come all the ways down here to say hello to you and you treat us like this?" said Rayf. "I'm insulted."

"Hey Rayf, maybe we should just leave. Fuck him," said Cal.

Henry poked his head out the back window and said, "Where are we?"

"Norfolk," said Cal.

"Who the fuck is that?" said Beaks.

"Henry," said Rayf. "This is his car. We're drivin' him home to Florida."

"So how's the Navy been treatin' ya?" said Cal.

"Better 'n being on that dead-end corner, man. Why his car?" said Beaks.

"Someone stole ours," said Cal.

"Shithead over here left the keys in it."

"Fuck you, Rayf."

"Now we're using this guy's car," said Rayf.

"Yeah, that's how we felt, too," said Cal.

"About what?" said a confused Beaks.

"About leavin' that dead-end corner," said Cal. "So we decided to go to Florida. First drop Henry off at Orlando and then continue down to Miami and the warm weather."

"I thought you had a good book goin' fer yerself?"

"Hey, I gave it up. What can I tell ya."

"You could tell me you're full a shit. That's what you could tell me."

"Some friend, huh Rayf?"

Beaks looked closer at his two friends with the beat-up car and the guy hanging out of it.

"Wha'd'ya need?" said Beaks.

"You don't see us in six months and that's the first thing you ask?" said Cal.

"Wha'd'ya need!?"

"Money, food, and clothes," said Rayf.

"I fuckin' knew it. I fuckin' knew it!" said Beaks. "There ain't no way in hell you two'd just stop by for a visit, especially lookin' as bad as you do now. You two on the lam or what?"

"You got a commissary here where we can talk?" said Cal.

"Maybe I ain't got no money. Did that ever occur to you two bastards?"

"You with no money?" said Cal. "That's like the earth without a sun. Are you gonna take us for somethin' ta eat or do we hafta tell everyone downtown that you left your friends stranded in Virginia?"

Beaks searched for a retort, trying various scenarios on how best to protect his reputation and his cash at the same time. But it was a defeated Beaks that finally said, "Let's go."

He waved to the guard as they walked towards an off-base cafeteria. Henry stayed in the car.

In the cafeteria Rayf and Cal drank coffee, ate toast and eggs, and pulled Beaks' leg about his uniform and how much bigger his nose now looked with that stupid haircut. But he never laughed at their familiarity. Instead, he just watched as they'd make trip after trip to the lunch counter.

He picked up the tab, gave them twenty bucks, and stuffed two pairs of denim pants and shirts into a brown paper shopping bag. They took it in stride.

Beaks did not smile until they were safely within the Ford; he had gotten off cheap.

Rayf leaned over into the back seat to hand Henry a sack of breakfast just like they had eaten, minus the coffee. *Because*, Rayf thought to himself, *Henry never touches the stuff.*

"Well," said Beaks. "Sorry to see you leave. Don't let the gate hit ya in the trunk."

Cal, who was behind the wheel picking at his teeth said, "We'll never forget this, good buddy."

"Me neither. You owe me seventy five."

"How the fuck do you figure that?" said Cal.

"Including interest," said Beaks.

"Ya know you're worse than those bastards in the back room," said Cal.

"Hey, we're all entitled to make a living."

Cal started up the Ford and began backing out of the parking space. Beaks walked close to the driver's side.

When the car was nose-out to the street, Cal leaned out his window and said, "You're lucky if you ever see that twenty again, shithead."

And then he hit the gas.

Beaks watched the clap-trap Ford slowly roll away in a cloud of exhaust fumes. He spit after them, cursing and kicking the ground with the toe of his Navy regulation boot.

The Ford was now wandering around Norfolk looking to break free of the city in order to continue with its southbound trek when Henry, who was having breakfast in the back seat, said, "Le's go to D.C."

"D.C.?" said Cal. "But that's north!"

Rayf, checking his map, quickly deduced, "Yeah, one-hundred-ninety miles north."

"So, it's ma car ain't it?"

"Why d'ya wanna go to D.C.?" said Cal.

"Gots ma reasons," said Henry chomping on his fried egg sandwich.

"What about gas?" said Cal.

"What about it?" said Henry.

There was a long pause as they meandered around the main drags and back alleys of Norfolk looking for Highway 17, and by time they found it, Rayf had come up with a plan that would accommodate all concerned. Since this part of the country was loaded with sailors coming and going, they'd pick them up, ask them for gas money, then after a short ride tell them that they had made a mistake and had to turn off a lot sooner than expected. Drop the sailors off and pick up another batch, and so on and so forth.

The plan met with instant approval. So, off they went on Henry's mission toward Washington D.C.

***

Beaks couldn't rest. He felt like a man taken. Twenty dollars to him was like two thousand to the average man. So when he decided to put a call in to his buddy Punky in Jersey City, he felt somewhat relieved.

It was one o'clock in the afternoon in Miranda's Coffee shop. School hadn't let out yet. It was still very quiet.

Miranda was doing her cleaning chores while Soapy sat at his stool with nothing going on in his head, nothing at all.

The phone rang three times before she yelled, "Soapy, Madonna Mia, you hear the phone ring and you just sit there. Pick it up for God's sake, before it drive-a me nuts."

Soapy, shaken from his vacuous daydream, walked from the counter to the rickety phone booth, picked up the receiver, and in a very bored tone, said, "Miranda's."

"Who's this?" said the electronic voice of Beaks on the other end.

"Who da fuck you wanna talk to?"

"Soapy, this you?"

"Yeah. Who's dis?"

"It's me, Beaks."

"Hey, Captain Ahab! How da fuck are ya?"

"Not too good. I'm calling long distance."

"What can I do for ya?"

"Is Punky there?"

"Hold on, I'll go look," said Soapy as he let the phone dangle on its cord. Out to the sidewalk, searching the faces in the crowd of perpetual hanger-outers,

"Any of you jerks seen Punky?"

"He ain't around," yelled Chubby.

Soapy went back to the phone, picked it up, and said, "Punky ain't around, Cap'n."

"Shit!" then after a very slight pause said, "Soap, Soap, do me a favor will ya?"

"Depends, might cost ya. What is it?"

"Tell Punky next time he sees Cal or Rayf to get twenty bucks from them for me, OK?"

Soapy, now wide awake, grabbed the phone with new found strength and said, "Did you say Cal and Rayf?"

"Yeah, those two con artists just beat me for at least a hundred bucks worth a shit. And Cal said …"

"What da hell are you talkin' about?"

"They hit me up for all kinds of money and stuff. And …"

"Whoa! Whoa! Slow down. Slow down," said Soapy. "When'd dis happen?"

"Coupla hours ago. Why?"

"Where da hell are dey now?"

"I don't know. They were talkin' crazy. Said that they were on their way to Florida with some spade."

"Florida? What were dey drivin'?"

"Looks like a really old Ford or something like that."

"No Chrysler?"

"No. Why all the questions?"

"Those son-of-a-bitches."

"What?" said a confused Beaks.

"Never you mind, Admiral. We'll get your cash back fer ya. Don't you worry about dat. But first, tell me where you're at?"

Silence.

"Hello, Ahab… you still dere?"

"Yeah."

"Where are ya?"

"You mean like now?"

"No. Like tomorrow; yeah, now!"

"I'm. I'm at the Norfolk Naval Station. Why?"

"Is dat in dis country?"

"Yeah it's in … it's in Norfolk, Virginia. Why?"

"Whatever you do, don't ship out."

"What're you talkin' about?" said Beaks.

"Just stay right where you are. Don't hang up I'll be right back."

Soapy left the phone to dangle on its cord, bashed open the wooden-framed glass door of the booth, and ran towards the back room.

Miranda, watching the noisy Soapy run off, said to herself, "Madonna mia! Justa like a bull in a China phone booth. Sumunabitch, one a dese-a days he's a gonna wrecka da place."

~ 5 ~

BEYOND CAMELOT

They drove north on US 17 out of Norfolk. On the way they stood by
their plan: pick up sailors, ask them for gas money, and after a few miles
dump them off. They pulled this scam four times for a grand total of three
dollars and eighty-five cents.

Gas was averaging twenty-five cents a gallon.

They picked up two sailors south of Loretto who told them that if they
were sightseeing they should go see George Washington's birthplace near
Oak Grove, Virginia in Westmoreland County just over the Rappahannock
River. But Cal, now driving, told them that they were on a time schedule
and had to bypass that particular tourist attraction, and asked, "By the
way could you all spare some change for a little gas?" The sailors asked
to be let off.

They were dropped off eleven miles later near Port Royal. This experience proved to the boys that even with a service as valuable as theirs,
they could still not expect to meet up with a one hundred percent success
ratio. Cal was flabbergasted that "these two creeps" could expect to ride
through life for free.

They spent the next fourteen miles, up to the US 1 intersection at Fredericksburg, talking about the behavior of these two sailors who refused
to pay for their ride.

"You haven't been in the Armed Forces," said Rayf, "so you how can
you expect to understand these guys?"

"Neither have you."

"Yeah, but at least I got compassion."

"Compassion?" said Cal, "It was you who came up with this scheme in the first place."

"So, can't a businessman have a heart?"

"Truthfully?" said Cal, "No."

"You got a big problem, Cal."

"Me? It's you who's got the problem."

"You see," said Rayf, "these guys don't have that much money so they rely on the kindness of the American public."

"Sheet," said Henry, just now sitting up behind Cal's seat, "good luck w' dat one!"

"What're you bitchin' about back there?" said Cal.

Rayf turned in to split the difference between the two guys, and said, "You been in the service, Henry'?"

"Wot fo? To fight the white man's wars? You think ah'm a real foo'?"

Cal looked into his rearview mirror. Henry was wide awake.

"So, uh," said Cal, "is everybody like happy now?"

"It was you who started it, man," said Rayf.

In the Ford there was silence, the sound of the road, and the smell of the bay.

"Pull over," said Henry. "Let's get us a jug."

"That," said Cal, "is the best idea I have heard all day."

They had enough of this driving business, philosophizing and the gathering of gas money. They needed a break.

Outside of Stafford, they pulled over and bought two bottles of wine. It was cold outside so they got back into the Ford, opened one bottle, and passed it around. Cal lit up a Cigarillo and blew smoke rings up towards the high-ceilinged Ford.

The wine made them feel good to be alive. Henry's thinking under the influence went something like this: *Hell, here I am with a couple of crazy white boys out on a scramble*; and Rayf's went, *Fuck work. I needed this*; and Cal's went, *This sure beats marriage.*

The wine made them forget all about their past, their future, or where they had to be at five o'clock. It numbed them, making them only aware of the moment and the world as they wished it to be.

They passed the bottle until it was bone dry. Rayf rolled down the window and flung the dead soldier into the bushes.

Cal fired up the Ford, nosed it onto US 1 North, and started ambling leisurely, once more, toward Washington D.C., which was fifty miles dead ahead.

***

"And there, right below us," said the tinny voice of the 707 pilot over the speaker system, "is the capitol of this great land: Washington D.C., home of the brave, land of the free." The asymmetrical city of the District of Columbia showed itself through the lacework of clouds below as the pilot droned on, "The official map of Washington D.C., completed around 1790, was drawn up by white US surveyor Andrew Ellicot and, according to legend, was assisted by free Negro mathematician Benjamin Banneker."

Soapy, in the aisle seat, stood. "Where? Where's it at?" he said, stretching to look.

"Somewhere down dere, behind doze clouds," said Ali Baba.

"I don't see nuthin'," said Soapy, sitting back down.

"Maybe it's too cloudy or somethin'," said the other, staring blankly out the plane window.

"Hey Babs, get a load a da legs on dis one!" said Soapy, leaning out into the aisle.

Instead, Ali Baba studied Soapy, who was tracking this stewardess as she came and went.

"Ya know, I tink you got a sickness," said Ali Baba.

"Sickness? What da hell're ya talkin' about, sickness?"

"Brawds; thems all you ever dink about"

"Ya got somethin' better ta dink about?"

"Yeah."

"Like what?"

"Like baseball, fer one," said Ali Baba.

"Baseball? Baseball!? I dink you're da one dat's got da sickness, man. Ya can't fuck a baseball, dumbo."

"Who you callin' dumbo?" said the man with the hair-trigger mentality.

"Sorry Babs. It's just dat ...Yeah. Yeah. Ya know, ya just might be right! Maybe I do got too many brawds on da brain."

"Maybe you should go to a shrink. I hear dat dey got all sorts uv cures for over-sexiness an' stuff like dat."

Soapy gave the giant a sidelong glance to see if he was pulling his leg. But the concrete face of his current partner never revealed what little brain activity was taking place behind that rock-like forehead of his. His huge frame blocked out the entire 707 window.

"A shrink?"

"Yeah," said Ali Baba, "either dat or a priest." He turned to the window.

Soapy, now looking at the back of Ali Baba's head bit his tongue and raised a clenched fist as he pantomimed throwing a punch at his partner's medulla oblongata. *That*, thought Soapy, *should finish off this giant for sure.* And now, once again, he turned his gaze to the aisle in search of his short-skirted entertainment.

"Baseball!?" said Soapy, under his breath, "Un-fuckin-believable." He looked down the aisle and caught sight of a skirt bending down to pick up a dropped liquor cap. *Ah*, he thought, settling back to enjoy the show, *dis, is more like it.*

***

At this very same moment, in the back room at Miranda's, Pietro d'Alloro was just finishing up some business with Mike Russo, the nineteen-year-old nephew of local politician Marc Russo.

Mike, on the strength of his name alone, had taken out several large loans from Pietro's loan-sharking operation, but could not make his vig, which is a penalty fee for missing a weekly payment, the sum of which does not come off the principal.

Petey, it should be noted, filled a definite need in this neighborhood. People unable to get personal bank loans at the current twelve percent rate compounded daily, always had access to Petey's loan company, which provided rates at a modest six hundred percent, vig included. And the only compounds incurred from Petey's Loan Co. were fractures.

And now as Pietro was explaining to Mike Russo the compound-fracture clause of his loan, Mike's mother, Bertha—a large, loudmouthed Calabrian flushed with rage—charged into the office.

At first Bertha started scolding her son for borrowing "so much damned money without even having a job to pay it back," and then she turned her anger on capo Pietro for lending such a stupid kid such a large sum. Pietro knew this woman. He watched her in stone-faced awe. Here was a mother protecting her young. Her courage knew no bounds. The boss had no intentions of interrupting her tirade for he knew women, like hurricanes, always blew themselves out.

Pietro watched as Bertha slapped her son, pulled his ears, kicked him in the shins, pulled at his clothing, and then, as quickly as she had started, stopped, turned to the boss, and threw a stack of bills on his desk.

"Here Pete," said Bertha. "Is that enough to cover it?"

Pietro looked at the stack of bills laying there on his desk.

"Well?" said Bertha. "Aren't you going to count it?"

"I will. But first," said capo Pietro. "May I ask you a personal question?"

"What?"

"Where did you get this money?"

"I took out a loan from a bank," she said defiantly. "Why?"

"I see," said capo Pietro, now counting the money.

"Is it all there?"

He nodded pushing several bills back towards her.

"What's this for?" said a surprised Bertha.

"Because," said the boss very quietly, "when the bank gets through with you, you're going to need it."

"She picked up the money and said, "Thank you mister d'Alloro."

"Thank you, Bertha!"

She grabbed her son by the ear and as she walked him out of the office said, "You're welcome, Pete." To Mike she said, "And you, you stupid son of a bitch…"

Then they were gone.

Slowly, Pietro readjusted his tie and suit jacket. The four men-in-waiting watched their leader for a sign. He chuckled. They laughed. The boss shook his head, pulled open a smooth-railed desk drawer, deposited the money into it and pushed it closed.

There came a frail knock on the alley door.

Dum-Dum peeked through the peephole, looked back at Pietro, and said, "It's your daughter, boss."

Capo Pietro gave the signal to let her in. Then with another gesture, he cleared the room.

The men left through the coffee shop door.

Angela, entering from the alley door, walked in with her head hung down.

Now father and daughter were alone in the makeshift office.

"To what do I owe this visit?"

Angela, very meekly, said, "I ... I ... want you to ... to spare Cal's life."

The capo did not reply, but instead started to stroke his smooth chin. Angela stepped closer, repeating her request, "I want you to call off your orders."

"Just like that?" He studied her, wondering what things Cal could have said to her. Did he retaliate with a threat to her life? Did Soapy or Ali Baba get wind of why the contract was implemented? He thought on in this manner and then noticed his daughter sobbing softly. He handed her his handkerchief. She took it from him and brought it up to her teary eyes.

Pietro sat back.

"What you are asking for is very difficult to accomplish. It's like trying to retrieve a rock after it has been thrown into a lake. Even if you do find the rock, you can never recall the ripples that it has caused."

"I just want you to bring him back alive, father. Is that asking too much?"

"I know what you said. Did you hear what I said?"

"Yes father, I heard you. You said that you couldn't stop the order ..."

"I didn't say that. I said it would be hard to recall what has already been set into motion."

Angela sobbed softly. To Pietro, those sobs were like keys to a great room wherein kindness was kept. And this much Angela knew: he would do anything within his power for her, his little princess.

Capo Pietro watched his little girl crying there before him, but he could not stop wondering about the gender of his soon-to-be grandchild. *Will it be a boy to take over the rule of my small fiefdom and, with a good education, enlarge my domain?* He mused on in this manner while rubbing his chin for reassurance as he always did in moments of great decision.

"What matters now, Angela, is that you take good care of yourself and the child that is growing within you. You're my blood and the child that lives within you must be given all the proper medical attention that money can buy. There within you is our future. And right now that is all that matters. The rest I will take into consideration."

Angela dried her eyes and looked into the loving and wise eyes of her father. She knew that her request was above and beyond all the tears that she could muster, for an honorable solution had to unfold and the yearnings that grew from a lover's quarrel held very little weight.

She stood up straight, held her chin as high as she could, and walked over to him. He stood up. She kissed him on his cheek. "I'm sorry to bother you. It won't happen again."

Capo Pietro nodded, held her out at arms length, and said, "It is not your fault. A woman knows not the workings of a man's world, therefore it is not a woman's place to interfere in matters pertaining to men. What must be done shall be done."

He kissed her gently on her forehead.

"I love you, Daddy."

They embraced.

"I love you too, sweetheart. Now, if you will excuse me."

She walked to the side door, stopped, and waved a strong hand back to her father. He sat down behind his desk, nodded, and watched as she closed the door gently behind her, and in so doing closed out the world on the lone man within.

***

Their plane landed at Patrick Henry International Airport, Virginia. From there they took a cab ride across the James River to meet with Seaman First Class Edward "Beaks" Cellini at the Norfolk Naval Station.

They picked Beaks up outside the gate and had the cabby take them to a little waterfront dive of a bar. Soapy told the cabby to wait.

They walked into a bar filled with sailors. The room got quiet. Beaks gave the sailors an all-clear sign, the noise resumed.

Soapy and Ali Baba, in their suits, ties, and greatcoats, were in sharp contrast to the sailors now gathering for some serious drinking.

Beaks, who stood five feet eight, felt out of place and conspicuous with these two large men who he thought looked a lot like gangsters, even though he knew that is exactly what they were. He looked around the room and smiled a frozen smile to four of his mates at the next table. Beaks ordered three beers.

"We don't drink beer," said Soapy.

"That's all they serve here," said Beaks.

The nondescript waitress brought the three beers. Soapy took a small sip, held the glass up to the light, studied it, and said, "What da hell d'ya call dis shit?"

"Beer," whispered Beaks; feeling stupid as he said it, and then with a shrug of the shoulders gave a frozen grin to his mates' questioning stares.

"What kind? It tastes like piss ta me," said Soapy.

"Who gives a fuck about beer," said Ali Baba. "We're here ta talk about Cal."

"What, do you want to know, Babs?" said a nervous Beaks.

"Like where dey are right now?"

"I don't know. Like I told ya they beat me for over a hundred bucks worth a shit."

"What'd dey get ya for?" said Ali Baba.

"Money, food, clothes ..."

"I'm tellin' ya Babs. Taste this shit. G'head, taste it."

"Fer Christ sakes!" With that, Ali Baba downed his own glass. He swallowed, licked his pallet, burped, and then said, "He's right." Smacking his lips, "What is dis shit?"

Beaks, a little embarrassed, leaned in and whispered, "It's three-point-two."

"Never heard of it," said Ali Baba.

Soapy took another mouthful.

"It's not a brand name," said Beaks. "That's the alcohol content of the beer."

"Tree-point-two," shouted Ali Baba.

"Yeah."

Soapy spit a mouthful out.

A fine spray of beer landed on the four sailors at the next table. One by one they stood up to face the two strangers.

Beaks jumped up and ran over to his four friends.

"Hey guys, relax. They didn't mean anything by it. They're just not used to the beer down here, that's all. Ain't that right, Soap?" said Beaks through a nervous laugh.

The four six-foot-tall sailors looked over Beaks' head readying to get on with a good fight.

Ali Baba and Soapy did not stand up, but instead just looked at the four young men.

The two thugs did not see the rest of the bar looking their way. That didn't matter. They turned their chairs to face the four standing sailors at the next table. Now, very slowly they peeled back their greatcoats just enough to give the four swabbies a peek at their shoulder ware.

Beaks, with his back to the thugs, was still pleading with the standing four to forget it, as one by one they sat down. Their slack jaws told the story.

Slowly, Beaks turned around and looked towards the two men who were just now readjusting their coats and grinning back at him.

Beaks excused himself from his mates and walked back to the two thugs.

"Hey, what the hell did you guys come down here for in the first place? First those two fuck ups come and then ..." catching himself in mid sentence, reevaluating the situation. "They said they were going to Florida, Orlando, or Miami. They had this colored guy's car. They hit me up for money. Cal said he gave up his book and was takin' a vacation. I don't know any more. That's it! Now would you please go, before I wind up in the fuckin' brig?"

"Touchy kid," said Ali Baba, to Soapy.

"L-Look, I'm sorry I raised my voice. But I gotta live with these people," said Beaks.

"What're you, a fag or what? You live with all a dese guys?" said Ali Baba.

Beaks hung his head. He knew nothing could be said to these two men; time had to take its course. They would have to make the next move if he expected to see tomorrow's detail.

He heard their chairs sliding against the hardwood floor and, without moving his head, watched the two men as they stood up. And now he felt the presence of Ali Baba over his right shoulder. He waited and waited and then Ali Baba tapped him and said, "Come on. Let's go. Outside."

Beaks stood up and, with a frozen smile, nodded good-bye to his four mates as he walked out of the bar between the two large men.

The three men stepped out into the parking lot under the late afternoon overcast sky.

"You're a good kid, Beaks."

"Thanks, Babs," said a shaky Beaks.

"But sometimes when good kids hang out with shit, dey get treated like shit," said Ali Baba.

"Let it be known that I am not hanging out with those two bastards. I'm tellin' ya the truth. They beat me for over a hundred and ten bucks." Now pleading, "Look if you ever find 'em could ya at least please try an' get me back twenty of it," hopefully with hesitation. "OK, Babs?"

Ali Baba turned his back on Beaks and said to Soapy, "Take care of him."

Soapy reached into his greatcoat. Beaks pissed in his pants.

"Here," said Soapy. "Here's a few to carry ya over till pay day,"

Beaks was now holding two twenties in his sweating palm.

Then once more Soapy reached into his pocket, pulled out another bill, handed it to him, and said, "Go back inside and buy doze four kids all a da tree-point-two shit dat dere stomachs can hold. After all, dey's protectin' us, ain't dat right Babs?"

"Soap, like I told ya, you need a shrink. Come on, let's get outta here."

Beaks, with a wet crotch and sixty dollars in his hot little hands watched Ali Baba and Soapy walk back to their waiting cab; they got in, Soapy waved. He waved back. They drove off.

Here he was, still alive and ahead of the game. This called for some sort of celebration.

He ran back into the enlisted man's bar and yelled, "Drinks on the house," but then correcting himself, "Make that, whatever twenty bucks'll buy."

For it is told that Beaks is a very wise man with a buck.

***

It was dark when Rayf, behind the wheel, found his way down Constitution Avenue. It was a wide-awake Henry who told Rayf to slow down as they approached the Lincoln Memorial.

"What for?" said Rayf.

"I just wanna see it," said Henry, half hanging out the back window.

"See what?" said Cal.

"Stop!" yelled Henry.

Rayf hit the brakes.

"OK, you could move now. But go real slow like."

They moved at a snail's pace.

"Dat's where da King spoke."

"What're you talkin' about? We got a president in this country," said Rayf.

"Martin Luther, man. He spoke here a few months ago and dere was like over two hundred tousand people listenin' to 'im." said Henry, half talking to himself.

"Oh him!" said Cal.

"Yeah, him," said Henry. And then he said softly while still looking out the window, "I have a dream ..."

Rayf readjusted the rearview mirror to get a better look at Henry, who was staring off at the Lincoln Memorial monument with its reflecting pool. Then he looked over at Cal, who was also looking back at Henry. Rayf and

Cal then looked at each other before turning to look towards the monument. They all fell silent. The monument slid by.

And here's where Rayf thought, *If they were now the stuff that movies were made of, they'd probably be ghosted-over with some newsreel footage of the two-hundred-thousand people who had gathered here at the Lincoln Memorial back on August 28th. And there'd be Martin Luther King reciting his "I Have A Dream" speech.* And of course he and Cal would be portrayed as Freedom Riders carrying a destitute young Negro boy back home to his poor old sick and dying mammy way down south. The camera would come in close to scrutinize their determined faces, and now with a nod of deep understanding, punctuated by just the right violin-enhanced, heart-wrenching crescendo, the viewing audience, sitting out there in the dark, would all understand and there wouldn't be a dry eye in the house.

But this wasn't a movie, and his ego-driven daydream was broken when he saw a real poor person lugging all of her life's possessions in two rag bags as she moved stoop-shouldered and aimlessly through the cold, November, Washington D.C. night.

This very real scene looked nothing like one of those clean-cut cowboy action movies that J.F.K.'s dad, Joseph "Joe" P. Kennedy, had produced back there in the good old roaring twenties—movies that helped make him a millionaire several times over. Instead, this scene looked more like the continuation of the great depression—a depression that, according to Rayf's dad, Joe, helped aggravate and further depress without any regard to anyone but himself. "He was just makin' money," Rayf's dad would say, in the same tone as he'd say, "Pass the pork chops, please."

They now had a clear, unobstructed view of the White House all lit up in the night.

"I'll bet J.F.K.'s in there right now plannin' another one of those fancy dress balls with all the tax payers' money," said Rayf.

"At least they're tryin' to bring culture to this country," said Cal.

"It's his wife that I'd like to ball," said Rayf.

"He's our president, man. Cool it," said Cal.

"So? I can't dig his wife?" said Rayf.

"Dems dat got," said Henry, as they cruised past the White House.

"Who knows?" said Rayf. "Maybe, we do have a king for president."

"I'd settle for a measly ten percent of the Kennedy's money," said the rational-minded Cal.

"We is definitely in a class system, boys. All da world over, dems dat got, party. Dems dat ain't, either watch or serve," said Henry. "Well boys, I have seen e-nuff. Let us go to 0-lando. I have paid my respect."

"You mean you made us drive an extra 380 miles just to look at a couple of crummy monuments?" said Rayf.

"We have just passed over holy soil, boys. Now we got us some good luck. Say Hallelujah!"

Rayf and Cal looked at one another, shrugged their shoulders, and in unison and without much emotion at all said, "Hallelujah."

Rayf, at the wheel of the dilapidated car, aimed it southward once again in search of US 1, which would take them into the real America and leave behind forevermore the media-fabricated province of Camelot.

Cal turned on the radio and started dialing for a station. Henry leaned over into the front seat and selected a station of his own choice. The song he found playing over the air was "Our Day Will Come" by Ruby and the Romantics, a slow ballad with a group of soulful background singers wailing out a hopeful tune.

It was a hit song.

***

Meanwhile, Soapy and Ali Baba, with one of their many false IDs, rented a car from Hertz. It was a black Lincoln Continental.

They headed the car towards Florida.

***

Rayf, Cal, and Henry, on the other hand, found US 1 and pointed the old Ford south. Just south of Fredericksburg, Virginia, they picked up a hitch-hiking soldier. He told them that his name was Leonard and he also told them that he was a full-blooded Cherokee Indian, one of the five civilized tribes—the five being Cherokee, Choctaw, Creek, Chickasaw, and Seminole. The term civilized was used because these five tribes had adopted many colonists' customs.

Leonard was stationed at Fort Dix and had just received orders for Vietnam as a crew member on an H-21 Shawnee helicopter nick-named "The Flying Banana." He was on leave and felt a need to visit his ancestral homelands, which he had never been to.

"Where's that?" said Rayf.

"The Allegheny Mountains in West Virginia," said Cherokee Len.

"Why?" said Cal.

"To talk with the spirit of my people who were uprooted from this area and driven to Oklahoma. I have to walk among the trees there and on the land of my ancestors. I have to breathe the moist, cold air of the great mountains and walk through the valley of Shenandoah."

"That sure is a pretty word," said Henry, "Shenandoah."

"In English it means, the Daughter of The Valley of Stars. And only after I walk in that valley can I can go to Nam," finished Leonard, the American soldier.

Henry offered Len some wine but he refused, saying that his system was unable to metabolize the alcohol. Then he asked to be let off just north of Richmond.

He got out of the car, closed the door, and started walking west. He disappeared through the trees over which a thin sliver of a moon had just gone.

They were quiet as they watched Len walk away. And then Henry said, "If you ask me, maybe, just maybe we come all a dis way just ta give dat guy a lift. An' fer dat we's gonna git us some good luck. Garunteed, man. Garunteed."

"Yeah," said Cal. "I hope he finds some, too."

They were very quiet now as they drove off towards the South. They never did ask Cherokee Len for gas money, these two white boys from a northeastern urban ghetto and the southern black stable hand from O-lando.

They drove on.

~ 6 ~

BREATHIN' AND HOPIN'

Soapy, unaccustomed to reading maps, took Highway 58 out of Norfolk and went as far west as La Crosse, Virginia, where he took a left turn onto US 1 south.

Ali Baba, comfortably ensconced in the plush interior of the black Lincoln Continental, was busy studying the wrinkled map.

"Where da hell're ya takin' us?" he said.

"Ta Florida." said the driver.

"Why da hell'd ya take us all da way out here, fer Christ sakes?"

"Cause we're goin' south, dat's why."

"We'd been a hell of a lot better off on 301 if ya ask me."

"I'm not askin' you."

"Well, I tink you took us way out a da way, asshole."

"You wanna take da wheel, Columbus?"

"I'd get us dere a hell of a lot sooner 'n you," mumbling out loud, "All da ways out ta US 1."

"Dat's it! I'm tired of you always tellin' me what ta do, who ta fuck, how ta drive," he said, pulling over just north of Raleigh, North Carolina. "Here, take da wheel."

Ali Baba, now behind the wheel, drove through the capital and continued for forty miles down US 1 to Sanford, where he then took a left onto State Highway 87 east, with the hope of hitting US 301 in Fayetteville, NC.

Just below Olivia, they saw a bright orange neon sign shining among the trees. It buzzed the word, "PIZZA."

"Well look a dat," said Soapy. "Dey got pizza down here, too. How da hell d'ya like dat?"

"Let's give it a try," said Ali Baba. "I'm starvin'."

"A little taste a home. Let's do it," said Soapy.

It was 11:15 p.m. when they pulled up to a gravelly stop in front of the one-room roadhouse. They got out of the Lincoln and, while standing half in and half out of the car, gave the place the once over.

Slightly confused, they looked toward one another across the shiny black roof, shrugged their shoulders, and slammed closed the car doors one after the other. Immediately, the night became quiet with a stillness they were not even aware of. They crunched up the gravel walkway to the roadhouse's door all a clutter with advertisements for soda pop, cigarettes, beer, sandwiches, ice cream, and hanging there among all that visual cacophony was the sign that read, OPEN.

Soapy pulled the door toward him. A tiny bell warned of his entrance. They both looked up to the tinkling sound.

The place was barren and empty of customers. Randomly scattered about the small, one-room eatery, on a clean but well worn linoleum floor, were six mismatched, bare wooden tables with accompanying chairs in varying states of disrepair. The room was lit up by several naked light bulbs that hung overhead. Two neon beer signs advertising Atlantic Beer buzzed away in the windows to the right and left of the wood-framed glass door where the two men stood.

They looked around for signs of life. There were none to be seen. Cautiously and instinctively they walked to a table near the window, better to watch their car.

Ali Baba was studying the cream-yellow ceiling which he figured must have been white about six or seven years ago. Soapy, on the other hand, was casing the room, looking for various escape routes, when all of a sudden the swinging door opened from the back room.

Both men, out of habit, went for their shoulder ware, but stopped when they saw a pretty Chinese girl walking through the doorway towards them.

She had no idea how close she had come to meeting her Buddha.

"Y'all wanna see a menu?" sang the Chinese waitress to the two bewildered men.

"Y-Yeah," said Soapy haltingly.

Ali Baba, studying the girl standing there right in front of him said, "It says pizza outside. Right?"

"Y'all want a pizza? Large?"

"Yeah," said Soapy, with some hesitation, "large."

And then Ali Baba said, "Make dat wit' everything on it."

"Drinks?"

"Yeah," said Soapy, "How's 'bout two Dewar's on da rocks."

"Dewar's?" said the waitress.

"You know," said Soapy flirtatiously, "like, Scotch?"

"Sorry, but we only serve pop and beer."

"Pop?" said Soapy. "What's dat?"

"You pullin' ma leg?" said the waitress.

"No. But I wouldn't mind."

"Bring us two beers," said Ali Baba.

"It ain't no tree-point-two stuff, is it?" said Soapy.

"No sir. It's Atlantic, 'The Beer of the South'," said the pretty Chinese waitress slinging the slogan with a sweet Southern drawl.

"Never heard of it," said Soapy, moving in for the score.

"It comes from Charlotte, North Carolina."

"Just bring us da pizza and two beers," said Ali Baba with a finality that ended Soapy's amorous advances like a branch breaking clean from a tree.

"One large pizza and two Atlantics," said the efficient waitress. She walked back towards the swinging kitchen door.

Soapy sat back and glared at the giant who was still studying the roadhouse. *Dey got da nerve to call dis joint a restaurant?* thought Ali Baba while looking around the room. "Fer a minute dere I daught she was gonna bring us Chow Mein. A Chink rebel! How da hell da ya like dis? What'll dey tink of next, jeez!"

Soapy, with locked jaw, did not answer his partner but instead, through squinted eyes, just stared at him.

Ali Baba stood six feet four and weighed 280 pounds. He was balding, with brown hair that he combed straight back and parted, what was left of it, on the right side. He was missing his right front top tooth and bottom left front tooth. He wore a suit and tie, and filled out the broad shoulders of his greatcoat without any shoulder padding whatsoever.

Soapy watched as the dumb giant looked around the room and tattooed a steady beat on the table top with the stubby fingers of his right hand, a ham of a hand that had seen the soft side of many a head.

He studied Ali Baba in this manner until he heard the squeaking back room door open once again. Out walked the waitress with the two beers.

She put the glasses down and started to fill them. Ali Baba grabbed the beer out of her hand and started to drink it right from the can.

The girl was not in the least bit interested in people's drinking habits, for she had seen more than her share of Friday night beer bouts when the good old boys would come in with their hot rods parked out front, drink their beers, eat their pizzas, and race up and down Highway 87 from Olivia to Pine View, four miles east of here. Or when the college boys from State would come down and try like the dickens to impress one another with their drinking prowess. She left the two silent men to their thoughts, which in Ali's case was nothing at all, and in Soapy's case was a severe hatred for Ali Baba.

Several minutes later the pizza came.

She placed it down in front of them. They stared at it as it just lay there in the center of the table.

"Anythang else, boys?"

"Anything else?" said Ali Baba. "Where da hell is da pizza?"

"You're lookin' right at it, sir."

"Dat ding?" said Ali Baba.

"That's what you ordered, sir, one large pizza with the works."

"You call dis pizza?" said Soapy. "You gotta be kiddin'!"

"What's wrong?" she said.

"Hey," said Ali Baba, "I ate a lotta dings in my time, from tripe to cap-pozzelle ..."

With knitted brow, she asked, "What's that?"

"What's what?" said Ali Baba.

"Cappo ... What's that?" said the waitress.

"Cappozzelle? Baked sheep's head," said Soapy. "Why?"

"Yuck."

"And nothin' I ever ate looked as strange as dis," said Ali Baba.

"Hey, what ken I tell y'all," said the Chinese Southern belle.

"You can tell me dat dis ain't pizza," said Ali Baba.

"Well it is."

"I come here fer a taste a home, and I get dis slop," said Ali Baba. "You ever taste Italian pizza?"

"Fer your information," said the waitress, "Marco Polo brought back the pizza from China."

"Must a been cold as hell when he got it home," laughed Soapy.

"Who told you dat?" said Ali Baba to the girl.

"M' pa."

"Was he dere wit' him?" said Ali.

"With who, sir?"

"Wit' dis Marco Polo guy."

"No sir. He jest figured it out."

"Could it be dat he figured wrong?" said Ali Baba.

"No sir. You see in China it was called pinza."

"So dat's what dis is!?" said Ali Baba.

"No sir. This here is pizza. The only thing that the Eye-talians added was the tomato sauce."

"De on'y ding!? Dat's da whole ding." said Ali Baba; then after a slight pause, "Look, sweetheart, not ta be rude or anything, but a good tomata sauce is what makes pizza pizza."

"Is that right?" said the waitress.

"Yes, dat is right. Look," said Ali Baba the teacher, "Next time you go up ta New York, taste da pizza, 'cause dat's where it got purfected.

"Maybe you could learn how to make it da right way. No offense, but dis ding here looks more like chop suey on a disc." Now pushing it away, "Don't worry we're gonna pay fer it."

"I'm sorry you don't like it."

"How's 'bout two hamburgers," said Ali Baba, "You make dem with beef, right?"

"Yes sir, we make 'em with beef," said the dejected waitress.

Soapy pulled out his cigarettes and was fishing around for a match while the waitress started to remove the exotic pizza from their table.

"You got a match?" said Soapy to the girl.

She pulled out a book of matches from her apron pocket, handed the book to Soapy, and with the untouched pizza in-hand headed back to the kitchen.

"Pizza from China!" said Ali Baba, more to himself. "I guess somethin' musta got lost in da translation."

Soapy picked up the matches and saw the name written on the cover: *Bamboo Pizza Palace.* He tore off a match and struck it to life. He closed the book and continued reading the name on the cover while bringing the lit match up towards the cigarette hanging from his lips. A light flashed in his eyes. He killed the match, jumped up, and said, "I got it! I know where dey's headin'!"

"Where who's headin'?" said Ali Baba.

"Cal and Rayf! Dey's headin' to Johnny's joint in Miami, da Pink Flamingo!"

"How da hell d'ya know dat?"

"Call it a hunch, call it anyting, but I know dat is where dey are goin'. I gave Rayf a book a matches and told him dat he'd do good if he went down dere. You can call me crazy, but I'll bet dat's where dey's headin'."

"So what da hell are we waitin' fer? Let's go," said the other as he stood up and slapped a twenty dollar bill onto the table.

They ran out amid clinking bell and slamming door.

The Chinese waitress peeked out of the back room just in time to see the big black Lincoln start up and skid off in a hail of gravel. *Just like those crazy ol' white boys do on weekends,* she thought. She yelled back into the kitchen with a sweet Southern drawl, "Hold the burgers, pa."

***

The boys in the Ford had taken US 1 south and, just before Richmond, caught a short section of Interstate 95, a branch of the brand new interstate highway system that would eventually link the entire United States. They took I-95 down to Richmond, then merged onto US 301, and without so much as one wrong turn continued on their journey.

They were making good time. Cal had calculated that since leaving the Rag Doll the night before they had traveled 707 miles, 380 of which were back-tracked for Henry's D.C. tour. This, he figured, gave them a grand total of 327 miles, the distance that separated them from Petey.

Virginia, where the first permanent English settlement was established in Jamestown back in 1607, had slipped by and folded into their own historic gray-matter recording devices.

They hit the North Carolina border in full stride and cheered. The car was holding up.

In Fayetteville, Rayf once again resumed with their gas-plan idea and picked up a gaggle of hitchhiking sailors. Cal was sleeping in the shotgun seat and Henry, who was sleeping propped up against the rear right door, almost fell out when the four sailors piled in.

Rayf asked the sailors for some spare change and received one dollar and twenty-five cents with nary a qualm. And since the four guys were just going up the road a piece he decided to give them the full treatment and take them all the way.

But all things do not always go according to plan.

The interior of the old car was huge; the back seat was big enough to fit the four sailors and Henry in cramped comfort. Henry, now propped up between car and tar fell back to sleep.

It is rumored that sailors are perhaps the horniest of all the armed forces, hence the nickname coined by British sailors, randy tar. Henry, who had never heard the term, was about to learn the true meaning of the phrase first hand.

After much adjusting and readjusting, the five men in the back seat finally fell quiet, and one by one either dozed off or stared out at the dark shadowy trees that they passed in the night.

Henry once again drifted back into a deep sleep. Soon a dream began to form within the void. In this dream he saw a beautiful young wisp of a dark skinned girl appear out of the mist. She beckoned to him with curled finger and pointed to her moist spot that was covered with a tan, curly patch of hair. He moved in slow motion towards her, and slowly she ran towards him, her supple breast bouncing ever so gently. They met; she reached down to his crotch. He squirmed there in the back seat, a smile on his lips. He dreamed on. Now the girl, fondling his pecker made it hard. But alas, he awoke, and soon realized that he was not in the midst of a dream at all, but was, instead, in the back seat of his very own car.

And then he felt it. It was a hand groping around for his zipper. He stopped for a moment, did not even breathe, and then checked to see where his own hands were. Now with both hands accounted for, he thought, *If I gots ma hands here and dere, and neither one of 'em is down dere, den who da hell's holdin' ma ...?* And then, very slowly, politely, and diplomatically he reached down and removed the randy tar's roving hand.

Now wide awake, he sat bolt upright and started coughing himself into a fit. The sailor on his immediate left started snoring.

Henry shouted, "Help. Pull over, Ah'm chokin' ..."

Rayf pulled the car over to a dusty stop.

Henry jumped out of the car and said, "Dat's it fellas! We is turnin' off right now. Sorry 'bout dat, but y'all hafta bail out now, hear?"

The sailors, while stepping out of the car, asked questions like, "But I thought you were takin' us all the ways up the road," and, "What kind of con job is this?" And so on and so forth.

Rayf, who was just as surprised as the sailors, did not interrupt, but instead, watched as Henry urged the swabbies out of his car. *No big deal*, thought Rayf, *We already got the one dollar and twenty-five cents and, after all, it is his car. Shit, he can do whatever the hell he wants. And anyway, the lighter the load the less gas we'll use*, went Rayf's rationalizing.

The car, several inches higher and a couple of hundred pounds lighter, drove off.

"What happened?" said Rayf over his shoulder to Henry in the back seat.

"Let's jest say dat boy's got some balls," said Henry who was now looking back at the four sailors standing there beneath a street lamp—three forlorn and somewhat confused sailors, unaware of their mate's infringement. and blaming, so he thought, those three wise-ass con men as they drove off without them after taking their one dollar and twenty-five cents for a ride that never happened. Henry couldn't make out the culprit from this distance. In uniform they all looked the same. And he thought, *Dey'll wonder 'bout dat ride dat night in North Carolina and why it ended so quickly wit'out any reason—all of 'em dat is, except one.* They became smaller and smaller as they drifted into the past.

He turned back to face front and breathed one last, "Jeez!" before pulling his horse blanket up off the floor.

He lay down, stretched out full and covered himself with the blanket.

"You OK?" said Rayf.

"Yeah, I'm OK," said the voice from deep down in the darkness. "But do me a favor, will ya."

"What's that?"

"Don't cho go pick up no mo' hitchhikers, 'K?"

"Whatever you say," said the driver. "It's your car."

"Tanks."

They drove on through the night: Rayf at the wheel, Cal sleeping in the shotgun seat, and Henry lying down in the back seat.

Everything is back to normal, thought Henry as he drifted back to sleep, wondering that maybe all of this was just a dream and perhaps what he thought had happened had never really happened at all. And with any luck, he still might be able to catch up with his dream girl. He snuggled down, a smile on his lips, and imagined real hard.

Several miles later, aglow in the night, Rayf saw a brightly lit gas station. The warm, orange and white bath of light from the tungsten lamps seemed a welcome and pleasing sight as they illuminated the dark trees that surrounded the place to within fifty feet. Looking at his gas gauge, which was never more than an eighth full, he decided to pull in. Cal, who had slept through the entire preceding event, woke up as they came to a bumpy stop next to the pumps.

"Where are we?" said Cal, wiping the sleep from his eyes.

"Just south of Fayetteville."

"Why'd we stop?"

"Gonna get some gas."

"How much?"

"A dollar and a quarter."

"Cool, man," he said, as he fell back to sleep along with Henry, whose snoring from somewhere in the back sounded a lot like a band saw.

Rayf, now outside the car, was talking to the friendly kid who worked the all-night shift. He told the attendant where they were from and where they were going and asked the kid what he did in the daytime. "Oh, so you go to college! That is great. Stay in and beat the draft." And, "Yes, the Ford does look bad, but it's got a whole lot of life left in 'er—anyway, we hope it does. It's gotta get us all the way to Florida. Oh you've never been there? You should take a vacation and go there sometime." And, "What is that strange looking billboard with the sleeping Mexican guy on it that comes up every couple of miles and says, South of the Border? Oh, it's a tourist attraction that sells fireworks, coffee, and road trophies! Oh, they've got a motel, too! Maybe we'll sleep there tonight. Oh, it's just over the border!" And so on and so forth.

The pump was slow; it took a few minutes to put in the five gallons of gasoline, but they were having a good old time exchanging stories and, besides, the kid was happy to have someone to talk to in the middle of the night. Anyway, it gave him an excuse to take a break from his homework. And it gave Rayf a chance to meet the locals.

While all of this was taking place, Ali Baba and Soapy had since discovered US 301 at Fayetteville and were at this very moment driving past the four hitchhiking sailors under that street lamp. Soapy was sleeping; Ali Baba was still at the wheel. He saw the four ghost-white hats on the side of the road and thought he'd have a little fun. He aimed the car right at them and punched his steering wheel dead-center. The blast from the powerful horn sent the four sailors scattering like dust particles before a beam of light. He laughed.

"Wha' da hell happened?" said Soapy, jumping up from his sleep.

"Deer in da road," said the other.

"Jeez, I'd liked ta've seen dat. I never seen a real deer in my entire life," said Soapy now studying the trees all around them. "Hey Babs, ain't it pretty down here? I never seen so many trees in one place. Ain't it somethin', man?"

"Yeah, it's OK I guess."

And dead-ahead, the gas station with the Ford parked by the pump loomed up out of the darkness.

"How we doin' on gas, Babs?"

"Half a tank."

"Let's fill 'er up, no?"

Rayf, leaning back against and concealed behind the high-topped Ford that stood between him and the road, continued talking with the kid.

The Lincoln slowed down. Soapy and Ali Baba looked at the gas station. The driver started to turn in, but then said, "Nah, we'll fill 'er up at dat 'South uh da Borda' place."

"Whatever," said Soapy as he snuggled back down to sleep in the comfortable shotgun seat.

The Lincoln drove on.

***

The drizzle had turned to rain, and by the time they hit Saint Pauls, North Carolina, it was a deluge. The Lincoln's wiper blades removed the droplets of rain with sudden and swift dispatch.

The slow, rhythmical tic-tic-tic-tic of the windshield wipers, along with the warm air and soft, syrupy music coming from the radio made Ali Baba drowsy. He shook Soapy awake.

"Wha'?" said the groggy passenger.

"I'm fallin' asleep."

"So, go ta sleep."

"Take over da fuckin' wheel, wise guy!"

"What time is it?"

"It's almost two," said the driver.

Soapy, fighting the map, said, "Where da hell are we?"

"Just past Saint Pauls, North Carolina."

"OK, OK. Let me see … let's see …" said Soapy, buried in the map. "OK! Next big town coming up should be Lumberton. We stop dere and get us some coffee, OK?"

Ali Baba pulled over.

"What're ya doin'?" said Soapy.

"Drive!"

A sleepy Soapy climbed into the driver's seat.

Two minutes later, Ali Baba said, "An' no local shit, ya hear me? From now on we eat at one a doze chain joints."

"A chain joint? Wha' da hell is dat?"

"You know, one uv doze chain restaurants!"

"Oh, right," said Soapy, now straining his eyes to keep the big car on course.

Here were two city men unaccustomed to bouts of extended driving, who would need all the caffeine they could get their hands on if they had any intention of staying awake on this chase.

Twelve long miles later, in Lumberton, on Capuano Drive, Soapy located a Howard Johnson.

He pulled into the parking lot and killed the engine. They got out and, with coats pulled up and over their heads, ran through the rain into the warm, dry diner.

Following a short distance behind the Lincoln, and unbeknownst to everyone, was the Ford with Rayf still behind the wheel. He shook Cal.

"Wha' da ya want?" said Cal, retreating deeper into his seat.

"I can't see. The wipers are broke."

"What're you tellin' me for? I'm no fuckin' mechanic?"

"Reach out and pull on the blades. Maybe they're stuck."

"What blades?"

"The windshield wiper blades."

"It's fuckin' pourin' out there."

"No shit," said Rayf.

"Fuck," said Cal, as he rolled down his window, reached out, and pulled on the wiper blade—both wipers moved simultaneously.

"Great!" said Rayf, "Keep it up."

"Close dat window!" shouted Henry, from the back as he changed sides to get out of the pouring rain.

The windshield wipers on the Ford were useless and Cal had had enough of this "hand jive." He closed his window and said, "I'll drive. You work the wipers."

Instead, just south of Lumberton, Rayf pulled off US 301 and headed east along the Lumber River. He found a place alongside the river and parked.

The rain was still coming down hard. Cal fished around for the clothes that Beaks had given them and came up with a denim shirt and a pair of denim bell bottom trousers. He dried off and put them on.

"Now all you need is the nose and you'll look just like the Beaks."

Cal didn't laugh, but instead threw his wet clothes clear back onto the rear window ledge where they landed with a damp thump.

The metallic music of the rain upon the roof, less the stress of driving, helped Rayf to fall asleep in no time at all. Henry woke up to check on why they had stopped, looked around, and went back to sleep. Cal lit up a Cigarillo, swung his bare feet onto the dashboard, and dreamed along with the rivulets of smoke that rose up to and drifted out his open inch of window, dreams and smoke melting into the night.

The Ford, nestled among the trees by the winding river, shone as if it were brand new.

***

The rain stopped around five a.m., but the boys did not rouse from the sleepy Ford until six thirty. Cal was the first one up. He got out and sat on the right front fender taking in the clean, fresh smell that a good rain always leaves in its wake. Rayf was next. He opened the front door and joined Cal on the fender. They looked down at the slow-moving river. Henry was the last one up. He stepped out of the back, stretched his arms wide, and said, "It's great to be alive." He dug around in the back seat, found a bar of soap, and walked down to the river's edge.

"Hey, you guys, come on down an' wash up."

They stripped to their drawers, tumbled down the hill, and joined him, washing in the cold water. They were waking up, and the warm feeling of "it's-great-to-be-alive" welled up within all three. Rayf was the first one to see them up there on the bank.

He was cupping a couple of handfuls of water into his eyes to wash away the stinging soap when he saw them. More water into his eyes. Now his vision stabilized, and sure enough, there they were.

He shook his head, hoping they would go away. But they did not. He signaled Cal. And when Cal looked up, he too froze. This is when Henry noticed Rayf and Cal frozen like statues. He followed their gazes up the riverbank and that's when he saw them, too.

There were four men standing near the Ford with shotguns at the ready, looking down their barrel sights at the three bathers. The trickling of water was all that could be heard. The hunters knew they had their prey praying and smiled to one another through the corners of their eyes.

The only thing Rayf could think was, *Who would know if they murdered us? We're strangers in these parts and could be killed and buried along this riverbank with no one being the wiser.* And now the cold water chilled him to the bone.

Henry knew that he was about to meet his maker and, therefore, did not give it any further thought, for he had been here many times before—and even if he did survive this one, he would surely meet up with another situation just like it sometime down the road. He only had one wish—that he was holding a machine gun instead of this bar of soap.

Cal still wasn't sure if this was actually happening, and then he heard himself say a shaky, "Howdy!"

No response. Had he used the right term for hello? *They do say howdy down here, don't they?* he hoped.

"You boys always wash with niggers?" said the big one up front. Rayf and Cal looked at Henry, then back to the four gun toters. "He's our friend," said Rayf.

"Now do ah detect," said the big leader, "a Nawthun accent?"

"Sho sounds dat way ta me, Luke," said the little one.

"Yeah. ..." said Cal. "And, uh, we're like, uh, on our way ta Florida, man. And, like, we don't mean to be causin' you any trouble, pardner..." Again he wondered if he had used the right term—or was it brother, or br'er? He promised himself that if he ever got out of this alive, he'd study the greetings and dialects used throughout these United States.

"Well, well," said Luke, "looks like we got us a couple a Freedom Riders, Jed."

"Well, how do you like dat," laughed Jed, the ugly, skinny one on the right.

"No, I don't think you understand ..." started Rayf.

"Oh yes we do," said Luke, the leader. And they all broke out laughing.

"Look, man," said Cal, "We're not Freedom Riders."

"We were hitchin' to Florida," said Rayf. "And this guy was nice enough to give us a lift."

"Well, how do ya like dat boys; we's got us a charitable nigger here," said the leader, who then, quick as a flash pointed his rifle at a bush to his left and squeezed off a round. The shot made the bathers jump.

The little one ran off towards the bushes and held up the carcass of a dead rabbit.

"Nice shootin', Luke," said the skinny one.

"You boys plannin' on stayin' 'round these parts?" said Luke as he reloaded.

"Us?" said a squeaky Cal, trying to get the echo of the shot out of his ear. "Hell no, we were just leaving your beautiful state. Ain't that right boys?"

Rayf and Henry nodded.

"If you give us the room mister Luke," said Cal, "we'll be outta North Carolina within forty minutes, sir."

"You make that thirty and I might consider not killin' the whole lot a ya," said Luke.

"Would you believe, twenty minutes?" said Rayf.

The big man looked at his watch and said, "Well, wha'choo waitin' fo' boy, you already blew thirty seconds." And with that, they scrambled up the hill, hopped into that Ford, cranked it up, and skidded out toward US 301.

The hunters laughed and squeezed off a few more rounds into the air. But the boys in the Ford had no idea where, what, or who they were firing at, because Cal was all balled up on the front floor while Henry was flat out on the back floor and the only thing that could be seen of Rayf were his hands on the steering wheel and his head popping up and down. It looked as if it were a self-propelled car heading west in a cloud of gray exhaust.

And it was good-bye to North Carolina and hello to South Carolina, whose motto is: *Dum Spiro, Spero*—While I Breathe, I Hope.

And that is exactly what they were doing inside that Ford.

***

The night before, Soapy and Ali Baba had found South of the Border, ordered two separate rooms, and hung out do-not-disturb signs on their respective doors. They were going to sleep in even if it killed them.

***

By eight thirty that morning, Rayf drove in under the giant cut-out sign of the siesta-taking, sombrero-wearing Mexican known as Pedro, an oversized replica of the same sign that they had seen on billboards strategically placed a few miles apart on US 301 for the last one hundred miles.

Pedro slept while sitting on the ground, his back leaning up against a huge cactus tree with sombrero on his head and his chin resting on chest.

It had taken Rayf only thirty minutes to drive from the Lumber River to this South Carolina roadside attraction. The place teemed with services and facilities that catered to the motor trade. Rayf and Cal, attired in navy denims, jumped out of the car. Henry, in the back seat, was buttoning up his one and only faded yellow cotton shirt when Cal opened the rear door, reached onto the back ledge and grabbed his clump of wet clothing. He laid out the wet clothing on the right front fender.

The sun, rising in the clear blue South Carolina sky, burnt off the early morning chill.

Henry, pulling inspection on his car, first kicked the four tread-bare tires, and next lifted the hood to check the oil. Just then a swarthy, skinny kid with a pencil-thin mustache and black, slicked-back hair approached the three guys who were pulling maintenance on their meager possessions amid exaggerated tales of pure bravado.

"Yo!" said the skinny kid.

Rayf, who was laughing, stopped, turned around, and saw the kid, whom he figured to be about eighteen. An eighteen-year-old Gypsy.

"Hey you guys. What's new?"

"What's it to ya?" said Rayf.

"Hey, after all of those bumpkins, it's hip to see three cool cats."

Rayf and Cal puffed up.

"You boys traveling?"

"Yeah," said Cal. "Why?"

"It's cool, man—just asking. You boys looking for some amphetamines?"

It was only a short pause, but long enough for the kid to recognize who he was dealing with.

"Uppers!?" said the kid.

"I knew what you meant," said Cal.

"I knew you knew, man. That's why I approached you. You guys are cool."

"So?" said Cal.

"Well, like I said, I seen a lot of hicks out here and you guys ... you're from up north, right?"

"Yeah," said Rayf, proudly. "Why?"

"Hey man, you like radiate big city, dig?"

Their bell bottoms, which they had borrowed from Beaks, were two inches too short and the matching denim shirts were much too tight.

"What're ya sellin'?" said Cal.

In the kid's palm was a cellophane cigarette pack cover; it contained ten pills.

"What're those?" said Rayf.

"Man, this stuff'll get you to your destination before you even start."

"That right?" said Rayf.

"Damn right. It is good, shit."

"Drugs?" said Rayf.

"No, man, this is like stuff you can probably get from your doctor. The only difference is with me you don't need a prescription."

"What's it made of?" said Cal.

"Amphetamine," said the Gypsy. He winked when he said the second ingredient, "With a trace of lysergic acid diethylamide."

"What's that?" said Cal.

"Speed with a trace of acid."

"You mean LSD?" said Cal.

"That's right. The amphetamine keeps you awake, and the other entertains you while you're up there," said the underground pharmaceutical salesman, with a grin.

"LSD's legal?" said Rayf.

"Ain't no law against it, man," said the hustler. "Where you boys from? New York?"

"Yeah," lied Cal.

"Cool. Well?"

"Well, what?" said Cal.

"You buyin'?"

"How much?"

"Ten bucks."

"Ten bucks … hmm," said Cal, figuring.

"Yeah, man. It's a steal at twice the price."

"Let me talk to my friends."

Cal put an arm around Rayf and Henry. They turned their backs on the kid.

"Well?" whispered Cal, "What're we gonna do?"

"Ten bucks?" said Rayf. That's a lot of cash, man."

"That's what he's askin'."

"I'm aware of that," said Rayf.

"So? Are we buyin'?"

"What are we gonna do with them?" said Rayf.

"Eat 'em!"

"Like hell, man, not me," said Rayf.

Cal turned around and said, "Why'd you pick us out?"

"Cause like I said, you guys looked ..."

"Knock off the cool shit, OK?"

"Alright," said the kid, leveling. "I sell these things up and down the road. Sell them mostly to truckers. And sometimes to people who look ..."

"Cool?!" said Cal.

"Right."

"One sec, man," said Cal.

Back in the huddle, Cal said, "OK. So here's what we do. We buy 'em and turn 'em over for a profit."

"Buying them for ten bucks ain't gonna leave us much room for profit," said Rayf.

"OK, so we work him down," said Cal.

Henry was in awe.

"Let me talk to him," said Rayf.

"OK," said Cal. "Your move."

Rayf turned around, big city style. "So, uh ... You know Jackie Weaver?"

"Who?"

"Some Gypsy guy I know. You are Gypsy, right?"

"I'm Greek."

"Bullshit," said Rayf. "You're a fuckin' Gypsy. Be proud of it."

"OK, so I'm Romany, so what?"

"Just askin'," said a calm Rayf.

Henry watched the two cats, readying to pounce or run, he wasn't quite sure which.

Rayf was thinking he didn't know much about the Romany people but more than the average white guy did. He had first-hand experience with a tribe of Gypsies when he was a kid. He remembered hiding in Jackie's mom's fortune teller's storefront office behind a curtain with Jackie while Madam Pauline, Jackie's mom, read cards and told fortunes. He remembered when Jackie Weaver turned fifteen how he came back from wintering in Florida driving a brand new, 1956, fire-engine red Cadillac convertible and how Jackie wasn't allowed to play with Rayf any longer because now that he had become a man, he had a business to attend to. Jackie had purchased his wife and got half of his cash back when she proved financially non-productive (a used wife among the Gypsies had a bleak prospect in finding another husband and a very poor resale value). He also knew that Jackie's first male child would be turned over to his mom for her to raise as her own—a tribal pension fund.

He didn't know if this kid's tribe adhered to any of Jackie's customs, but that's all he had to go on.

"Your name Weaver?" said Rayf.

"What're you up to, man?"

"Are you a Weaver?"

"What are you a cop?"

"No," said Rayf.

"Then what's with the third-degree?"

"Three bucks," said Rayf.

"You are out of your freakin' mind! Three bucks!"

"Hey, then keep the stuff."

"Bye," said the kid turning to leave.

"Hey, wait up," said Cal.

The kid stopped, turned around, and said, "What?"

"Four bucks," said Cal.

"I'm goin', man."

"Four-fifty," countered Rayf.

"Seven bucks."

"Four."

"Man you eastern guys are too much. Six."

"Five," said Rayf.

"Five'll get ya four tabs."

"OK," said Cal. "Five-fifty."

"You still got four," said the dealer.

"How do we know its not aspirin?" said Rayf.

"'Cause I work this place, that's why. I got a reputation to protect."

Rayf recalled a phrase that Jackie Weaver always used: "You can't cheat an honest man, because an honest man isn't looking for a steal." Rayf said, "Look we're down to our last few bucks and don't wanna get burned."

"You're not gonna get burned. Trust me," said the kid.

After a long moment of silent thought, Rayf said, "OK, we'll go six."

After an extended pause, the Gypsy kid said, "Fuck it! Deal. Give me the money, man."

Rayf pulled out three dollars, looked to Cal who chipped in two and then to Henry who forked up the other dollar. Rayf held the six bucks out to the kid who very slowly extended the cellophane wrapper. They met, released, and grabbed—Rayf the bag, the Gypsy kid, the money.

He pocketed the money and said, "It's good stuff. I got regular trucker customers up and down 301. A quarter of a tab'll get you five hundred miles. You are gonna have a ball. Just wait and see."

And as quickly and as silently as he had appeared the Gypsy kid was gone.

Cal now handling the crinkly package said to Rayf, "You call that dealin'?"

"Hey, at least I got him down to six, hot shot."

"And you almost lost it, too."

"Almost doesn't count. What the hell are we gonna do with these things?"

"Simple. We take some and we sell some," said Cal.

"Bullshit!" said Rayf. "I ain't takin' none of that shit. You heard Doctor Benny, fuckin' stuff 'd drive ya crazy."

"You believe what that nut says. Come on, let's have a few laughs," said Cal, holding the bag out to Rayf. "Just take one."

"After you."

"What're you chicken or what?" said Cal.

"No. I'm just hip to your shit. You take one first."

"Oh, man," said Cal.

"G'head take one," said Rayf. "I dare ya."

"Darers go fir ..." said Cal as he dropped like a rock behind the car.

"What's a matter? You look like you saw a ghost," said Rayf.

"Get down!" croaked Cal.

The fear in Cal's voice made Rayf react without thinking. He just ducked.

Henry looked at Cal and Rayf down there behind the Ford's front shotgun-side fender.

Now he looked off in the same direction that they were looking in.

He didn't see anything unusual, just two big men in wrinkled white shirtsleeves with loosened ties carrying their suit jackets over their shoulders with crooked fingers.

"What's wrong, boys?" said Henry to the two guys now peeking out from behind the right front tire.

"Nothin'" said Cal, in a harsh whisper. "Be quiet. Act like we're not here. Look the other way."

All people pick up on reality transmissions. Without even so much as a question, Henry did as he was told.

The boys watched as Ali Baba and Soapy went into the restaurant to get some breakfast, or so they supposed.

"Holy shit," said Cal. "How the hell'd they get down here? Fer Christ sakes if those guys ..."

"Fuck!" said Rayf. "I told ya those guys had reach, man."

Cal stood up and ran away. Rayf followed.

Cal yelled back to Henry, "We'll be right back. Don't leave."

Cal found a public phone booth, jammed into it, dropped a dime, and dialed 0 for operator. The operator answered and connected him to Jersey City.

The phone rang twice in Angela's apartment before she picked it up. "Hello," said Angela into the phone.

"Collect call from Cal," said the operator.

Angela froze.

The operator, once again, "Collect call from Cal, will you accept?"

"Huh?"

"Angela, accept ... Accept ..."

"Sir, please, I'll have to ..."

"Angela ..."

"... I'll have to disconnect you."

"I'll accept, operator. I'll accept," blurted Angela into the phone.

"Thank you," and the operator was gone.

"Angela, what the hell's going on?"

"What do you mean?"

"Soapy and Ali Baba are tracking me down. These guys are gonna knock me off if you don't do something."

"I don't know what you're talking about."

"Angela!"

Silence.

"Angela, are you still there?"

"Yes, I'm still here."

"Look, Angela, if we get married we'll," and then he remembered, and with the delivery of a TV soap opera narrator he said, "Angela, Rayf told me a true story about his poor sister who had a shotgun wedding. And the guy she married disappeared leaving her all alone in the world with two children to support."

"What happened to him?" said Angela.

With a dramatic pause "He just ran off," pause, "Four lives destroyed because of one mistake."

Now there was silence on both ends.

Cal hoped that what he had just said was working its way into her emotions and would eventually affect her logic.

"Cal?"

"Yes, Angela."

"I'm sorry," she hung up.

He slammed the phone into its cradle and was now sweating profusely as he stormed out of the booth and said, "Fuck!" His dime returned. He pocketed the change.

He started pacing up and down, up and down, like a lion trapped in a cage and then he stopped, looked towards the car with Henry standing next to it, and called out, "Henry. Henry, come over here, hurry."

Henry trotted over to the phone booth.

"Henry, I got a plan," said Cal. "I want you to listen. Listen closely."

***

Angela, sobbing, threw herself onto her bed and in a very short time was crying.

She shifted from crying to sobbing and then to wiping her eyes and blowing her nose. Now she was under control. She picked up the phone and dialed.

After several rings the phone was answered. "Hello, you have reached La Madonna Del Lume, Convent. I'm Sister Mary Elizabeth. How may I help you?"

"Yes, sister," said a hesitant Angela. "May I please speak to Sister Camille Joseph?"

"One moment," making the connection, "May God bless you," finished the nun.

***

Henry was near the entrance to the diner, adjusting himself to look as presentable as possible. He looked across to Cal and Rayf hiding there behind his Ford on the far side of the parking lot, a place where he wished he were. Cal gave him the three-ring sign a sign that meant everything was OK. *Easy for him to say,* thought Henry. And then the door swung open, and he turned to see the two big men walking out. As they passed, he called out to the smaller and younger of the two, "Psst. Hey, you drivin' far, man?"

"What's it to ya?" said Soapy.

"Hey man, like I got some amphetamines. Uppers! Stuff's script-legit, man. It makes caffeine look like sleepin' pills, man," said a well-rehearsed Henry.

"Dat right?" said a now very interested Soapy.

"Come on, fuck dis spook," said the other.

"Wait up, Babs. Dis ain't no drug. You heard da kid—it's like legal wit' a doctor's prescription. I know a couple a fat brawds dat use da stuff regular. Keeps 'em wide awake an' skinny, dey say."

"So you want it. Get it," said Ali Baba. And he walked away towards the far parking lot behind the building.

"How much?"

"Dirty," said Henry weakly.

"Dirty?"

"Yeah, dirty bucks. And dey's real good, man," said Henry the salesman.

"How many do I need to take?"

"Only two or three at a time," said Henry. Or was that a third or a quarter? He wasn't quite sure. Confused, he wiped his face with his big, brown hand.

Soapy peeled off one twenty and a ten. "Here."

And this is where Henry performed the same careful exchange he had seen Cal and the Gypsy kid perform one hour before. Soapy, on the other hand, watched this guy doing this strange dance and wondered if maybe this kid was a total "nut-case" and was having second thoughts, when all of a sudden the exchange took place and now Henry was holding the thirty dollars and Soapy was left holding the bag, which he pocketed, then turned and split.

Henry flashed a smile across the parking lot. The warm sun danced off his silver filling, and the sparkle in his eye radiated "mission accomplished." And when he held up that money, the guys near the Ford knew that he had scored. Soapy, running after his partner, now heard a confident Henry calling out after him, "Hey!"

Soapy stopped, turned around and yelled back, "Wha'd'ya want now?"

"You goin' north or south?"

"None uv your business. Why?"

"'Cause if you're goin' south on 301, you could stop in and visit Claxton, Georgia."

"Why dere?" yelled Soapy.

"It's the fruitcake capital of da world, dat's why."

"Danks fer da tip. But we got no time to tour your hometown," said Soapy as he disappeared behind the building.

By the time Rayf and Cal ran across the parking lot to peek around the corner, Soapy and Ali Baba were gone.

"You see which way they went?" said Cal.

"No," said Rayf.

"You think they're really trackin' us?" said Cal.

"No. They're followin' Henry."

"I mean, maybe they're down here on some other business. Maybe this was just a coincidence."

"Coincidence my ass," said Rayf.

Just then Henry ran over,

"How much'd you get?" said Cal.

"Dat cat handed over dirty dollas like he prints da stuff."

"We should've kept a couple of tabs for ourselves," said Cal.

"You don't need any of that shit. You're crazy enough," said Rayf.

"Ya know, I just realized, we got nothin' to worry about," said Cal.

"How d'you come up that?" said Rayf.

"After they take that shit, those two guys are gonna be gah gah, man."

"That is *if* they take it."

"They spend thirty dollars and they're not gonna take it!?" said Cal. "Come on use your head, man."

"You sure you didn't take any?" said Rayf.

"I wish I had," said Cal.

"Man," said Henry, "I am starved."

"What're we waitin' for," said Cal. "We got money, now let's eat."

"Food!" said Rayf.

And off they went towards the diner.

At the door Henry stopped dead in his tracks. The other two guys kept walking, but when they noticed he wasn't with them they stopped, turned around and called him on. He wouldn't budge. He just stood there by the door.

"What's a matter with you?" said Rayf.

He didn't speak.

Rayf and Cal walked back to him

"You're hungry, right?" said Cal. "Then come on, let's go eat."

Henry just stood there and nodded toward a sign posted in the window. It read, Whites Only.

~ 7 ~

WASTED

Ten miles south of South of the Border, near Dillon, the Ford pulled into a gas station/mini-mart combo. Rayf and Cal went in to buy some groceries. Henry did not go in with them; they did not ask him to. They bought cold-cuts, bread, pickles, small individually wax-paper-wrapped pies, potato chips, pretzels, gum, soda, and two one-quart bottles of ninety-nine cent wine.

Back in the car Henry said, "Let's do Georgia by night. Dat's da best time a' day to visit dat particular state."

"And, since your license is still in the mail, I'll take it all the way through Georgia," said Rayf.

"OK," said Cal, "I'll drive to the border."

With all in agreement and thus provided for, they headed south: Cal behind the wheel, Rayf riding shotgun, and Henry in the back seat, all feeding their faces and singing into the warm air that rushed in through the four open windows as they rolled, well within the speed limit, on US 301 through South Carolina.

**

Thirty-five miles south of South of the Border, at Pee Dee, South Carolina, Soapy and Ali Baba popped two pills each.

Soapy was at the wheel.

Ali Baba, punching the air conditioning unit, said, "Wot's wrong wit' dis fuckin' ding."

"Here," said Soapy, reaching over to fiddle with the lever, "maybe if I jiggle dis here ding-a-ma-jig ..." The lever broke off in his hand, "Fuckin' junk! Dey got da balls ta rent us a piece a shit like dis!"

Ali Baba rolled down his window. Hot air blew in.

"Pull 'em all down, Soap."

Soapy, at the master control, opened all windows. The hot, humid breeze on their sweat-beaded faces helped cool them down.

"Here," said Soapy, handing Ali Baba two more pills. "Take a couple a more. Dey seems like dey's weak."

Ali Baba held the two little white pills in his huge hand and thought to himself, *Shit, look at dese little suckers. Dey couldn't keep a dwarf awake. Who's dat spade kiddin'? He conned dat stupid bastard inta buyin' aspirin.* He popped them into his mouth and swallowed hard. The driver did likewise. That made a total of four LSD-laced amphetamine tablets digesting within the stomachs of these two men.

Within fifteen miles, Soapy began to feel the effects of the drug.

The sweat was stinging his eyes. He rubbed them with the back of his hand. Now he started to see things in the road. He blinked a few times, rubbed a few times, but they didn't go away; they were still there—strange things, like lizards and buzzards. Then he thought he heard Ali Baba criticizing him. "Wha' da fuck did you say!?" said Soapy.

"Nothin'," said Ali Baba, eyes glued to the road.

Surreptitiously, the driver studied his passenger. Ali Baba seemed to be changing into some sort of animal. Soapy shook his head and slapped his own face, then he looked back and sure enough, a bear was riding shotgun. Soapy almost shit his pants.

"Babs!?" said a frightened Soapy, "Is dat you?"

Ali Baba, unable to speak, looked at Soapy, who now had a bird's beak where his nose used to be. He did a double-take. Soapy's nose returned. "Jeez, I feel strange," said Ali Baba.

"Take it from me, Babs, you look strange." But this time when he sneaked a peek at Ali Baba he was back to normal. *It's gotta be da heat*, thought Soapy. Now a feeling of euphoria filled his entire being. He felt as if he were flying high above the road. He stuck his head out the open window; the breeze felt great. Now when he looked down at the earth far below, he became entranced with that white-dashed line way down there. He couldn't take his eyes off of it.

Ali Baba, on the other hand, was feeling a sensuality that he had never felt before; it was thrilling, and yet at the same time frightening, for he had never experienced anything remotely sensual in his entire life. *What is this good feeling?* he wondered. *I feel great*, he thought, *but why? I hate feeling good. Oh glory be to God! God!? Who da hell is God? Ah, I'd love to fuck dat tree … Holy Christ, it's coming right at us!*

"SOAPY!"

Soapy jerked his head up from the hypnotizing white-dashed line just in time to see the tree coming right at them. He pulled the wheel hard to the left, narrowly missing a head-on collision with an unyielding black walnut. Now he cut a hard right. Ali Baba slid over to him.

They started laughing. The whole thing, which had taken only four seconds, flew past like an old-time movie.

"That was too funny," said Ali Baba through tears of joy.

"You looked like a fuckin' bear," said the other, between ripples of laughter, as he shoved Ali Baba back over to the other side of the seat.

"And you … you had a fuckin' bird's beak for a nose, you ugly son of a bitch."

"What kind a' bird?" said Soapy, still laughing.

"How da fuck should I know? One wit' a beak, I guess," said Ali Baba, scratching his own head.

"You know what I mean! Was it like a pigeon, a sparrow, a eagle? I'll bet it was probably a eagle's beak, right?"

"I wouldn't know an eagle's beak from a bee's dick …" Now half to himself, mimicking "What kind a bird's beak!?"

"Well, you looked like a fuckin' cub," said Soapy.

"What kind uv a cub?" said Ali Baba.

"How da fuck should I know? Da only bear I ever seen was a stuffed teddy bear."

"A cub is a kid bear, right?" said Ali Baba.

"Yeah, and dey're a baseball team too, why?"

"'Cause you probably saw me as a grizzly bear cub, dat's why."

"You were a fuckin' gorilla, dat's whatchoo wuz."

They broke into a fit of laughter. They got pains in their sides. Ali Baba's diaphragm locked in cramp, he couldn't breath. He leaned forward and motioned to his back. Soapy punched him between the shoulder blades as hard as he could.

Ali Baba, catching his breath, said, "What da fuck're ya tryin' ta do, kill me or what?"

"You were dyin', wha'd ya expect me ta do? Watch ya die?"

Now through teary eyes Soapy saw a billboard alongside the road. He read it out loud, "'Visit Woods Bay State Park just west of Olanta and see da alligators

swim in da Carolina Bays. Ya wanna check out dat place, Babs?"

"Yeah, dat sounds like a really nice place ta visit … alligators, hmm. Too bad we don't have dem up in da neighborhood."

"What da hell d'ya want alligators for?" said Soapy.

"Dey'd make a really great disposal system, no?"

It took a while before Soapy got it, but when he did, he started laughing just like before. And then he said, "Yeah, let's go see doze alleygators."

They took the Woods Bay State Park exit near Olanta, in search of alligators and the elliptical-shaped, swampy depressions known as the Carolina Bays.

The drug had only just started to work its alchemy.

***

The Ford was rapidly approaching Olanta. Cal was the first one to notice the sign for the alligators.

He called out over wind and radio, "Hey you guys up ta seein' alligators?"

"Keep drivin'," yelled Henry from the back seat.

"Those things give me the creeps," said Rayf. "Who the hell'd wanna see those things anyway? Do you know in Florida every once in a while one of 'em comes up in somebody's backyard and eats a kid?"

"Just an idea, for crissakes," said Cal.

So instead of searching for alligators, they continued driving towards Georgia, which was approximately one hundred miles south of this very spot.

Cal, behind the wheel, slowed down, being careful to obey all the rules of the road.

It was four hours till nightfall.

***

Soapy and Ali Baba were now completely lost and going in endless circles looking for the ancient geological phenomena known as the Carolina Bays. They had stripped down to their shoulder-strapped T-shirts, but forgot to take off their ties.

Everything seemed to be going by too fast for Soapy. He couldn't say what he thought. His mind was at least six paragraphs ahead of his mouth, so when he said to Ali Baba, "I ... we're ... how ... say ..."

Ali Baba heard the workings of his own mind which said, "Lost ... try ... fuck ... hot ..."

They were in a state of extreme anxiety and had forgotten all about the alligators, South of the Border, and the pills. They were in free-fall.

Soapy knew only one thing as he kicked off his shoes and loosened his belt: he had to get back to some sort of main road. He thought to himself, *But what is da main road? Why and where da hell are we? Oh, look—a sign up ahead. What's it say? Fuck! It flew by too fast. Make a U- turn ... shit, such a narrow road ... oops, dere goes a little paint off a' da fender ... fuck it ... no air conditioner ...*

"What ...?" said Ali Baba, to no one in particular.

"Alligators ... hot ..."

"Huh?" said an almost comatose Ali Baba.

Another U-turn and there's the sign: US 301 straight ahead.

"Fuck," said Soapy, softly to himself. "Dat looks familiar ... hmm, 301 ... Yeah, I'll go fer dat one. Right, Babs?"

"Huh?" said the other.

And in a flash they were on US 301. He was relieved until he saw the sleeping Pedro billboard that read: South of the Border ten miles ahead; this, he was almost positive, was in the wrong direction. So, with a sudden pull on the wheel, he made a sharp and screeching left-hand U-turn. Finally, they were heading south.

He hunched over the wheel and concentrated. Right! Now it was coming to him: he was heading to Florida to have a few drinks with Johnny at some bar. *But what is da name uv dat joint?* And then he gave up thinking about that as he looked over to Ali Baba who, was now staring wide-eyed at the road dead ahead with his jaw hung open and white knuckles showing as he clutched the door handle. He was in some sort of toxic shock, but Soapy didn't care about him right now. The only thing he cared about was driving. Oh, how he loved to drive. He could drive up to the moon right now if only he knew the way.

Soapy, so possessed, at the wheel of the Lincoln, aimed it due south towards Miami, which was located, he figured, someplace at the very tip of the continent upon which he was driving.

***

They were rapidly approaching the town of Claxton, Georgia when Cal twisted around to face Henry in the back seat and said, "What's this bit about Claxton being the fruitcake capital of the world?"

"Dat's what I said. 'cause dat's what it's known for."

"Should we stop off and get us one?" said Rayf, the driver.

"Not on my account," said the back seat driver.

"I gotta go bad," said shotgun.

"So, I take it we pass up the fruitcake and get us a shitter," said the driver. The passengers agreed.

A restroom was now on the immediate itinerary.

***

In the meantime, the Lincoln had just flown through Statesboro, Georgia, twenty-five miles north of Claxton, and was barreling south fast. Ali Baba was still wired with no sign of relief in sight; so was Soapy.

"Man, I got a headache that'd kill a horse," said Ali Baba.

"Me too, man," said Soapy, still at the wheel and loving every minute of it.

"Ya got anything fer a headache?" said the passenger.

"Yeah, I got a aspirin in here someplace."

He dug around in his pants pocket and came up with the last two pills. He looked at the little white tabs gleaming there in the palm of his now-dirty hand and tried to remember if they were the last of his aspirin. And as he studied them with furrowed brow, he was sure that they were. He popped one and said, "Here." He handed the other to his wasted partner. "Dis should lighten up ya headache."

Ali Baba took the pill, swallowed hard, and said, "I need a drink to wash dis here ding down."

"I'll find us a gas station; get us a coke or somethin'. My mouth feels like a rat's ass," said Soapy.

And now there were five tablets dissolving within each of the two men's stomachs.

***

Meanwhile, inside a shabby gas station shack between Claxton and Glennville, a small black-and-white television set was tuned to the local eleven p.m. news. Rayf saw the all-night gas station on his left, the only one he had seen open within the past twelve miles.

A neatly attired news anchorman was telling his unseen TV audience of three wine-drinking men that J.F.K.'s national Democratic Committee fund-raising tour would include a trip to Vice President Johnson's home state of Texas and the city of Dallas, wherein he hoped to bring together the liberal and conservative factions of the Democratic Party in order to get that much-needed Texas vote in '64. The announcer segued into a news bite of J.F.K. giving a stump speech.

As Rayf pulled in to the gas station, all he could see through his insect-splattered windshield were three guys sitting inside the small room looking at a TV set.

Inside the office a large, gnarly hand reached in to turn off the TV as the attendant mumbled, "Trash." Kennedy's twelve-inch likeness faded to become a bright white dot center-screen before going completely to black.

Rayf parked the Ford between the two rows of pumps, shut off the engine, killed the lights, swung out of the car, and started stretching and doing some simple deep-knee bends. Cal was doing the same on the opposite side of the car.

"Man," said Cal. "It is hot!"

The clanking of a cow bell got their attention. They turned to see a 250 pound gas station attendant slam closed the screen door of the shack and start moseying toward them. Cal couldn't tell the guy's age—he just kept getting bigger and bigger with each step. The guy had his hair cut like a recruit in basic training, the tree stump of a neck that held up the huge block of a head was beet-red, and plastered there upon his face was a smile that couldn't be deciphered.

"Who the fuck is this guy?" whispered Cal. "King Kong!?"

"Ug-ly!" whispered Rayf.

"What ken ah do fer you boys?" said the somewhat friendly gas station man.

"We just want to use your bathroom facilities," said Cal.

There was a sudden change in the man's demeanor when he said, "Oh, is dat so?"

"Yeah," said Rayf. "Is it OK?"

"You free, white, and over twenty one. I see no reason why you kain't."

"Great!" said Rayf. He slammed the car door closed. "Where's it at?"

"But it's on'y fo' customas. You buyin' sumpthin'?"

Just then the back door of the Ford opened and out crawled a groggy Henry, wiping the sleep from his eyes and stretching the kinks out of his body.

"Well, wot duz we have here?" said the gas man. And before he could get a response he let out a holler to the other two men who were inside sucking the jug.

Rayf and Cal looked to the sound of the clanking bell and saw two other 250 pound guys squeezing through the small gas station office doorway.

"Wot is it Darrel? You gots some truble?" said the smaller of the two giants.

"Looks to me like we got us a couple a' Freedom Riders, Cyrus," said the gas pump guy.

"Well, don't jest leave 'em standin' dere, Darrel," said the larger of the two approaching men. "Why'n't you invite 'em inside for a little taste. Ain't choo got no hospitality?"

Cal turned to Rayf and said quietly, "Man, right now, I would rather be facing Soapy and Ali Baba instead a' these three."

Rayf turned to the three large men and said, "Thanks just the same guys, but we're kinda on the wagon."

And in a flash they were pulling out amid bluish-white exhaust smoke and slamming doors.

The guys in the Ford figured it would be best to find a friendlier place to relieve themselves. So they bought a roll of toilet paper and headed into the woods to go where the wild things go.

The good ol' gas station boys were still laughing with knee-slapping abandon when the Lincoln pulled in to a screeching fifty mile an hour stop. They turned to see two large men jumping out of the car wearing nothing but pants and neck ties.

"Yo!" shouted Soapy, "you got a soda machine in dis joint?"

The three looked back and forth toward each other.

Darrel, the working attendant, yelled back, "If you mean pop, we got that." He now pointed to the machine next to him near the office door. "It's right over here. Come an' git it."

The bare-footed Soapy and Ali Baba, digging around in their pants pockets, ran towards the soft drink machine. Ali Baba came up with a fifty dollar bill and said, "Hey, any a yous guys got change uv a half a yard?"

Darrel, to his compatriots, "Well, well, ain't we lucky? Two sets a' Freedom Riders in one night."

Ali Baba stopped in his tracks. Now very quietly said, "What'd you call me?"

"Freedom Riders," said Darrel through rotten clenched teeth. "Wanna make sumpthin uv it?"

"Dat's what I daught you called me," said Ali Baba as he flew at the leader and nailed him with a right hook that sent him flying right through the plate-glass window. Darrel landed out cold on the office floor amid shards of glass and splintered sash. The crickets went silent.

Now Soapy, with the strength of three men on an amphetamine high, jumped in. And then, as quickly as it had started, it had ended.

The crickets resumed their night song.

"What's a Freedom Rider, anyway?" said Ali Baba.

"I dink dey's somethin' like Beatniks or somethin' like dat."

"Beatniks!? Ain't dey da ones dat got Vandykes and bongos?" Now, hitting the nail on the head, "And dey's dirty too, ain't dey?"

"Yeah, dat's dem," said Soapy, adjusting his tie.

"Dat no good rotten sonovabitch callin' us dirty Beatniks—why I should break ..."

Blocking his way, Soapy said, "Dey ain't woith it, Babs. Come on, let's get outta here."

"Not yet," Ali Baba said, stepping in through the broken, office picture-window frame. "I didn't get what I came fer."

He walked over to the desk, picked up the jug, held it to the light, and read the label out loud, "Georgia Peach Wine." He took a long, deep swig of the sickeningly sweet wine, wiped his mouth with the back of his forearm, handed the bottle to Soapy, burped, and said, "Ah, just what I needed. Come on; Florida's on'y a hun'red miles away."

They got into the Lincoln, started it up, and peeled out, leaving their three Southern counterparts to sleep off their slight concussions.

***

It was like breaking into a jungle clearing. Gone were the oppressive trees, lush undergrowth, and stagnant, gnat-filled air that left its impressions all over the Ford's windshield. Gone was the low overhead-visibility and apparent poverty conditions of an obviously poor state that showed itself off to travelers on US 301 with decrepit shacks that were slapped together with cardboard, scrap wood, and corrugated iron sheets. In place of this squalor came well-maintained lawns, houses painted to perfection, and a long, low-to-the ground, lacquered wooden sign that read: Welcome to Florida.

Florida, with its clear, clean, warm, aqua-blue waters, semitropical breezes, and very proper and straight-laced royal palms that tickled the crystal-clear blue sky filled Rayf and Cal with a promise of good things to come.

They cheered as they crossed the border at Folkston, Georgia, just six miles east of the great Okefenokee Swamp—Florida.

Twenty miles later, at Hillard, they merged with US 1.

The sign read: 515 miles to Miami.

They followed the coast route down through Jacksonville, over the Saint Johns River, which flowed north, and past St. Augustine, the oldest, continuously inhabited city in the US of A., founded by the Spanish in 1565, only 398 years before this Ford's arrival.

North of Daytona Beach, Henry said, "I'm home. I kin smell it."

On the west side of Daytona Beach, Rayf pulled over.

The fork in their road had come at Highway 92. One leg of the fork headed south to Miami; the other, southwest to Orlando.

It was six a.m.

Rayf and Cal gathered up their one change of clothing and stuffed it into a brown paper shopping bag. Henry got out of the back seat, stretched, looked up at the clear, blue, cloudless Sky and said, "Smell it! Tell me dat ain't a fresh breath." And, as if on cue, Rayf and Cal breathed deep. They could smell the Atlantic Ocean two miles east.

"Well boys," said Henry. "It was real."

"Can't deny that," said Rayf.

"Thanks for the lift," said Cal.

"Think nuthin' of it, boys; be seein' you two around, K?"

"Yeah," said Rayf and Cal simultaneously, "Be seein' ya, man."

But they knew that they'd never see him again, for they knew him only as Henry-the-Ford and he knew them only as Rayf and Cal. *And let's face it*, thought Rayf as he shook hands with Henry, *there's gotta be millions of Rayfs, Cals, and Henrys in this world.*

Henry got into his car and yelled back to the two guys waiting there by yet another roadside, "Y'all take care now, hear?" They nodded and waved back to Henry as he drove off towards Orlando, which was less than sixty miles away. They watched long after the car and its blue exhaust smoke disappeared.

Funny, thought Rayf, *this thing called life. No matter how well you get to know somebody, it always turns out the same. We all have our own solitary existences, and every once in a while we happen to share a few brief hours with someone else—and then it's always the same, always just good-bye.*

Neither man had anything to say. They just nodded, turned around, and walked through the outskirts of Daytona Beach towards the coast and US 1, Rayf kicking rocks and Cal swinging the brown paper shopping bag.

At US 1 they sat down on the soft, warm, green grass, laid back, laced their hands behind their heads, looked up to the clear blue sky, relaxed, and breathed deep.

Suddenly, Rayf sat up and said, "Shit, I left my jacket in the car!"

"Good," said Cal.

"What the hell're ya talkin' about, 'good'?"

"Now we're even." said Cal. "I traded his jack for gas."

"You did what?"

"I got a buck's worth of gas for it up in North Carolina."

"What if we got a flat?" said Rayf.

"Jack wasn't gonna do us any good."

"Why not?"

"He never had a spare, man."

"Shit," said Rayf, "that was a brand new jacket!" He lay back on the warm, green grass.

By six forty-five a.m. they were up and hitching.

By seven o'clock they remembered what it felt like to be ignored and invisible. But with such great weather, who cared.

***

The night before, Soapy and Ali Baba bought and drank one quart of scotch whiskey in the hopes of leveling off their amphetamine-LSD-laced high. Their remedy failed. It only intensified matters. They wandered aimlessly throughout the night. They misplaced US 301 and never found it again.

They saw a sign for the Okefenokee Swamp and this they knew must be in the wrong direction. So instead of going west, they turned east and cut across twenty-five miles of rural Highway 40, connecting them with US 17 at Kingsland, Georgia, which they took south into Florida—speeding right past the visitor's welcome center thirteen miles south of the state line.

They continued on 17 through Jacksonville, where they met up with US 1 South and were finally back on course.

South of Daytona Beach, Soapy saw two shabby hitchhikers roughhousing alongside the road. They were sword fighting with palm fronds and not paying any attention to the oncoming traffic. Soapy, being exhausted, under the influence and traveling at seventy-five miles an hour, did not recognize just who those two hitchhikers were until twelve miles later.

Then it dawned on him. He hit the breaks and skidded into a U-turnaround stop heading in a northerly direction.

"What da hell're ya doin'?" said Ali Baba.

"I just saw doze two bastards back dere."

"Who?"

"Who da hell d'ya think?!"

"Where?"

"Dey was hitchhikin'."

"But I daught ..." said Ali Baba.

"We got doze two in our fuckin' clutches," said Soapy.

He hit the gas and peeled out northward.

Rayf, playacting, was now on one knee pleading with the oncoming traffic while Cal followed each passing car with a plaintive thumb and face to match.

And then it happened.

An elderly couple in a two-tone green and cream 1962 DeSoto pulled up to a gentle stop. The old gent behind the wheel called out, "You fellers goin' south?"

"And how!" said Rayf. They both ran to the DeSoto.

Just as they were climbing into the back seat of the large, four-door sedan, the Lincoln came up out of nowhere. Soapy saw the two hitchhikers half in and half out of the car.

Soapy yelled to Ali Baba, "Hold tight!" He made another screeching, two-wheeled U-turn across the highway. The old-timey driver, looking into his rearview mirror, was the only one who saw the big, black car as it disappeared in a westerly direction. He mumbled to himself, "Strange, I don't recollect seeing any road goin' off that a-way. Hmm." He drove on.

But the one thing the old man did not see was the Lincoln crashing into a forty-foot tall coconut palm. The impact dislodged several coconuts that landed with different musical pitches upon the car's metal roof.

Ali Baba jumped out of the totaled car and ran to see the two-tone, green and cream car cruising southward. He turned back around to see Soapy crawling out of the heap of bent, black metal.

"Oh, my fuckin' head. I dink I broke it."

Ali Baba ran over to Soapy. "Broke it!? I'll break it for ya, you dumb fuck." He cuffed him hard to the back of the head. "Who da fuck taught ya how to drive?"

And then they got into it. The dust engulfed them as they fought—two men in trousers and neckties rolling around on the warm Florida turf, beating the shit out of each other.

~ 8 ~

WOMEN, WINE, AND MILK

The Daytona Beach Police would eventually find the trashed Lincoln Continental. The Hertz people would eventually have it towed in. But the registered driver would never be located.

***

Soapy and Ali Baba cleaned out the car and took a cab into Daytona Beach where they checked into a beachfront hotel to recuperate from one hell-of-a hangover. While they were registering at that hotel, the DeSoto drove on. In Hollywood, it took a left onto Hollywood Boulevard and then a right down Collins Avenue.

The pair in the back seat craned their necks. The palm trees that lined the avenue went straight for the sky. Cal elbowed Rayf, and they looked left towards the warm, pristine Atlantic, its waves gently lapping golden-white sands, while blue skies melted into aqua-green seas—conditions that made the folks in the front seat glad they had chosen and saved for their retirement years to be spent in Miami Beach and the guys in the back seat glad they were still alive.

On their right, as they cruised down this thin slip of land, was Biscayne Bay, teeming with bottle-nose dolphins and Florida manatees.

Cal looked over to Rayf and said, "I told ya so."

"Miami Beach, here we come!" said Rayf.

The DeSoto pulled over across the street from the Fontainebleau Hotel on Collins near 44th Street in Miami Beach.

The boys got out and walked up to thank the couple. The lady handed Rayf a ten dollar bill. He tried to give it back, but she insisted that they have

122

a "good-luck drink" on them. Rayf slipped the greenback into his dungaree pocket, stepped back, and waved to the old timers as they puttered off down Collins Avenue. Technically, their retirement years had officially begun.

The boys walked over to the little park with its perfectly manicured lawn, which was directly across the street from the Fontainebleau. They flopped down onto the soft green grass and stared at the famed hotel.

The Fontainebleau was right there on the opposite side of the street, the same hotel that Frank Sinatra, Peter Lawford, Sammy Davis Jr., Dean Martin, and Joey Bishop, hung out in, or sang in; they weren't quite sure. But one thing they were sure of was: here they were in Miami Beach. And to think that just three days ago, they were hanging out on that cold, northeastern Jersey City corner that was, they were also sure, now covered in the cold, dirty, gray November dusk.

In front of them the Fontainebleau; behind them a gentle slip of water from Biscayne Bay, Indian Creek.

Cal pulled out two Cigarillos and handed one to Rayf. They lit up, lay back, and watched the sky through palm trees while drifting off into their own individual dreams. They had finally arrived. Now all they had to do was figure out their eating and sleeping arrangements. *No big thing*, thought Rayf, *after all, we do have twenty bucks.*

They weren't there for ten minutes when they heard a young woman sobbing. Rayf sat up and looked. She was sitting on a park bench.

"Hey, Cal, Dig the chick."

"What chick?" said Cal, leaning up on an elbow.

"Over there. She's crying."

"Bad news," said Cal as he laid his head back down on the brown paper shopping bag that served as a pillow.

To Rayf she looked like a young executive on vacation.

"I'm gonna see what's wrong."

"Not a good idea," said Cal, not moving.

He stood, and approached her cautiously. Cal watched.

Even the classical cut of her clothing couldn't disguise her age. Rayf figured her to be about twenty-something. He sat on the grass facing her. "Is there something wrong?" he said. *A very dumb question*, he thought, but too late; it was already out.

Cal shook his head and thought, *Now, if I were over there …*

But it was Rayf's sincerity that caused the young woman to look up from her sobbing. She dried her eyes and, after some difficulty, said, "I'm sorry to disturb you."

"You're not botherin' us. What's wrong?"

"No. I can't get you involved."

"Why not?! We just got into town, and hey, we don't have nothin' else to do. Ain't that right, Cal?"

Cal looked the other way.

"Believe me, he's cool," said Rayf.

The friendless girl opened up and told him about last night—how she was almost raped by some conventioneer right over there in that beautiful hotel, and how she was here all by herself on vacation, and that she was an Anglo-Canadian from Montreal, "where it may be colder, but at least it's a heck of a lot saner than it is down here."

Rayf listened. He felt guilty about his mixed feelings. He wanted to help her, true, but that part about sex crept into his libido. He slapped it down and called out, "Yo, Cal. Get over here. We got some business to take care of."

Reluctantly, Cal picked himself up and walked over to Rayf, who had now taken a seat next to the young woman on the bench.

"What is it?"

"We got to teach somebody a little manners."

"Oh, yeah? Since when'd you become a teacher?"

"This chick almost got raped last night. And we're gonna get the guy."

"Oh, *we* are?"

She sobbed.

"Yeah, we are," said Rayf.

"Why doesn't she just call the cops?" said Cal.

Here was a practical thinker, one whose dreams did not include chasing rapists.

"Oh, forget it," she said, crying once again.

"OK? See what you did, man? You made her cry. You happy now?"

"I'm splitin', man."

"Wait up, man. She's from Canada and we've gotta help her."

"Did you lose your marbles, or what?"

"Did you lose your balls?"

"Boys, please don't argue over ..."

"Are you with me or not?" said Rayf.

"What're you gonna do?"

"Cal, we are going to help this lady."

"Victoria. Call me Victoria."

"… to help Victoria," said Rayf, "and to find the guy that caused all of this shit! Uh, excuse me … trouble. We're, like, actin' like ambassadors, dig?"

"Where are we supposed to be going, Victoria?" said Cal.

"If you want to help, he's probably at the bar right now."

"What bar?"

"At the Fontainebleau."

"I see," said Cal as he turned to face the huge building.

Rayf walked over and whispered to him, "This chick's all alone. We gotta give her a hand, man. What if your sister was in trouble in a foreign country, huh?"

"I don't have a sister."

"Use your imagination."

"Look, I'm not gonna risk my neck for some strange brawd, who … How do I know she's not crazy, huh?"

"Are you with me, man?"

"If you get us arrested or killed, I swear to god I'll beat you over the fuckin' head with a bat, so help me."

Rayf turned to the girl and said, "Let's go, Victoria."

She got up and very slowly led them across the street.

Here we are, thought Rayf, *in Miami Beach not a half hour and we already have a friend in need.*

In front of the hotel, the doorman watched the neatly attired young lady with the two shabby guys in dungarees and dirty, long-sleeved cotton shirts that they wore rolled up to the elbows. The darker of the two men was carrying a brown paper shopping bag with … *with their life's possessions in it*, figured the doorman. And he also wondered, *What the hell is a sharp-looking chick like that doing with those two bums?*

He stopped them at the door and said, "Excuse me," forcing the next word, "gentlemen … are you staying here?"

"Nah, we're with her," said Rayf.

"I'm registered."

"I'm sorry Miss, but the … uh, gentlemen are not allowed in the hotel without accommodations."

"Look buddy, we're helpin' out this chick …" said Rayf.

"There he is!" said Victoria.

She pointed to five very large men walking across the spacious lobby. "Wh ... which one?" stuttered Rayf.

"The one in the middle."

Rayf looked from the man to Cal. "That guy's bigger than a Buick."

"I know," said a very demure Victoria.

"You and your hero complex," said Cal.

"Uh, Victoria," said Rayf pulling her over to the curb, away from the doorman, "those are some pretty big dudes. There's no way we can handle them."

"I told you," she said, sobbing once again, "I told you I was in big trouble."

"Look, Vickie," said Rayf. "Can I call you Vickie, Victoria?"

"Vickie," interrupted Cal, "look, the guy is too big for us. If we had a gun, maybe ... but listen, my suggestion is you either, like I said, report him ..."

"No! I don't want to go near that animal."

"Or, your other options are to change hotels or go home."

Thinking while dabbing her eyes, "I'll check out and go home. But will you at least wait for me? Please."

"Sure," said Rayf. "We'll wait."

"If I'm not out in fifteen minutes, please come up to room 5005. I'm frightened. Please."

"If you're not out in fifteen minutes," said Cal, "we'll come up and get you." Then, referring to the doorman, "Don't worry about him."

She went in.

After she disappeared into the lobby, Rayf said, "You gettin' soft?"

"Maybe," said Cal, as he walked over to the doorman.

"You workin' here long?" said Cal.

"Yeah, what's it to ya?"

"We're from up in Jersey City and we're, like, lookin' for some rich Jew brawds. I hear they come down here without their husbands and like to party."

"So you're big spenders from the east, eh?"

"Yeah," said a cocky Cal, "I guess you could say that."

"You Lansky's boys?"

Cal, catching the rib, said, "Yeah, Meyer sent us."

"Hey, you could've fooled me."

"Well?"

"What you're lookin' for is South Beach, down around 7th Street. There's a whole lot of boarding houses down there. It's the lower rent district."

"And the Jewish brawds!?" said Cal.

"Yeah, they're down there, too," said the doorman, tiring of the game.

"Thanks," said Cal as he walked over to Rayf, who was watching and listening.

"What's this about Jewish chicks?"

"They, my good friend, shall be our salvation."

Just then Victoria came out of the hotel dragging one very large suitcase. Cal ran over, grabbed the bag, and winked at the doorman.

Rayf couldn't figure out what Cal was up to.

"Victoria," said Cal, "do you have a car?"

"Yes, I've a hired car. Why?"

"Could you give us a lift?"

"Of course. Where to?"

As he said, "South Beach," he looked back at the doorman who was now pointing with white-gloved hand in the same direction.

"It's down that way," said Cal. "Will it be out of your way?"

"No problem at all. I'd be glad to take you. That's the least I can do." They walked towards her car. Cal turned and saluted the doorman.

The doorman saluted back.

***

They were now standing at the very tip of Miami Beach. Any further and they'd be in the Atlantic Ocean. Victoria let them off at 1st Street and Washington Avenue. They thanked her for the lift; she thanked them for their help. Rayf and Victoria exchanged addresses and phone numbers. They promised to keep in touch. She went west over the MacArthur Causeway to Miami International, and a 707 did the rest.

A short time before, while driving down Collins Avenue, Rayf pointed out a sign at one of the beach entrances that read: Whites Only. Victoria said, "We've got a similar problem in Canada with the French."

"Damn," said Cal, "I got nothin' against any of those people. As a matter of fact, the only thing that I'd like to hold against Eartha Kit or Bridget Bardot is me."

By now, Miss Victoria was up in the sky flying in *l'avion* while they were in the low rent district looking for a different kind of miracle.

They walked along studying the signs that were sticking up from, into, and out of the well-maintained front lawns: Apt. to Let; Room for Rent; To

Rent By Week, Month, or Season. They knocked on several doors and asked the price. It was more than they could afford. They pressed on.

Six blocks later, it happened. It was a boarding house on Michigan. Rayf knocked on the door and waited. It was a balmy eight o'clock evening, and the stars made them feel right at home. He knocked again, no answer. Just as he turned to leave, the front door opened. He turned back to face the light and there, framed in the doorway of this squat, two-story clapboard cottage, was a tiny gray-haired lady. Rayf thought she looked a lot like his grandmother. She stood there, in the doorway, Rayf on the pathway, and Cal on the sidewalk, in silence. And then she said, "Hello, boys. I've been expecting you. Come on in, why don't you." It went just like that.

Rayf looked towards Cal and then back to the little old lady before saying, "Us? You sure you got the right guys, ma'am?"

"Oh, I'm sure alright, I can tell by the light that you give off that you've come to help me with my chores in order for me to open in time for the season."

"How much do you want for a room?" said Rayf.

"Lordy, lordy. I wouldn't take a red cent from you two. I'm telling you, the Lord told me to look for you two boys. He told me that two young boys would come in the middle of the night to help me with my work. Now you don't think that I could take any money from two such as you now, do you?"

"He told you about us?" said Rayf.

"Yes, He did."

They couldn't believe their ears. Here was this old woman inviting them into her house. For the first time, they gave themselves the once-over. They were shabby and scruffy, and were amazed that she would even be talking to them never mind asking them in. They charged past her before she changed her mind.

"Your rooms are at the top of the stairs. Come, I'll show you."

They followed and kept looking at one another. Were they dreaming? What the hell, they'd follow anyway; what did they have to loose, their lives?! A cheap price to pay for a hot shower and a soft bed, went their thinking, as they were shown to their individual rooms.

Rayf's room overlooked the front pathway that led out to Michigan Avenue; Cal's, the alleyway on the north side of the house. She showed them where the bathrooms and toilets were and told them that she always left the back door open. They didn't know how to thank her.

She said, "Save it for the mornin', boys."

Rayf felt like kissing her goodnight, she was that familiar—it was uncanny. She walked away with her back to the two strangers, and when she got to the staircase and turned around to go down, there upon her face was the most beatific smile that either had ever seen. She blew them a kiss. They blew one back.

Here they were, after three grueling nights on the road, with a clean bed under them and a roof over their heads, neither of which moved. Cal stood by his door and looked at Rayf standing by his. They started to laugh with relief. Tonight they would sleep the good sleep. They turned, entered their respective rooms and closed the doors behind them.

Rayf pulled back the covers on his bed, felt the crisp white sheets, and breathed in the clean, fresh smell. The room smelled of Pinesol. He walked over to the window and opened it. The warm, southern tip of Miami Beach air flowed into the room. He kicked off his shoes and fell back into the sack. He couldn't believe their luck.

Cal, in the meantime, was doing the same thing in his room with one exception; he lit up a Cigarillo and studied the matchbook cover—Pink Flamingo, Miami Beach's Coolest Hot Spot, "Hmm," he mused to himself out loud.

***

The crystal-clear, blue waves gently lapped Rayf's ankles. He walked through the warm surf. A cloud on the far horizon, beyond the end of the white finely-granulated sandy beachhead, backlit a clump of distant palm trees. Near the water's edge, centered in that cloud, walking very slowly towards him with undulating hips was a bikini-clad girl—Victoria, her soft, creamy skin blending ever so gracefully into the tropical tapestry. Rayf slowed down to longer appreciate this vision. He walked deeper into the surf. She did likewise. And now the two bodies were on a collision course. Up to their thighs in the warm Gulf Stream waters, hers glistening ivory white, his shiny deep tan, her bikini a soft green, and his low-cut tank trunks a sparkling white.

She grew closer; their eyes met and locked onto each other's gaze. Two beings on a deserted tropical beach—the stuff dreams are made of. He reached out with his right hand, she with her left. They met, clasped hands, and moved deeper into the warm, playful surf. Her lips glanced off his cheek, his going straight for the mark, they kissed. Swirling in the warm bath of sea water, locked in a lover's embrace, confirming their individual existence with each passionate kiss. The cloud grew larger and darker. It moved from the distant horizon to block out the warm, life-giving rays of sun. Rain started to fall, and then came thunder. It grew louder and louder. He awoke. Someone was banging on the door.

"Hey, you alive in there?" yelled Cal, through the locked door.

Rayf saw the white ceiling. His dream vanished.

More knocking.

"Hold on." said Rayf as he sat up, swung his legs off the bed, walked over to the door, and opened it. Cal walked in.

"For a minute there, I thought she might've killed ya or something."

"Who's that?" said Rayf, wiping the sleep from his eyes.

"The old lady. Come on, we're going out," said Cal.

"I wanna get some sleep, man."

"Fuck sleep."

"What time is it?"

"Ten-thirty. Come on, we're wastin' the night."

"Where we going?" said Rayf through a yawn.

"There's this place that I wanna check out. Come on."

"Christ, man, you really know how to spoil a wet dream," said Rayf while putting on his shoes.

"Hey! We're young and alive; fuck sleep. Let's grab Miami by the balls and show these Southern belles how to really swing."

"I gotta wash up first."

"Yeah, and comb your hair, you look like shit," said the freshly washed Cal.

As they walked down that hallway, Rayf made a mental note to call Victoria next time he got back up north—that is, if he ever did.

The Pink Flamingo Nightclub was located on the Biscayne Bay side of Miami Beach at 16th Street and Bay Road. Behind the long bar was an all-glass wall that looked out onto the Bay and the Venetian Causeway that connected Miami to the Beach. In the foreground was Belle Island. The barroom itself was done up in tropical kitsch. There were pictures of pink flamingos wading along the water's edge amid reeds and rushes. Some of the birds stood on one foot, some preened themselves, and others, with their heads underwater, bobbed for krill. Outside on the patio, just beyond the picture window, in huge bowls and hanging pots, were tropical plants, rubber trees, and potted palms. Behind the bar was a large aquarium with eight bulldog-snouted piranhas that looked out of their environment into the human one.

Rayf and Cal walked past the Cadillacs and Lincoln convertibles that were parked in the lot and through the wild plum hedges that funneled them into the dark innards of the Pink Flamingo. They waited at the door until their eyes adjusted. They looked around the room. The first thing that came into view was the causeway with its tiny auto lights coming and going. A few couples sat at small round tables here and there. At the bar sat a beautiful, dark-skinned island woman in a colorful, skintight dress that exposed very ample cleavage. Their eyes were now fully adjusted as they walked up to the bar and sat not two stools to the right of that lovely figure.

"What're we doin' here?" said Rayf.

"What the hell d'ya think," said Cal, nodding in the bar girl's direction.

"Where do I know this place from?" said Rayf half to himself.

Just then the bartender approached.

"What'll it be boys?"

"Scotch, White Horse. Mine's on the rocks, his with water," said Cal. "What kinda fish are they?"

"Piranha," said the barkeep while fixing the drinks.

"Piranha! Do they really eat living things?" said Cal.

"When they're hungry enough."

"I heard of 'em but I never saw 'em before," said Cal.

"You guys from up north?" said the bartender, while setting their drinks down in front of them.

"Yeah. We're from New York," said Cal, lying. "Why?"

"No reason. Just thought I detected an accent. That'll be two-fifty."

"Yeah, we're thinkin' of relocatin' down here, like for permanent." Now to Rayf, "Ain't that right?"

"We're lookin' for work," said Rayf. "Any ideas?"

"I'll tell ya the truth," said the bartender. "Since that Castro guy took over in Cuba, there ain't no more decent wages in Miami for Americans no more. I mean it, so help me."

"You sound like you're from up north yourself," said Cal.

"Yeah, Brooklyn; name's Johnny."

Johnny, thought Rayf, *that really sounds familiar.*

"Used to live in Sheepshead Bay," continued Johnny, "Know where that's at?"

"Nah," said Cal, "we don't get out into the boroughs that much."

"You miss it?" said Rayf.

"Sometimes. But then you run across some beautiful babe from Kansas who's lookin' for some tropical excitement and wham! You're over that homesickness in nothin' flat. Wha' da you boys do for a livin'?" said Johnny, taking an elbow to the bar.

"I used to tend bar up in Union City," said Rayf.

"That ain't in New York," said Johnny, catching the mistake.

"He used to commute. Ain't dat right, Rayf?"

"I moved there in '62," said Rayf, confusing Cal's fabrication.

"Union City, huh?" said Johnny. "I used ta know ..."

"How does one go about gettin' woik down here?" said Cal, interrupting Johnny with the best Jersey accent he could muster, while throwing a five dollar bill onto the bar.

Johnny, walking to the register with the money said, "Well there's a whole lot a cheap labor down here now, like I said, 'cause of da Cuban influx. But if I were you two; what's ya names?"

"I'm Cal and dis here's Rayf; and yours again?"

"Johnny."

"Good ta meet cha, John," said Cal.

"Likewise," said Johnny.

"Me too," said Rayf. They all shook hands.

"G'head, John. What would you do?" said Cal.

Rayf's head was spinning. Where did he hear that name? And in connection with this very place? It was on the tip of his mind. Where and when? It'd come to him, he was sure of it; if he'd just let it slide, it'd come to him.

Johnny was droning on, "I'd pack up and head ta New Orleans, now that's where da action's at."

"What's happenin' there?" said Cal.

"Oil rigs and shrimp boats. There's lots of work over there."

"Hey," said Cal, "If things don't work out down here, maybe we'll give it a shot. Sounds cool, huh Rayf!"

"Yeah," was Rayf's distant reply.

"But just supposin'" said Cal, "you wanted to stay in Miami Beach. I mean we're not in town ten minutes and we got dis here chick from Montreal drivin' us all over the place. And den dis little old lady over on Michigan and 7th gives us a place to stay for zip, man, just 'cause she said, like, it came to her in a dream, like, dat we were comin' over to help her out with somethin'. Man, I am totally in love wit' dis place. Dis burg is, like, too much, man."

Rayf looked at Cal with his newly acquired accent and was hip to the game.

"Well," said Johnny softly with elbow on the bar, "first thing ya gotta do is register with the Dade County Police Department."

"Why's dat?" said Cal, suspiciously.

"'Cause that's how it goes down here. You ask me, I'm fillin' ya in. But if you ever wind up in New Orleans, you gotta check out da Cat 'n' Fiddle; it's a bar offa Bourbon street. You just tell 'em dat I sent ya—Johnny from da Pink Flamingo."

There it is again, thought Rayf. Those names; where did I hear them before?

"'Scuse me fellas," said Johnny as he walked away, "I gotta freshen up da lady's drink."

"Hey, is this great, or what?" said Cal to Rayf. "This guys fillin' us in to the whole scene down here. Oh man, this town is like magic."

"I can't help feeling that I've been here before," said Rayf.

"You mean like in that deja vu stuff?"

"Maybe … it … it just feels like … maybe I'm just imagining it."

Just then Johnny came back.

"You guys ready for another?"

"Yeah," said Cal. "Two uh da same."

"So like I was sayin', first you register with da police an' den you look for work."

"Sounds great, danks!" said Cal.

"At your service," said Johhny, wiping the bar.

"Johnny," said Cal, nodding towards the lone woman seated at the bar, "where's all uh duh … de action around here?"

"Gamblin' or brawds?"

"Brawds."

"Nowadays it's all in Little Havana."

"Where's dat at?" said Cal.

"Over in Miami."

"Cuban chicks?" said Cal

"Yeah," said Johnny as he ducked under the bar to get something. Cal's nod to Rayf said, "Watch this!"

As soon as Johnny came up with his corkscrew, Cal said, "Hey John, could I ask you somethin'?"

Johnny leaned in, "What is it, kid?"

"Could you spare a few bucks for a couple a' hometown guys?"

Johnny, now pulling his elbow back from the bar, stood up straight and studied the two East Coast sharpies. He had seen many before them and he would undoubtedly see many more after them. "Look boys," said the barkeep very softly, "the lending of capital is no way to start a friendship."

"Hey," said Cal, "no harm in askin'."

"Oh yes there is," said Johnny as he walked away from the two panhandlers.

"So," hollered Cal to Johnny, referring to the causeway outside the window, "is that Miami on the other side of that bridge?"

Johnny, who was now tending to the lovely bar girl, did not speak, but nodded instead.

"You fucked up," whispered Rayf.

"Hey," whispered Cal, "you win some, you lose some. What can I tell ya?" In full voice to Rayf, "You wanna give Miami a shot?"

"How we gettin' there?"

"Walk, hitch; how else?" said Cal, as he stepped off his stool. Now loudly, "Come on, drink up." They downed their drinks.

"See ya around Johnny," yelled Cal. "We're gonna check out some a dem Cuban brawds over in Miami. Thanks for da tip."

Johnny waved a lazy hand that, if properly understood, would've said, "Yeah, yeah. Don't let the door hit ya in da ..."

Once again they were out and under the stars.

Rayf looked back at the neon sign that read, Pink Flamingo, and racked his brain to no avail.

Halfway across the causeway at San Marco Island, Rayf stopped dead in his tracks. "Holy shit!"

"What's a matter?" said Cal.

"I remember that bar!"

"You been there before?"

"No. But why the fuck did you take us to *that* joint?"

"I saw it on a matchbook cover. Why?"

"Where'd you get it from?"

"From you, up at the Rag Doll. Why?"

"You dumb fuck. That's one of Soapy's people!"

"How the fuck was I suppose ta know that?"

"You weren't," said Rayf, now deep in thought.

"So what!? What does he know? We're clean."

"We gave him our names and a whole bunch of other information."

"Man, that dude sees like tons of people. How the fuck is he gonna spot us out of all the other shit that comes in ta that joint? You see how dark it was in there? Use your head, man, be practical. And besides, those two guys are probably in the nut house or dead by now."

"That is a wish, not a fact."

"You heard what Doctor Benny said about LSD. Forget about those two—they're history, man."

"What the fuck are you up to now?"

"*We* are going to Miami to score on some a dem Cooban babes, mon."

"The Pink Flamingo, of all places. I don't believe it," said Rayf, half to himself.

"So I fucked up, alright. What d'ya want from me, blood? Relax, will ya? Come on, enjoy yourself for Christ sakes," said Cal, as they started walking over Biscayne Island towards the mainland on the opposite side of this two-mile span.

"This walkin's for the birds," said Cal. "Let's hitch."

***

Cuban bar girl, Rayf; Cuban bar girl, Cal. Behind the bar, a Cuban bartender spoke English well enough to tell the two boys that the two girls, who barely spoke any English at all, only drank wine. To Rayf and Cal, who had just left Henry off not twelve hours before, wine was a very cheap libation. And "Hey, if they want another little split, why not? Sure, go ahead—give 'em whatever they want."

Rayf was trying to communicate with his girl who could only say, "Yes." And this, he thought, was a very good word considering what he had in mind. Cal, on the other hand, was deep in conversation with his girl.

"Your J.F.K. is just anuder Batista," said Cal's bar girl.

"Who's Batista?" said Cal.

"He let all de rich do as dey please."

"That's not all true," said Cal. "Kennedy started the Peace Corps."

"I had a brudder dat was betrayed by your J.F.K. when he deserted us in de Bay of Pigs invasion. Dat's all I know."

"Hey ... hey," said the Bartender, "enough uv dat political talk in dees place. Dees boys are here to party. Hain't dat right, big guys?"

"You got that right," said Cal. "Give the ladies another bottle of wine."

The ladies were well tanned and trim. They had black hair and deep black eyes that could take a man as far away from his reality as he wished to go. They had deep red lips and rouged cheeks. Their breasts were held captive in tight-fitting, strapless halters. Cal's bar girl wore a red top and a black skintight skirt with a slit that ran all the way up the front of her well-formed right leg, showing off a tanned thigh laced in wide-mesh black stockings.

Rayf's girl was dressed the same except for the colors: her top was black and her bottom was red. They were both covered in sparkling costume jewelry, which consisted of large earrings and necklaces that got lost in their cleavage.

When Cal ordered another round of drinks, the girls giggled, crossed their delicate ankles in the barstool's rungs, and hung their heads back to shake out their hair. This gave the boys an opportunity to study more fully their out-thrust breasts. They looked at their girl's tits and then towards each other with pained expressions that showed both at once their pleasure and their dreams of a night fat with promise. The bartender brought the drinks and the bill.

"Here cho go girls," now to the men. "And dis," handing Cal the check, "ees por cho."

Cal, who was drinking a Dewar's on the rocks, picked up the tab with the aplomb of a man of the world, but upon reading it, choked on his mouthful of scotch.

"What the hell is this?"

The bartender, with a slight frown as though he had made a technical mistake, took the tab and looked at it for a split second and said, "Watt ees 'rong, sir? I don't see any problem here. Heet ees chor check, which also includes *dee* wine por dee two joung ladies. No?"

Cal looked at the mirror behind the bartender. It reflected the entire room: the red and black that the girls wore was repeated throughout while the two red neon signs in the small fortress-like windows buzzed Club Cuba on and off every two seconds. He looked for an escape route. Rayf was still conversing in Pidgin English with his date.

Cal, with a reassuring smile to the bartender, said, "Gotta talk to my friend over here." Now with a nod to his girl, said, "Dear, if you'll excuse me for just a moment." He walked over to Rayf.

"Yo, Raul," said Cal. "I got us a little present." He showed him the bar tab.

Rayf spit his drink out onto the bar. "What the fuck is this?"

"Hit ees chor tab, senor."

"What the fuck kinda wine did they drink?" said Rayf.

"Champagne uv course."

Now, as if on cue, the girls stood up and melted into the dark empty room. In their places were two very large bouncer-type men.

"Choo got trrouble, Ricky?" said one of the bouncers to the barkeep. "No," said the bartender. "Dees here har two big spenders from dee east. We hab no trrouble." Now to Rayf and Cal, "Hain't dat rite, boys?"

Rayf, sizing up the room, said, "No prroblem, Ricky baby."

And with that, they ran out the front door. Behind them they could hear the panting breaths of the three out-of-shape men and the clicking of taps upon the hot concrete pavement. Their pursuers were cursing at them in Spanish as they chased them down 14th Street and up Biscayne Boulevard, where they now heard one less pair of metal-tapped heels. They turned east and saw up ahead the Venetian Causeway with a sign that read: Pedestrian Toll. Rayf looked over his shoulder to see Ricky the bartender and one bouncer still in pursuit.

Up ahead, the toll collector outside his booth was blocking their path. Rayf ran right up to the toll guy and, with a halfback maneuver that would've made his high school football coach proud, faked him out and left the causeway monitor empty handed.

"A fuckin' toll to run over this thing," said Cal. "They gotta be out of their fuckin' minds, man."

"Get back here!" yelled the toll collector.

"They're payin' for us," yelled Rayf. "Get the money from them."

The bar men stopped at the causeway tollbooth and shouted what sounded to the vanishing men a lot like obscenities. After a few more minutes, Rayf and Cal slowed down and went from running to jogging and finally to walking at a normal pace. As they neared Belle Island they could see off to their right, in the near distance, the Pink Flamingo's lights shimmering and reflecting on the bay. Near the shore they leaned over the ocean-side railing and looked down at the warm water. The waves, not fifteen feet below, gently lapped the pilings.

"Hey Rayf, what's that sound down there?"

"Sounds like fish to me."

"What kind, d'ya think they are?"

"Could be Barracudas, maybe," said Rayf.

They listened more intently.

"Wow!" said Rayf. "Listen to that, will ya? You can actually hear fish jumpin' around down there. Man, if I was a fisherman, I'd have me a ball down here."

"Hey, if we run outta money, maybe we should just get us a couple of fishing poles," said Cal as he tore the bar tab up into little pieces.

"Not a bad idea," said Rayf.

Cal threw the little bits of paper into the bay.

"Eighty-five dollars for a couple of scotches and two wines!? They gotta be out of their fuckin' minds," said Cal.

"They wanna be crooked then they deserve to get fucked. Let's get goin', man. I gotta get some sleep," said Rayf as the little pieces of paper floated gently into Biscayne Bay to be mistaken for fish food by the local inhabitants.

The 'cudas spat it out.

***

They found their way back to the Michigan Avenue boarding house, walked down the alleyway, and entered through the back door. They climbed up the steps and went to their respective rooms. They opened their doors, turned on the lights, looked inside, stopped, turned around towards each other and in unison said, "Holy shit!" And there, in their rooms, right next to their beds, setting upon their end tables, was a big glass of milk and a small plate of cookies. They smiled, nodded, and closed their doors behind them. The last two lights on the second floor of this boarding house on Michigan Avenue went out. It was two a.m., November 21, 1963.

~ 9 ~

WORKIN' THE BEACH

The smell of breakfast greeted them as they walked into the yard. "Come and get it, boys," sang the old lady.

They rubbed their eyes.

She was setting a makeshift table. "I got ham, bacon, eggs, hotcakes, and lots of coffee."

"You didn't have to do that," said Rayf,

"Son, with all the work you got facin' you, that is the least I can do." She pointed to a huge stack of window screens piled high in the yard.

"We certainly appreciate this, ma'am," said Cal.

"My pleasure, and please, call me Irene. That ma'am business makes me feel too old."

Rayf looked at her standing there by the table and thought about the night before up in his room—after devouring the milk and cookies, he fell asleep studying a painting on the wall. It was a picture of a beautiful young girl wading in an aqua-green sea. The gentle clouds that stretched and pulled overhead cast their delicate shadows over the girl and honey-colored sand. She wore a white linen dress with a wide brimmed linen hat that caused a faint shadow to fall over her young, healthy face. The painting looked amateurish. It was the last thing he remembered before fading off.

"That's a real nice painting hanging up in my room," he said.

She grew far away then said, "That's me in that painting. My late husband painted it." After a pause, "He did it back in the fall of '38 when we first got here from Chicago." Now partway back, "My, how time flies." Gone again, "That's all he left me." Back again, "We call them our children, those paintings, 'cause that's what they are. They're all over the house." Halfway gone again, "God, how he loved it down here."

"Well, what're we doing reminiscing like this?" she said. "Lordy, lordy, you boys eat up and get some of that energy that you're gonna be needin' to get this place shipshape, like Walter used to say."

"Walter?" said Rayf.

"Mister Grabowski, my husband."

"And these clothes?" said Rayf referring to the coveralls that they were wearing.

"Walter's," she said, proudly. "Now you eat up and I'll come back to show you what needs to be done." And with that, she walked back into the house with the spry step of a teenager.

"Well, how do you like this?" said Cal, tilting back on the wooden box that he used for a chair. "This is too much, man. It's like somebody up there is lookin' out for us, huh?"

"Yeah," said Rayf, leaning into a mouthful of hotcakes. "How lucky can we get?"

"That's a hell of a lot of screens to paint," said Cal.

"Nothin' to it man."

"You did this before?"

"Yeah."

"Where? When?"

"At my grandparents' when I was a kid. They had a couple of bunga-lows in Keansburg."

"Down the Jersey shore?"

"Yeah, and we had to do this stuff every season."

"Where do we start?"

"First we eat," said Rayf.

A half hour later Irene returned with a tray to remove the dirty dishes. "OK, boys, let me clean up this mess."

"Irene," said Rayf, "that was delicious."

"Why, thank you."

"Just in case you're wondering, my name's Rayf and this here is Cal."

"Glad to make your acquaintance boys." After a short pause, "Hope you don't mind me askin', but where'd you ever pick up handles like those?"

"They're nicknames."

"Is that right!"

"Yeah. We come from a neighborhood where everybody gets a nick-name," said Rayf. "They'd probably call you Irene-room-and-board."

"Which" added Cal, "would probably be shortened to, Irene Rooms."

"So's not to mix you up with another Irene," said Rayf.

"Irene Rooms. Hmm, sounds nice. So where'd Cal and Rayf come from?"

"My real name is Tommy Califano."

"And of course Cal is short for Califano."

"Right!"

"And my name's a combination of my first and last names."

"Which are?"

"Raymond Falcone."

"I see. Very interesting."

"That's just the way it goes in our part of the world," said Cal.

"Sounds kinda friendly if you ask me."

"It depends," said Rayf.

"Just remember boys, friendship is good medicine. And don't you ever forget that."

She started to pick up the dishes.

"Here, let us help you with that, Mrs. Grabowski."

"Why thank you Rayf. But you really don't have to ..."

"We insist," said Cal. This he knew how to do.

After the leisurely breakfast and the clearing away of the dishes, they started on their chores. Rayf would take a fine, steel-wired brush and scrape all of last year's paint and salt from the screens, and then pile the good ones over to one side of the yard and all of those that needed patching he'd pile over on the other side. Cal would then take the good screens over to where he had a canvas drop cloth set out on the grass and paint them with a light coat of dark green paint. And then he'd set the wet screens to dry out near the six foot tall hedge. Cal worked hard at learning his task. Some of the paint went right from can to brush to screen, and some of it sprayed right back onto his light-skinned face. So when Rayf looked over at him, he saw a green-freckle-faced Cal looking back.

"I'd like to know how come I always get the dirty jobs." said Cal.

"Hey, it could be worse."

"Yeah? How's that?"

"We could be wearing our own clothes," said Rayf.

"Some consolation."

After scraping all the screens, Rayf then set about patching up the torn ones by making little patches out of an extra piece of screen. Then, with a spool of fine wire, he would sew the patches onto the torn ones to make them whole once again.

When all the screens were cleaned and patched, he went over to help Cal with the painting.

They were all done by nine-thirty.

Irene re-emerged from the house.

"My, my, but you boys sure are quick. I didn't think that you'd be through till at least lunch time! You must a done this sort of work before, eh?"

"*I* did," said Rayf, wiping his hands with a rag.

"Where at?"

"My mom's folks had two bungalows on the Jersey shore."

"Your grandparents still alive?"

"Nah. They're both gone."

"Oh, that's too bad. Well at least you've still got the place to remember 'em by, right?"

"Not really."

"Sold 'em?"

"No, eminent domain. The state wanted the property back, so they took it."

"Why'd they do that?"

"They wanted to build parking lots or something like that."

"And?'

"And that's all she wrote," said Rayf. "When the state wants it back, they take it back. They get it, one way or another."

"Such a pity," said Irene.

"Yeah," said Rayf. "What're ya gonna do."

"Revolt," said Cal.

"Good luck," said Rayf. "Look, Irene, as soon as they're dry, we'll hang them up, OK?"

"Right Rayf," said Irene, "hang 'em high. First, you start on the second floor and then work down, OK?"

"OK," said Rayf, "You're the boss."

"And as the boss lady, I say that you boys should take a break right now."

"Good idea," said Cal. He hit the grass. Rayf did likewise.

Within an hour, in that hot sun, the screens were dry enough to hang. Cal carried them into the house while Rayf hung them in place and by eleven-thirty they were all done.

"Well, that's that," said Cal.

"Yeah," said Rayf, dusting his hands on his coveralls, "that does it."

While they were admiring their handiwork, Irene came down the back steps with a pitcher of ice-cold orange juice and three glasses.

"Here you go, boys. Some Florida-fresh orange juice to whet your whistles."

"Thanks," said Cal reaching for a glass, downing it in one gulp, and then quickly pouring a refill.

"Not a bad job, if you ask me," she said. "Not a bad job at all."

Rayf held up his glass to toast.

"Here's to you, Mrs. Grabowski. May your screens hang as long as your house stands and may your dreams outlive us all."

"*Our* dreams," she said.

"Our dreams," said all three.

They clinked glasses and toasted the good toast.

***

It was half past noon when they finally got around to showering and shaving. They were getting ready to go over to the I.D. and Records Department at the South Miami Beach Police Station. They were putting on their freshly washed and pressed old clothes that Mrs. Irene Grabowski had made look like new.

At the same time that they were combing their hair and whistling along with their own reflections in the mirror, Ali Baba and Soapy were just passing the Fontainebleau Hotel in their newly rented, fire-engine red 1963 Buick convertible.

Irene wished the boys good luck and said, "When you get back I got some more chores for you."

"No problem," said Rayf.

And with a smile, they headed off down Michigan Avenue towards 1st Street.

"Holy Christ," said Cal. "That old lady's got enough work ta kill a mule. It's no wonder that old Walter kicked the bucket!"

"It's our rent, man. Remember?"

"I don't dig this barter bit. I'd rather pay and split. This feels too much like home if you ask me."

"So we register with the police, get a job, and pay rent. It's that simple."

"That sounds more like it."

The boys found the police station, climbed the one flight of stairs to the second floor, and waited for the clerk to sign them up.

In the meantime, Soapy and Ali Baba had just parked their car in the Pink Flamingo's parking lot and were just now walking into the cool interior of the bar. Johnny was dangling a frog over the red-bellied piranhas. Two New York ladies were watching in mock horror. In front of each woman was a colorful drink with a tiny parasol sticking out of it. Four tiny parasols lay on the bar in front of them. They were howling at Johnny's antics as Soapy entered. Johnny saw Soapy and let the frog fall. The girls squealed with pleasure.

"Soapy! Back so soon?" said Johnny wiping his hands in a bar rag.

"Yeah."

"Can't stay away from the beach, huh?"

"Yeah, I guess so. Yo, John, dis is my partner, Ali Baba. Johnny, Ali Baba; Ali, Johnny,"

"Good ta meet ya, Ali."

"Same here," grunted Ali Baba.

They shook hands.

"What a strange name," said the squeakier of the two women.

"Da betta to screw ya wit, my dear," said Ali Baba.

The tanked ladies giggled.

"What brings ya back so soon, Soap?"

"Business. Give us a couple a Dewar's, neat."

And while Johnny was pouring those drinks, Rayf and Cal were just being called up to the desk at the Miami Beach Police Station's I.D. and Records Department. The clerk behind the desk wore a white, short-sleeved cotton shirt with a red, white, and blue striped tie. He had thick, horn-rimmed glasses and a shirt pocket full of pens and pencils. He wore his blond hair in a crew cut. He was cheerful and very happy to have such a job. He bubbled over with enthusiasm for Miami Beach, his foster home. *Didn't everyone in the whole wide world want to live here?* went his booster mentality. The room was cool and clean. The floor shone with a deep, rich luster. The Venetian blinds cut the sunlight into thin little slivers of dark and light that lay across the long counter and onto the clerk who stood behind it.

"You boys new in Miami Beach?"

"Yeah." said Rayf. "We heard that we have to get IDs to work down here. Is that true?"

"Yes, you do. Where y'all from?"

"We're from Jersey City, New Jersey," said Cal.

"Jersey City?" said the clerk, looking up from the form. "Jeez, I'm from North Bergen, myself."

"Get out!" said Cal.

"No, really," said the clerk.

"What a small world," said Rayf.

Cal said, "Ain't this somethin'? I used to go out with a girl from North Bergen."

"Really?" said the clerk.

"Really."

"What was her name?"

"Mary Scarpolleti."

"Hmm," said the clerk, "Doesn't sound familiar. What school did she attend?"

"Got me. It was only a summer romance. But *what* a summer!" And with that, all three of them laughed.

"You guys intend on staying down here long?"

"As long as it takes," said Cal sending up another peal of laughter.

"No. All kidding aside, I need to know for the record."

"Well," said Cal, "we came down here because of the weather."

"Isn't it great?" said the clerk. "See this shirt that I'm wearing?" holding out one of the short sleeves, "I had this thing on for the past three days, and it's still clean. I'd just like to see you try a stunt like that up in Jersey City; by now this shirt would've been a black rag."

"Jeez," said Cal. "Would ya look at that! It doesn't even have any dirt around the collar. I am truly amazed! How long you been down here?"

"Three years."

"You like it here?" said Rayf.

"Like it!? I love it," said the wage slave.

"You get outside much?" said Cal.

"Yeah. In the summer the sun doesn't set till late, so I get a chance to walk the beach. And in the winter I really don't mind being inside, because

I get out at four o'clock. And the rest of the time, including weekends, is mine to do with as I please."

"You're not a cop?" said Rayf.

"Nah, I'm just a city employee. Although I wouldn't mind being a policeman. The security's great and you get lots of benefits. Where are you guys staying?"

"On Michigan Avenue at Irene Grabowski's boardinghouse," said Rayf.

"The address?"

"I think it's 715 Michigan," said Rayf.

"What's goin' on in New Orleans?" said Cal.

The clerk stopped writing, looked up, and said, "Jeez, I don't really know that much about New Orleans. Why do you ask?"

"'Cause this bartender friend of ours told us that that's where the money's at," said Cal.

"Got me," said the clerk as he went back to his clerking, "I just stay here on the beach."

"Well, if we don't score here, we just might try our luck on the shrimp boats or the oil rigs on the Gulf," said the worldly Cal.

"Good," said a disinterested clerk. "Now if you'll just put your ages in the box and sign on the 'X,' we'll get your photographs."

As they were doing this the clerk said, "You ever been arrested?"

"Not yet," said Cal.

"That makes two of us," said Rayf.

"Good. And you're both citizen's of the US, right?"

"You better believe it," said Cal the patriot.

"Well, that just about does it. Soon as you're done filling it out, I'll take your pictures."

"Why do you need our pictures?" said Rayf.

"To put on your I.D. cards. This way, whoever you show it to will know that it's really you to whom they're talking," finished the young bureaucrat.

"I'm ready," said Cal, handing in his form.

"OK, now just stand over near that wall and I'll shoot you."

"Why do we have to do all of this stuff in the first place?" said Cal.

"To catch illegal aliens and crooks who think Miami Beach is their playground." Now to Cal, "Say cheese."

Cal smiled. The clerk snapped. Then Rayf stood there and the clerk snapped once more. They were through with the formalities.

"Your cards will be ready in a couple of weeks. Until then you can use this receipt. This'll show all prospective employers that you've registered with the police."

"Great!" said Cal, grabbing his receipt.

And now they were all set to join the work force that kept Miami Beach up and running neat, clean, and smooth.

"Oh," said Cal, folding away his receipt, "do ya think that you could spare ten bucks for a couple a neighborhood guys?"

The clerk stopped breathing with the thought of departing with ten dollars. He pulled out his wallet and, after much deliberation, finally dug out a bill. He looked lovingly at Lincoln's likeness and said, "Will five dollars do?"

"Anything you can spare, neighbor," said Cal.

"Please," said the clerk, handing Cal the bill, "please send it back to me. Here … here's an envelope, with my name and address on it. Just pop the five dollars into it and drop it in any mailbox." And then, on second thought, he pulled out his wallet once again and fished around for a stamp. "Look," he said while licking the stamp, "you don't even have to buy a stamp." He stuck it to the envelope. "Please, I don't make that much money." The boys thanked the clerk and shook hands. The clerk's heart sank. He had the feeling that he could just as well kiss Mister Lincoln good-bye.

They took the bright shiny steps down two at a time. A blast of humid, hot afternoon air welcomed them outside. "Jew brawds, here we come!" said Cal. And in no time they were walking towards Collins Avenue and their date with destiny.

In the meanwhile, a well-oiled Soapy and Ali Baba were talking with their Miami Beach confederate. "So," said Johnny, "these two young guys come in ta the place last night, and say that they're from New York. But I feel somewhat suspicious considering that they're not even familiar with Sheepshead Bay. You ever been to Lundy's Fish House in Sheepshead?"

"Go on with the story," said Ali Baba.

"OK. So then the other one says that he works in Union City, which I know as well as the next guy that that is in Jersey. So, when I go ta tell 'em that I know some people from Union City—namely you, Soapy—I was getting ready to say that, the other kid cuts me off. This added to my suspicion, especially after the lighter one of the two puts a lean on me for a few bucks. Of course I say, 'no way Jose.'" Soapy and Ali Baba are hanging on to every word.

"Did dey say where dey was stayin'? Where dey was goin? Anyding else dat you can remember?" said Ali Baba.

Johnny leaned on the bar and very confidentially said, "What'd dey do?"

Ali Baba leaned closer into Johnny, and said, "None of your fuckin' business."

"Hey, I'm just tryin' to be helpful," said Johnny pulling back and becoming more business like.

"Good," said Ali Baba, "It's a lot healthier dat way."

The two soused girls had since picked up some guy who was also on vacation. The three of them were causing a ruckus. Johnny excused himself when the drunken man with the ladies called out for another round.

"Well," said Ali Baba to Soapy, "wha'd'ya make a dis?"

"I was right. Just like I said, 'dey's here.'"

Johnny returned.

"What more da ya know?" said Soapy.

"I know for sure that they're livin' on Michigan Avenue at a boardin' house or somethin' like that," searching his memory, "and I told them that things were tight down here since those Cubans flooded the market. You won't believe it, but I could get me a bartender for half the price of what it costs me to hire an American; or a cleaning lady; or a good lay. But you gotta be careful with the chicks, some of 'em'll give ya jungle rot, make ya dick fall off."

"You sound like dis sick bastard," said Ali Baba. "I don't give a fuck about no brawds. I'm askin' ya about doze two fuck-ups."

"Right," said Johnny. "I told 'em that if they wanted some real action, they should try New Orleans. I also told 'em about the Cat 'n' Fiddle, like a dumb bastard."

"What about da Cat 'n' da Fiddle?" said Soapy.

"It's a joint in New Orleans—belongs to one of the boys. And, like a stupid bastard, I tell 'em that if they ever get there, ta tell 'em that I recommended them. This is all before they tried to put the bite on me."

"Anyding else?" said Soapy.

'Yeah, one other thing."

"What is it, John?" said Ali Baba.

"They were askin' about getting some work down here."

"And?"

"And I told 'em that there's a law down here: everyone that works the Beach has got to get carded."

"So what am I gonna do wit' dis information?" said Ali Baba.

"Hey, with the right persuading, if they did register with the police, one could possibly get the info that one desires, no?" said the wise barman.

"Johnny," said Soapy, "you are a angel. Give us a couple a more Dewar's," turning to Ali Baba, "So now all's we gotta do is locate da police station an' take it from dere."

"I'm allergic ta police stations," said Ali Baba.

"Hey, we go in like a couple a businessmen inquiring about a couple a guys dat are seekin' employment with us. And we tell 'em dat we got rea-son ta believe dat maybe da two dudes who came ta us lookin' fer woik are criminal types. Yeah! And den we say we dink we saw dere picture on a Wanted poster at da local post office or somethin' like that."

"Jesus," said Ali Baba, "I'm even startin' ta believe ya."

"Johnny," said Soapy. "Where is dis police station?"

Johnny pulled out a telephone directory, looked up the address, and said, "It's at 120 Meridian. That's just south of here near 1st Street. Here," pulling out a map, "I'll show ya."

***

South Beach: the Jewish fountain of youth discovered.

"This place looks like Bushwick Avenue back in the old days," said Cal.

"You must be blind!" said Rayf.

"You *know* what I mean, with all of the vegetable stands and all."

"When'd you ever see a juice bar in the Village?" said Rayf.

True, it did resemble the old days of the old neighborhood with its fresh fruit and vegetable stands and lots of older people haggling over the prices, but the big difference between this neighborhood and theirs was the phenomenal cleanliness. This place sparkled under the warm sun, and the live food stands gave off only sweet, clean, and wholesome fragrances, not like the ones back there in the good old days where every once in a while one would catch the pungent smell of something long gone bad. Here, everything smelled like a natural perfume and they breathed in the mixture of Atlantic Ocean, fresh fruit, and suntan lotion worn by the old Jewesses who congregated about these stands squeezing and testing each piece of fruit until the thing developed little brown spots and had to be removed by the Cuban produce boys who worked for the transplanted Brighton Beach Jews who owned these stands.

Rayf and Cal slowly and provocatively strolled the avenue—theirs was more of a swagger than a walk. At first glance they looked just like two ordinary guys out for a very leisurely and nonchalant stroll. But upon further examination one would have noticed that they moved very unnaturally with long, slow strides, constantly checking themselves out in the nearby store windows and continuously adjusting their hairstyles before moving on with furrowed brows and roving eyes in search of big game.

They made their best eyebrow forms and mixed them with grins that would've made James Dean roll over in his grave. They were on the make, Hollywood style. By the time they hit 6th Street, Rayf asked (under his breath and without disturbing his grin), "Where the hell are the chicks?"

"They're here," said Cal. "You just gotta look for 'em."

"All's I see is a bunch a dried up old ladies with a ton of makeup."

"Relax," said Cal, the professional poacher.

"I'll let you handle it," said Rayf, tiring of the game.

Cal moved over to one of the fruit stands and stood opposite a fifty-year-old Jewish lady who was appraising a selection of apples.

"Nice fruit, eh?" said Cal, fondling an apple.

"Excuse me? Are you talking to me?"

"Yeah," said Cal with his best Don Juan smile.

"I think they're goddamned rotten," said the matronly Jew. "Look at the prices on these. The bum should be ashamed of himself, calling this fresh fruit! The nerve of him."

"You down here on vacation?" asked Cal, the undaunted.

"What's it to ya?" snapped the woman.

"Well, I was. ... you know ... just askin'."

"You don't think I'd live in this hell hole do you?"

"I'm from up north myself," said Cal, hoping to conjure up images of a big spender on the prowl.

"That's too bad," said the woman as she went on her way.

"Well, how'd you do?" yelled Rayf.

"Hey, I'm just warmin' up. Gimme a break."

Meanwhile, just a few blocks away, Soapy and Ali Baba parked their Buick convertible around the corner from the police station on Washinton Avenue and walked down 1st Street to 120 Meridian. They opened the front door, and walked up the shiny flight of steps to the second floor, directly over to the desk clerk who told them that they'd have to wait their turn. But after Soapy explained that they were potential employers checking up on a couple of guys who, they believed, just might be wanted by the police.

The on-the-ball clerk dropped everything and told them that he'd be with them as soon as he took care of a Cuban refugee who was having trouble translating his form.

They took a seat on an empty bench and looked around. There, sitting on a bench facing them on the opposite side of the narrow room, sat six dark-skinned men. Ali Baba showed his distaste for being in this place with all of these foreigners by nudging Soapy and, of course, Soapy agreed. The two men fidgeted away their five minute wait until the blond, short-haired clerk said, "OK, gentlemen, I can talk to you now."

Ali Baba did not know who he was referring to until Soapy said, "He's talkin' to us, meathead."

Ali Baba wanted to punch Soapy right then and there, but he was in a government building and would have to wait for his revenge. They stood up and walked over to the desk.

"How may I help you two gentlemen?" said the friendly clerk.

Once again, Ali Baba looked over his shoulder for the gentlemen.

"Well," said Soapy, "we're part owners in a bar down on Bay Avenue, and just last night a couple uv guys come in lookin' fer a job. And bein' gud citizens and all," with a distasteful glance towards the Cubans on the bench and a nod of mutual agreement from the clerk, "I wanted to make sure dat dey weren't criminals or woist yet," whispering now, "wetbacks. Ya folle me?" finished Soapy.

Ali Baba was very impressed.

"Well sir," said the clerk to Soapy, "that's what we're here for, to help the business community at large. Now, do you have the names of these two, uh, men—I suppose?" asked the clerk.

"Uh, yes. Dat is correct … two men. Dere names are Ray Falcone and Tommy Califano."

The clerk looked through his files and came up with the just-completed forms.

"As a matter of fact sir, they were in here just a few minutes ago." Now studying their forms, "And I dare say, sir that everything seems to be in order. We are currently checking our police files and should have their clearances within a couple of weeks. If you can call back then …"

"Great!" said Soapy to Ali Baba. Now to the clerk, "Now if I can just …" as he yanked the form out of the clerk's hand, "Look at dis …"

"Hey!" said the clerk, going for the forms, "That's confidential."

Soapy turned his back on the clerk, who was now leaning over the counter and clawing the air for the forms. Ali Baba pushed him back down.

"Hey!" said the clerk to Ali Baba, "What do you think you're doing?"

"I daut you lost you're footing or somethin'," said Ali Baba, the thespian. By then Soapy had all the information he needed. He handed the forms back to the clerk.

"You're right. It is all in order. Dank you, sir," said Soapy.

The clerk, now holding the forms and not really sure what had just happened said, "You're … you're quite welcome, sir." They nodded to the clerk and to the six Cuban refugees waiting there on the bench as they walked very upright and business-like down the shiny staircase that led them outside.

Walking toward their car, Ali Baba couldn't help but look up to his physically smaller partner. "Man," said Ali Baba, "You even had me believin' ya. You were just like a actor. Unfuckin' believable, man."

"Hey, ya know I coulda been a actor if I wanted ta leave da corner. But I like da block too much ta give it up."

"You're full a shit."

"I'm tellin' ya, I'm a natural. I coulda been a …"

"Where da hell're dey stayin'?"

"At 715 Michigan Avenue."

Cal, in the meantime, had just cornered another Jewish woman. This one he figured to be no more than forty-five. "I'm from New York," he said to the window-shopping woman.

"Is that so?"

"Yeah, I am. Hey, have you ever noticed how clean your shirts stay down here compared to up north?"

"I'm afraid I don't wear shirts."

"Well, you know what I mean … By the way, where're you from?"

"None of your business!"

This shot to the ego did not stand in the way of the relentless Cal. He questioned on: "You down here with your husband?"

"Grow up, sonny," she said and walked away from the window, leaving Cal all by himself to admire the latest women's fashions direct from the exotic garment district of Manhattan. He turned around and saw Rayf watcing him from over near the curb—he was leaning against a parked Dodge.

"What the hell are you laughin' at?" shouted Cal. "At least I'm tryin'; you just stand there grinnin'."

"Look, half of these women I wouldn't fuck with your dick and the other half I wouldn't fuck at all."

"That's not the point, jerk-off. A gigolo doesn't only fuck 'em, he escorts 'em, acts like their friend. He's like their pet, dig?"

"I'd rather be on relief, man."

It was four-thirty p.m. and evening was being painted in the Miami Beach sky with streaks of red, orange, and purple. They decided that they had had enough and would retire to their quarters to see what new tortures Mrs. Grabowski had in store for them. They walked easily through the darkening, semitropical night.

"I'm tellin' ya Cal, some of those ladies were old enough to be your grandmother."

"Hey, if I scored, you'd be the first one to help me spend the money."

"You're a dreamer, Cal."

"That's where it all begins, wiseguy."

Now just as they were turning the corner of Michigan, Rayf stopped in his tacks and yanked Cal back.

"What's wrong?"

"Take a look."

Cal peeked around the corner. And there, across the street, he saw Irene Rooms standing on her front step yelling in Polish at two men. Soapy and Ali Baba were paying her no mind as they walked back to their car.

"Holy shit," said Cal. What the fuck are they doin' still alive?!"

"Fuckin' Gypsy probably sold us aspirin," said Rayf.

"Good!" said Cal. "At least we burned the bastards."

"Good?"

"What am I gonna do now?" said Cal.

"I? What happened to *we*, jerk-off?"

The Buick pulled away from Irene who, with clenched fist, was still yelling after them.

As soon as the car turned the corner and vanished, Rayf and Cal ran over to Irene and pulled her inside.

"Irene," said Rayf, "what did those two men want?"

"They said that they were the police and that they were looking for you two. They also said that you were escaped convicts. But when I asked them to show me identification, a badge, or something, they had nothing to show. And that's when I told them that *I* was going to call the police department to find out if they were really policemen."

"And?" asked a nervous Cal.

"That's when they left."

She was in a trembling rage, "To think that they could just come in here and scare me like that."

"Did you tell them anything?" said Rayf.

"Yes. I asked them who the hell did they think they were?"

"No, Irene. I mean, about us?"

"No. I just told them that you were two good boys and that you wouldn't bother anybody."

"So," said Cal to Rayf, "they know we're here."

"Irene," said Rayf, "we're gonna have to leave now."

"Why?"

"Because those two men," said Rayf, "are bad men. They're gangsters and they're after us."

"But, why? What did you do?"

"It's a long story," said Cal. "We just have to leave so that you don't get into the middle of all this."

"But you are such good boys."

"Thank you Irene," said Rayf.

"Will you be coming back?"

"Someday," said Rayf. "Maybe someday, Irene."

"The house looks so nice with the screens all painted and fresh. Walter would be so proud."

"Irene," said Rayf, "Walter has a good woman and he *should* be proud."

"What about your denims?"

"Hang on to 'em," said Cal. "You might need 'em next year."

"Will you come back next year?"

"We'll send you a postcard," said Rayf.

"From New Orleans," said Cal.

"You promise?"

"Promise," said Cal.

And now she studied the two strangers, who just the night before she had let into her house and into her life. She smiled at them in their clean clothes and shaved faces and thought back on how raunchy they had looked less then twenty-four hours ago. She reached up, brought their heads down and placed a gentle kiss upon each of their cheeks. A tear formed in her eye, and she quickly wiped it away with her colorful hanky. "You've got to take care of yourselves for Grandma Irene, hear?"

"We'll take care," said Rayf. "And you take care too, OK?"

"Yes, yes. Now go. And stay away from those two bad men."

"Thank you for everything, Grandma Irene," said Cal.

And then they were gone, leaving behind them Beaks' clothing, the house, and Irene Rooms.

~ 10 ~

Movin' On

Under the cover of darkness they drew up a plan: Rayf would stake-out the house, Cal the Pink Flamingo.

Slithering through the parking lot, Cal saw the fire-engine red Buick convertible. Carefully, he worked his way up to one of the many tinted windows of the building that showed off tiny flickering candles on the tables within. This was not good; he could only see shadows. Around the back of the building on the patio deck that was built out over the bay, he got a better look.

His view was now over Johnny's shoulder and he could look right into the faces of Soapy and Ali Baba not ten yards away. They were at the bar in deep discussion. Johnny, in the meantime, was tending to his business and was having all he could do to keep up with his hostess who kept bring-ing back more orders for him to fill—she would first read them to Johnny from her pad, and after he prepared them, she would then give him the bill so that he could tabulate it in his shiny, chrome-plated cash register. Then she would take the drinks and tab back with her to the individual tables.

Ali Baba, on the other hand, was using very expressive hand gestures to Soapy; gestures that Cal could easily understand. There were hands strangling, hands pounding the bar, hands going through messed-up hair, and hands grabbing Soapy by the front of his brightly colored Hawaiian shirt. One did not have to be versed in the art of sign language to under-stand that the larger of the two men was in a rage, and if he did not get what he wanted, and soon, somebody, anybody, who got in his way was going to get the short end of a very mean stick. Cal stood very still behind the potted palm and watched. Soapy got up and walked out of the bar. Ali Baba was alone.

Cal quickly scampered over the patio deck's railing in time to see Soapy jump into his Buick and drive off. Cal watched as he headed south on Bay Road. Not three minutes later the big, red Buick parked obliquely across from 715 Michigan. Rayf watched as Soapy turned off the engine, pulled out a cigarette, and lit up.

Cal, in the meantime, went back to his potted-palm position and watched, in his opinion, a very dumb ox sitting there like a lump on a log. And then an idea came to him—vague at first, but then it started to take on form and color. Now he could almost taste it. Once again he scaled the deck's railing and walked quickly through the parking lot. The first part of his plan called for a dime, which he did not have. At this same moment a lovely blond in a 1962 white T-Bird convertible pulled into the parking lot. She parked and was just getting out of her car when a very casual Cal approached and said to the startled woman, "Excuse me ma'am, but could I trouble you for a pin?"

"A pin?" said the long-legged lady.

"Yes," said Cal. "Silly me, I just tore my trousers and I'm so embarrassed. I'll have to have the maid sew them as soon as I get home, but until then, do you have a safety pin that I may borrow?"

The woman, no longer afraid, just confused, looked through her glove compartment; anything to get this guy off her back and out of her life. She was in luck, she found one. And not wishing to make physical contact, she tossed it to the young vagrant.

"Why thank you, my dear," said Cal, in his best English gentleman accent. And then he was gone. The leggy blond watched Cal run out of the parking lot and head north on Bay Road. She shrugged, slammed her car door shut, and headed toward the safety and comfort of the Pink Flamingo.

Cal got into a public phone booth on the next corner. He jabbed the safety pin through the wire and ground its tip against the metal coin box. This gave him a dial tone, and from information he got the Pink Flamingo's phone number.

Johnny, who was now up to his ears in fancy drinks, which he could handle with no problem, had to let the phone ring at least ten times before yelling to his waitress, "Hey Annie pick up that goddamned thing, will ya?" The waitress picked up the phone and said, "Hello, Pink Flamingo."

Cal, with his shirt over the mouthpiece, spoke into the phone in a deep, guttural voice, "I want to speak with the big guy sitting at the bar; his name is Ali Baba. Get him for me."

"Ali Baba!?"

"You heard me."

"Look is this some sort of joke?"

"No joke, lady. Get 'im."

At this very moment the long-legged hooker was saying, "I'm telling you, Johnny, I've been asked for a lot of things in my time, but never, 'Hey babe, you got a safety pin?' It was funny, man. I'm telling you."

That's when Johnny overheard his waitress talking at the phone: "Next thing you're going to ask me for is the Forty Thieves, right?"

"Who you talkin' to?" said Johnny to Annie.

With her hand over the mouthpiece, she answered, "Some joker wants to speak to Ali Baba. I told him to go rub his lamp."

"Don't hang up," said a frightened Johnny. "I'll get 'im."

Annie, with a double-take from Johnny to phone, said with a change of voice, "One second sir."

She put the phone down, shrugged, picked up her booze order and walked away with her tray.

Johnny leaned in to Ali Baba and told him he had a phone call and that he could take it in the privacy of his office.

Ali Baba, following Johnny into the office, couldn't help wondering who wanted to speak to him. After all, Soapy was the only other person who even knew that he was there.

Johnny, with a reassuring nod, left Ali Baba alone in the small room. He picked up the phone and said, "'Lo."

"Hello, is dees Ali Baba?"

"Yeah, what's it to ya?"

"Señor Ali, hi ham calling choo on a grreat danger to my hown life. For hif dee boys know dat hit ees choo dat hi ham calling, for sure dey would have me dead. You must leesen, señor. Leesen very closely. Hello, are choo still dere?" finished the baritone señorita.

"Who da hell is dis?" growled Ali Baba.

"Señor, hi can only tell choo dees much, dee two choung men dat choo are looking for can be found rright now at dee Club Cuba on 14th Street een Miami."

"Who da hell is dis?"

"Eef choo look out dee bar window, you will see dee Venetian Cause-way. You should take dat up to Biscayne Boulevarrd where choo will den take a left and go up to 14^(th) Street. Den choo will take a right, and eet is dere dat you will see dee Club Cuba—and heenside you shall find dee two choung men dat choo are looking for." He hung up.

Ali Baba looked at the phone, thought for a second, and then hung up. On his way back to the bar he wondered what that phone call was all about. Who was it? And how did she know that he was sitting here at this bar? *Is it Soapy fuckin' around,* thought Ali Baba, *or is it one of those two fuck ups? But how can it be them? They don't even know that we are here? Or do they?* It was in this confused state of mind that Ali Baba found his way back to his seat at the bar.

Johnny walked up to him and asked, "Everything OK?"

"I don't know, I'm not sure," he said as he stared out the picture window to the causeway with its cars coming and going, "Hey Johnny."

"What's up, Baba?"

"Da name uv dat causeway? Venetian?"

"Yeah, why?"

"No reason," then on second thought. "Dose two assholes, last night dey talk about goin' ta a Cuban joint?"

"Come ta think of it, they did. When they were leavin' last night, the blond kid said that they were gonna try out some of those Cuban tomatoes. Like a real wise ass he says it. And here I am, I got this classy Cuban hustler workin' the bar and he says somethin' stupid like that."

"Dey say which joint dey was goin' to?"

"Nope. Just that they were goin' to look for some Cuban chicks."

"Where would ya find Cuban chicks around here?"

"They're all over the place."

"How's bout 14^(th) Street in Miami?"

"In Little Havana! By the thousands."

"Danks, Johnny. By da way, I need a ride. Call me a cab."

"Hey, for you I could do better than that." He waved the long-legged blond over.

"Wanda, this is a friend of mine. He needs a lift. Take care of him."

"Sure," said Wanda-the-pin. "Whatever you say, big John. Where you goin', big boy?"

"Just down da block."

"Well what are we waiting for? You from New York?"

"Yeah," said a disinterested Ali Baba as they walked out of the bar.

Cal was running back towards the Pink Flamingo and had arrived just in time to see Ali Baba and the blond pulling out of the parking lot in her white convertible. He clapped his hands. His stomach was a little queasy. Later for that—right now he had to move fast.

Back at the phone booth he asked the information operator for the phone number to Club Cuba in Miami. While waiting for the number, he almost threw up. He wished he had a Tums. The operator came back with the number. He memorized it and dialed. The phone rang in Club Cuba. In a matter of seconds Cal heard, "Hello, Club Cuba."

Cal, in a guttural voice, said into the phone, "Listen, is dis Ricky?"

"Yes."

"Good. Listen jerk, I got some business to finish up wit' you. You hear me, Cisco?"

"Who ees dis?"

"Doze two guys who ran out on dere tab last night?"

"The bartender with a new-found interest said, "What about them?"

"I'm sending over two big white guys to take care of dat tab. You hear me, Pecos?"

"Who ees dis?"

"You fuck wit' dees guys and dey'll send you back to Cuba in a cement rowboat!" He hung up.

Now, Cal ran down Bay Road toward 7th Street.

In the meantime, Rayf saw the convertible pull up with Ali Baba riding shotgun. Soapy stood up in the Buick to get a better view of the blond. Ali Baba jumped out of her car and into Soapy's, where he pulled Soapy back down into the driver's seat. Soapy yanked his arm from the other's grip.

After some discussion the T-Bird pulled out, and the Buick followed it up 7th Street. Rayf did not leave his post, but instead waited. Within five minutes Cal came running down Michigan Avenue. He ran up to meet him. Cal bent over to catch his breath.

"What happened?"

"We ... we ... got the fucks good this time," said a panting Cal.

"What'd you do?"

"I ... set them up at ... Club Cuba."

"How'd you do that?"

"I called the Pink Flamingo and spoke to Ali Baba like I was a Cuban chick, and told him that we were in the Club Cuba. Then I called Club Cuba, and told the bartender that two big guys were comin' to square up our tab." He sat down on the curb with his head between his legs trying to catch his breath and then he said, "Now all's we got to do is wait and see."

"Good fuckin' work," said Rayf slapping him on the back. Cal threw up this morning's breakfast.

***

The reason sharks have remained around for as long as they have lies in their ability to smell out danger and to attack only when the odds are heavily in their favor. If, while stalking their prey, the slightest problem should arise, they will back off and wait. By hunting in this manner, the prehistoric shark has been able to survive longer than most other animals on earth. Soapy and Ali Baba were not sharks.

Ricky got ready. One could never be too careful in Miami. In the back room he had three goons on hold. Perhaps Ricky was related to the shark. The three armed bouncers waited for the signal from Ricky and could respond within a matter of seconds.

The red Buick convertible parked in front of Club Cuba. Out stepped Ali Baba and Soapy. Ali Baba waited for Soapy to walk around the car. They met by the right front fender, checked their pockets, and then walked towards the open door of the bar. Soapy walked in first, looked the place over, and saw two bar girls and one bartender; other than that the place was empty. He waved Ali Baba in. Ali Baba walked in behind him.

True, Ricky was impressed with Ali Baba's size, but he knew that the big ones made a louder noise when they hit the floor. He hit the buzzer under the bar. The boys in the back room saw the warning light flash one time. One flash and they would prepare; two and they would respond. They prepared. Very nonchalantly, Ricky said in his most servile voice, "What ken hi do por choo two genteelmen?"

It was Ali Baba who spoke first, "Where's da shitheads?"

"Hi beg chore pardon, señor, wheech sheetheads are you referring to?"

"Don't give me dat señor shit, Jose," said Ali Baba.

"My name his Ricky," said the bartender, proudly.

"Dickey, Rickey ... I don't give a fuck what your name is. Where da fuck are doze two fuck ups?" said Ali Baba.

"Har choo tawken about dose two choung boys from New Jorrk?"

"Dat's dem," said Soapy.

"Well, well, well, hain't dis a coincidence. Hit just so happeens dat hi got a leettle tab dat dey owe me, and frrom what hi understand, choo boys are going to peek it up. Is dis correct?"

"Where did you hear dis shit?" said Ali Baba.

"Someone just called to tell me dat two big men were coming over to pay hit off."

"Is dat right," said Ali Baba, "Well, I just got a call from some spic chic dat told me dat dey'd be here. And I come here to bang doze two bastards."

"Verry interesting," said a thoughtful Ricky, "Now let me get dis straight: choo get a call from a Hispanic woman who tells choo dat dey are here?"

"You heard da man," said Soapy.

"Hain't hit funny dat hi should get a call from a New Jorrker who tells me dat choo two would be comin' over to pay for dere tab, hmm. Dis ees verry interresting."

In the meantime, Cal had done his phone trick one more time and was waiting for someone to pick it up. She awoke from a very deep and relaxing sleep, picked up the receiver and said, "Hello, whoever this is, I'm sleeping."

"Angela, this is Cal," said the metallic phone voice into her sleepy ear. She jumped out of bed.

"Cal, where are you?"

"Yeah, like I'm gonna tell you, right?!"

"Cal, it's so good to hear your voice. I'm so glad that you're still alive ..."

"That's more than I can say about your father's goons, baby doll."

"Cal, what are you talking about?"

"You can tell your dad that his two top bloodhounds are history; that they have bought the farm."

"Cal!?"

"And don't forget to pass on the message. Hear me?"

"What are you talking about?"

"Do I have to spell it out? Soapy and Ali Baba are probably at this very moment barracuda chum." He hung up.

"Cal ... Cal ..."

Gently, Angela laid the dead phone into its cradle. Bewildered, she sat down on her bed and, with a set of rosary beads clasped in her small hand, started to rub her belly. If one had the ability to look into her mind, one would notice that a very big change was taking place deep within. This game that she was a part of—the one Cal, Soapy, and her father were still playing—did not concern her as much as it did before, for now another reality had taken its place, a reality that was perking away in her womb—compared to this, all else seemed trivial.

Cal walked out of the booth. He was a little shaky. To steady himself he put a hand on Rayf's shoulder and said, "Now that that's all taken care of, what d'ya say we check out New Orleans. I mean, ding-dong the witch is dead, eh?"

Rayf, disengaging himself from Cal's hold, said, "We'll see."

Meanwhile, at Club Cuba it didn't take long for Ricky, Soapy, and Ali Baba to figure out that they had been set up. Ricky offered them one drink on the house, and they accepted. And since they were here, why not introduce them to the two bar girls? After all, went Ricky's motto, a man should never drink alone.

In the meantime, Rayf and Cal were walking over the Venetian Causeway towards Miami. Halfway across Cal sat down on the curb. "Damn, it feels like a ton of bricks just fell on me." His face was covered with beads of sweat.

"You look bad, man."

"I feel bad!"

"What happened?'

"How the fuck should I know? I just feel sick."

"Look, we can't stay out here in the open. Come on, stand up."

After much effort, Cal stood. Just then a hot rod pickup truck with orange and yellow flames painted on the hood and fenders pulled up alongside them. The young Cuban guy inside yelled out, "Hey, you guys need a ride?"

"Yeah," said Rayf.

"I'm heading to Little Havana. Is that any help?"

"We're just going over to the other side," said Rayf.

"Cool. Hop in."

Rayf helped Cal in and took the shotgun seat himself. They peeled out. Two miles later, Rayf got out, thanked the Good Samaritan, and helped Cal out. The hot rod pickup truck turned south towards Little Havana.

Rayf didn't watch; he was too busy with his heavy load. Finally, he set Cal down on the cool, soft grass under one of the three sixty-foot coconut palms that stood in this small, triangle corner park at the foot of the causeway. Cal, with cramps in his stomach, rolled himself up. Rayf didn't know what to do, so he just sat there and watched as Cal went deeper and deeper into delirium.

But the scene at Club Cuba, not five blocks away, was very different.

Soapy was dancing some sort of rumba with his girl, and Ali Baba was still at the bar with his hand up his girl's skirt, playing with her pubic hair. The music was loud and Ricky was in a joyous mood, for here were two real big spenders. The gang in the back room was now deep into a game of dominoes. Like cats, they relaxed and would spring into action if the need ever arose. It was unusual for Ali Baba to let down his guard as much as he did here, but he did have a very deep fixation on dark-skinned women and this beauty, with her red lipstick and green-blue mascara, drew the big man deep into her dark Spanish eyes where he found himself in freefall. It was good to relax, was Ali Baba's last sober recollection.

Back at the tropical triangle park, Cal was still rolled up like a ball, and Rayf was gathering up two real coconuts. He walked over to Cal and showed them to his friend. Cal mumbled, "Leave me the fuck alone, will ya?" So Rayf proceeded to open the one coconut with the other, entertaining himself until Cal either got well or died, whichever came first.

The music in Club Cuba stopped and a laughing Soapy, along with his girl, returned to their seats at the bar. Ricky thought this was a good a time as any to present the two soused men with their tab. And with a smile, he handed it to Soapy, the celebrant. At first Soapy ignored the tab, but his girl slipped it gently into his view. She was very helpful in these matters. She worked on commission. And now, as though it were his idea, Soapy picked up the tab and stared at it waiting for his vision to stabilize. And when it did, Ricky the bartender saw the sobering effect that his addition had upon this drunken reveler.

"What da fuck is dis?" said a very loud Soapy.

It was a very smooth Ricky who took the tab and studied it for a while before saying, "Why, hit ees chor tab señor."

"You gotta be fuckin' kiddin' me, man! Dis says four hundred and sixty-fi' dollars. We on'y had four rounds. How da fuck'd you come up wit' a number like dat?"

"Dee girls, dey hab been drrinking champagne," said the very business-like Ricky as he pressed the button one time.

In the back room the single flash of light snapped the three bouncers to attention; they checked their weapons. And now Ali Baba was called back from those Spanish eyes and was once again sitting here on a bar stool in Club Cuba with the red neon lights that blinked on and off every two seconds in the small, fortress-like windows. He reached over his girl and grabbed the tab out of Soapy's hand and, after much squinting and readjusting of the distance between his arm length to his eyes, he finally focused on the cash-register-printed numbers and said, "Who da fuck broke a window?"

"Hit is no weendoe, señor. Hit ees chor bill," said Ricky.

"I told you fuck-o, knock off dat señor shit before I knock you the fuck back to Cuba." It was here that Ali Baba laid his piece on the bar, and it was here that Ricky hit the button twice. The three cats in the back room sprung into action, quietly joining the five in the front room.

"Do hi sense dat señor is hangry weeth me?"

"You got dat right," said Ali Baba.

The three bouncers kept well within the shadows, waiting.

Soapy was the first one to notice something moving back there in the mirror behind the bar, but he didn't say anything. He just kept the shifting, silent clump well within his peripheral vision as he watched Ali Baba and Ricky in deep discussion.

"You got a better chance a collectin' ya pension tamara den collectin' dis here tab tonight," said Ali Baba.

"Hab hit chor way señor," said Ricky the calm, who gave a slight nod.

Soapy saw the clump as it emerged from the shadows to become three men going for their guns.

With one swift motion, Soapy spun around, drew his gun, and fired. One of the Cuban gunmen kissed the dusty floor. The other two stopped in mid stride with their hands still in their belts.

Ali Baba saw Ricky going for his gun lying on the bar. He grabbed the flyweight by his shirt front and, with one swift motion, picked him up, dragged him over the bar, and slammed him head first onto the floor. He then kicked him in the face. Ricky took a nap right there among his broken teeth. Ali Baba grabbed his gun, spun around, aimed at the last two standing bouncers, and said, "One fuckin' step and you're all dead." No one moved.

In the meantime, Rayf had peeled off the first layer of hairy coconut and was shoving it into Cal's face, "Look at this, Cal. It's a real live coconut. Can you believe this?" Then twisting Cal's head, he pointed to a clump of remaining coconuts a full sixty feet up in the tree, silhouetted against the bright, neon-lit sky.

"Fuck those coconuts," said a fast-fading Cal.

"You know what your problem is Cal?" You got no desire to learn how things happen. You don't give a fuck about life. Therefore, you're never gonna grow." Now, with full force, he threw the coconut against the nearest tree. "You like coconut milk?"

***

Soapy and Ali Baba, with guns in hand, were just backing out of Club Cuba. Soapy jumped into the car and started it up. Ali Baba, at the barroom door, said to the four remaining people left alive and awake, "You follow us and we'll blow your fuckin' brains out. If ya know what's good for ya, ya stay right here." He backed up to the car and hopped in. Soapy peeled out and made a screeching U-turn.

The two bouncers ran to the door. Ali Baba opened fire. The bouncers ducked back inside until the car turned the corner. Then they ran across the street, leaped into their brand new 1963 purple Pontiac Bonneville convertible, and peeled out.

Rayf now had Cal propped up against one of the palm trees and was forcing him to watch as he attempted to juggle the three large coconuts. Cal was thoroughly pissed off at his friend, but couldn't do a thing about it.

The screeching tires made Rayf drop his coconuts. He turned to face the action. That's when he saw the fire-engine red Buick convertible careening around Biscayne Boulevard on two wheels, heading right at them. He ducked behind Cal's palm tree and saw the purple Bonneville convertible take the same turn.

The Buick went speeding right past the tollbooth. The toll man jumped out with raised fist yelling after it. The roar of the other oncoming car sent him scampering back for cover. The pursuers flew past. Now it was a very cautious toll collector who stuck his head out to watch the two cars speeding off toward Miami Beach.

Rayf ran into the middle of the road to watch the car chase. Gun fire sent him running back to take cover behind his palm tree.

The Bonneville caught up with the Buick just before Belle Island. Amid gun fire and gnashing fenders, the Buick was forced over the side. Soapy's last shot blew out the Pontiac's front tire. Both cars, with all four men, went crashing into Biscayne Bay.

"Cal, you did it, man. You fuckin' did it."

"Whaaa?" moaned Cal.

He helped him stand, slung his arm over his shoulder, and started walking. The distant sound of sirens was music to Rayf's ears.

***

He struggled with his friend up Venetian to North Miami Avenue where he then turned north. They went past the city cemetery and then up Northwest 20th Street, where he found an all-night drug store. He sat Cal down in the drugstore parking lot, propping him up against the wall. "I'll be right back," he said, "Don't move." He went into the store.

Cal was too weak to move. He tried to stand, but couldn't, so he lay down and tried to sleep.

In the store, Rayf was walking up and down the aisles. His clothes were no longer clean and pressed.

He looked around for the hidden two-way mirrors and found them near the ceiling. He looked for the spotters: the plain Janes and Joes that walk the aisles with carts that never made it to the cash registers. He didn't see any, and with quicker-than-the-eye-can-see hands, stashed a box of cough drops, a jar of Vicks, a package of No Doz, and other assorted over-the-counter drugs into his pockets. At the cash register he paid for only one package of gum.

Outside in the parking lot, he looked over to where he had left Cal. He wasn't there. Then he saw someone staggering around on the far side of the parking lot. And when that person walked under the street lamp, he recognized the cotton shirt and yelled out to it, "Hey Cal, wait up."

***

Soapy, talking on the phone in the emergency room's phone booth, watched the paramedics as they wheeled one of the unconscious Cubans past.

"We had a little accident. No, we're at da South Shore Hospital, Miami Beach. No, I'm OK." Looking down at his left arm hanging in a sling he said, "Just broke my arm. Yeah, he's OK, dey're workin' on him right now … a slight concussion. He's got a thick head … should be OK by da mornin'. What? Oh, yeah it's cool. We took a little swim, went back ta our place, and changed clothes before cumin' over here. Told 'em we got inta a fight … guys ran away. Yeah, dey fell for it. Dose two bastards set us up in some Cuban joint. Yeah, we lost 'em, but we got a couple leads. We still got dis old lady ta see. Nah, I ain't messin' around … come on, boss, she's like seventy years old fer crissakes. Yeah dey were stayin' at her place. Yeah, sure … In da mornin' we get us anuder car. Right, OK. Talk ta ya later."

He hung up, stepped out of the phone booth, sat down, and felt his tender left arm. Silently, he counted the cars that had gone to that big junk-yard in the sky since he had started chasing Cal, and he dreamed of getting his one good hand around that rat bastard's skinny neck.

After Cal took the medicine, they continued walking up 20th Street and then went northwest up North River Drive. Soon they found themselves on Okeechobee Road. By now the medication was working its wonders and Cal was too high to remember that he had ever had the twenty-four-hour flu. They both walked on with newfound strength.

Cal felt so good, he said, "Hell, we can walk to New Orleans."

Just then an old pickup truck pulled over. The middle-aged man behind the wheel hollered out to the two fast-paced walkers, "Where you boys headin'?"

"New Orleans," shouted Rayf.

"Hop in the back. I'll lift yer up as far as Alligator Alley."

"Much obliged," shouted Cal.

They hopped into the back.

Twenty-five miles later, when the driver pulled over and said, "Here's where I turn off, boys," the patented medicine had completely run its course.

Rayf jumped down onto the spongy Florida sod and reached up to pull Cal out.

"Somethin' wrong with the boy?"

"Nah. He's just tired."

"You sure?"

"Yeah, I'm sure."

"OK. Now in order for you to hit N'orleans you gotta continue on up 27. Or ya could take this here Alligator Alley, which you is on right now, and then you swing on up north."

"Thanks."

"No bother," yelled the disappearing pickup-truck driver.

And then there was silence at the crossroads of US 27 and Alligator Alley.

Rayf looked after the long-gone pickup truck and thought how that driver was probably laughing his ass off right now as they sat out here in the middle of nowhere. He dragged Cal off to the shoulder of the road and leaned him up against the fat trunk of a live oak. He then lay down a few feet away under the low-hanging branches and looked up at the stars twinkling between the tree's blunt-tipped, leathery leaves.

He slapped and killed a mosquito that had made the fatal mistake of landing on the back of his neck. He breathed in the thick air and listened to the strange sounds of the night. He stared off into the all-encompassing darkness and waited for the first alligator to come loping out. And if one ever did, he figured he'd be forced to sacrifice Cal.

The night wore on.

~ 11 ~

OTHER WORLDS

The morning light found them alongside the road on a pine land ridge. The ridge, six feet above sea level, was composed primarily of pine trees, palmettos, and cabbage palms that rose one hundred feet into the air. Off near the edge of the ridge were stumpy saw palmettos waving spiny, finger-like palm fans that, during the summer rainy season, called all to come and take refuge.

There, in this prairie of grassy waters, Rayf saw hardwood hammocks: islands that stood barely three feet above the water of this sixty-mile wide river. Islands composed of trees, the names, some of which he had never heard—live oak, gumbo limbo, hackberry, willow, magnolia, sweet bay, fiddlewood, and orange.

This river, which started up around Lake Okeechobee, would drain almost imperceptibly and lazily for over one hundred miles before emptying into the Gulf of Florida, where the brackish waters of the mangrove swamp played host to the largest population of mosquitoes in the continental United States.

Cal slapped another mosquito, "Where the hell are we?"

"At the intersection of US 27 and Alligator Alley."

"Alligator Alley! Where's that?"

"About fifty miles northwest of Miami Beach."

"Fifty miles!? Looks more like a thousand from nowhere. How the hell'd we get here?"

"Hitched."

"Hitched!? I don't remember anything after the phone call to Angela."

"You were a load of fun, man."

"You carry me?"

"You got that right."

"Sorry, man. I don't know what happened. I just lost it."

"Good to see you up and alive. I had my doubts there for a while."

"That makes two of us. Man, it sure is quiet out here. Pretty, though, in a strange kinda way."

"Yeah, I know. If I could only get those alligators out of my mind."

"Alligators?"

"There must be alligators out here someplace if they call it Alligator Alley, no?"

"Shit, they can't climb trees—can they?"

"I knew you'd be good for something besides bait."

"Hey, the way I feel right now they'd probably spit me out. I gotta rest a while."

"Well, you can rest in peace, man."

"Wha' d'ya mean by that, wise ass?"

"Soapy and Babs … last night, they crashed over the Venetian Causeway."

"They what?"

"You heard me, man."

"I kinda remember you telling me something like that."

"A car was chasing them, and both cars crashed through the railing."

"Get out!"

"No! Really."

"Then it worked!"

"You did it."

"Oh man, I wish I coulda seen it!"

"Take it from me, it was beautiful."

"Then they're gone?"

"Right now they're probably shark shit."

"And I feel like mosquito food."

"You? I'm just about sucked dry," said Rayf, slapping another one dead on his neck, "I wonder where Marlin Perkins is."

"Who?"

"That guy on TV who's always running around in the wilderness? I mean, I expect to see him out there chasing some water buffalo or somethin'. I mean, come on, look at it. It looks just like the African plains, doesn't it?"

"Where the hell'd you ever see an African plain?"

"On TV in that Wild Kingdom show."

"Come to think of it, it does look something like that."

A car meandered past, giving off a warm, welcome breeze to the two hitchhikers sitting thirty feet from the road. They were relaxing, taking in the quiet beauty that is the eastern border of The Glades.

Rayf laid back and looked up at the puffy white clouds against the blue sky. He played mind games with the shapes.

Cal, leaning against the live oak, lit up and said, "Maybe the smoke'll keep the bugs away."

He looked at the surrounding beauty and listened to the incredible quiet that permeated this part of Florida. Then he thought about home and his bookmaking operation. It seemed strange to him that that life, which was so real to him back there, felt like only a dream to him out here. No matter how hard he tried to visualize that previous life, he would always come drifting right back here to this very real location—here, at the crossroads of land and glades. And then he noticed, way up there in the blue sky, a long-legged great white egret flying southward. He watched its gentle, undulating wings as it flapped off over the flat plains vanishing into a distant cloud. He saw a car moving slowly towards them. He didn't even put out his thumb; instead, he waved a lazy hand, pulled in another lung full of nicotine, and thought how nice it would be to have a cup of coffee just about now. This is the way they spent the first few hours after waking—just relaxing and taking in this very different and, to them, very strange vista.

It was almost two o'clock when the black funeral hearse pulled over. The passenger's door flew open, a blast of radio news shattered the pastoral scene, and hanging half out of the car's door was its driver, a kid no more than eighteen years old wearing a cheap black suit, white shirt, and black tie. He was calling out to the two guys sitting off near the trees, "Hey, you guys hear the news?"

They looked the other way. For one neighborhood superstitions said never to look directly at a hearse; it was bad luck. So they completely ignored the vehicle and driver, who was now yelling, "Hey, you guys deaf?"

Cal broke first and yelled back, "Wha'd'ya want?"

"The news! You heard it yet?"

They shook their heads and pointed to their ears. Now he waved to them to come on over and then ducked back inside to turn up the volume. Rayf and an unsteady Cal stood up and walked slowly towards the long, black car. As Cal approached the open passenger's door, Rayf looked into the rear of the vehicle. To his relief, it was empty. The kid with a gapped-tooth smile blurted out, "They got Kennedy. J.F.K. got hisself assassinated. He's dead. Somebody killed the president."

There was an awkward moment of silence as they stood there listening to the electronic voice of the radio spewing out the news from people on the scene and from people off the scene. Then he changed stations and here was news from Washington D. C.; and now here was a schoolgirl being asked how she feels about it. And now here was a schoolgirl crying over the radio in the big, black hearse.

"Is it true?" said Rayf.

"Damn right! Where y'all headin'?"

"Where'd he get killed?" said Cal.

"Dallas."

There was a moment's hesitation before Cal said, "Dallas. We're goin' to Dallas."

"What?" said Rayf, "I thought we were going to New Orleans?"

"Sure wisht I could join y'all, but I'm a workin' stiff," said the kid, laughing at his own joke. "Well hop in, I'm headin' down Alligator Alley. Somebody'd have to jump in the back, though."

They stepped back from the hearse, "But we're goin' up 27 toward Orlando," said Rayf.

"Hey, come on," said the impatient driver, "I'll take you up near there. Anyway, I need me sum comp'ny; come on, hop in."

"Choose ya for it," said Cal to Rayf.

Rayf called odd, Cal even. They made a fist, counted to three, and threw out one hand of fingers each. The fingers totaled six. Reluctantly, Rayf hopped into the back and Cal, with a sigh of relief, jumped into the shotgun seat.

The hearse took a left onto Alligator Alley and headed west. The kid, like a ghoul, kept tuning the dial, gathering as much information as he could about the murder of President Kennedy. And somewhere in there, between static and commercials, they heard a local news bulletin: "Three men missing and feared drowned. Late last night, two cars crashed over the Venetian Causeway into Biscayne Bay. One man, Hector Lopez, was found and is reported in critical condition. The other three remain miss ..."

"Damn Cubans!" said the kid, changing the station.

Cal turned to Rayf. Did they just hear something?

***

The rented 1963 gold Cadillac Eldorado convertible cruised very slowly down Michigan Avenue and parked across the street from 715. Ali Baba, riding shotgun with bandaged head, looked at the quaint, two-story, white boarding house with its newly painted, green screened windows and then over to Soapy, who had his left arm in a sling, and said, "G'head."

Soapy got out of the car, slammed the door shut with his good right arm, walked across the wide concrete street and up the neat little pathway that led to the front door, and knocked. There was no answer. He knocked again, waited, looked back at Ali Baba, and shrugged. He knocked harder. Slowly, the front door opened and there, in a flowered-print house dress with handkerchief pressed to weeping eyes, was Irene, "What do you want?" said the sobbing landlady.

"Sorry ta bother ya ma'am, but, uh, we gotta talk ta Cal and Rayf. Ya see, we know dat ..."

"Don't you have any respect for the dead? You really don't have any feelings, do you? Yesterday and now today. I'm telling you I am going to call the police if you don't leave me alone."

Soapy looked back towards Ali Baba with a gleam of hope in his eye, and then said, "Excuse me, but did you say dat dey was dead, ma'am?"

"Not them, you idiot." Now breaking into tears. "The president."

"Oh," said Soapy, flatly. "Too bad. But what about dee udder two guys?"

"You chased my boys away, you no good bums. Because of you, they're gone. Gone to New Orleans." Pounding him on his chest, she said "You chased my good boys away. You should be ashamed of yourselves."

Soapy, backing down the pathway towards the sidewalk said, "Danks, lady."

"Why, the audacity!" Now slapping his left cheek with her right hand, a whack he could not block.

Soapy could take no more of this abuse, so he grabbed both of her tiny wrists in his one large right hand and said, "Lissen lady, we got no beef wit' chew, OK? So be cool and we'll leave it dat way." He dropped both of her arms and walked towards the gold Cadillac. Irene raised the hanky to her nose and watched through tear-filled eyes as the Cadillac moved off quietly down Michigan Avenue, turned west on 7th, and vanished.

Inside the car, Ali Baba said, "Well?"

"Dey're gone. Dey split town."

"Where'd dey go? She say?"

"Yeah," said Soapy, looking straight ahead. "She let da cat outta da bag."

"Where?"

"New Orleans."

"Hmm," mused Ali Baba as the car turned north on Bay.

For a while they rode on in silence and then Soapy said, "Hey, d' ja know dat J.F.K.'s dead?"

"No! Really? Who told ya dat?"

"Da old lady."

"Get out!" said Ali Baba.

"I'm tellin' ya dat's what she said. Here, let's turn on da radio." And that's what Soapy did.

He tuned the dial finding bits and pieces of what the world had already known for the past three hours—that John F. Kennedy, 35th president of the United States of America, born in Brookline, Massachusetts on May 29th, 1917 was now rapidly fading into ancient American history.

***

Inside the Pink Flamingo. Johnny was setting up three shot glasses. "Well, how do you like that? I mean if they kill the president, none of us are safe, he said."

"Yeah," said Soapy, "you're right."

"Where'd he get it, again?" said Ali Baba.

"In da head," said Soapy.

"I mean what city?"

"Dallas," said Johnny. "Some guy up in a tower hit him. What a terrible way ta go, right there, with ya pretty wife sitting right next ta ya."

"Yeah," said Soapy.

Except for these three and the tanked piranha, the bar was empty. They lifted their shot glasses.

"To life," said Soapy.

"Yeah," said Ali Baba, "I'll drink ta dat."

And they did.

"Give us anudder one, John," said Soapy. Johnny poured three more shots of scotch.

After three rounds, Ali Baba said, "Enough mourning. Let's get down ta business."

"I'm wit'cha, Babs."

"Now what's dis about New Orleans?" said Ali Baba to Johnny.

"I told them that that's where they should go if they wanted some real work."

"An' tell me about dat 'Cat and da Fiddle' place again," said Soapy.

"It's a joint one of the boys own."

"Right. And how da ya get ta New Orleans from here?" said Ali Baba.

"You go to Miami International Airport and hop a plane."

"Dey ain't takin' no plane," said Ali Baba. "How da ya drive dere?"

"Well, the quickest way would be ta take 27 up ta the panhandle and from there you go due west through Tallahassee and all, I guess. I never drove it myself,"

"What da hell are we waitin' fer?" said Ali Baba, "Give us one last belt fer da road and den we're outta here."

"Right," said Johnny, "Three Dewar's neat."

***

"Wow," said Rayf, while reading a road sign from the back deck, "'Big Cypress Seminole Indian Reservation'. A real Indian reservation. This is cool, man."

"Sheet," said the driver, "Dey ain't no big deal. Dey's jest a bunch a lazy good fer nuttins. Man, dey'd a lived in dat swamp forever and not done nutin' 'bout it." With a bony left hand he crushed a mosquito that had landed on his neck. He peeled it off, and between thumb and middle finger, flicked it out the open window.

"Why do you say that?" said Cal.

"'Cause it was us dat put in da canals so as to try and drain dis dang place so's we could get us some good pasture land fer grazin' cattle and da likes. Sheet, if it was up ta dem, dey'd still be out dere in da wild huntin' down all of da game fer demselves before we could even git us a crack at it. Dat's why we got 'em all cooped up out dere; so's we can make dis place civilized."

"How long they been out there?" said Cal.

"Who's dey?"

"The Indians," said Cal.

"Da Seminoles? Sheet. dey broke away from da Creeks and was chased down here when da Spanish had da place. And when we took 'er over and told 'em to move, dey damn as hell went ta war wit' us and have been holed-up here in dis god forsaken swamp ever since," said the driver slapping another mosquito. "Dey been here a long time, since the seventeen hunnerds. Why?"

"Just wonderin'," said Cal.

" how the hell they live out there with all these mosquitoes?" said Cal as he slapped his own neck and flicked another one out into that huge compost heap just beyond the window.

"Don't rightly know. Some people swear dat dey use magic and such. Me?! I think it's because dey's too filthy. No self respectin' mosquito worth his salt'd wanna bite one of 'em."

"I see," said Cal.

They were now driving through a small patch of dark trees that lined the road of the reservation. Here they saw walking towards them on the right-hand shoulder two "squaws," fully garbed in long, flowing dresses that had all the hues of the rainbow woven into them. Under these dresses were oversized petticoats that swept the ground as they walked. And up around their necks were strings of turquoise beads that wound round and round right up to their chins. Their skin looked like the earth. *It's as if*, thought Rayf, *they grew right out of it, like plants that learned how to walk and talk.*

"Dere, see dose two?" said the driver. "Ain't dey filthy? Man, I'm tellin' ya dey's filthy. Yuck!"

The "squaws" turned their faces from the oncoming vehicle and looked off into the swamp to avoid the white man's probing eye. The hearse drove deeper into Big Cypress Swamp. Passing through a low evergreen swamp made up of bay, pop ash and custard apple trees, they saw turtles and young alligators basking along the banks of a canal that paralleled the road. Now passing a prairie, the kid pointed to a large group of herons, egrets, and ibises knee deep in the grassy waters.

"You boys should come fishin' out here," said the kid.

"In that black water? You gotta be kiddin'," said Cal.

"Hell I am. Dere's good eatin' tarpon out dere, dat is if dose damn Indians ain't got 'em all by now."

He stopped the hearse right there in the middle of the road and real quietly got out and motioned for them to follow. They got out of the car as he hunched over and pointed to a speckled, seven-foot long king snake lying across the road. Now with finger up to pursed lips he said, "Shhh. Jes look at 'im. Ain't he beautiful, man? Jes look at 'im." And that's what they did for the next few minutes.

"Seminoles keep 'em as pets; dey eat rattlers dey do."

"The Seminoles?"

"Yeah, but da king snakes do, too," said the kid. And then, with a stick, he started goading the snake back into the canal. It swam off into a patch of bushes. "Look at dat water, will ya?" he said.

Instead, Rayf looked over to the skinny kid saying it. Here was a kid still young enough to truly love this natural beauty, yet impressionable enough to voice his father's opinions. It was here that Rayf wondered about his own opinions—which ones were his and which his parents? The kid broke off this train of thought with his high-pitched voice:

"It's as clear and as black as fresh brewed coffee."

Rayf and Cal looked into the water and there on the bottom they could see a whole stack of long, skinny fishes that looked like cigars. Rayf said, "What kinda fish are they?"

"Da ones wit' da long snouts are called garfish. Dey look just like a woodpile don't dey?" said the kid with a small laugh.

Yeah, thought Rayf, *they do look like skinny logs.*

The kid pointed out a green tree frog sleeping on a vanilla orchid leaf; a slender striped lizard bobbing on a moonvine stem; and a thin, green snake that rested across the tips of a waxy leafed tree.

The sounds of the swamp were many and varied: chirps, squawks, squeals, grunts, brush moving, tree branches swaying and, off in the distance, water splashing. They felt that they had just journeyed back in time, back before people had even started measuring time. The kid threw a rock into the crystal clear black water and said, "Come on, I gotta git dis rig back to da barn."

Rayf and Cal looked around at the dark channels of water that led through arched ceilings of ash, maple, and pond cypress trees, back to where only little rays of sunlight came in and gleamed green, gold, and amber on the leaves and glossy water. They breathed in the smell of rotting roots, orchids, and a thousand and one other fragrances that the swamp gave up as an offering to the visiting strangers.

The boys got back into the hearse. The kid started it up, pulled out, and said, "I'll show y'all where da 'gators live."

As they drove out of the swamp and took a right hand turn up State Highway 29, the kid pointed out a couple of clumps of trees out there in the sawgrass and said, "See dose willow heads? Well right between dem is a hole, and dat's where you'll find 'em. Dey weed dose holes and fill up on garfish. Wanna take a run out dere? Water's only two or three feet deep. What'd ya say?"

Cal was the first to answer, "I say you are out of your cotton pickin' mind, pardner."

"Hey, I was jest pullin' ya legs."

"Glad to hear that," said Rayf from the back ledge.

"Where we goin' now?" said Cal.

"This side a La Belle where y'all could continue straight up and meet wit' your US 27."

Driving steadily north up around Immokalee, the sawgrass gave way to a drier expanse of prairie. It was just after four in the afternoon when they pulled into the town of La Belle, the Hendry County seat. The kid gave them his famous smile and said, "Hope y'all liked da tour, y'all come back now, hear?"

"Hey!" said Cal, "Where the hell are we?"

"Git out cha maps and see fer yerself. You jest gotta go up dat road over da Caloosahatchee River and foller it north ta 27. Dat's 29," said the kid pointing toward the road they had just turned off, "da same road we been on after we turned off uv 'Gator Alley."

"Oh, I see," said a hopelessly lost Rayf, as he climbed out, stretched his legs, and looked off in the direction the kid just pointed.

"Thanks for the lift," said Cal.

"'Y'all welcome now! And next time I'm up east, which may be never, y'all best do da same fer me now, hear?"

"Yeah," said Rayf, "we hear."

He pulled away, waving his black-coated arm out the driver's window while looking at the two road apples in his rearview mirror. He took a right and was gone.

"You catch the name of that river?' said Cal.

"Yeah, except I don't think I could ever pronounce it again."

"Ya know," said Cal, "This looks like a great place to have us a good cup of coffee. Wha' d'ya say?"

"I say coffee," said Rayf.

And off they went to bum some good road jack.

***

At five-fifteen p.m., the part of the earth upon which they were sitting was rotating rapidly away from the sinking sun, revealing in the eastern sky a first quarter moon. The darkening, glowing, coal-red streaked violet and indigo expanse above made visible once again the first stars of night.

Cal and Rayf had talked themselves out about the assassination. They had listened to the radio at the lunch counter in the restaurant where they had their coffee, and had heard stories from people who had seen the television reports. These people spoke about the event as though they had actually been there and, indeed, they had via the tube. The media was transmitting all over the world, even down here in La Belle, Florida, thirty-three miles west of Lake Okeechobee.

As night approached, the more desperate became their need for a ride; a ride that would, hopefully, allow them to sleep away the night on a soft car seat while traveling north; a ride that would give them time; time to plan anew with the dawn's early light their continuing trip to Dallas. They were pointing north on Highway 29, a sparsely traveled route towards US 27.

Cal spoke about Angela and apologized for causing Rayf so much grief. Rayf accepted the apology and said, "Fuck it." This had Rayf perplexed, why wasn't he angry with Cal? Could it be because of the soft, warm, sultry air? Could it be the distance from the neighborhood corner? Could it be the adventure of living life on the edge, with starvation and death looking them right in the face and them laughing at it? Or was it delirium? He couldn't understand why he was almost happy about being forced down this fork in the road of his life, one that he would never have chosen, but happy just the same. It was as if he was supposed to be out here, away from the familiar surroundings of home and family, in order to experience this land on a first-hand basis by walking over it.

At five-thirty an old rattletrap of a 1950 Dodge pickup truck pulled over to the side of the road. Rayf got up and walked over to it. In the pickup he saw the face of a smiling Indian looking back at him through the rear window. As Rayf pulled open the squeaky door, the friendly, pony-tailed driver said, "Come on, hop in."

Rayf waved to Cal who was already casually strolling towards the dark gray, beat-up pickup truck. The climate down here was gradually working its way into the muscle and bone of these two city dwellers. They were slowing down.

"Where y'all headed?" said the cheerful driver.

"To Dallas," said Cal taking center seat.

"You got jobs up there or something?" said the young Indian as Rayf hopped in and closed the rattling door behind him.

"Naw," said Rayf. "We wanna go see where the president got killed."

"Who's that?" said the leathery skinned driver as he maneuvered the large pickup truck back onto Highway 29 north.

"J.F.K., our President," said Cal. "He got assassinated this afternoon up in Dallas. Haven't you heard?"

"Nope," said the cheery driver. "No radio. Anyways, he ain't my president."

Now here was something; what did this happy guy behind the wheel of this pickup truck that was so large inside you could almost hear your echo mean by '... he ain't my president'? Cal shot Rayf a sidelong glance.

Rayf said, "How's that?"

"How's what?" said the driver.

"You said that he wasn't your president, John F. Kennedy."

"That's what I said. Where y'all from?"

"Jersey City," said Rayf. "But if you live in the United States, then he's your president."

"I'm a Seminole Indian, direct descendant of Chief Osceola of the panther clan, and we ain't never signed no peace treaty with you crackers," said the Native American.

Cal and Rayf quickly looked around the cab for tomahawks and the like. The Indian said, "So technically speakin' we're still at war with you pale-eyes."

For an instant, Rayf and Cal wished their eyes were brown.

Well," said Cal, "we didn't have anything to do with it, man."

"Yeah, that's the whole crux of the white man's value system: it ain't us, it was them. Your values and ethics are always in a flux, and always based on earthly possessions which vary from generation to generation."

"So what's wrong with that?" said Cal.

"Well, for openers, ain't no one can posses the earth. And your needs are always changing. First you want gold, then oil, then land and minerals. So you sack and plunder to get as much as you can get and, without fail, the next generation comes along and refuses to accept responsibility for their parents' perversities, saying that what they did was not right. So they build their own set of ethics, but in reality it is always the same: it leaves their children rich with money and an escape clause of their own to continue with the plundering. Get what I mean?"

Rayf looked out at the stationary scenery as they moved past and wondered how they had gotten onto this topic in the first place. "Why are we talking about this?" he said, "I mean what good is it gonna do?"

"Plenty," said the Indian, "if you listen to your inner voice."

Here was another concept they had never heard of. *An inner voice?* thought Cal and Rayf.

Cal said, "I always thought that if you heard voices you were crazy." They both laughed at Cal's joke. Their driver did not.

"Yeah, that's another one of your weaknesses. That voice you hear is the voice of all creation."

The earth had rotated further from the sun, and now there were many more distant suns millions of light years away, sparkling through the earth's atmosphere.

"Man," said Cal, "are you tellin' me that I can, like, hear all of creation? Me? Why me? Who am I? I'm like a nobody."

"Why do you call yourself an 'istee toko?'"

"I didn't say that," said Cal.

"Yes, you did. You called yourself 'a person not.' That is one of the worst insults that my people would use on another. Yet you hurl it at yourself. You're not a nobody," said the Seminole. "Even the ant is somebody. Study them sometime and you'll notice how busy they keep themselves and how organized they are. They hear the voice. It directs them to do whatever it is that ants are supposed to do. That's how come panthers don't ever act like sheep, 'cause they're guided by the all-powerful spirit. We are all individual rays coming from the one spirit. Dig?"

They were amazed that this Indian from somewhere deep down in Florida, the same place where everybody from New York and New Jersey would love to retire, was hip enough to say, 'dig'.

"You mean to say," said Rayf, "that you can even get along with a mosquito?"

"They live here too, don't they?"

"But how do your people live with them?"

"Same as yours."

"No," said Cal, "How do you repel them?"

"With OFF!"

"Is that a magic potion?" said Cal.

"No, it's an insect repellent. You buy it in a store and spray it on. Why all this talk about mosquitoes? I'm getting itchy."

"But you didn't have OFF! in the old days," said Rayf. "What'd you use then?"

"Fish oil, smudge pots, smoke, nets; same as today."

"I see," said Rayf. *One sane answer*, he thought. Now he'd try to steer this conversation back towards familiar ground. "So, uh, where're you headin'?"

"To bring the magic mushroom to your people."

The driver would've used the word sacred instead of magic, but he knew by the pale-eyes' complete disregard for the earth and its creatures that the word sacred held absolutely no power.

So they do use magic, thought Rayf.

"What's a magic mushroom?" said Cal.

"It's a fungi that allows one to hear the voice of the Breath Maker."

Now the driver looked at them, and there in the darkening cab they stared into his deep, black eyes that were set between high, smiling cheekbones with lines of crow's feet that ran off towards his large ears. Out of his right eye came a glint of light as he winked. They flinched. He saw it. And now very softly, he said, "Wanna meet him?"

There was lots of hemming and hawing from the two passengers. "But you've got to get to Dallas. Maybe next time, right?"

"Yeah," said Rayf, "maybe next time."

The driver turned to face the road, becoming deathly silent. He was like a stone sitting there behind the wheel driving through the night with its millions of stars twinkling all around them. He remained quiet. All they could hear was the sound of the wind and the hum of the motor. The silence that his voice once filled had left a chasm that could not be filled with their limited field of experience. They had heard of drug pushers, like John Cangi, and how they lured people into the abyss of drug dependent states that caused them to steal and lose their self-worth, shooting-up families, homes, and jobs—cashing it all in, enslaved to their own physical desires, that led to a solitary, death-like existence. They were sure they had fallen in with such a pusher of dark dreams; dreams that once experienced would lead them to wander forever in a hell-on-earth. They feared for their psychological lives, and now the warm breeze gave them a chill, Cal nodded for Rayf to close his window. He closed it all the way, and that's when the driver looked at the two shivering young men.

They look so naked, so white, so frail and lonesome, he thought, a small representation of the entire white culture, all alone in a fearful universe which is set against them; a life that isn't fair, where death rules all. How little and helpless they look, yet how brave they appear for all the world to see, this facade that they hold up for other pale-eyes who are just as blind and afraid as they are. He said, "What're your names?"

At last, thought Rayf, a sensible question, one that I can sink my real mind into. He blurted out, "I'm Rayf."

"And me, I'm Cal."

"I'm called Wolf Who Wanders."

"That your real name?" said Rayf.

"That's what I said, didn't I?"

"Right."

"But you can call me Billy Wolf from Big Cypress." He put out a weathered hand and said, "Glad to meet ya, Rayf and Cal."

They shook hands and when they did, the bird of fear flew from the cab. They laughed and were certain that this Indian guy was not a drug pusher at all, just someone who had been someplace that neither of them had ever been. Rayf rolled down the window, for the night had become warm once more.

The pickup continued up 29 and caught US 27 north.

Just before Palmdale, Billy said, "Let's pull over for a few minutes."

"Where are we now?" said Rayf.

"We're at Thlothlopopkahatchee Creek."

"The ... thlo what creek?" said Cal.

"Fish-eating Creek to you," said Billy.

"That other name? Seminole?" said Rayf.

"Yup," said Billy as he guided the truck alongside the creek and stopped. They all got out.

It was a bright evening on the south end of the Kissimmee prairie. They were able to see low, flat meadows set with strands of saw palmettos and the corpses of live oaks with groves of cabbage palms and mixed hammocks made up of various trees. Billy gathered up a few small logs for a fire. Loaded with wood, he pointed with his chin to a small herd of wild Kissimmee ponies. They watched as the ponies galloped eastward. He lit the small fire and invited them to come on and sit by it.

They did. They rubbed their hands with fingers splayed and held their palms toward the flames; what else is a body supposed to do in front of an open fire?

"Ever look into the living flames?" said Billy. "You can see things in there, things that can help you with your life."

"Really?" said Rayf.

"Really. Whenever we take the magic mushroom, we treat it with great respect. We ask for visions that will teach us how to live in harmony with the elements."

Rayf and Cal felt strange. Here they were being tempted into partaking, wanting to accept, and yet afraid of losing their tenuous hold on this reality. They looked deep into the fire where they saw many things—Rayf saw Soapy's red Buick and the purple Pontiac that was chasing it crashing over the causeway into Biscayne Bay; Cal saw Angela spilling her hot pink nail polish onto the tan leather seat of her powder blue Corvette. But out there in the night, right now, they heard a bone-chilling sound.

"What's that noise?" said Cal.

"Owl," said Billy. "When you hear the hoot of an owl at night it could mean that someone is lost in their dreams and can't find their way back, or a spirit who has left this life is now heading for the other world."

The owl hooted again. Rayf and Cal felt a chill and drew closer to the fire. Billy got up, walked over to the back of the pickup, reached in, and brought back some wood chips. Sitting back down, he threw the cuttings into the fire.

"This cedar wood will keep away the bad spirits."

"Cool," said Cal not knowing what else to say.

"So," said Rayf, "I guess you want us to try this magic mushroom thing, eh Billy?"

"I don't want you to try anything, Rayf. But if the voice within you is calling, then I would be willing to show you the door. Why? Do you hear something?"

"Will I go, uh, like, crazy from this stuff?"

"No," said Billy. "You won't go crazy."

"I don't know," said Cal. "The strongest thing I ever did was scotch."

"There is no comparison. One leads to self-delusion, the other to self-illumination."

Cal looked to Rayf on the opposite side of the small orange, red, and yellow-blue flames. They nodded to each other.

"We'll do it," said Rayf.

Now the quiet of the night was split once again by the screams of other animals. This time, one was struggling for its very life while another was trying to take it. One sustaining its life off the life of another; the life and death struggle of the wilds.

Billy untied a small rainbow-colored sack from his belt loop, he removed six dried dark little caps of the psilocybin mushroom, and handled them between thumb and fingers as though he were gauging their magic or putting magic into them. Then he blew on them.

"Why're you doing that?" said Cal.

"Giving thanks to the Breath Maker—The One Who Lives Above."

"God?" said Rayf.

"The One who gives life," said Billy. Now he handed two to Cal, two to Rayf, and the last two he kept for himself.

The little fire alongside Fish-eating Creek burned brightly in the night, and the reflection of its flames danced off the face of the slow-moving water as Billy held up his cap and then put it into his mouth, chewed, and swallowed. He looked at Cal and Rayf; they followed his lead. *It has the consistency*, thought Rayf, *of dry, stale bread, but it tastes more like musty Parmesan cheese.* They ate the other caps and waited.

A multi-veined splash of silent lightening split the eastern sky, turning the night into an electric-blue photographic negative.

And now Soapy, behind the wheel of his newly rented gold Cadillac, driving north over Fish-eating Creek, looked off at the eerie, witch-like, electric-blue fingers that touched down somewhere beyond Lake Okeechobee. He also noticed a small orange fire on the northern shore of the creek, but paid it no mind as they drove on, insulated through the night, in search of the elusive duo.

Meanwhile, by the creek, Rayf said, "I thought you said that this would empower me. I feel totally naked." He drew closer to the fire.

"You still got your clothes on," said Billy, "not to worry."

Cal had wandered off to a small spur in the creek. There he picked up a pebble and threw it into the glassy calm; the water's face broke like glass. He saw each particle of water as though he were looking at it through a microscope. Now he saw the molecular structure of the water. It was composed of many independent molecules that were themselves made up of smaller and smaller particles. The pebble's splash now formed a second ring and a third and so on and so forth. He stared transfixed with the wonder of the realization that all things in existence, including him, were made up of non-solid particles: atoms made up of smaller parts, which were made up of even smaller parts, and so on and so forth. The entire visible creation supported by the invisible. Nothing was solid. He found himself in a reality where nothing existed. This is as far as he could go, for now his thought processes moved too fast for him to grasp. Everything blended into one: all of nature was totally porous. And for the first time in his life, he realized that he, too, was just a part of nature, composed of many molecules all with independent existences of their very own. Chemistry 101 had never gone this far.

Back at the fire, Billy cocked an ear and looked off to where Cal, not fifteen yards away, was staring transfixed into the creek. He stood and ran past him through the ankle-deep waters. The splashing water was music to Cal's ears. Billy stopped on the other side of the creek near a small bush. There at a spider's web he reached in and removed from it a struggling butterfly. He held it out on his weathered hand. The delicate footing of the butterfly caught hold onto the creases in the Indian's finger and flapped its wings several times before taking flight. The butterfly, for the moment, had been spared.

Billy walked back to the fire. Cal followed.

Rayf asked Billy, "What was that all about?"

"I heard a butterfly scream."

"How does a butterfly sound?" said Rayf.

"It's a direct experience, another sense," said Billy.

Rayf thought that maybe all of this was just a sham, but when he looked over to the bush where Billy had run off to, all that he could see was total darkness. He pulled closer to the fire.

Now Billy started rocking back and forth to an inner rhythm. He started chanting into the bright orange flames:

"They are taking us beyond Miami
They are taking us beyond the Caloosa River,
They are taking us to the end of our tribe.
They are taking us to Palm Beach, coming
Back beside Okeechobee Lake,
They are taking us to an old town in the
West ..."

Then half to himself, "That was the dirge that some of the people sang as they were captured and driven out west, but several hundred of us dug deep into the impenetrable sawgrass rivers of the Glades, where we remained. We were never defeated. As Chief Coacoochee said during the wars against my people, 'The white men are as thick as the leaves in the hammock—they come upon us thicker every year. They may shoot us and drive our women and children night and day; they may chain our hands and feet, but the red man's heart will always be free.'

"We are the Seminoles, the wild ones, the runaways, the Unconquered People. We are born to be free, and we are," said Billy Wolf Who Wanders.

After some silence, Cal said, "Did they actually take your people out west?"

"Yes."

"Why?" said Rayf.

"It was a common practice of the Americans to remove the people from their soul-land. Stealing their land was not enough they wanted their spirit, too. The pale-eyes have forced themselves upon the indigenous people of this land. We have suffered under their ways, and have died from their diseases, guns, and cruelty. Yet we have come through it all. And now, with hope, this medicine that you have taken will reach you and teach you how to live in harmony and balance with the elements. And in so doing, at last you will find the thing that has driven you to search, has always eluded you, and yet has been within you always."

A silence fell over all three men. The only thing that could be heard was the crackling of the small logs on the fire.

It was then that a very strange thing began to happen to Rayf. It felt as if it were starting from way off out beyond the stars in the blackest of space or from deep within the universe of his own mind, he was unsure; he could see it out there and yet feel it right here. It came on like a tickle, a tickle of the mind. He sat there at the fire expectantly, awaiting its arrival. It was moving at the speed of light and heading right at him. He waited, jaw unhinged. And then it struck and he was convulsed with laughter. He couldn't stop laughing. *It feels so good*, he thought, *Good!? Hell, it feels great!*

It was the greatest, healthiest feeling he had ever experienced. The laughter was cleaning out his mind of ancient cobwebs, dusty from years of accumulated dogma. In an instant, he understood the human cosmic joke, the absurdity of man's amassing fortunes—vagrants on a vagrant planet spinning aimlessly through space. And as quickly as it had started, it stopped.

Through gasps of air he said, "It felt like I was going to sneeze, but instead I laughed. Now I know where laughter comes from!"

"Where's that?" said Cal.

Rayf tried to explain, but it was beyond his ability to do so. Words, he discovered, like steam vapors coming from a boiling kettle, gave off only a hint of the scalding turbulence taking place within. And it was here that he got his first inkling of a vocabulary of the senses—a solitary communion with something beyond, or was it within? How limited, then, our human vocabularies. Words and pictures, in their wake, left only a very brief outline of the total picture. All human attempts at communication, art included, only amounted to creative residues. And he wondered where the hell that thought came from … His mind? The mushroom? A combination of both? He was still tripping when he heard Billy saying:

"So how many things, then, are really beyond the grasp of the intellect?"

And as they pondered that question, Billy stood up and, with creek water in cupped hands, doused the fire.

Rayf asked him, "What is the difference between good and bad medicine?"

"The good strips you of your ego, aligning you with all of creation, while the bad gives you false powers that trick you into believing that you are above and beyond everything, and, in so doing, you are misaligned with your natural birthright."

"And what's that?" said Cal.

"You have a right and a duty to your home," said Billy,

"By home, do you mean, Jersey City?" said Rayf.

"By home I mean the planet, the universe, life and death. It's all within you, you are all within it," said the Indian, kicking soil onto the dying embers with booted foot.

"You make it sound so simple," said Rayf.

"And you make it so hard, when in reality it is very simple. If you are a panther, act like one. If your nature is that of a sheep, act like one."

They walked back towards the pickup truck, leaving no trace of the fire. At the truck Rayf said, "I think I'll ride back here."

Billy reached in behind his seat and grabbed a woven, rainbow-colored blanket. He handed it to Rayf, who laid back and covered himself with it. With fingers interlaced behind his head, he studied the cloud-dusted, starry nighttime sky. They drove on through the night—Billy behind the wheel, Cal riding shotgun, and Rayf out back under the stars. Within minutes, the rocking of the truck put the man beneath the rainbow weave to sleep. In this sleep, he dreamed.

He dreamt he saw many people rolling boulders, huge heavy boulders, to the edge of a cliff where they pushed them over the side. This they did over and over again. He asked, "What is this all about?" Now the echoed, deep voice of the Dream Maker answered, "These are people who live their lives, then die." Then Rayf noticed another man scratching a mark into a boulder. "And him? What about him? What is he doing?" "He is trying to leave behind a record of his short existence to tell how he saw it."

Rayf saw the air as he had never seen it before. It was pure and clean. The sun shone brightly, glistening off pristine waters. The clouds were white and unblemished. He breathed in this crystal clear virgin air and realized that this was the first time that he had ever experienced such a perfect breath.

Deep down inside, he knew that he was nearing wakefulness and that this was only a dream. And it was here that he felt a terrible sadness to think of what had become of the air and what was becoming of the entire planet.

Then he woke up, for the earth had rolled around once again to face the daytime star. Its warm rays shone brightly through his eyelids, calling him back once again into the world of dreaming men. He breathed in the warm breeze of the Gulf Coast air, sat up, looked around at the side of the road with its multi-colored foliage, and noticed that the air in this part of Florida was still warm, clear, and clean. This filled him with hope.

He knocked on the Dodge's rear window. Billy pulled up to a stop. Cal slid over, and Rayf jumped in.

"Where are we?" said Rayf.

"We're up near Old Fields," said Billy.

"Old Fields? Never heard of it. Where's that at?"

"That's the English translation for Tallahassee. It's a Seminole name," said Cal.

"He tell you that?" said Rayf.

"Yeah," said Cal.

"Sleep good?" said Billy.

"Yeah," said Rayf.

They all settled into a contemplative space as the Dodge jostled its passengers up US 27. Several miles later, Cal pointed off to some guys working by the side of the road. Billy slowed down to give his passengers a better view. Up there on the approaching right were fifteen men wearing white work suits with powder blue horizontal stripes, they were wielding pickaxes and shovels. A guard sat atop a pickup truck, rifle at the ready.

"What's that?" said Cal.

"Chain gang," said Billy.

And the northern boys looked out in wonder. Up until then, they had thought that chain gangs were just in the movies. Yet here it was, guys in striped suits breaking rocks and repairing the highways in this Florida heat.

And they were thankful they were not shackled as they passed these prisoners of the state on the west coast of Florida, up near Tallahassee, on the morning of November 23rd, 1963.

~ 12 ~

ROAD WARRIORS

In Tallahassee, Billy drove north up Monroe Street, turned west onto New Quincy Highway past Florida State University, and continued clear on out to Capital Circle Northwest, where he pulled into the parking lot of the Old Fields Diner.

"Come on," said Billy, "I'll buy you a cup of coffee."

They hopped out of the Dodge and walked into the small roadside eatery. Billy ordered three coffees.

"You know, I been thinkin'. I need me a good commercial handle. Something like Johnny Apple Seed."

The waitress with the three coffees asked, "Anything else, boys?"

Rayf and Cal, salivating, said, "No thanks."

"I've been thinking of a trade name, one that'll go down in history. How's this sound? Billy Fungus Spore!"

The two guys, each dumping three teaspoons of white, water-soluble crystalline carbohydrates into their steaming coffee for a combined caffeine-sugar-rush, never looked up.

"Well?" said the Indian.

"Well what?" said Rayf, stirring his coffee.

"My handle: Billy Fungus Spore!?"

"Sounds like a disease," said Cal.

"He's right, Billy," said Rayf, taking a sip of hot, sweet coffee. "It just doesn't have it, man."

"I think you're gonna have ta go back ta the drawing board with that one," said Cal.

"Yeah. Maybe you're right. It doesn't trip too lightly on the ears," said Billy. "Coca Cola'd never get behind that one, eh? No secrets to conceal." The boys chuckled politely but kept swilling down that coffee.

They drank and talked about the night before—how they had no hangover from the magic mushroom and how lucid Rayf's dream seemed.

"That dream sounds more like a vision to me," said Billy.

"Wha'd'ya mean by that?" said Rayf.

"It could be a message."

"What does it say?" said Rayf.

"It's best if the dream hunter finds his own answers; tracks it down, finds out what it means to you and to you alone."

"Ya mean analyze my own dream?"

"Analyze. Hunt it down, same thing. Maybe you're to compose some talking leaves."

"What the hell are talking leaves?!"

"They're books, man."

"Oh," said Rayf, now thinking about his dream.

Billy, through the steam of his coffee, said, "You had better make up your minds boys; panthers or sheep, which one you be."

That statement was clear enough, and they thought about it as they finished up their coffees.

Outside, they walked up to Billy's pickup.

"So Billy," said Rayf, "I guess we'll be seein' ya in the happy hunting grounds."

Rayf and Cal laughed at that.

"That's right, boys," said a serious Billy, "Y'all take the Good Road, and we're sure to meet up in the land of shades."

He jumped into the Dodge, cranked it up, rolled down the window, and yelled, "Hey, Falcone."

"What?" said a confused Rayf.

"Live up to your namesake, man."

"Right," said a still unsure Rayf.

Billy winked that wink, turned to face the road, and slowly drove off into the warm Florida morning.

Rayf, still watching the pickup, said, "How the hell'd he know my last name?"

Cal, also watching as the vehicle faded into the distance said, "I mentioned it last night."

"That's better. I thought he was a real magician."

And then together they raised a right hand and waved to Billy Wolf Who Wanders, who was rapidly growing into his own future while simultaneously becoming a part of their past.

They stood there for a while lost in their own thoughts when all of a sudden, from behind, they heard a high-pitched voice saying, "You boys been hitchhiking the countryside?" They turned to face a tall, skinny man in his mid-fifties. Rayf took him for a bum. They didn't answer.

"Hey, I kin sympathize with y'all," said the lanky stranger, "I bin dere, boys. I did my own hard travelin' back in the thirties durin' the great depression. Y'sir, I bin dere awright. 'Cept'n I still kain't figure out why in the world dey ever called it great! Hell—was nuthin' great about it."

Rayf looked over this sorry-looking man speaking cliches and said, "We're headin' to Dallas."

"Jest like rollin' stones, huh?" Now with a dream in his eye he said, "Gawd, it seemed jest like yesterday, I tell ya; jest like yesterday. Y'all look over Tallahassee yet?"

"No," said Cal.

"Well, it's a pretty city. Some parts of it look jest like dat Gone With the Wind movie. It's got some big old beautiful antebellum houses, jest like in dat movie, I tell ya. You seen Gone with the Wind?"

"No," said Rayf and Cal one after the other.

"Well, you still got time. I'm sure it'll be around for a long time to come," said the depression-era roadie. He handed Cal a quarter. "Here, maybe this'll help ya along."

"Thank you, man," said Cal, looking down at the shiny twenty-five cent piece in his dirty hand.

"My pleasure, son. Y'all take care now, hear?" said the stranger over his shoulder as he long-stepped between the rows of parked cars in the Old Fields Diner parking lot.

"Thanks again," shouted Rayf.

"Looks like our luck is changing," said Cal.

Ten minutes later with backs to the oncoming traffic, donuts in right hands, and left hands thumbing the breeze, they walked west on US 90.

Within five minutes a faded blue 1956 Oldsmobile sedan pulled over. They trotted off to meet their ride.

Cal got there first, opened the front door, leaned in and said, "We're headin' to Dallas."

"Hop in," said the driver.

Rayf went to open the rear door; it was locked. The driver yelled, "Git in the front. We'll all ride up front. Its best dat. way." He hopped in, and Cal squeezed into the middle.

The car took off like a rocket. Their heads whipped back. It leveled off at ninety miles an hour. Cal looked at the speedometer. Rayf, hanging onto to the door handle, sized up the driver: He was at least six foot three with an elongated head that started a good eight inches above his shoulders. He had a fire going on in his eye as he asked the first of the "W" questions: "Where you boys from?"

"Je … Jer … Jersey City," said a petrified Cal as the rocket hurled down the highway.

"Oh, so you boys is Nawthiners, eh?"

"Yeah," said Rayf "We're sight-seeing the United States."

"That right?"

"That's right," said Cal. "And at this pace we're just gonna see a blur."

"You jest hold on tight, boy," said the driver. "Where was you last?"

"You mean where'd we just come from?" said Rayf, eying the rapidly approaching horizon.

"That's what I mean, boy," said the driver craning his long neck to get a better view of his passengers.

"Uh," said Cal, "don't ya think ya aughta keep your eyes on the road?"

"Gotdammit! I ain't 'bout ta have no Nawthin boys tellin' me how ta drive. Hear?"

"Hey, we ain't tellin' you how to drive, mister," said Rayf, now nudging Cal. "Ain't that right, Cal?"

"Right! We never mess with anybody's drivin'. Swear to god."

"God! You have dee audacity to use dee Lord's name in vain; you two sinners of Satan's order!"

"Well …" said Rayf, "What my friend over here was trying to tell you, sir …"

"Gotdammit, boy, I heard the blasphemy. Don't you go tryin' ta talk me down. You hear?"

"Yes sir!" said Rayf

"That's a whole Gotdamn lot better. And you had best not go meddlin' with my people while you're down here, either. Hear?"

Before they could answer, the man pulled out a long-barreled, chrome-plated Smith & Wesson .44 from under his seat. Waving it under their noses, he said, "I am a man of dee Lord and I aim to bring you two boys back into the fold. It is my ability as a preacher that made me see that you two boys was covered in sin as I saw y'all standin' by dat roadside an' Jesus—say it!"

"Say what?" said Cal.

"Say Jesus!"

"Jesus," said Rayf and Cal in unison.

"Dat's right. Jesus. He said to me: 'pick up them sinners and git dee Holy Spirit back inta 'em', an' I said, 'I am yo instrument, dear sweet Jesus'—say it."

"Sweet Jesus!" said the sweating congregation.

The Olds, at ninety miles an hour, was now passing through Quincy and heading up towards Chattahoochee. The boys were praying hard.

"Like I asked, where you boys comin' from?"

"M ... Mi ... Miami Beach," blurted Rayf without turning his head.

"Downstate, huh? Jest as I suspected. Well, let me be the first ta welcome y'all back t' da South. For you have just returned and have left behind the wicked ways of the North forevermore. Miami has been takin' over by Nawthiners and Cewbins. But y'all mark mah words: we will take it back when the South rises. And rise it shall once again like the great Phoenix bird from the ashes. Hallelujah! Say hallelujah!"

"Hallelujah!" said the captured congregation of two.

He stuck the huge .44 revolver up on his side of the dashboard and pulled out a black Bible with a large red cross emblazoned across its front cover. Holding it up high, he said, "I am a man of dee Lord, I am thee Reverend T. Bob Wilson and I come to you, oh Lord, to deliver dese two sinners from Satan and into the glory o' thine own house. I command thee—say Jesus!"

They both said, "Jesus!" Rayf with white knuckles holding the door handle and Cal with outstretched arms holding back the dashboard.

Reverend T. Bob hit Cal over the head with his Holy Bible and yelled to Rayf, "Git chore hands off a dat do' handle boy, before I kill you and your friend over here and have you both be meetin' up wit dee Lord in about five seconds flat. Hear?"

They were like two bug-eyed road apples, nodding. Rayf pulled his hand away from the door and clasped it with his left hand onto his lap.

Muttering a silent Hail Mary with Cal doing the same, both guys moved their lips in silent prayer, eyes glued to the road.

The Apalachicola River came and went, the Olds doing ninety five.

From his pulpit behind the wheel, the Reverend kept hard at his preaching: first with the Smith & Wesson, then with the big black Bible. His passengers feared that the end was near as he'd zoom up to a car, truck, trailer, or bus and, at the very last moment, pass them or trash them on the left or the right or whichever other way he chose to go; for here was a man of the Lord who was beyond the laws of man and land. He would do as he damn well pleased. The scenery flew past as he preached on about the North, the South, the crooked politics in Washington D.C., the lack of religion in the whole damn country, the niggers and foreigners who were invading *his* United States and messing up *his* great land, all the while holding up either Bible or pistol and on one occasion, both at the same time. There was no escape.

The roadside was a blur. They prayed—Reverend T. Bob, to his God of fire and brimstone, and his passengers, to their God of happy endings.

It happened somewhere between the towns of Galliver and Holt, about sixty miles east of the Alabama border. *It* first made itself visible in the Oldsmobile's rearview mirror in the form of flashing red lights. The passengers became aware of this fact when Reverend T. Bob said, "Gawd damn those sons a' bitches. Ain't they got nothin' better ta do than ta be messin' with a man a d' Lord?"

Rayf turned his head slightly to the left. He could see Cal staring dead ahead, eyes glued to the onrushing road. Rayf, blocked by Cal's head, sneaked a peek over his own left shoulder and saw at least ten police cars from various parts of Florida, all with flashing red lights and sirens blasting. Rayf gave a silent thanks to his God, but reminded Him about the happy ending part.

The Reverend, before pulling over, said, "If you two even so much as breathe one word about ma gun under ma seat, Ah swear in da name uv d' Lord y'all'll be dinin' with him tonight. Hear?"

They nodded.

"Now put your hands on dis here Bible and swear to it!"

They swore.

The Olds pulled over. Rayf and Cal jumped out of the car. And within seconds the police swarmed over the Reverend like ants on grease.

One cop pulled the Reverend out of the Olds and spread-eagled him against the left side of the car while another cop came out from under the front seat of the Olds with the shiny .44 wrapped in a handkerchief. Another cop was taking down the license plate number while another was taking note of the dented front fenders. Another was on the radio microphone and two others, with their guns drawn, covered the frisking cop. Rayf and Cal took this busy moment for their exit cue.

Sneaking away from the scene, they took one last peek back at the Reverend. There he was assuming the position and yapping away to all and none. They turned the bend in the road and the Reverend T. Bob Wilson channel was off the air.

They were all shook up. Cal pulled out a Cigarillo, put a match to it, and walked off the road's shoulder. Rayf followed. Now all they had to do was lay low until the cops dispersed.

Off behind the trees and out of sight, Rayf and Cal spoke about their own private fears during their harrowing ordeal with the Reverend T. Bob, whom they hoped would eventually pull some long time in order to save the souls of his jailed brethren.

Meanwhile, the commotion was drawing lots of attention. Traffic had slowed to a crawl. Heads were bobbing and weaving to get a better view of this roadside attraction. And in this long line of rubberneckers were two men who had gotten a late start after a long night in a crummy Tallahassee motel.

"Looks like a accident or sumthin'," said Soapy, behind the wheel.

"Jesus K. Christ," said Ali Baba. "Guy must a' committed moida or sumthin'. Geezus! Would ya look at all a dem dere cops!"

The guys in the gold Cadillac saw among the many police cars a truck, a bus, and three other civilian cars. And milling around all those vehicles was a mob of angry people. One man was gesturing frantically towards his dented pickup truck, while a uniformed bus driver pointed from the faded blue Oldsmobile to his bus loaded with passengers; three other drivers were doing similar things regarding their own vehicles. And there, intermingled among all these people, were the policemen who were interrogating and filling out reports.

Just as Soapy and Ali Baba were about to make the bend in the road, they saw the handcuffed Reverend being stuffed into a squad car. The guys in the Caddy had a good laugh. And not fifty yards from this westbound gold Cadillac, hiding in the bushes, sat Rayf and Cal.

All the cops were gone within an hour. And fifteen minutes after the last patrol car drove off, the boys returned to their hitchhiking positions. They were now arguing about work and leisure. For what frightened these guys more than guns was the thought of trading their lives for dollars.

"I mean," said Rayf, "how the hell can a guy pay you X amount of dollars for your hours? Your hours are priceless, man. To give you an idea: how much is your last second of life worth?"

"Hey, I don't have a job. You're the one with the job, man."

"You call tending bar work?"

"Look, if you have to be there by a certain time, then it is work," said Cal.

"And you don't have to hustle your book?"

"Hey, man, that's different."

"Fuck work," said Rayf. "They lock you up for forty, fifty hours a week for twenty or thirty years and then if you're lucky, you wind up with a pension. Know what you could do with that pension? My grandfather, my father's father, comes from Italy, works his whole life in a steel smelting mill to feed nine kids. His whole life he works, then he retires, and within six months—six months, man, not eight months, not a year, but six months and he's dead. Some pension, huh?" said Rayf as he stuck out a brave thumb into the breeze. It wasn't too long after taking the shoulder with bravado that another ride soon materialized in the form of a beat-up Pontiac. It pulled over to a very slow stop.

"Looks like it's being held together with bailing wire and tape," said Rayf.

Cautiously, they approached the car. Rayf got to the car first and pulled open the door. The smell of raw alcohol assaulted his nostrils. Inside he saw a very tipsy driver trying to focus on him.

"Where you goin'?" said Rayf.

The drunken driver said, "Alabama. Wanna lift?"

Rayf looked at Cal and then back into the car before saying, "Sure, why not."

Cal climbed into the back seat, and Rayf took the front. He slammed the door closed. There was no inside door handle; it could only be opened from the outside. Rayf rolled his window down.

"Hey, whyn't you close dat window?" said the driver. "I'm freezin."

"I'm not," said Rayf.

The Pontiac weaved back onto the road, narrowly avoiding a head-on collision with two eastward-bound cars. Now he veered into his own lane. Alabama, dead ahead.

Rayf looked at the drunken driver. His dirty-blond hair was all messed up, his red face was covered with two days of stubble, his clothes were dirtier than theirs, and on the seat beside him was a bottle of unlabeled booze. He was clutching the wheel with both hands.

"Where y'all headin'?" said the dirty driver, without taking his eyes off the road.

"New Orleans. We're going to get laid. Why?" said Rayf.

"No reason. Jess thought Ah'd ask," said the driver, struggling with the road.

"And I told ya," said Rayf.

"N'awlins, check."

That was the end of that. They drove on in silence from their pick-up point outside of Holt and all through Alternate 90, which took them around metropolitan Pensacola and clear on out to within five miles of the Alabama Welcome Center.

"Where you boys from?"

Here, then, was the second W.

"We is Nawthinas," said Rayf. "Why?"

"Sheet, I'd a knowed it even ifn I was soba."

"But you ain't never soba, are ya?" said Cal.

Then, real friendly like, he picked up his bottle of water-clear booze and said, "Here, take a hit. It'll do ya good, boy."

Rayf took the bottle.

"Hit the bottom," said the driver. "G'head, hit it 'gainst yer palm!"

Rayf hit it against his palm.

"Now hold 'er up to da light."

Rayf held it up.

"See dem shiny little thangs floatin 'round in dere?"

"Yeah," said Rayf."

"Das d'lead, man. Das d'stuff dat really gits ya up and over d'top, man."

"What the hell is it?" said Cal, from the back seat.

"Li'tnin', boy ... das white li'tnin'. Gaw'head, take a swalla."

"Nah," said Rayf. "Think I'll pass."

He set the bottle down between them.

Just as they were crossing into Alabama, the driver said, "You fuckin' Yankees don't know what's good fer ya. Even ifn it was put right into yo fuckin' faces, know dat?"

"Nah, we don't know dat," said Rayf.

"Ya know, we used t' own our own slaves, but danks t' y'all, now we gotta rent 'em." He laughed at his own joke. They did not.

"I gots me a philosophy," said the driver.

"Fuck you and your philosophy," said Cal.

"It's called the shitbag philosophy."

Rayf gave Cal a get-ready nod.

"The way I sees it is dat you eats and drinks and den produces shit. Dat is your main function. You may walk and talk, but in reality, all dat you ever make is shit. To shit, dat is your main function on earth. Dat's it: To shit! Well? What d'yall dink 'bout dat?"

"You are what you eat," said Cal.

"Ya see," said the driver, "many religions make da mistake dat consciousness awareness is a reality. Whereas I see it as people catching thoughts in their brains and then shitting and dying anyway. Dat's all dere is to it."

Cal tapped Rayf; he was ready. They were doing forty miles an hour. Cars passed them as they meandered by magnolia, oak, sweet gum, and hickory.

"You boys lookin' fer women, right?"

"What's it to ya?" said Rayf.

"Well, ma daddy's got dis here pretty little nigger housekeeper who needs her some white meat. You guys'll do. Wha'd'ya say?"

"Thanks anyway," said Cal. "Maybe next time."

"Well Ah'll be turnin' off a dis here road up here ta get us up near Stapleton where I live. An' it jest so happens dat we is havin' us a big ol' fashion cook-out. What say? Care ta join us?"

"Nah," said Rayf. "I don't think so."

And up there at the State 59 junction the Pontiac took a right and headed north.

"I said we were going west," said Rayf.

"You heard the man," said Cal. "We're going west."

"But we got us dis here cook-out and you boys'd be da guest uv 'onor."

"Stop the car," said Rayf.

Instead, he hit the gas and said, "I don't dink you boys gets da picture. We's gonna be cookin' y'all up. See, we love Nawthin meat down here. All cooked up nice an' well dun. "

"I don't think *you* get the picture," said Cal. "We ain't goin' with you."

The driver was laughing hard. Rayf looked at Cal, nodded, and then punched the driver in his temple. The driver wobbled. Rayf now hit him in the jaw. It broke. Now Cal was strangling him from over the back seat: the driver let go of the wheel. Rayf grabbed it and turned it to the left. They were cutting across the other lane when the driver hit the gas; the car took off. Rayf aimed at a tree stump; it was a direct hit. The car came to a screeching stop, fan blade tearing into radiator, hood popping open, a plume of steam. Rayf gave him one last kick to the chest. The drunk was out cold.

They got out, slammed the door closed, and walked around to the driver's side. Cal grabbed a handful of dirty-blond hair, picked up the unconscious head to make sure he was still alive, he was, and said, "Sorry to spoil yer appetite, pal." He let it fall back onto his chest.

"Maybe we should walk the rest of the way," said Cal.

"Maybe you're right."

They gave one last look back at the Pontiac with its hood reaching for sky and a stream of steam vanishing into thin air.

On US 90 they turned right and started walking westward towards New Orleans. A dusty haze was on the November highway, the sun was setting off beyond the Gulf, and the sweet fragrance of magnolia called to them as they walked along the red earth kicking rocks, stones, and beer cans. Two miles up US 90, a black BMW pulled behind and started trailing them. They moved off closer to the shrubs and waved it on. The driver tapped his horn; they looked in and saw a young, preppy-type guy waving to them.

Rayf, without looking back, waved him off and said to Cal, "Bad things run in threes."

The BMW pulled up between them and the roadway.

The driver leaned across the passenger's seat, opened the window and said, "Hey you guys want a lift?"

"Thanks anyway," said Rayf.

"Where y'all heading?' said the driver.

"OK," said Cal under his breath. "Now we get the queer ride." To the driver he said, "None of your business."

"Don't have to be so hostile," said the driver.

"We're going to New Orleans," said Rayf.

"Hop in. I'm going through there myself."

"Thanks anyway, but we're walkin'."

"Don't be silly. Come on, I'll take ya," said the driver in a healthy and positive tone.

"Wha'd'ya think?" whispered Rayf to Cal.

"Fuck it. Let's go. But this time I'm riding shotgun," said Cal, turning towards the car. He opened the door and pulled back the seat; Rayf crawled in.

"No funny stuff," said Cal to the driver as he got in and closed the door behind him.

"What do you mean by that?"

"We just had two of the worst rides of our lives. That's what I mean."

"How's that?"

"One guy tried to shoot us and the other wanted to cook us," said Cal.

"Sounds like you met up with a couple of Chattahoochee escapees."

"What's that supposed to mean?" said Rayf.

"Chattahoochee is a prison for the criminally insane. It's in Florida up near the Georgia border."

"That just about explains it then," said Cal.

"What's that?" said the preppy driver.

"Nothin'," said Rayf.

"You boys from up east?"

"Yeah. What's it to ya?" said Cal.

"Welcome to the Cradle of the Confederacy."

"What's that supposed to mean?" said Cal as the BMW pulled out smoothly into the easy flowing traffic.

"It means," said the well dressed young professional, "that this is the birthplace of White Supremacy."

"And what're we," said Rayf, "purple?"

"Hey, when these people mean white they mean white Anglo-Saxon."

"Who's they?" said Cal.

"Man, you boys are traveling through the South and you don't even know the basics."

"This is America, ain't it? What's there to know?" said Cal.

"Well for openers, never get caught driving at night with a Negro in your car."

"Why not?" said Rayf.

"Because they'll figure you for an integrationist."

Cal looked back at Rayf and in an instant they understood why Henry the Ford rode the twelve-hundred miles from New Jersey to Florida mostly lying down on the back seat. Henry knew the South. Had he been sitting up they probably wouldn't be alive and riding in this BMW right now. After a moment of silence Cal said, "Where you from?"

"Corpus Christi, Texas."

"That anywhere near Dallas?" said Rayf.

"Far from it. We're on the Gulf. You got Dallas on the brain?"

"Just wonderin'," said Rayf.

"J.F.K. put that city on the map, didn't he?" said the driver.

"We were thinkin' about going there to check it out," said Cal.

"Cool. So, what do you guys do?"

"Like work?" said Cal.

"Yeah."

"I'm a bartender."

"And I'm a bookkeeper," said Cal, stretching the truth.

"And you?" said Rayf.

"I'm a computer programmer."

"A computer programmer?" said Cal.

"Yeah. It's the way of the future. In twenty or thirty years this whole world's gonna be running on computers. If I were you guys I'd get into it now, on the bottom floor."

"Hmm," said Cal to himself, ruminating on the concept of computers, sports, and gambling.

"Hey, you've got two good trades. No machine is ever going to take the place of a good bartender's ear. But I am afraid all the bookkeepers of the future will be plugged into computers."

The night seemed warmer as they spoke with this person. They were actually letting their guard down and started to stretch out and enjoy the ride. Only time would tell if this was another variation on the Southern nut theme.

"What kind of car is this?" said Cal.

"It's a BMW. A fine machine; runs like a clock. Those Germans really know how to build cars."

"Yeah," said Rayf, "it might run good but it doesn't have any ..."

"Pizzazz!?" said the driver.

"Yeah," said Rayf.

"Yeah, said Cal, "that's what it's missing."

"It might not have the gaudiness but it sure makes up for it under the hood. Anyway, flair is all that American cars have—fancy covers and nothing substantial. It's like a diet of all sugar: it gets you up all right, but man, it is going to let you down real hard."

"Tell me more about these computers." said Cal.

He proceeded to tell them all about computers and their role in the future. The two passengers listened in wonder. He was speaking another language, a language based on scientific fact, one that was beyond color, race, gender, and physical limitations—a language that seemed to be coming from the future. And in this future that he spoke of, there would be ample opportunity for everyone. He seemed to be coming from another place in time. *Maybe the guy is from outer space*, thought Rayf, as he checked him out. He wore a short-sleeved, thin, green vertical-stripe-on-white shirt with a shirt pocket full of pens. He had a crew cut and thick-rimmed glasses, was clean shaven, and radiated cleanliness. Compared to them he looked totally civilized. They, on the other hand, looked as though they had just crawled out of the primordial soup.

The weeping willows waved lazily in the Alabama night as the BMW passed them by. A fine rain started misting the windshield, and the driver turned on his wipers. They cleaned the glass effortlessly, precisely, and quietly.

"So who are these white people down here?" said Cal.

"Undiluted Anglo-Saxons, the sovereign gentry—the same people that took the land away from the Indians, the French, and the Spanish—this is their land, and they don't want you to ever forget that."

"Hey man," said Rayf, "the Civil War is over."

"Right. Not even a hundred years ago. But the wound is still open down here. The Stars and Bars are still flying higher than the Stars and Stripes up in Montgomery."

"Where's Montgomery?" said Cal.

"The Alabama state capital."

"Alabama," said Cal softly to himself.

"None other," said the driver. "Alabama, the state that seceded from the Union three months before the Civil War to form the Confederate States of America. A lot of people down here think that the last battle of the Civil War was fought just last year."

"Last year?" said Rayf.

"September '62 up in Oxford, Mississippi; Ol' Miss turned into a battlefield when James Meredith, a young Negro man, tried to register for school. Thirty-two US Marshals were shot and two foreign correspondents were killed. It was the old South's last gasp."

"Shit!" said Rayf.

"But personally, I think the war is still going on. Look at Medgar Evers, that Negro Civil Rights worker that they killed in an ambush just last June. That was only five months ago."

"I think I'm starting to get the picture," said Cal.

"Not totally. Now if you really want to get the picture, you've got to visit the local gentry. And the best place to do that, as you in the back seat already know, is the local lounge. So what do you guys say we stop in and look over the locals and share a glass of cheer with them."

"Uh ..." said Cal, "I ... uh, don't know about that, man. We almost just like got our asses tarred and feathered, and I don't really want to meet up with anymore rebels. Thanks anyway, man."

"Relax. You're with me. I'm from the South. I can handle these people. Just stick close and everything'll be all right. I've got your back."

"But we don't have any cash," said Rayf.

"It's on me," said the driver.

They had no more excuses.

"If you think it's cool," said Cal.

"It's cool."

"OK," said Rayf. "What the hell. Let's do it."

"So it's decided."

"Alright," said Cal. "I'm in."

"Before we go in, my name's Smitty."

"I'm Cal."

"I'm Rayf."

"Glad to meet you boys."

"Same here," said the two at the same time.

The air was heavy with humidity as they approached Mobil Bay, a well-protected port off the Gulf of Mexico. Smitty turned right off US 90. He went a little way north towards Spanish Fort searching for a roadside lounge. He didn't have very far to look. They pulled into the parking lot of a one-story building.

The lot was filled with pickup trucks and big American cars. The pickups sported rifles in rear-window racks. The BMW looked like a toy. Smitty paid no attention to the ostentatiousness surrounding him, but instead parked, pulled off his glasses, placed them carefully behind his visor, stepped out of the car, stretched his legs, and said, "Well, let's go."

They walked up to and into the one-room whiskey bar. The building was functional. It was built of cinder blocks and felt more like an army bunker than a bar. Three hardwood tables with chairs were on their left as they entered and a few more tables and chairs were down below near the bar. Behind that bar was a cabinet filled with miniature whiskey bottles, the same ones served on airplanes. To get to this small bar they had to step down one step and walk around a pool table, the room's dominant feature. There were no mirrors in the place. The room was indestructible.

Smitty walked straight to the bar. They followed, and felt that they were transmitting for all to see: we are Nawthinas. But in reality, they fit in better than Smitty did, for this was a blue-collar bar and everyone was still in work clothes, celebrating.

Smitty asked the boys what they would have. Rayf looked around the place, saw an advertisement, and ordered a can of Regal beer. Cal and Smitty did likewise. They got their beers, and Smitty led them over to a table near the bar. On the way they heard a group of guys talking.

"Now alls we gots to do," said one of the revelers, "is git Wallace inta da White House and den, by God, it'll be a White House fer sure."

"Wallace?" said Rayf, quietly, "George Wallace?"

Smitty nodded and put his finger up to pursed lips. Another guy in the group picked up his glass of whiskey high above his head and shouted, "Hear, Hear! Long lay Kennedy!"

Everyone in the room stood and cheered.

"They're celebrating J.F.K.'s assassination," said Smitty very quietly to the two Northerners. "Join in, otherwise they might get a little suspicious."

Smitty raised a glass while Rayf and Cal turned to share a swig of con-dolence and the thought passed through their minds: was Smitty really one of them and would he expose them? Paranoia crept in.

"So, uh, this," said Cal, "this is the South."

"This is it," said Smitty. "I'll bet seventy-five percent of these kids are Kluxers." Before they had a chance to ask what that was, he answered, "K.K.K."

"Get out! Really?" said Cal.

"At least," said Smitty. "There's been a revival in the Klan with the Civil Rights movement.

"Do you know what happened in some of the schools down here when they got news of J.F.K.'s assassination?"

"No," said Rayf "What happened?"

"Some kids actually got up and started cheering. Just like these guys are doing right here and now. They were that happy about it."

Rayf studied the crowd of drinkers. These were not like the drinkers in the Rag Doll. These were professional drinkers; nothing could get in the way of their liquor—liquor was a way of life to them. They made it, they bought it, they sold it, but mostly they drank it.

One guy staggered over to the table and said to Rayf, "Where you from, boy?"

"What's it to ya?" said Smitty.

"Boy's got a tongue. Let 'im speak," said the stranger.

"He's got one all right, 'cept I talk for 'im. You wanna make somethin' of it?"

Rayf looked at Smitty, who stood there holding his ground.

The redneck stared him in the eye and then said, "Y'all want a little nip a ma hooch?"

"Thanks jest the same, bro, but we're drinkin' suds."

"Wotever," said the redneck as he staggered away.

"Smooth move, Smitty," said Cal.

"Nothin' to it. Come on, drink up. Let's get out of here."

They drank up, put their empties onto the bar, and left by the same door that they had entered. The Northern guys were happy to be outside in the hot, humid air. They breathed a sigh of relief.

"You know," said Smitty, "I believe all this violence has to do with a vanquished people fighting for their last vestiges of respect."

"Who's them?" said Rayf.

"The Scotch-Irish who settled here in the South; they've always had a penchant for family feuds, a love of whiskey, and a warrior ethic that demands revenge. Now a lot of people might say all this violence stems from their losing the Civil War, but how do you account for Benjamin Franklin, America's first internationally recognized statesman, referring to them as "White savages" at least one hundred years before that war?

"This is a culture based on honor. And with slavery, one group is honored at the expense of another. Now here are their former slaves seeking equality. Who do you think they blame for this state of affairs?"

"Not me," said Rayf.

"Yes, you," said Smitty. "According to a lot of these people it's you Yankees who are to blame for destroying their way of life."

"You one of them?" said Cal.

Smitty stopped, looked Cal in the eye, and said, "I'm of Irish decent if that's what you mean."

"And you're talking against your own people?" said Cal.

"Look," said Smitty as they crammed into the car, "we're not all like that." He started the car, pulled out, and found US 90 west.

"For instance, take Alabama. Now even though it seceded from the Union, Winston County seceded from Alabama and sided with the North. So, you see, even down here in the heartland of the South, it still isn't all one way. I'm sure you've got a few rednecks up North too."

"Yeah," said Rayf, "we know a couple of guys who'd be right at home down here."

"I'm sure you do," said Smitty. "You know, I'll bet there's some guy down here right now sitting in his room writing all about these dunces."

They were now forty-five minutes from Mississippi.

"You guys read much?"

"Used to," said Cal, "in school. Why?"

"If you want to read a brave Southern writer, try Erskine Caldwell. He's one of the most censored and banned writers in the US. And believe it or not, the guy was the son of a preacher man."

"Preacher man!?" said Cal. "Thanks anyway. Think I'll pass."

"Try some of his short stories. You just might change your mind."

"Why was he banned?" said Rayf.

"They say it was because of the sex in his stories. But I think it was because he wrote about Kluxers, and lynchings, and killings—things Southerners don't care much to publicize."

"Does that make him brave?" said Rayf.

"When you consider that the late US Senator Teddy G. Bilbo, who was Governor of Mississippi when Caldwell started writing, had for his Governor's election slogan: 'It was every red-blooded American's duty to get out and see that no nigger votes,' then you get an idea of how brave Caldwell really was. It could be that today's saints have taken up the pen. I mean, look at Henry Miller, Mark Twain, Boccaccio. Now those guys were seminal writers and all of them had books that were either banned or ignored."

"Boccaccio?!" said Rayf.

"Yeah, he was the first writer to write about the common man, long before the common man could even read. And he did it in longhand."

"When did he write?" said Rayf

"Mid fourteenth century," said Smitty.

Deep in the dark of the back seat, Rayf thought about all he had just heard and remembered his vision-dream. He pondered its significance. It was the middle of the night as they drove through Mississippi. Rayf didn't want to think about how this night could have turned out without Smitty.

Cal and Smitty got to talking about everything up there in the front seat, from cars to numbers to computers and what would be the wave of the future, while Rayf just stared out at the oncoming traffic's white headlights. The glare would flash into the dark interior and, with a slow roll, for a brief moment illuminate all within before finally leaving them once again in total darkness.

As the night wore on, Rayf, lying down, got to think his own private thoughts back there: about the Kennedys; J.F.K.; Jacqueline and their kids; J.F.K.'s brothers; his mother, Rose, and his father, Joe. True, Kennedy was president of these United States, but wasn't he also a father, a husband, a cousin, an uncle, and all the other things that men become? Sure he was. But there was one thing he'd never become, and that was a grandfather rocking his grandchildren on his knee.

Then he thought about the people who did these things—assassins and sociopaths. He thought about rulers and kings, of which J.F.K. was one. Didn't they order young boys off to war? Sure they did. And didn't some of those kids get killed protecting philosophies that were forever changing?

Sure they did. And didn't a lot of those kids get killed before they even had a chance at becoming fathers? Sure they did.

Then he thought about those kids who would never live to play catch with their sons, and of the sons who would never even have a chance at being born. Wasn't this a form of extinction? Sure it was. He tried to find the humor in this cosmic joke. But try as he might, he could not find it. Maybe tomorrow with the sun he'd find it, but not tonight. Tonight was only heavy with the question: Why? This then was the way in which his thoughts wound on as they drove on through the dark Mississippi night in the Deep South.

~ 13 ~

AIN'T SO EASY

Rayf awoke to the brassy sounds of a slide trombone's music gliding all around that of a trumpet, a saxophone, a clarinet, and a banjo as a drummer banged, banged, banged away to a happy Dixieland Jazz version of "When the Saints Go Marching In."

Very slowly, he opened his eyes from deep down there in the cramped back seat and saw, just beyond the windows, a silver-gray cloud. And for just one very brief moment he wondered if he had died in his sleep and was just now being heralded into heaven.

He pulled himself up and saw Smitty and Cal seated in the same places where he had left them the night before.

The BMW was stopped in the middle of a street, at an intersection, to let an all black marching band pass in front of it. The musicians, in tuxedos, danced as they played.

"It's a jazz funeral," said Smitty to Rayf. "We're in luck."

"Maybe for us," said Cal. "But not for the guy they just buried."

Rayf rubbed the sleep from his eyes.

The band shuffled off through the early morning fog.

They drove on.

"This is Bourbon Street," said Smitty, their self-appointed tour guide.

"It looks a lot like Greenwich Village," said Cal.

"Yeah," said Rayf.

"Never been there," said Smitty.

"It's got that same European flavor," said Rayf as he looked out at the tawdry street. "What time is it, anyway?"

"Nine o'clock," said Smitty.

"And the bars are open already?"

"Already!?" said Smitty, "They never close."

"Oh man," said Rayf, hanging out the back window. "This is my kind of town."

The fragrance of deep fried cooking, perfume, booze, and strong coffee filled the air.

He could see couples staggering on the "banquette"—the French word that Smitty told them locals used for sidewalk—while inside some of the clubs, pickup bands played their music.

And over there, sitting on that banquette curb, with his head down between his knees, was a Bourbon Street reveler throwing up last night's party in order to make room for this morning's gig.

"We're in Vieux Carre," said Smitty.

"That French?" said Cal.

"Yes it is."

"Say it again," said Cal.

"V-yer Kar-ray. It means Old Square or the French Quarter to us tourists," said Smitty. "It's the original site of New Orleans, the heart of the city."

From their moving car they could see the old, high-styled Southern buildings with their cast- and wrought-iron-laced balconies, and hear the sounds of jazz, Dixie, swing, blues, ragtime, zydeco, and rock 'n' roll spilling out onto the street and filling their ears. And to their noses went the sweet aroma of deep fried foods—foods that were, unbeknownst to them, prepared with enough grease to clog the sewers of a small American city, not to mention the arteries of its inhabitants; aromas that caused them to murmur in unison the satisfied sound of, "Ah." And to the man, their palates salivated after that sweet smell of atherosclerosis.

They felt as if they were in a French village with its carefree charm and devil may care attitude. Yes, this town actually gave off an attitude that said: "I have been here through floods, pestilence, and wars, and I am going to stick around as long as that river keeps on flowing." This town, five feet below sea level, which buried its dead in wet graves or above ground in hermetically sealed tombs within cemeteries that doubled as tourist attractions; this town whose people danced and sang behind the grim reaper as if they were dancing over to Storyville, the infamous red-light district of old, to celebrate life over and over again. This town's attitude was one of laugh, live, eat, drink, create, procreate, and die for there will be others to take your place.

Smitty, parking the car, said, "This is Carnival town, the home of Mardi Gras, where they celebrate the coming of Lent with such a vengeance that the media actually publishes and broadcasts the number of homicides that take place here during the festivities. Welcome to the town they call New Orleans." He stepped out of the car and said, "Laissez les bons temps roulez!"

"What's that mean?" said Cal.

"Let the good times roll."

"Sounds good to me," said Rayf.

"Let's get something to eat," said Smitty, "I am starved."

Rayf now knew he was in heaven.

At Cafe du Monde near the levee, they had coffee and beignets. They sat outside near the fountain pool and ate their square fluffy, doughnut-like pastries covered with powdered sugar, drank their chicory-flavored coffee, and smoked their Cigarillos.

They felt like artists or writers in some Hollywood movie as they sipped, smoked, and dunked while learning from Smitty all they needed to know in order to stay healthy and alive down South. They relaxed and learned that this cosmopolitan town was an international city and melting pot long before the term had been applied to the rest of the country. It was a city with a global point of view, a city with a multi-national gentry, a city with a sense of humor.

They smiled at the fact that all the original women of this town were either hookers or prisoners released from *gai* Paris jails, as were the men who were deserters, smugglers, and scoundrels, but frowned to learn that through the years over one-hundred-thousand people were wiped out by the now defeated and once dreaded yellow fever. And that Jefferson Davis, the first and only president of the Confederate States of America, died here and was buried at Metairie Cemetery, one of the cities of the dead, as the natives affectionately refer to the thirty-one cemeteries that are within greater New Orleans. Another notable buried in one of these cities was voodoo queen, Marie Laveau. Her grave upkeep, according to Smitty, is paid for by a special preservation fund. Jefferson, on the other hand, was later exhumed and sent off packing to Richmond, Virginia, the old capital of the Confederacy, up around where Rayf and Cal let off Cherokee Len. This last fact was their own and not Smitty's recollection.

They ordered another cup of strong New Orleans chicory coffee.

"This full-bodied blend goes really great in this semitropical climate. Doesn't it?" said Smitty.

"Yeah," said Rayf.

"And how," said Cal, as he swallowed deep and sucked in another lung full of Cigarillo smoke.

"You like those cheroots?" said Smitty.

"No."

"Then why smoke 'em?"

"'Cause they're eighteen cents a pack," he said.

"I see," said Smitty.

"You want one?" said Cal.

"Thanks anyway."

"You're welcome."

So there they sat with Smitty, drinking their coffee, smoking their small cigars, and champing at the bit.

***

And while Smitty was doing his history thing at Cafe du Monde, Soapy and Ali Baba were parking their car across the street from the Cat 'n' Fiddle.

The Cat 'n' Fiddle was a rundown, all night, twenty-four-hours-a-day, seven-day-a-week, serious drinking, blue-collar bar situated on the northwest side of Royal Street.

They walked through the invisible odor-curtain of stale alcohol and tobacco smoke. On their right was a long bar. They dragged out two stools and sat up front near the picture window that looked out onto Royal Street.

On their left at the far end of the bar were three sailors drinking shots and beers, their backs to the black-velvet curtained doorway of the back room,.

"What's da big deal about dis place?" said Soapy to All Baba. "I mean it's just an old rundown waterfront town."

"Yeah. I feel like we's in Hoboken or sum udder dump city," said his partner. "Dey should tear it down and put up some classy joints. Dey'd make a bundle in real estate."

The bartender, in his late twenties, walked up to the two realty appraisers, put down two coasters, and in a congenial tone said, "What'll it be boys?"

"Scotch and water," said Soapy, "Two of 'em—and put lots a' ice in da glasses."

"Right." And off he went to work.

"Friendly guy," said Soapy to Ali Baba.

"So, how's it going, guys?" said the barkeep as he began preparing the drinks.

"Not too good," said Ali Baba, wiping under his bandaged brow with a handkerchief, "Too damn hot and humid down here."

"Where you guys from?"

"Jersey," said Soapy, the spokesman.

"New Jersey, huh? Where abouts?"

"Jersey City," said Soapy as he swung his slinged left arm onto the bar.

"That right!?"

'Yeah."

"Don't worry, you'll get used to the climate down here. You've just got to learn to take it nice and easy. You'll be just fine."

"You Louie?" said Soapy.

"Louis de Bienville, at your service."

"We just left a friend of yours down in Miami Beach."

"Is that so?" said the bartender as he set the two drinks down in front of the men.

"Yeah. Johnny at the Pink Flamingo on Bay Street sends his regards," said Soapy.

Louis stopped to think this over for a minute. Soapy watched as the wheels started turning inside his head, then they stopped, and when they did he saw two cherries register in the windows of the barman's eyes. "Johnny!" said the bartender. "How the hell do you like this!? I haven't seen him in, what ... must of been two ... three years ... last time I was on the Gold Coast. Great guy—how's he doing?"

"Not bad; said to say hello," said Soapy.

"Let me tell you something, he's one hell of a guy."

"Yeah, I know. He said that you could be of help to us."

"Hey, any friend of Johnny's is OK in my book. What do you need?"

"We're lookin' fer a couple a' wise ass young punks."

"Town's loaded with them. Where do you want to start?"

"We'll start right here," said Ali Baba.

"What do they look like?"

"Dey stand about yo high," said Soapy, standing while bringing his right hand up to his top lip.

"Hmm. Any other distinguishing characteristics?"

"Yeah. One's got blondish hair and dee udder ones got like, brown hair."

"Color of their eyes?"

"I ain't never got dat close." Now to Ali Baba, "You know?"

"Dee ony ding I know is dat dey's gonna be bloodshot when I gets tru wid 'em," said Ali Baba, chewing on an ice cube.

"Where they from?"

"Same place. Jersey City," said Soapy.

"So I'm looking for two guys about so high, with dark and light hair. They talk like Jersey or what?"

"Yeah, dey do."

"And what do I do if and when I locate them?"

"If we're not here, you call us at the Holiday Inn and ask fer Soapy. Dey'll get ya tru ta us."

"So, uh, you're Soapy I presume?"

"Yeah. And dis here's my partner, Ali Baba."

"Glad to meet you gents." He stretched out a hand.

"Good ta know ya, Louie," said Soapy.

"Me, too," said Ali Baba. They all shook hands. "Give us two more, and have one fer yerself, kid."

"Right," said Louis as he went off to get more ice.

Soapy, called out to Louis, "We're gonna be callin' dis place our headquarters."

"No problem, we're open twenty-four hours a day. Just find a corner and crawl into it."

"Danks," said Soapy.

"Where's a good place ta eat?" said Ali Baba, "We're starvin'."

"You into Cajun cooking?"

"Whatever. Just as long as it's good," said Ali Baba.

"Well," said Louis, bringing over the three drinks, "they've got a great three-drunk gumbo right around the corner."

"Is dat da number uv drunks it takes ta make it?" chuckled Soapy.

"Nope. That's how many times you can get drunk before it's ready to eat." They all guffawed.

"What is dis here gumbo made uv?" said a skeptical Ali Baba.

"It's a soup made up of seafood, chicken, and all kinds of vegetables. It's delicious, take my word for it. You'll love it."

"If you say so, we'll try it," said Soapy.

They toasted.

"Now," said Soapy, "how do we get dere from here?"

He gave them directions.

Soapy threw a twenty dollar bill onto the bar and said, "Dis is fer you, Louie. Keep ya eyes open."

"Thanks," said Louis.

Soapy and Ali Baba stepped out into the hot, humid day in search of brunch.

***

The blur that was Smitty's head came slowly into focus and then with a quick click, vanished. The precision mechanism reset and he reappeared. But within that millisecond between his coming and going, his likeness, along with the fancy lace iron grillwork that he stood in front of, was captured for posterity on a thin sheet of photographically sensitized celluloid.

"Now get me in front of this one," said Smitty to Cal who was taking the photo from over near the curb.

With arms crossed, Smitty leaned debonairly against a building loaded with iron curlicues interlaced with cast-iron angels to form a complex pattern, one that Rayf and Cal didn't take too seriously, but fine craftsmanship nevertheless—craftsmanship that Smitty wanted to show the folks back home in Corpus Christi, Texas, folks who had never been to New Orleans. He wanted to show them not only how good the old French Quarter looked, but how good it looked with him in it. "Just focus and hit the top button," said Smitty, standing under a balcony. "Can you get it all in from there?"

"Yeah. Now just stand still."

Click, whiz, whir. Click, whiz, whir.

"OK. Now I've got to take one of you two guys. Come on get over here."

Cal handed him the camera; they changed places and he snapped twice.

And, perhaps, somewhere in a Corpus Christi attic fifty years from today around 2013, someone will come across that photo and wonder, "Who the hell are those two ragamuffins standing in front of all that fine architecture?" And if it'll be of any help, that's Rayf and Cal posing with their thumbs strung in their front dungaree pockets for Smitty's souvenir book.

"Well, boys, thanks for everything. Sure you don't want to come to Texas with me?"

"Thanks," said Cal, "but first we gotta dig this place."

"What about Dallas?"

"Later," said Cal. "It ain't goin' nowhere—and anyway, this might be the last time that we're ever here."

"Whatever you say," said Smitty, packing up his camera. "It's really been fun. Thanks guys."

"Thanks!?" said Rayf. "We're the ones who should be thankin' you. You like saved our lives."

"Come on, you're making too much of it. It was nothing."

"We'll never forget what you did," said Cal.

"Glad to be of assistance," said Smitty, shaking Cal's hand. And when he did, Cal felt something pressing between their palms.

"Hey, Smitty, man, you don't have to do this," said Cal, holding up two five dollar bills.

"I know I don't. I want to," said Smitty now shaking Rayf's hand, "Y'all take care now, hear?"

"Right," said Rayf, rubbing his empty palm against his pant leg.

"See ya later, Smitty," said Cal.

He walked over to his BMW, opened the driver's door, and yelled back to the two guys standing near the wrought-iron lacework, "Hey, if you're ever out near Corpus Christi give us a look up, hear!?" They nodded, he got into his car, slammed the door closed, started it up, and pulled out towards Common Street and US 90 west.

"I think we blew it," said Rayf.

"Why's that?" said Cal.

"We had us a ride right into Texas."

"Yeah, but now we got ten dollars and the Quarter is calling to us. Don't you hear it calling, man?"

"No. What's it saying?"

"Its saying, 'Laissez les bon temp roulez'."

"And five dollars of that better roll my way."

"Bullshit! We're gonna invest this money."

"In what?"

"I got a plan."

"It better include eating."

"Better than that. But first, we are going to combine these two Lincolns into one Hamilton."

"What for?"

"You'll see."

Cal walked away. Reluctantly, Rayf followed the money.

Now when they walked up Saint Peter's Street from Jackson Square towards Royal, Cal could feel a change coming over him. He felt like one of those soldiers of fortune who might have been thrown out of France back in the seventeen hundreds, or a pirate, like Smitty had talked about, who swaggered down these same streets way back when. He was smitten with the sense of adventure, smitten as never before as he shared his plan with Rayf.

"I don't think we should do it," said Rayf.

"Relax. Look, if it'll make you feel any better, we'll use Southern accents, OK?"

"Accents?"

"As disguises."

"I think we should just stay clear of the place."

"Not to worry," said Cal as he walked into a smoke shop to exchange the two fives for a ten.

A few minutes and a couple of blocks later he saw it.

"There it is, man," said Cal. "Right on the sunny side of the street."

"I got a bad feeling here," said Rayf.

"Hey, you said you saw them go into the Bay yourself, right?"

"Right," said Rayf, weakly.

"'We heard the radio report, right?"

"Right."

"So stop worrying, fer crissakes. Come on," said Cal.

They crossed the street, walked into the sunlit room, and took a seat at the corner of the bar up near the picture window.

"This is a good spot," said Cal. "We can see people comin' and goin'."

"Look, whatever you do, don't mention Johnny Flamingo, okay?"

"Wha' do I look like, a real idiot?" said Cal.

"I'm not gonna answer that one."

They waited on the bartender while outside the window the passing parade of humanity flowed by.

The barroom was old. The wooden floor creaked when walked over. There were tables lining the left wall as one entered, and the scarred and ancient bar that ran along the right wall with its hard-seated, backless stools told of days gone by as did the deep-red-stained, wooden-paneled, beveled mirror on the wall behind it. Three tiers of liquor bottles, on narrow glass shelves, stood in front of the mirror, the more popular brands on the bottom. And the smell of the place, if you had a nose for it, also had a history.

Hanging on the center back bar wall was a large, gaudy, gold leafed, framed portrait of a guy from colonial times with the subject's name engraved underneath upon a brass plate: 'Bloody' Don O'Rielly.

Sitting at the far curve of the bar was a young, blond woman framed against the black velvet curtain that served as a door to the backroom.

"What'll it be, boys?" said a cordial Louis.

"Dewar's and water. Two," said Cal.

"Right," said Louis.

Now Cal in his best Southern drawl said, "Who's dat a picter uv?"

"Oh," said Louis fixing the drinks, "that's the second Spanish Governor of Louisiana."

"O'Rielly!? Spanish?" said Cal.

"Well he wasn't Spanish. He was an Irish soldier of fortune who became a General in the Spanish Army and then became Governor."

"Why 'Bloody'?" said Rayf.

"Because he had a bunch of French Revolutionaries shot when they rebelled against the Spanish, back around 1769."

"Dat's like two hun'r'd years ago," said Cal.

"That's right."

"So why you keep him hangin' up there?" said Rayf.

"A conversation piece. Where you boys from?"

"Oh, uh, we is, uh, from Mont-gum-ery, Alabama. Why?" said Cal.

"Just asking. We get a lot of people in here from Montgomery. You boys on a tear?"

"No," said Rayf. "We're lookin' fer work. Any leads?"

"Well, they're always hiring down on the oil rigs. You into that sort of work?" said Louis while setting the drinks down in front of the two young counterfeit confederates.

"We's into anythin' dat pays," said Cal.

"Well," said the barkeep taking an elbow near the two. "You work out there on the platforms for fourteen days straight and then come in for a week. That's about the size of it."

"Hmm," said Rayf, and with that hmm it was understood; rough necking as an occupation was definitely out.

"How's 'bout fishin'?" said Cal.

"Shrimp boats?"

"Okay."

"Yeah, that's happening too. Mostly Cajuns do it. I gotta tell you, though, it is a lot of grunt work."

"The hours?" said Cal.

"About the same as oil," said Louis.

"Hmm," said Rayf.

"Have a drink on us," said Cal. "An' give dat sweet little yella haired thang down at dee udder end uv da bar one while you are at it."

"Right."

And when Louis moved off to fill the glasses, Rayf whispered. "Wha' the fuck you doin' buying all these people drinks with my money?"

"Your money!?"

"Yeah. You heard me. Half of that's mine."

"Look, you spend big, you make a big impression. This way he'll remember us if we ever need him. Dig?"

"I think you're losin' your fuckin' mind, man."

Louis returned to claim the house's portion of the Hamilton that lay in front of the two impostors.

"That'll be four dollars even."

Rayf flinched.

"Take it out of here," said Cal, pointing to the lone bill lying on the bar.

And since that was the only money laying on the well-worn bar's surface, he took it and brought back one Lincoln and one Washington in its place.

They downed their drinks, slid their stools out, and stood up. Cal pushed a one dollar bill into the trough and said, "Thank ya fer the info regardin' work, neighbor. Much obliged."

"Best of luck to y'all."

Cal did his big spender's wave, and they stepped out into the warm sunshine.

"Five fuckin' dollars, just like that," said Rayf, snapping his fingers.

"Easy come, easy go," said Cal as they strolled back down Royal towards Conti Street.

"Look, if we ever get split up for any reason, we'll meet back there in the 'Cat'. Dig?"

"Five fuckin' dollars."

At Conti Street they hooked a right and walked very slowly towards the Mississippi River. They were starving.

"Why don't we get something to eat?" said Rayf.

"Because."

"Because why?" said Rayf.

"Because we need the money for tonight."

"What the hell are we doin' tonight that we can't do now?"

"Bourbon Street rocks at night."

"Not even a hot dog?" said Rayf.

"Forget about food. Think about something else."

"Like what?"

"Like look at that street sign, will ya," said Cal, "Exchange Place. Just like in New York."

"Hey man, you can't eat a street sign."

They turned up Exchange Place and there, in the middle of the block on the other side of the street, they saw a gaggle of young runaways and social misfits.

"Maybe we could hustle them for a few bucks," said Cal.

"You're not thinkin' clearly," said Rayf.

They continued walking.

On Canal Street they headed towards the river and walked and walked and walked. On this walk they saw a blood bank with a hand scribbled placard that read: $5 for blood. They walked into the blood bank's waiting room, took their seats, and waited just like the sign on the wall instructed them to do.

In a few minutes a lady dressed in white, like a nurse, came up to them and said to Rayf, "Follow me." He followed closely looking at her lovely buttocks in that tight-fitting white skirt. She reminded him of that nurse at the Jersey City Medical Center, where he had gone three years before for a chest x-ray. That lovely young Jersey nurse told him to strip from the waist down—for a chest x-ray!? Hey, who was he to argue with the medical profession? He did as he was told. Physically, this one looked just like that one.

She led him over to a clean cot and said, "Please remove your shirt and shoes. Thank you."

He did as he was told.

"Make yourself comfortable," said the nurse-type lady as she closed the curtain around his cot.

He was now all alone in his white-curtained, makeshift, hospital-like bedroom.

They had a good time back there, him and that Jersey nurse. *Who knows*, went his thinking as he lay back on the clean sheets, *maybe something nice'll come out of this one, too.*

In a short while he heard Cal being led into the cot-room next to his. He heard the same nurse as she started questioning Cal, "Have you ever had any contagious diseases?"

"Come to think of it," said Cal, "yes I have."

"What was it?"

"Yellow fever."

Rayf's ears perked up.

"Yellow fever? Are you sure it was yellow fever?" she asked.

"Yeah, it was something deadly like that. Why do you need to know that?"

"Well, I'm sorry sir, but we can't take your blood. You'll have to leave."

"But ..."

"I'm sorry, sir. Health code regulations."

She led him back to the waiting room.

By time the nurse returned to Rayf he was already dressed.

"Where are you going sir?"

"I've changed my mind, ma'am."

Cal was already smoking a Cigarillo out on the sidewalk when Rayf came walking out of the blood bank.

"So soon?" said Cal.

"Yeah."

"You get the five bucks?"

"Nah."

"What happened?"

"They found out that I had malaria," said Rayf.

"You had ma ..."

"Yeah when I was a kid. You mean you didn't know that?"

"No," said Cal blankly. But Rayf registered the very slight change that came over Cal's face—it showed the workings of his mind: Does he know? Did he hear me? In the meantime Rayf's face was saying: I know something, and you don't know if what I know is what you just pulled, do you?

"Did you get the five bucks?" said an innocent Rayf.

"No. Man, those people are really particular. They wouldn't take mine neither. How do ya like that?"

"Oh really? Why not?"

"I told 'em I had a cold once, and they didn't want to take any chances. Can you imagine that?" said Cal. "A friggin' cold!"

"Isn't that somethin'?"

Now Cal studied Rayf. But whatever was going on inside Rayf's head never showed up on his face.

"Let's get outta here," said Rayf.

They turned around and started walking back up Canal Street, unaware of the ghosts that surrounded them. To the rear, the white-supremacy obelisk monument commemorating the victory overthrowing the reconstruction government of 1874, and ahead of them Matiere Cemetery, final resting place of voodoo queen Marie Laveau.

It was two o'clock in the afternoon.

They didn't speak. They just walked.

Rayf, to take up the slack in his now loose-fitting dungarees, tied two belt loops together. Cal followed suit. They had lost a good two inches apiece.

They were starving to death and had no idea where they were going or why. They had forgotten all about the chase, Angela, or Petey.

Rayf only knew one thing; Cal was holding out on him. And Cal knew nothing of what Rayf knew.

***

Her body was right there: not too thin, not too fat, just right there. She has beautiful legs. Her thighs and calves look like that of a dancer's or a. … nah. Rayf dismissed that other *or* and elbowed Cal to watch his style. Cal assed up onto a parked car's front fender in order to get a better view of the proceedings.

She's cruising, window shopping, thought Rayf as he approached and joined her at the large, plate-glass shoe store window on Canal Street.

"Nice shoes," he said.

She cocked her head and smiled a crooked smile.

He patted down his hair. He was on a roll.

"You from New Orleans?" he said.

"No. Ah'm from Opolusus," she said very sweetly.

"Where's that?"

"Lowizianna. Bayou country. Northwest a here, 'n' you?" She spoke as slow as Southern honey poured.

"We're, uh. I'm from, uh, Jersey City. Know where that's at?"

"Now that's not in England, now is it?" she said with a smile in her throat.

"Nah, it's up around New York City—'bout twenty minutes east of it. Excuse me, but I couldn't help but noticing, you got some great looking gams." There, it was out.

She smiled at him and said, "Bien merci."

She spoke French, too. What a score!

She stepped into the shoe store foyer, formed by two display windows. He followed. They were off the street. Cal had to stretch his neck to keep them in view.

"You come to New Orleans much?"

"Jest to dance," she said even slower while lowering her eyes. "You dance?"

"Uh ... yeah, I guess," said Rayf. "Slow dances mostly."

Now they were on the other side of the foyer working their way back out to the main Canal Street display windows.

"I'm working on becomin' an exotic dancer."

"You sure don't have to work too hard on the exotic part."

"Why, thank you. Maybe I could teach you a few steps. Looks like you could use a little carin' for."

"I ... uh ..." He felt like the dog that caught the car—what to do with it?

She put out her hand and said, "Come on, honey pie, Ah'll sho ya a real good time."

Piss on the tire, that's what he'll do.

And now when they stepped out onto Canal Street they were a couple. She, built to perfection in a mid-thigh tight skirt; he, looking like something the cat just dragged out.

Cal turned his head, and when they were a half block away, he followed.

***

She was a hustler, but was not going to charge him for her services. She was down here on the second part of a two-week vacation. The first part was spent in Puerto Rico, where she was supposed to have had an abortion, paid for by the old guy who puts her up. The old guy didn't know that she was a hooker or that she wasn't even pregnant. But she needed a vacation and would be going back to Opolusus tomorrow morning. She gave him her phone number just in case he ever got up that way. Rayf told her, as they lay there naked on the huge bed, that he had no intentions of going into the bayous.

Sucking on one of her king-sized mentholated cigarettes, he stared up at their reflection in the mirrored ceiling. She looked even more beautiful as she lay there by his side, not even bikini marks to spoil that golden tan her red hair cascading onto his chest. Sharing his smoke, she said, "Do you like these satin sheets?'

"Uh, they're all right, I guess. Why?"

"Jest askin', silly," said the sweet redhead, "Y'all know that you were just fabulous."

"Thank you, I guess. So were you."

"Mercie. But Ah mean, compared to ma ol' man, who jest lays there," she hit a higher note on the word lays.

How anyone could just lay alongside a girl like this was beyond Rayf's wildest imaginings. And he told her so. She thought he was cute and nice, and then she snuffed out his cigarette and the band played on.

Outside, across the street from the hotel, Cal perched atop a Cadillac's street-side front fender, bouncing heels against rubber tire with eyes peeled to the doorway that his friend and the redhead had walked into not a half-hour before.

***

"Well, how was the gumbo?" said Louis.

"Not bad," said Ali Baba.

"Great stuff," said Soapy.

"You got a Tums, Louie?" said Ali Baba. "I got a heartburn dat'd kill a horse."

They pulled up to the bar, pushing away the stools along the rough wooden floor. Louis gave Ali Baba a glass of seltzer, then poured two scotches. They picked up their drinks and walked over to a table down in the corner of the barroom near the black velvet curtain to set up shop.

Soapy put his drink on the table and went over to the phone booth to check in with Jersey City.

Ali Baba tilted back on his chair and, with a toothpick and darting tongue, searched out his rear right upper molars for a concealed piece of shrimp—or was that chicken, or crab, or oyster, he thought, as he dug it out for one last chew and swallow. He was beginning to enjoy this trip.

It was five p.m.

At five-thirty Rayf walked out of the hotel. He saw Cal sitting on the Caddy, nodded to the doorman, and walked across the street.

"Well, how'd we do?" said Cal, jumping off the Cady's fender.

"What do you mean, 'How'd *we* do?'"

"Money. Did ya get any?"

"Do I look like a gigolo to you?"

"No money?"

"No."

"Shit."

"Come on, let's go," said a revived Rayf.

"Go!? Where?"

"To the Quarter."

"With what?"

"With our five bucks. We still got it, don't we?"

"Yeah," said a deflated Cal.

"Then let the party begin."

"With fi' dollars!?"

Rayf put his arm over Cal's shoulder and said, "It's all in your attitude, man. It's all in your attitude."

"Easy for you to say. You just got laid."

"Now let us get drunk."

The sun was setting out over Panama as they crossed Canal Street and stepped into the time machine known as the French Quarter, where the present becomes the past and where Rayf and Cal were about to become history.

***

They sat there on the southeast curb of Bourbon Street sharing a large bag of greasy potato chips and a brown-paper-bagged bottle of Thunder Bird. This repast served three purposes: first, to put something into their stomachs; second, to get them drunk; and third to have some spare change left over to party. The rotgut was hard to keep down, hence the potato chips—a banquet of modest means, to be sure.

The sounds of the night were starting to intensify as the sidewalk traffic began to increase with lots of tourists and people who either catered to or preyed upon them.

A drunken middle-aged couple stopped by the two curbside drinkers. "Oh honey," said the drunken woman, "look at those two poor boys." Rayf looked up at the woman staggering over towards them. "Here honey," she said as she handed Rayf two one dollar bills, "you take this money and get yourselves something to eat. You two boys look terrible."

"Thank you, ma'am," said Rayf, "And may God bless you."

She gave a saintly smile as they staggered back into the throng of drunken revelers.

"You lucky fuck," said Cal.

"It's more than luck, Cal. It's looks, man."

"One of those dollars is mine."

"Bullshit! Gimme that bottle."

Cal passed the paper bag that held the bottle.

Rayf, taking the bag and stashing the bills, said, "Ya know, I think I like this town."

Cal was chomping a mouthful of chips and Rayf was swilling the wine when they heard a voice that came from behind, "Hey mon, you look like you needs some woe-men. Is dees true, mon?" whispered a black-as-coal young man whose face shone with the additional color of the many neon lights that now lit up the Quarter.

By the looks and sound of this guy, Rayf pegged him for one of those Caribbean natives. "Come on. Here, have a swig," said Rayf as he passed the paper bag.

The stranger refused with straight arm as he pushed his ass down on the curb between the two guys. "Hi gots dee charm dat chu needs, mon." He pulled out a small, shiny pebble.

"That's a fuckin' pebble," said Cal.

"Ehey, mon," whispered the black man. "Hi ham a voodoo doctor and dees is dee magic to brring you woomen, mon. It ees dee stone found een dee swallow's nest. It restores dee sight of its fledglings. It is dee lucky charm, mon." He stopped, looked around, and said, "Two dollar, mon."

"What for!? A fuckin' pebble?" said a drunken Rayf. "You're out of your fuckin' mind. You know," now referring to Cal, "you're worse than this guy, over here."

"One dollar," said the voodoo man.

"Here, have a slug," said Rayf to the doctor.

"No tanx, mon." Now to Cal, "What chu geev me por dis charm, den?"

"A fuckin' potato chip. That's what. Here, take one. They go great with the wine."

"Chu boys get no woe-men!" said the frustrated voodoo doctor about to stand.

"Here, let me see that thing," said Cal. He grabbed the pebble, fondled it, and rubbed it as if he were putting luck into a pair of dice. Then he spoke directly to it, "Hokus pokus, get us some WO-MEN!"

"Gimme back dat charm, mon." He tore the pebble from Cal's grasp and stood up. "Hi take back dee gris-gris spell dat you have conjured. It shall not stand. It shall not stand."

"Take a fuckin' hike," said Rayf, to the voodoo doctor.

And as mysteriously as he had appeared, he was gone.

They closed ranks on the curb. Rayf passed Cal the bag of wine and said, "Wot a hustle, mon."

A few more swigs and everything returned to normal. Here they sat, getting drunk, watching people, and listening to the music that came from every which way to fill the night with a backbeat that kept everyone swinging up and down the street.

One of the carousers was a tipsy twenty-year-old woman on vacation. She had separated from her friends and was now wandering around the Quarter aimlessly, in search of her lost compatriots. Had she been in any other city she would not have done what she was about to do, but the charm of New Orleans was working its spell on her also and, anyway, she could always say it was lagniappe—that extra measure.

She saw the two young men sitting on the curb, swallowed hard, walked over to them, tapped Cal on the shoulder, and said, "Do you know the way to Jackson Square?"

She's sweet, Southern, and extremely feminine, thought Cal. He slid over, tapped the curb, and said, "Come on, take a seat. I'm Cal and this here's Rayf."

What the hell, thought the prim and proper young lady as she threw all caution to the wind and sat down between Rayf and Cal. To her, this was high adventure and definitely something to talk about when she got back home.

She told them that her name was Lee Ann and that she was from Louisville, Kentucky. And, "No," she said, "I'm sorry Cal, but they do not manufacture the Louisville Slugger baseball bat in Louisville, but just across the river in Jeffersonville, Indiana." Another American marketing myth bit the dust in the already weakening psyches of Rayf and Cal.

They told her that they were from New York City, and that they were traveling the country in search of material for a novel. They passed the bottle, then the chips. She drank and ate along with them. The chips she could handle, but the wine, she thought, was sickeningly sweet.

She asked where they had been and where they were going, and they told her their route, right up to this very banquette, and all about their going on to Dallas.

"And yes," she sobbed, "wasn't that a terrible thing that happened out there?"

In the way that can only happen when one is young, drunk, and in the French Quarter of New Orleans, they became fast friends and, "Yes, of course we'd love to help you find Jackson Square and your lost friends," said Cal.

They stood up, one helping the other, and staggered off down Bourbon Street in search of the Square, excitement, and high adventure—these two pirates and one lady of the night.

The three adventurers walked up Bourbon Street to Saint Louis and down towards the levee where they took a right onto Chartres Street. They walked up Chartres, and just off Conti they found a cheap little bar that was set off the main drag via a long alleyway with walls covered in sweet-smelling vines. They staggered down it towards the open-doored bar with its bright insides beckoning to them.

The colorful flagstone walk of the alleyway continued right into this dive to become its floor, the floor being the nicest feature of the room. There were chairs and tables scattered here and there with an ugly wooden bar pressed up against a brick wall; it was this brick wall and bar that served as the main focal point from alley and street, a flame for drunken moths.

Lee Ann, it was agreed upon, was Cal's, without her even knowing. So when they stepped into the dimly lit barroom, it was Rayf who had to turn this party into a foursome.

The entrance to this joint was through a double-wide doorway that was jammed open and remained that way twenty-four hours a day, seven days a week, except during hurricanes.

There was one lone woman sitting at the right end of the bar. The bartender, reading *The Times Picayune*, was seated behind the bar at the opposite end.

The only other people in the room were four black-leather-jacketed customers, who sat out of street view, huddled around one table off in the corner.

When the three drunks entered the bar, one of the leather-jacketed men peeled off the pack and walked over to the center of the bar; the other three leathered ones remained at the table and watched their leader standing up at bar-center.

Rayf walked up to the far left side of the bar. The bar was now balanced.

Rayf ordered three bottles of Dixie beer. The bartender gave him the beers. Rayf took two back to the table near the double wide door where Cal and Lee Ann were getting better acquainted.

The lone leather-jacketed guy sized up the three tourists and nodded to his three cronies.

Rayf returned to the bar to pick up his beer. He stopped and, just for the sport of it, told the bartender to see if that lovely young lady down at the other end of the bar would like to have a drink on him.

A flash of eyes between barkeep and jacket bar-center; the barman walked over to the blond decoy at the far end. She nodded.

And when Rayf went to raise his glass to the lady, he was very surprised to find that he now had the company of two black jackets, one on his right and one on his left.

He went to excuse himself from the men in order to get back to his table. But they insisted that he drink his beer right there with them.

Then center-bar jacket said, "So! You like m' woman, huh?"

It didn't take Rayf that long to figure it out. He was about to become a mugging statistic in greater New Orleans and it wasn't even Mardi Gras.

"Is that your girl? Jeez, am I sorry about that, man. I really didn't know. So help me! Here, let me buy you a beer, too. Hey bartender, how's about giving that gent over there a nice cold one. Wha' d'ya drink? Bottle? Draft? Name it. Jeez, your girl!? Well how do you like this? Hey, we all make mistakes now and then."

"Buddy," said the man in black, "this jest might be your very last one."

"Hey ... love your sense of humor. Sure you won't have a drink?"

He tried to signal Cal, who only had eyes for Lee Ann.

"OK, sucka," said the guy on Rayf's right, "Ah'll have a draft."

"You want one too!?" said Rayf to the mug on his right, "Of course you can have one."

The bartender came down the bar and drew a glass of Jax beer and put it in front of the masher on Rayf s right.

"How's 'bout my buddies over here," said the ingrate. "Ain't you gonna' buy dem a drink too?"

"Well, let me see if I can cover it first," shouted Rayf.

This time Cal heard him and looked up to notice that Rayf had attracted to himself two very large and very ugly men who were standing unusually close to him in this otherwise very empty barroom. He looked around the room and noticed that the other man at the corner table held him in his gaze. Now it became crystal clear to Cal that they had ventured into a den of thieves right here in good old New Orleans.

Lee Ann did not know what was happening and continued talking about this and that to an otherwise distracted Cal.

Rayf, on the other hand, was playing the happy drunk, counting his change and saying, "Oops, can't buy all of you boys a drink. Not enough pennies. But here, take a Cigarillo; puts hair on your chest. Hey, barkeep, buy 'em whatever they'd like, provided I got enough up here." Then to the thugs, "I gotta piss. Where's the head in this place?"

"Over there," said the cat on the left of the mouse. "And make it snappy."

"Oh," aiming this one directly at Cal, "I'll only be a minute."

He walked into the men's room, leaving the Cigarillos and change upon the bar.

The men's room was narrow, filthy, and damp. On the left, bolted to the wall, was a dirty, rust-stained sink with a dripping, cold water faucet; next to that was a stinking urinal; and at the far end of the room sat a grimy, greasy, seatless toilet bowl. Above the bowl was a very narrow window. He climbed on the bowl, looked out, and saw, beyond a grubby garden, an alleyway that emptied out onto Royal Street with its bars and pulsating red neon signs advertising exotic dancers.

Three minutes had passed and not only were the four thugs becoming suspicious, so was Cal. It was now decided by the leader at center bar that "thug nearest toilet" would go in to check on "creep inside head."

Thug nearest toilet stood up, walked over to men's room, yanked the door open, looked in, spun around, and yelled, "The bastard's gone!"

And faster than you can say "skip town," Cal, with Lee Ann dragging behind, was hauling ass down that quaint little flagstone alleyway towards the safety of the milling crowd on Chartres Street. They melted into the crowd and didn't stop running until they hit Royal around the corner.

On Royal, Lee Ann had to stop to catch her breath. Cal also caught a few while covering her.

In the meantime, Soapy and Ali Baba had come to terms with Louis and had access to his back room where they were now taking a little rest from their boring surveillance work. They were napping on two cots that a generous Louis had set up for them back there—any friend of Johnny's.

Rayf got to the Cat 'n' Fiddle in nothing flat. He looked around to make sure he wasn't being followed, entered, walked up to the bar, and leaned against it with outstretched arms. He was gasping for air.

Louis, walked over and said, "What's the matter?"

"Nuthin'," said the winded confederate.

"Looks like you been runnin' for your life."

"Have you seen ... mah ... mah friend?"

"Who's that?"

"You know, thet guy I was in here with earlier this mo'nin'?"

Now Soapy, in the back room, opened his eyes. He didn't know if he had heard it or dreamt it. He reached over to the next cot and shook Ali Baba awake.

Louis was racking his brain trying to recall the other big spender that Rayf was describing, when all of a sudden his face lit up and he said, "Is that the guy?"

And when Rayf turned around to look in the direction that Louis was pointing in, he saw Cal running past the plate-glass window and into the bar with Lee Ann in tow.

"Yeah, dat's him," said Rayf.

"What the hell happened?" said Cal.

"They were gonna mug me."

"I think they chased us, too," said Cal, and then his face froze.

Rayf turned around to follow Cal's frozen stare and that's when he saw, standing there in front of that black velvet curtain at the far end of the barroom, a sling-armed Soapy and a head-bandaged Ali Baba with their hands snuggled into their suit jacket pockets and pointing directly at them.

"I thought you said they were dead," whispered Cal.

"I saw it with my own eyes. I swear."

"Hello boys," said Soapy, "What a pleasant surprise to find you two here. Why not come on down and join us for a little drinky poo. Take your goilfriend, too."

True, Lee Ann was looking for excitement, but this was excitement overload. She had had enough.

Louis watched as Rayf, Cal, and Lee Ann walked very slowly and reluctantly over to join Soapy and Ali Baba, who were now dragging several chairs away from another table for them to sit on.

"Not in here," said Louis.

Soapy nodded not to worry, everything would be all right.

And just as the three tourists were about to join the two bounty hunters at their table, way down back near the black velvet curtain there came a shout from the doorway up front, "Don't you take another fuckin' step you two son of a bitches."

Rayf and Cal turned around to face the hollering. And there, framed in the Cat 'n' Fiddle's doorway, were the four black-leather-jacketed thugs. They were now caught between four rocks and a couple of guns.

Rayf sized up the situation and yelled, "Fuck you. Come and get us."

That's all it took. The four men charged.

Rayf ducked behind Soapy, who didn't have the slightest idea of what was happening. Cal jumped behind Ali Baba —Lee Ann ran and hid behind the bar.

Thug-leader ran through the barroom and swung at Rayf, but hit Soapy instead and with that blow, all pandemonium broke out. Ali Baba and Soapy were in a barroom brawl of Rayf's design. Now Louis jumped in as did the four lone sailors who were sitting at the bar, itching to either fight or fuck, whichever came first. Now there were nine against four. *This*, thought Rayf, *was more like it*, as he pulled down Don O'Rielly from off the wall and crowned thug-leader with it before charging, with Cal, out of that ever-present open door onto Royal Street and up to Canal Street where they proceeded to get themselves lost.

But not so easy for Soapy and Ali Baba, who had to stay and fight it out or else get creamed. The fight raged on for a full four minutes and then it was over.

The sailors out on the banquette in front of the club were now piling the last of the four unconscious thugs on top of his other three sleeping buddies. In the meantime, Soapy and Ali Baba were inside talking to Lee Ann.

"Where'd dey go?" said Soapy.

"I don't know," sobbed Lee Ann.

"Look, if you know what's good for you, you'll tell us," said Soapy.

"The only thing I know is that they're from New York and that they're traveling around the country, writing a book or something, and they're ... they're going to Dallas to see where President Kennedy got shot." Now she broke down into a pile of tears and softness. *This lady-of-the-night bit is not as much fun as I had thought and if I ever get out of this one, I just might even marry that boy next door*, were some of her mixed thoughts.

She reminded Ali Baba of someone he had once known a long, long time ago, so far back that it was only her tears that he could recall, not even her face or her name, just her tears. It was a soft feeling, like the one he had in South Carolina when he saw that tree coming right at him. And, as with that tree, he also shook off *this* collision and said, "Would you like a coke or sumthin', honey?"

"No, I just want to get out of here and go home."

"It's OK sweetheart," said an extremely gentle Ali Baba. "You can go now."

Soapy looked at Ali Baba in total wonder as Lee Ann ran out of the place and up Royal. He couldn't believe his eyes or his ears. What the hell was going on here? Was Ali actually getting soft? *Strange place this New Orleans*, thought Soapy.

Ali Baba walked up to the bar and said, "Sorry 'bout da mess, Louie." He plunked down three one-hundred dollar bills. "But it was dose four bastards out dere dat did it."

"I know. Look, its best if you guys get out of here. The cops are on their way."

"Louie, danks for everything," said Ali Baba.

"Yeah, yeah," said Louis, looking over the torn portrait of Don O'Rielly amid the mess that was once the Cat 'n' Fiddle.

"C'm'on, Soap, let's go."

"Louie, one more ding," said Soapy.

"What's that?"

"Which way t'da airport?"

~ 14 ~

LIGHTS OUT

The driver of the paddy wagon pulled it over to the shoulder of the road. The cop riding shotgun stepped out of the cab, swaggered around to the back, unlocked the rear door, opened it wide, and told everyone inside to get out.

Out of the police van crawled the lowest of New Orleans' street life: hustlers, pickpockets, winos, hoboes, derelicts, and vagrants. The cop standing near the back of the wagon told Rayf and Cal to hurry it up. They were the last two men to climb down.

It was nine a.m. on the outskirts of Westwego on the west bank of the Mississippi River. The motley crew was given final orders: stay out of town.

For now, the bums had been given a reprieve. The crowd dispersed.

Rayf and Cal walked off down US 90 West, not speaking but thinking; thinking about the risen-from-the-dead zombie gangsters and their next ride.

They walked a while before sitting down by the roadside. Rayf pulled out his now dirty, dog-eared road map and traced their journey thus far. The cartoon characters of happy family groups and snappy gas station attendants were just as clean as they had been when he first bought the map back at that Howard Johnson on the New Jersey Turnpike up around Camden, New Jersey. Rayf and Cal, in the meantime, had lost fifteen pounds apiece and were now riding in paddy wagons with the social sediment of the United States of America. Rayf looked at the cartoon characters living their unchanged lives; he felt sorry for them.

Their first ride after the paddy wagon happened just south of Bridge City.

"Can't tell if that car's comin' or goin'," said Cal to Rayf as they walked up to meet their next ride.

"Just like I feel," said Rayf, folding away the map.

"Hop in," said the young driver reaching over to open the passenger's door.

Climbing into the back seat, Cal said, "What make car is this? Looks like an insect or something."

"It's a Volkswagen," said the T-shirted driver, "a German import."

Rayf climbed into the front seat and slammed the tinny door shut.

"You guys coming from New Orleans?"

"Yeah," said Rayf.

"So, how'd you like it?"

"New Orleans!? Well," said Cal, "the cops were friendly enough."

"The cops?"

"Yeah, they escorted us out of town."

"What'd you do?"

"Vagrants," said Rayf. "They were cleaning up the streets."

"You come back here with cash," said the driver, "and they'll be calling you sir. Believe me."

They were just now passing over Bayou Lafourche.

Rayf and Cal were exhausted and hung over.

"Where you all from?"

"Jersey City," said Cal, dryly.

"Cool. I'm from Connecticut, myself."

"What the hell are you doin' down here?" said Rayf.

"I'm a student."

"What're you studying?" said Cal.

"I'm at Tulane, majoring in political science. But eventually I'd like to be a social ecologist."

"A what?" said Rayf.

"A social ecologist! That's a person who studies the environment. It's a relatively new field. So I take it you didn't like New Orleans."

"What exactly does an ecologist do?" said Cal.

"We study the environment and try to correct conditions that pertain to its well-being—biologically, psychologically, and sociologically—they're all interrelated. So tell me about New Orleans."

"What's there to say?" said Cal. "Besides the cops throwing us out of town and four jerks almost mugging us and a couple of hit men trying to kill us, I guess it was okay."

"Hit men?"

"Did I say that? What I meant was big men."

"It's definitely a tough town."

"Country's more like it," said Rayf.

"No argument there. Where y'all headed?"

"Dallas," said Cal.

"Talk about tough towns!" said their driver, "Why you going there?"

"See where J.F.K. bought it," said Rayf.

"J.F.K., huh?"

"Yeah," mumbled Cal.

"Did you know that in 1959, Joe Kennedy, J.F.K.'s dad, was the ninth richest man in America? Did you guys know that?"

Here was a fact that had apparently escaped Rayf's dad.

"So?" said Cal. "What of it?"

"That was like only four years ago," said the driver.

"Yeah, I can count," said Cal.

"Money and power. They go hand in hand," said the driver. "You guys Italian?"

"We're American," said Rayf.

"Yeah," said Cal. "We're Italian-Americans. "Why, you got a barbecue planned?"

"I don't get it."

"He means, what's with the heritage thing?" said Rayf.

"Oh! You just look it."

"How do Italians look?" said Rayf.

"I'm just trying to make a point here. You see, we're all here because of money."

"Where do you mean by here?" said Cal.

"America. Oh. Excuse me. The name's Barry. Barry Peeples. And yours?"

"I'm Cal; he's Rayf."

"Glad to meet ya." They all shook hands.

"You see, it took money for Columbus to discover America—a country which is, by the way, named after another Italian, Amerigo Vespucci."

"What about Leif Erickson?" said Cal.

"Sorry, Cal. The burden of proof is with Columbus. He's the one with the maps, charts, and logs. The other guy!? Hearsay."

"We didn't have anything to do with it," said Cal. "We're innocent. And we can prove it."

"You see, in Florida," said Rayf, "we met this here Seminole Indian, and from what he says, the Indians were here a long, long time before any of us."

"Yeah," said Barry, "Poor people. Ignorance is the root of all prejudice."

"What do you mean by that?" said Rayf.

"Yesterday, in Nazi Germany, it was the Jews; and right here in America, it was the Italians; and before them and right up till now it's been the Negroes and the Indians."

"Whoa!" said Cal. "Back up—the Italians?!"

"Yeah," said Barry. "They lynched eleven of 'em in New Orleans back in 1890."

"Eleven?" said Cal.

"Yup. They were tried in a court of law and found innocent, but they were lynched anyway."

Silence.

It was one thing when the genocide was being performed on other people; but now that the other moccasin had fallen, they didn't feel so secure.

"How come they killed 'em if they were innocent?" said Rayf.

"It didn't matter what the jury said. The cry of the mob was: 'When the courts fail, the people must act.' Nine of the eleven were naturalized, so I guess you'd call them Italian-Americans, too, huh? Just like yourselves." After a dramatic pause, "Vigilantes," finished Barry.

"Why'd they kill 'em?" said Rayf.

"Dave Hennessey, Chief of Police back then, got gunned down and his friend, W.J. O'Connor, the first person on the scene, claimed that Hennessey's last dying word was, 'dagos.'"

"So," said Cal, "what you're sayin' is that the vigilantes acted on hearsay?"

"Right. They claimed that the jury was fixed and paid off."

"But that was a long time ago," said Rayf.

"By the turn of the century, Italians were open season. They hung 'em in Hanville and Talluah, Louisiana, too. And in 1927 there was Sacco and Vanzetti, electrocuted up in Boston."

"Never heard of 'em," said Rayf.

"Not too many people have," said Barry.

"What'd these guys do?" said Rayf.

"Sacco was a factory shoe cutter and Vanzetti a laborer who was 'black-listed' because of his pro union speeches at workers' rallies."

"I mean, what crime did they commit?"

"They were charged with armed robbery and murder. No witnesses, no evidence, nothing. When they were arrested for this crime they said to each other, 'Another deportation case.' They were sadly mistaken. Because you gotta remember, back then, and even now, the word union was and still is a very dirty word."

"So what you're saying," said Cal, "is that they were killed because they were talkin' union?!"

"That's what I'm sayin'. The guy who tried them, the honorable Judge Webster Thayer, called them 'anarchist bastards.'"

"Let's face it," continued Barry, "well-publicized lynchings and state-sanctioned murders have a strong tendency to keep people in line. It is a basic military procedure: divide and conquer. Once divided, they're easier to control to send off to work or to war."

"You make work and war sound the same," said Rayf.

"In a military-industrial complex, there's really not that much difference."

"You a communist?" said Cal.

"I already told you, I'm a political scientist studying to be an ecologist." They pondered his military-industrial statement, but were too hungry to argue and knew that listening was the fare they had to pay for this ride.

"So what you're sayin'," said Rayf, "is that prejudices are, like, planned."

"I think so," said Barry. "Look at the black folks today; Freedom Riders trying to help change things. If we don't do something about it now, who knows who'll be next: Mexicans? Alutes? This insanity has got to stop."

"But how?" said Cal.

"We've got to stop the killing and start talking. People are people. We're all the same. We've got to stop the fighting. Why do we fight? Go ahead, I'm asking you. Why?"

"Money?" said Cal.

"Governments?" said Rayf.

"You're both close. It's because of ignorance. The media keeps us ignorant. We are deliberately kept in the dark. Now I don't necessarily mean that there's a conspiracy here. It's basically just doing business. And them that's got want to keep what they've got; they're ignorant."

He was in orbit; they were still on the launch pad.

"Let me see if I can explain it. You see, the guy who buys the full-page ad is the guy who is calling the shots."

"Slow down," said Rayf.

"Okay. Now if I owned a company and you owned a newspaper and I took out full-page ads in your newspaper to get more business, and if there was a strike at my company and you ran a big story in favor of the union, then I'd really get pissed-off and pull my dollars out of your newspaper."

"Why?" said Rayf.

"Because it would show me in an unfavorable light. And what would that do?"

No answer.

"It could affect my business and make me lose sales. See what I'm getting at?" said Barry.

"A little," said Cal.

"It all boils down to money and power. My job as a political social ecologist is to try and instill an ecological conscience into corporations. Now do you understand?"

"Understand?! I am totally lost," said Rayf.

"OK. I'll try again. It's all related. Corporations will do anything to increase their profits, keep wages down, ignorance up, and even pollute. But you can't expect to make a profit at the expense of the environment; it's too fragile and it's usually the first thing to give out. And without a healthy environment, we're all poor. Wealth is a healthy ecosystem. The Indians were right."

"Ecosystem?!" said Cal.

"It's what sustains us; the whole ball of wax, or should I say earth. The word ecology comes from the Greek word *oikos*, meaning household. We've got to do a little housecleaning."

"Okay, I think I see what you're getting at," said Cal. "If you piss in the water upstream, then the people downstream will get sick and this sickness could eventually spread back to the people up stream."

"Hey, you're catching on!"

"Hey!" said Cal. "How do you like this, ten minutes and already I'm an ecol ... what was that word again?"

"Ecologist," said Barry. "You see, those people pissing in the stream are ignorant of the fact that whatever they do to this stream affects them, too. It all comes back around."

"Right," said Cal, "I think I'm catching on."

"You're on your way," said Barry. "What d'ya say we take an oath—right here, right now, in this car; all three of us take an oath. Wha'd'ya say?"

"It depends," said Rayf, "What's it on?"

"That we all vow to help save our earth. After all it's the only one we've got."

"But what about the lynchings and the murders?" said Rayf.

"We don't forget that; but we don't let it blind us either. We've gotta go to war against pollution," said Barry, "against ignorance. We've all got to join hands. All colors, races, nationalities, religions, all of us. If we don't win this one, we as a species are done for, finished, gone. And all of their gold and diamonds won't amount to a hill of beans. The days of ignorance are coming to an end."

Rayf looked at Cal; they shrugged.

"Okay," said Rayf, "what's the oath?"

Barry put his hand in the center, palm down, Rayf laid his hand on top of Barry's, and Cal piled on last.

"All for the planet, the planet for all," said Barry. "That'll be our pledge. Now let's all say it all together, OK? On the count of three."

He counted to three and they all said: "All for the planet, the planet for all."

The miles rolled on and he spun stories every inch of the way—to them, for them, and at them.

Half-heartedly, Rayf and Cal tried to understand this rabble rouser, but the loud backbeat of hunger drowned out most of the driver's song.

"We're starving," said Cal.

"Why didn't you say that before," said Barry. "We're almost at Morgan City—I'll buy you something there."

"Really!?" said Cal. "Ya know, all of a sudden, I think I could really get into this ecology."

"Good," said Barry.

Up near Morgan City they saw a stretch of Cypress swamp at the Gibson and Highway 20 junction with its green-gray-black, dense flooded forest, and he told them that this was part of the Great Swamp. And here they saw giant construction cranes higher than the trees and huge offshore oil platforms lying on their sides along the bayous. "This," said their driver "is the center of Louisiana's oil-drilling industry." And he told them that he was going to start speaking to the Cajuns in hopes of stopping this wanton rape of the bayous and the Great Swamp.

Then he turned onto Highway 182 just outside of Morgan City and said, "You guys have any chicory coffee yet?"

"Yeah," said Rayf, "in New Orleans."

"That, my friends, is strictly tourist mud. You haven't tasted coffee till you drink this stuff."

He pulled the Volkswagen over to a little roadside diner and waved them all to come on in and partake of some real Cajun coffee. Rayf and Cal felt conspicuous walking into that diner and imagined ropes tightening around their now skinny necks.

Barry put up thirty-five cents and ordered three cups of coffee and two donuts. The waitress took a quarter. The mugs held almost a pint of pure black liquid.

They sipped the coffee and sensed an immediate rush. It was an instant high. They now felt strong enough to walk to Dallas, and this was only after the first sip.

They spent the next several minutes eating, drinking, and talking about their travels.

Rayf said, "Before we go to Dallas we're gonna check on a friend of ours up in Opelousas."

"Well, if I were you, I'd take Highway 182 north. It's really pretty with not too much traffic. But between Calumet and New Iberia, it is the most scenic plantation road in southwest Louisiana. Highway 182 winds by the legendary Bayou Teche."

"Is Teche, French?" said Cal.

"No," said Barry, "it means snake in one of the American Indian tongues."

"Good idea to take 182," said Cal to Rayf, "Not too much traffic; winding road; nobody we know'd be driving on that. What do ya think?"

"Sounds good to me," said Rayf

Barry hoisted his mug and said, "You'll love it."

After he finished his coffee he said to the waitress, "Use that dime there to give these two boys a refill."

She filled them up.

And then, with a grin that could start a revolution, he said, "What better place to talk to the people than in a town that's named after J.P. Morgan, the most important financier in US railroad history—a man with a fat-cat lifestyle who enjoyed his meat red, his wine plentiful, and his cigars expensive." He paused, got real quiet, looked around, and said in a whisper, "Remember, 'All for the planet, the planet for all.' Got it?"

With serious masks, they nodded. Barry then winked and said, "Adios boys." And with that, he up and left.

They watched him walk out, get into his Volkswagen bug, and drive off. It was Cal who said, "Who was that masked Volksman?"

"That was no Volksman," said Rayf, "that was an e-col-o-gist."

The coffee was warm, full-bodied, and the best they had ever tasted in their lives. They vowed at that counter to someday come back down here with lots of money and time in order to drink this good coffee to their kidneys' content. Looking outside they noticed that the sun would not wait for them. So they drank up and hit that long, winding Highway 182 north towards Opelousas Marie.

With that jolt of strong Cajun coffee, they walked at a brisk pace through the outskirts of Morgan City and up to the Highway 182 junction. There, they followed it east to Verdunville, which borders on Six Mile Lake.

Highway 182 takes a very circuitous route to Opelousas by winding and weaving around Bayou Teche. They walked on this winding road until their nervous systems returned to normal. Then they crashed like a couple of giant cypress trees felled by an oil man's axe to make way for some serious drilling. They had to take a rest stop.

Parked alongside the infrequently-used highway was a little white rowboat resting on a trailer. They decided to sit on this rowboat with their legs hanging over the gunwale and hitch northward in this most leisurely fashion.

On the opposite side of the road, across from where they were sitting, they could see a glassy, calm bayou that was ringed with tall cypress trees and giant live oaks that were draped with Spanish moss. And out there in the middle of that calm pool of dark water bobbed a tiny, bright red rowboat mirroring itself in the reflecting water. In that tiny red rowboat was a fisherman with a straw hat pulled down across his eyes; he was lying back on the seat of the boat, fishing pole in hand, while basking in this sunny, warm, peaceful day. Rayf looked at this scene with its trees of varying hues of green, its black clean water, and its blue skies with big white puffy clouds that floated lazily over a tiny red rowboat with a yellow-hatted guy sleeping right smack dab in the middle of it all.

It looked to Rayf, just like that Norman Rockwell–type painting hanging on Gizzi's barber shop wall back there on Bushwick Street in downtown Jersey City.

But this is not a picture, thought Rayf. This was a living person out there, right now, living a lifestyle that these two guys would never ever get a chance to experience except in passing. So Rayf decided to absorb as much of this calmness as he could hold. He breathed deeply and felt the weight of the road lifting from his shoulders.

They did not speak at all during this idyllic state; they just watched and relaxed.

A half-hour passed before a pickup truck broke their meditation. It pulled up to a stop not fifteen feet ahead of them.

They hopped off their rowboat perch and fell to the ground in a heap. Perplexed, they looked toward each other. What had happened? Why couldn't they walk? They tried to stand up, but couldn't. They tried and tried again and again, but they didn't have one leg to stand on between them; so they did the next best thing—they crawled towards their waiting ride.

It was a strange sight the young waiting driver saw through his rear- and side-view mirrors: two guys in the dust crawling towards him. Rayf was the first one to reach the cab. He hauled himself up to meet the concerned face of the driver.

"You boys cripples?" said the driver.

"No," said Rayf, struggling to pull himself up onto the seat. "Our legs fell asleep."

"Oh," said the driver. And he watched and waited for the other hitch-hiker to pull himself up.

Once inside the cab, Rayf and Cal began massaging their legs. And as the kid drove off toward New Iberia, Rayf's and Cal's legs started to come back to life through the pain of a million stinging needles. There were lots of "Oooohs" and "Ahhs" coming from the two hitchhikers as Fats Domino sang "I'm Walking to New Orleans" over the pickup truck's radio.

The driver watched the hitchhikers as they frantically worked their hands over their legs. They rubbed and waited for the litany of Ws but none did come.

They drove on listening only to the radio. Soon their legs returned to normal. Rayf thought, *How inconvenient it must be to be crippled.* He made a mental note *never to take walking for granted ever again.*

Their driver didn't say a word, but drove steadily northward. *Here is a silent man,* thought Rayf, *one who wastes few words.* He was calm. They were hungry.

The twisting Bayou Teche came in and out of sight: one of many bayous that pierce the jungle of swamp that is southwest and central Louisiana.

They drove the thirty-five miles up to New Iberia and through its tree-lined streets of live oak with arches of moss-draped boughs. Here and there, past the great tree trunks, they saw the gleam of huge, white columns that belonged to the plantation-style houses. They could only imagine what life would be like inside those dwellings and how it must feel to be waiting on some sweet southern belle, waiting and watching as she would glide down those great curved staircases that surely must grace the interiors of those spacious places. And the sign that welcomed the travelers entering this town read: New Iberia, The Queen City of Teche.

Funny, thought Rayf, *how all your life you hear about a group of people—like the Cajuns— and never really know anything about them except their name. What a strong bunch of people these must have been to have survived in these jungle-like swamps overrun with snakes, alligators, insects, and all kind of diseases—not only survive, but flourish.*

"This is Cajun country, right?" said Rayf to the stoic driver.

"Yep."

"Do these Cajuns live in those plantation houses?" said Rayf.

"Some. Some live out there in the bayous in swamp shacks and out on the lovely prairies, and some even live in the cities nowadays."

"Who are they?" said Cal.

"Acadians."

"Where they from?" said Rayf.

"A lot of 'em come here directly from France and some others, they come here by way of Nova Scotia. That's an island up near Canada. English wanted the place so they ran 'em off."

To Rayf it seemed as though everybody was chasing somebody else in this country and he said, "When did all of this happen?"

"Long time ago; I don't rightly know exactly when. They walked from the East Coast and floated on down the Mississippi. They been settled out here in these bayous ever since."

"I see," said Rayf, "You Cajun?"

"Hell no. Ah'm a Heinz 57 variety special—Choctaw, Chicksaw, Spanish,

French, English. You name it, it's in there someplace." Then he paused and reflected a moment before saying, "Guess you'd call me all-American."

All that talk seemed to deflate the young driver. He became silent and distant once again. Then midway between New Iberia and Saint Martin-ville, the pickup truck had to turn east up a small, sandy dirt road where they were let out. Since they had nothing else to do, they watched that pickup truck go up that road trailing a screen of smoke, pebbles, and dust in its wake.

Rayf wondered *how must it feel to be familiar with that stretch of dirt road*, but soon hunger took over his and Cal's thoughts. *If it were not for those donuts we had up in Morgan City*, thought Rayf, *that strong coffee would surely have burnt a hole right through the lining of our stomachs.*

They searched their pockets for some money, but none was to be found. Rayf had absolutely nothing, whereas Cal, on the other hand, came up with a safety pin he had borrowed from that lady in the white T-Bird in Miami Beach. Ah, the memories that tiny pin conjured up for him, like cookies and warm milk, breakfast in the yard with Irene Rooms, and the smell of vegetable stands in South Beach. He looked at the pin and stashed it safely into the changeless change pocket in his pants. He dug deeper, and in his back pocket he found a crumpled piece of paper. It was an envelope, the one the guy at the Miami Beach Police Station had given him. And there in the upper right corner was a first-class stamp worth a full five cents. They had money after all!

Just this side of Saint Martinville, west of the Longfellow Evangeline Commemorative area, they found a small roadside fruit stand and traded the stamp for two apples, which they ate very slowly and with much gusto.

Cal said, "If that guy in Miami Beach had any idea on how his stamp helped save the lives of two road apples, he'd be very proud of himself." He stuffed the now stampless envelope deep into his back pocket. Someday he'd pay back that five dollar loan—someday.

Here in this magical land sat two Northerners chomping down on big old life-sustaining apples, feeling oh so happy to be warm, dry, alive, and eating.

After this early dinner, they decided to take the much more trav-eled US 90 North. They walked some, rode some, and in their travels saw shrimp boats and oil vessels cruising past the towns' backyards. At one bridge crossing they stopped to breathe in deeply, filling their lungs with damp, swampy marsh air. It cleared their heads of all negative thoughts; they were on the mend. And now the sun started setting in the west and they decided that this sunset out over the bayous was a most spectacular thing, unlike anything that Jersey City had ever produced—during their lifetimes anyway.

Up here, where US 90 went west, they got back onto One Eighty-Two North.

Just below Opelousas they noticed another great light off towards the east, near the region of the Atchafalaya River. This light glowed bright in the night as it shot flames high into the nighttime sky, giving off a plume of multi-colored smoke. They recognized those flames as the same ones that they had seen at the ESSO oil refineries back in New Jersey; this was fast becoming a booming oil-producing region and they turned their eyes away from those noxious flames and hunched their shoulders to the road. They still had a ways to go to reach Opelousas Marie.

***

Several hours passed.

They hitched some and walked some, but no ride appeared.

The earth continued rotating and once again darkness descended. Then, seemingly out of thin air, a ride materialized.

They did not hail down this rusty, faded-red pickup truck that pulled up just a few feet ahead of them, but they were happy to see it just the same. They trotted off to meet their next ride.

He was going up near Opelousas. They jumped in. Rayf took center, and Cal took shotgun and slammed the door shut.

"You boys must be from out of town."

"Yeah, we are," said Rayf. "How'd you know?"

"'Cause nobody here in dere right mind'd be out walkin' after dark."

"Why's that?" said Cal.

It seemed like the Ws were now on all lips.

"Werewolves, for one."

"What?" said Cal. "Like this is the twentieth century, man. And there ain't no such thing."

"Da Cajuns call 'em loup-garous. Dey say dat dey can change into many different forms, dat some entice young men as beautiful women and den ..."

"Aw, come on. You're pulling our leg," said Rayf.

"Now why would Ah do dat? Ah don't git no fun on makin' jokes on people Ah ain't never gonna see no more, hear?"

"Yeah, but ..."

"Dey hold balls out on Bayou Goula all da time; mens and womens. Dey got big red eyes and everything, just like a wolf, hair all over an' sharp nails, too. You see one, you t'row a frog at 'em; dey's 'fraid uv 'em. Dat's dee on'y way to chase a loup-garous. Bullets go right trew 'em. Da Cajuns say dat you must lock up inside at night for fear uv da dark spirits dat roam da bayous. Dey say dat da devil has been known to disguise hisself as a flower and have unsuspectin' young chillun pick him up and dat be all she wrote," said the weaver of dark tales in the night.

"Well," said Cal, "I for one do not believe in that stuff. There's no such thing."

"Dey cover theirselves in voodoo grease and come out jest like wolves. Dey fly big bats, big as planes and drop down when you're sleepin', den dey bite cha and drink ya blood and make you a loup-garous. Den soon you, too, be out on Bayou Goula dancin' wit' all d' udda lost souls."

They waited for a laugh, but none came.

Rayf was only able to see his own and Cal's reflections in the dark windshield before him, but not their driver's. So he turned his head this way and that trying to pick up the storyteller's image in the dark glass, but none appeared.

Cal said, "That's a pretty tall tale, mister."

The driver did not smile when he said, "Let it not be said dat you had not been forewarned, neighbor." He pulled over to the side of the road. "Remember, sleep indoors, lest da evil one jump up an' say," then he got real quiet, leaned in close between their faces, where Rayf could have sworn he saw a flash of red deep within his eye when he said, "Ah got cho now!" They flinched. Then he said, "And w'dat, he take away ya soul."

Then, after a dramatic pause, he said, "Last stop, boys."

Cal opened the door. They stepped down from the pickup truck into the pitch blackness. The faint slip of moon came and went behind cloud and tree. Then that driver let out a horrible laugh which stayed with the two guys as he drove off down the road leaving them covered in the deep darkness of a Louisiana bayou night.

The willows and tall cypress trees stood still in the darkness as did the two strangers listening to the new sounds of the night. There were animals out there, some settling down and some just setting out to hunt up their nighttime breakfast. The jungle-like swamps were teeming with life, and then they heard a shrieking howl. They jumped closer together and, wide-eyed, searched the night surrounding them.

With the bravado of the two Musketeers, minus muskets, they faced the night and the road ahead of them once again. They spoke bravely about things of the day—things like food.

It was after ten in the evening when they finally made it to the outskirts of Opelousas, walking all the way. They were filled with visions of big southern meals—wine, beer, coffee, barbecued shrimp, broiled crawfish, oysters on the half shell, fried chicken, and all of the other foods that they had either smelled or had seen advertised in the restaurant windows while coming up that highway. They were having feasting dreams as bright as the dark tales that had been told to them by that driver in the rusty, faded-red pickup truck.

They found a well used public telephone booth alongside the road. Rayf plunged the safety pin through the phone wire, grounded it out against the metal box, got the dial tone, and dialed Opelousas Marie.

Rayf blew on his cupped hands as he held the phone between shoulder and ear. The night was getting cold—colder than they had expected and colder than they were dressed for. Cal danced a keep-warm dance outside the phone booth.

It was a man's voice that answered the phone after five rings, saying, "Hello."

Rayf was taken by surprise, then after a pause he said, "Hi, is, uh, Marie there?"

There was a long silence on the other end. Rayf said again, "Excuse me, but is Marie there?"

"Who is this?" asked the deep voice.

"Uh … Marie said if I was ever in town to …"

"Where you at?" said the phone.

"How do you mean?" said Rayf.

"Well, Ah'd be on'y too happy to come by 'n' pick y'all up." Rayf's mind was in overdrive.

Cal was making signs to Rayf, signs that said: hurry-up, I'm freezing and starving.

"Where you at, boy?" said the phone.

Rayf was silent.

"You down on the highway at that outdoor phone? Where you at?"

Rayf knew, not by the words but by the feeling under those words. He hung up.

He stepped out of the phone booth.

"Well?' said Cal. "Are we eating or what?"

"Holy Christ." And with that Rayf started running.

Cal followed, shouting, "What is it, man?"

"We are in big trouble, man."

Still running, Cal said, "What? Who?"

"Her old man just answered the phone. And he didn't sound that old."

"So why're we running?"

"Cause he knew I was at that phone booth—probably the only one in town."

"Holy shit!" said Cal as he left Rayf in the dust.

They ran for several hundred yards. Then Cal jumped into a clump of bushes beside the road. Rayf followed.

In the dark, they sat silently, waiting and watching each and every car that went past. They stayed there for at least an hour before taking to the road once again.

They walked quickly, quietly, and very far from the road. And whenever they heard a car, they jumped back into the bushes. They kept this up for another hour.

As they walked on in this manner, the night grew darker.

"Let's run," said Rayf. "Just to be on the safe side. And anyway, running'll keep us warm."

They jogged through the outskirts of that bayou town and soon turned left onto US 190 West; here they continued at a quick trot for a few more blocks before slowing down to a fast-paced walk for two more miles. And now the sweat that once warmed them chilled them to the bone. It was here that they started thinking that perhaps they would freeze to death before this night was through with them.

At Lawtell they took a left turn onto Highway 35 South and walked further into the night."

"I think you really fucked up, Cal."

"Me?! You're the one who got us into this mess. Me!"

"I mean in New Orleans, with that voodoo doctor, when you pulled that magic charm out of his hands, and ..."

"Now you're startin' to believe in that shit?!"

"What about Soapy and Ali Baba? I mean, I saw those two guys crash into Biscayne Bay with my own two eyes; and now they're alive? Don't you see the connection?"

"Between them and voodoo? No, I do not."

They walked on and on down that dark, gloomy road.

"They could be zombies," said Rayf. "I mean why not? Stranger things've happened."

"Yeah, like what? Getting picked up by Martians?"

"No. Like this one story that I heard where this guy's young bride dies, so he goes down to the islands, probably the same island where that voodoo doctor comes from …"

"Knock it off, Rayf. I'm tellin' ya, knock it off!"

"What's a matter? I thought you didn't believe in the supernatural."

"I don't."

"So then this guy asks this voodoo guy to bring his young wife, who died, back to life …"

"… and she comes back from the grave all dead and fucked-up, right?"

"… with skin rotting and eyes falling out and grave-slime all over …"

"Yeah, I saw that comic book, too," said Cal.

The night grew darker and the giant live oaks with their Spanish-moss tresses waved ever so gently, shimmering like ghostly, lace-webbed veils in the all-consuming night.

Rayf raved on.

He talked about the possibilities of werewolves and vampires; he was now certain that Opelousas Marie was a vampire. "You heard that guy: 'they disguise themselves and turn themselves into …'"

"Maybe she turned you into one," said Cal. "And if you are, and you fuck around with my neck, there's really gonna be some big trouble out here. I'm tellin' ya, you fuck around with me, I will kill you with my bare hands, I swear."

"Man, I wouldn't bite your neck with Soapy's teeth."

This, then, was the manner in which they entertained themselves: scaring the hell into each other with ghostly tales and threats of vengeance, while deep within the recesses of their individual minds they wondered about this woman, Marie, and the man, and the telephone number that she had given Rayf and the sounds out there in the all-encompassing night. Was all this merely a figment of their imaginations fired up by hunger, exhaustion, and freezing weather? Or was this truly a separate reality?

The night was totally dark; so dark that at a hairpin bend in the road, they couldn't even see their hands, which they held up right in front of their faces. They stopped telling tales and, instead, listened only to their footfalls and to the sounds of the night—sounds out there in the swamps. Was that not the roar of a bull gator or a ...? Now they were positive that if the spirits did not get them, nature surely would.

Then they saw it while rounding another bend in the road, the most beautiful sight in their travels so far. There, on the opposite side of this rural highway was an all-night gas station. They broke rank and hauled ass towards the welcome sight. Rayf got there first.

There was a lone, lanky kid sitting inside the cold gas station office with his feet propped up on a dilapidated wooden desk. He was listening to a radio.

Rayf opened the door. A clanking cow bell warned of his entrance.

Rayf looked up towards the sound, then to the kid who was just now slowly turning his head in Rayfs direction. The first thing Rayf noticed about the kid were his eyes; those eyes were as black as the night, so dark that within those deep black orbs Rayf could now see Cal entering this dank office right behind him The kid did not speak. He just stared. And Rayf saw mixed in with that black shiny eye a hint of red. *Perhaps*, thought Rayf, *it's from that sign in the window reflecting in them*. The kid said, "You two want gas?"

"No," said Rayf. "We're freezin' out there."

"So?"

"So we need a place to stay," said Rayf.

"No car?"

"No, we're walkin'."

"And?" said the kid.

"We'd like to sleep in here if it's all right with you," said Rayf.

"Well, it ain't," said the kid.

"Oh, man," said Cal, "you don't understand. We're freezing out there. And if we don't sleep inside I am afraid ..."

"This ain't no hotel," said the sickly yellow complexioned kid.

"We realize that," said Cal. "But we're not dressed for this weather."

"You two don't look like you are dressed for any weather; you boys runnin' from the law?"

"No," said Cal. "We're headin' to Dallas. Please let us sleep in that corner. We won't bother you, I swear."

The kid looked them over from head to toe: their long-sleeved cotton shirts were filthy, as were their dungarees, which hung torn and loose. Their shoes, worn and scuffed, were as far as he could tell, made for dress and not for walking. He stared at them with his coal-black eyes for what seemed like an eternity before saying, "You ken sleep in the garage, on the floor," and with his chin motioned towards the wooden glass-paneled door that led to the garage in the adjoining room.

They thanked him, opened the door, and walked into the garage.

The kid went back to listening to the radio and staring out into the darkness.

Rayf found a large piece of cardboard in the corner of the room. He dragged it over near the four-hole Buick and placed it down on the cold, concrete floor. The flattened cardboard box served as a mat; it was big enough for both guys to sleep on. They lay down on it and balled themselves up, back towards back, into fetal positions.

They could not get warm. They rattled and chattered right there on that cardboard mat which lay upon that cold, concrete floor next to that old Buick parked right there in that frigid garage.

Every once in a while, the kid would check in on them to make sure that they weren't stealing anything; but as the night wore on, he became more accustomed to the two freezing bodies in the adjacent room and soon stopped checking. One time during the night when the gas station kid went outside to gas up a car, Rayf and Cal hopped into that Buick—Rayf, with knees meeting chest, balled himself up on the back seat, Cal doing the same on the front seat.

The last thing Rayf thought before passing out on the soft fabric of that back seat was we are still alive and, with any luck, we just might make it to feel the warmth and see the sun of another day.

~ 15 ~

SALLY FORTH

The gas station kid woke them up early in the dark morning. They greeted the Louisiana day sans sun.

Half asleep, they turned two cold thumbs southward on rural Route 35. They got several rides that took them in the general direction of Lafayette.

At Lafayette the country started to change. The bayous were now thinning out and with them went the French heritage which continued to diminish until it too disappeared completely, along with Acadia Parish.

At Rayne, they met up with US 90 West and hooked a right. They crossed the Sabine River into Texas at Orange, where a road sign read: El Paso 922 miles.

"Texas," said Cal, "is one hell of a big state."

"Glad we're not going to El Paso," said Rayf.

They were losing ground fast; the more they covered the worse it got. Hunger was their constant companion. Food was all they could think about as they hopped from pickup truck to pickup truck playing the five-W game as best they could.

Not far from the Sabine River, a one-armed black man in a beat-up pickup truck offered them a ride.

"Ah'm going a little past Beaumont. Any help?"

"Thanks," said Cal. They jumped in.

The driver, with his one good arm, pointed out the window to an area where, as he put it, "Oil men has chewed up dee earth." He then said, "Ah'm a Thicketeer."

"What's that?" said Rayf.

"Dat's me. Ah was born in da Thicket."

"What's the Thicket?" said Rayf.

"Dat," said the driver, nodding out the window.

"You mean all of those oil wells out there," said Cal.

"No. They is what's replaced da Thicket. Use to be millions uv acres uv trees out dere."

All they could see now were bulldozed dirt roads, ripped-up trees, and oil derricks in the distance.

"Use to be Texas black bear and red wolf out dere, too. Most uv 'em are gone now, dough. No place for 'em to hide, I guess," said the one-armed driver. "Oil and chemical plants taken over now. We is at the southernmost end uv da Big, or should Ah say was, da Big Thicket. Jest 'bout all logged out now."

"Is that right," said a drowsy Rayf.

"Yep. I'm a lumber man, ma self. Born jest north a here, south uv Saratoga. See dis arm? One day, me 'n' ma bro was drivin' north in a pickup truck, jest like dis one, when a lumber rig headin' south jack-knifes in front uv us and we gets broad sided. Damn, when I pulls ma arm back in from da window, like dis," and he pulled his left arm in, "it was a full eighteen inches shorter," finished the driver, laughing and waving his stump around the cab.

Rayf looked from the human stump to the scenery beyond the window. Out there he saw a clump of trees with roots drying in the sun.

"Is that how they log down here?" said Rayf, pointing to the carcass of a rotting tree.

"Hell no! Dem's is vandals, usin' bulldozers. Some people tryin' to prevent the conservationist from turnin' dis inta a fancy-assed national park. Kain't rightly blame 'em. We's gotta make a livin,' too, ya know."

"Which ones are the vandals?" said Cal, looking out at the desolation.

"Anybody's guess: Land developers, oil men, hired killers like da one dat got J.F.K. Hell if Ah know."

The term "hired killers" got Rayf and Cal to share a look; they had to keep moving.

Rayf continued looking out at the thousands of tree stumps and dead trees, whose only defense was to quit processing oxygen, a fact of which he was not even aware. As he looked out at the wholesale destruction of this natural resource, he just felt sad and sick to his stomach and he didn't even know why.

"We is at the easternmost part of da Golden Triangle," said the driver.

"Yippee," said Cal under his breath.

"Port Arthur's to da south and Beaumont's in da west."

Beaumont ... hmm, sounds familiar, thought Rayf.

"What's so golden about it?" said Cal.

"Used ta be lumber, now it's oil. Damn, on the Alabama and Coushatta Indian Reservation up on 190 jest north uv here, dey got over t'ree hun'r'd acres of primitive forest. Now if we could on'y get our hands on dat, it be sure ta give us a couple years more work," said the driver.

"That makes sense," said Cal, circling his index finger to his own temple.

"Know how Spanish moss got into da Thicket?" said the natural born story teller, eager to spin his yarns.

"No," said Rayf.

"Well, ya see, when da North and da South Winds got into a fight, da North Wind lost all uv its beard in da fight, and it got scattered all over da area ... and dat is how we got Spanish moss down here." And then he told them about how, "Some of da best-tastin' whiskey is bootlegged out dere in da Big Thicket. Dere are also magnificent magnolias way back in dere, some being over one thousand years old. And dere was a redbud tree, so called da Judas tree 'cause its flowers makes it look like it's bleedin'. And next to da Judas is da dogwood; folks round here call dat one da crucifixion tree, 'cause in da center of each flower is a blood-stained nail print wit' da likeness of da image of da crown of thorns; Could be," he continued, "jest could be dat good and evil is fightin' it out back dere in da Thicket. I mean, why not, eh?"

The driver rambled on.

Rayf looked out the window toward the Thicket and wished the Volksman back there in Morgan City all the luck in the world, because as far as he could see, it would take a hell of a lot of luck to put an end to this wanton destruction.

Nearing Beaumont, Rayf remembered why that town sounded so familiar. It was because of Buddy Gann, a guy he knew from high school who had gotten married, moved out to Texas, and who was now supposedly involved in the oil business, or something like that. And if his memory served him well, Buddy lived in, of all places, Beaumont, Texas.

The one-armed driver, still spinning tales, rambled into Beaumont. He dropped them off at the Greyhound Bus Station, wished them good luck, and with his one good arm waved good-bye through the paneless rear window. Weakly, they waved back.

Rayf got to a telephone, dialed operator, got information, and hit the ceiling when he was given "Mr. Gann's" phone number. He dialed, and within two rings it was answered.

"Hello," said Buddy, with his unmistakable, flat Jersey City accent; a sweet sound for sore ears and an empty stomach.

"Buddy … It's me, Rayf."

"Rayf!?" said the voice, searching through his memory banks, and then, "Rayf! How the hell are you? Wow, what a charge hearing from you!"

"Buddy, I'm in Beaumont."

"Down here!? Get outta here! What the fuck are you doing down here in this hell hole?"

"I'm calling you."

"This is too good. Where the hell are ya? I can't believe this: Ray Falcone in Texas. Hot shit! Where are you?"

"I'm at the Greyhound Station."

"What are you doing there?"

"Praying for a bus."

"Look, I'll be right over. Oh, man its great hearing your voice. I'm tellin' ya, this is unbelievable. Look, just stay put. I'll be right there," he hung up.

Rayf walked out of the phone booth and over to Cal who was sitting on the curb, holding up his head with both hands. "I got him. He's coming to pick us up."

"I'll believe it when I see it," said a fast fading Cal.

Within fifteen minutes Buddy pulled up in a shit brown Plymouth. "Hey you fuckin' bum," said Buddy as he jumped out of the car and hugged Rayf. "You look horrible."

"Thanks," said Rayf, breaking the clinch.

"Who's that?" said Buddy, suspiciously regarding the very slow-moving Cal.

"Tommy Califano. You know him … Cal!? From downtown!?"

"Doesn't look familiar."

"He's changed a little," said Rayf, "Lost a few pounds … you know."

Looking him over, "Hey, if he's with you, then he's OK in my book. You look like you're starving, fer Christ sakes."

"Really!?" said Rayf. "That's funny; we had a shoe for breakfast."

"Still the same old kidder, eh? Well, you're in luck. The old lady is makin' some of her famous green split-pea soup. You into that?"

"Buddy, in a very short while I will be into cardboard. Take us to your soup, please."

"Good. Come on!"

They piled into the Plymouth and off they drove towards Buddy's casa. Buddy's brand new split level ranch house was on a cul de sac in a brand new subdivision.

"What happens if you ever get drunk around here?" said Rayf.

"Wha'd'ya mean by that?" said Buddy, as they pulled into his driveway.

"All of the houses look the same."

"No they don't, not when you get used to them they don't. Look, see that statue near the mail box, the little brown cement Mexican guy leading that little cement burro?! That's one way I know that this is my house. Come on in. Mary can't wait to meet ya. I always talk about ya."

They followed him into the very cool air–conditioned interior of his split level ranch house, and there, in front of the television, sat his wife holding and bottle feeding an infant.

"Mary, remember I told you all about Rayf, the crazy bastard who I knew from when I was a kid?"

She turned her head very slowly and gave the three men a frozen glare. Everyone but Buddy saw it.

"Well," said Buddy, in true Ed McMahan announcer fashion, "here he is!" Mary did something with her chin that said, "Big deal."

Right then and there Rayf knew he was in no-man's land.

"And this here is Tommy, another guy from the neighborhood." No response.

"Hey, I was tellin' 'em all about your famous, green split-pea soup. Wait'll you taste it Rayf, you're gonna love it. You were makin' some, weren't ya hon?"

Now for the first time she spoke, "The cans are in the cupboard, and the pot is on the stove. Help yourself." And with that, she turned back to her TV game show.

"Right," said Buddy as he led the two guys down into the split level kitchen.

Everything in this house was new; it smelled perfect. It was the American Dream answered—a house of their own on the doorstep to the great American plains just downwind of a chemical plant.

Buddy opened up two cans of split-pea soup, dumped the contents into a pot, added the required amount of water, and turned on the electric range.

"Electric?" said Rayf.

"Yeah, cooks great. So, how ya been?"

"Okay, I guess. We've been on the road for a few days now."

"Where y'all headin'?" said Buddy, slipping into his recently acquired Texan drawl.

"Dallas," said Cal.

Mary turned around to look at the three guys near the electric range and yelled, "Don't burn the pot."

"Don't worry, honey. I won't."

There was something about the way he said "honey" that made Rayf think that maybe, just maybe, this marriage was merely a mirage.

"Dallas," said Buddy wistfully as he stirred the green split-pea soup on the electric range. "Hey, do me a favor when you get there, OK?"

"What's that, Buddy?" said Rayf.

"Shake Jack Ruby's hand for me if you get the chance, will ya? The guy's a hero if you ask me," said Buddy, stirring the soup.

"We'll do that, Buddy," said Rayf as he watched Buddy pour the hot soup into the new bowls.

"He used a .38 caliber Colt Cobra, ya know."

"That right?" said Rayf.

"Yep."

"So, you're a fan, eh?"

"Damn right," said Buddy as he set the hot bowls of green split-pea soup down onto the brand new yellow Formica and chrome kitchen table and laid out the all-new silverware spoons next to each bowl.

They gobbled up the first bowl and were working on the second one when Buddy, very quietly, said to Rayf, "Hey, listen, if you ever run into a guy out there in your travels who has been using my name to swindle people, let me know, OK? I am pissed off. I am tellin' ya, guy's ruinin' my rep. You do that for me, 'K?"

"What do you do, Bud?"

"Sales. I buy and sell old silver. Just keep an eye out, 'K?"

Rayf drained the bowl of soup and said, "Right." He then poured himself another bowl. Cal did the same.

After three bowls, they burped. Mary looked back from her game show and shot the two pigs a daggered stare. Rayf waved back an "excuse me" sign; she turned her head on him, stuffed the bottle back into the child's mouth, and resumed her televiewing.

"Your kid?" said Rayf very quietly.

"Yeah, that's Buddy Junior. Chip off the old block. Well," said Buddy, standing up, "all done?"

"Yeah," said Rayf. "Why?"

"Then I'll get y'all back to the Greyhound—wouldn't want you to miss your bus."

"But ..."started Rayf.

On that "but," Mary turned around and threw another one of her now infamous daggers. Rayf caught it right between the eyes.

"Right," said Rayf as he and Cal both slid their new, chrome-plated, plastic-seat-covered chairs away from the new table and said their good-byes to Mary and Buddy Junior.

Outside they all piled into the shit brown Plymouth and headed back towards the Greyhound Station. Rayf said, "Take us to the western end of town."

"But what about the bus?"

"We're hitchhiking."

"Oh."

They drove on silently for a while. Rayf felt a whole lot better as he looked over toward his pussy-whipped ex-friend who was leading a very mysterious life to be sure.

"Man," said Buddy, "I got this Mexican woman over in the barrio ... oh, she is good! Me and my wife, we don't make it that much anymore since Junior came."

"I see," said Rayf.

"Hey, the women are easy down here, man. Wait'll you see. I mean it."

"Maybe after we get washed up and all, then we'll go and look for some," said Rayf. The irony eluded Buddy completely.

"Yeah, you do that. By the way, stay clear of the wet-backs."

"What's that?"

"That's a term we use for Mexicans."

"But I thought you're makin' it with one."

"Yeah, the women; they're cool. But not the men—it's the men we don't like down here."

"Oh! I see. Thanks for the tip."

"They're like the spooks back home. Dig?"

"Dig," said a disinterested Rayf.

The Plymouth pulled up on the green, flat-landed outskirts of Beaumont. Buddy said, "This is it."

"Thanks, Bud."

"Think nothing of it, Rayf. Anything for a friend."

And just as Rayf was about to step out of the car, he turned around to face the driver and said, "Hey Bud, could you spare a couple of bucks?"

Buddy's face dropped, then picked up again as he searched his pockets. "Damn! I left my wallet in my other pants. I'm really sorry guys."

"That's OK, Bud. Thanks for the green split-pea soup, man. You were a lifesaver." He slammed the door closed.

"Hey, if you're ever down around the Golden Triangle again, y'all best stop by, hear?"

"Right," said Rayf.

"And y'all watch out for those Mexicans," hollered Buddy as he made a slow U-turn, heading for his split-level ranch house or the barrio. Rayf wasn't quite sure.

"Strange guy, your friend," said Cal, as they watched the brown car get smaller and smaller until it finally disappeared into Beaumont.

"Something's up with that guy," said Rayf.

"No!" said Cal. "Really!?"

***

With a stomach full of green split-pea soup, they felt much better and hitched with newfound gusto. Westward ho!

There was only one thing wrong with this picture. Dallas was north; next stop, Houston.

Several miles before Houston they realized their mistake, but figured "what the hell," they were already halfway to San Antonio, so why not keep going? Fate had other plans.

A Mexican guy in a dusty pickup truck picked them up and started complaining that, "Dees ees not dee American Southwest at all, but actually dee Mexican Northeast." They sympathized with him as he proceeded to tell them that these myths were perpetuated by the "stinkin' Anglos" in order to cover up their own evil deeds. They smiled and nodded along with this guy, but really did not care in the least about Anglos, Frenchmen, Mexicans, or any other men for that matter. They were totally disenfranchised anyway, and what the hell good would it do if they did care. All they knew was that they were dirty, dry, and hungry once again.

This last fact they shared with the friendly Mexican, who told them that they needed to see a little more of his Texas and that this would soon help them forget about their hunger. "Dees great state is more den just beef steak," he said. Then he told them to hang on, as he peeled out.

They crossed the Colorado River on US 90 and went south on Highway 71 past Garwood and into El Campo, and then west once again on Highway 59, where the Gulf of Mexico was less than sixty miles to the south.

The hombre then continued on into Victoria, where Rayf had a vision of a girl he once knew. *Or is she, too,* thought Rayf, *just a mirage, as perhaps all of life is,* as it flashed before his weary eyes. Outside Victoria, they started ripping through a seemingly random network of roads and highways that passed through towns by the names of Cuero, Pandora, and La Vernia; here the driver said, "If it were not for us Mexicans killing off most of dee Apaches and settling dees area, your people would not have had it so easy. We taught dem how to conserve, share, and treasure water; and do you know what dey did? Dey poisoned, captured, fought, killed, diverted, and laid claim to dee wells; dey used dee water as a power, dese Anglo savages. We show dem how to live out here and what thanks do we get? Manifest Destiny, dat's what we get."

Rayf and Cal kept nodding; they were well-trained in the protocol of the road guest: agree.

They drove through the town of Hedwig, and there up ahead was a sign that read: Fort Sam Houston.

"Tell me, now," said the driver. "Ees dees not Mexico?"

They had gone from green, flat, and wooded lands in east Texas into dry, hardpan, baked brown earth with clumps of sage and tumbleweed to the south. They were now entering a city that could very well have been, as far as they could tell, Mexico City.

"Are we really in Mexico?" said Cal.

"No, dat ees just dee point. We settled dis area first; dis ees San Antonio. Remember dee Alamo?" said the driver.

"Yeah," said Cal. "It was a battle cry."

"Well, we won dat battle. But dee school books tell you dat it was a patriotic victory for da United States. Bullsheet! It was a few rich gringo landlords fighting for dee land dat dey stole from us. We paid dem back but good."

"I see," said Rayf. "Now let me see if you understand me, OK?"

"Shoot."

"We are starving. Do you understand that? Mucho hungry-o."

"Why didn't you say dat een dee first place? You should check into dee Salvation Army. Dose people, dey will take good care of you."

And then Rayf and Cal said that they really did care about his people's plight and that they'd love to join in his fight, or revolution, or whatever it was that he was up to, and that maybe tonight, right after dinner, if there was a special place where guerrillas could sign up, they would be happy to do so. This is when the driver thought that perhaps he had picked up a couple of locos. He kept quiet, suspiciously eyeing his two passengers until he dropped them off in front of the Alamo, where his last words were "It was here dat General Santana kicked your asses, man." And then he was gone.

Here they were in San Antonio, the latest but surely not the last two desert rats to come crawling into town. Standing on the sidewalk they looked up and saw the Lone Star flag flying high above the mission.

Now they noticed a very strange sight. Standing there on the curb, pulling at his hair, was another wild man. This one was ranting and raving. They figured it had to be the climate, all these nuts. Then the man approached them with fire in his eye and yelled, "Look at what they did! Jest look at what they did!" He pointed to the ground.

Rayf looked down to the sidewalk and then back to the pointing madman and said, "Excuse me, but do you know the way to the nearest Salvation Army?"

The man just said, "Look at what they did! Somebody painted the sidewalk red! Some communists have painted the Alamo's sidewalk red!"

Rayf and Cal, having never seen that sidewalk, had no idea what color it was yesterday or the day before. And besides, they didn't care.

It was Cal this time who asked the raving maniac if he knew the way to the nearest Salvation Army. The guy did not pay any attention to their questioning, but just kept on ranting about the color of the sidewalk. Rayf thought that it looked a lot like the color of blood, the same color that was spilt all over this land, but he didn't say that, for that would only further incense this patriot, and he sure as hell did not wish to have any of his precious red fluid spilt on that sidewalk. So they left the man to his calling.

They walked on asking other people for directions. Eventually one woman pointed out the way and they found it. *Why*, thought Rayf, *have we not thought of this before?*

***

All she wore were fancy-cut cowgirl boots. She jabbed her heels into the fleshy sides of her pony-man as they played horsy in this ground-floor room at the Dallas Ramada Inn.

The bronco, with one slinged arm, reeled back on his knees. She grabbed tight about his neck, squishing her full bosom against his back.

"Woa, horsy!"

Neighing, he rolled over on top of her. She giggled out loud and thought to herself, *Don't these Eastern boys ever come up with an original idea?* The phone rang.

"Shit," said the horsy in his jockey shorts, as he crawled over, picked up the phone, and said, "What?!"

"What da hell are you doin' over dere? It's like eight o'clock!"

"OK ... OK," said Soapy into the phone while looking at his gold-plated wristwatch. "I got caught up in a little business, Babs." Now, with a wink to cowgirl May, he said into the phone, "Hold your freakin' horses. I'll be right dere." May giggled as he rammed the phone back into its cradle. "Fuck!" said Soapy as he stood up. "Gotta go, May."

"What's a matter, Mister Horsy?" said the pouting cowgirl.

"Gotta relieve my partner."

He pulled on his pants, yanked out a wad of bills from his pocket, peeled off a few, and handed them to her, saying "Here, this should cover it."

May stuffed the money into her just-pulled-on panties and said, "Well suga, you got ma numba, now don't chew be no stranger now, hear?"

"Yeah, I'll give ya a call later on. Now buzz off. I gotta get to woik." May dressed as quickly as she had peeled. Now she was half out the door kissing her right index finger and blowing it to Soapy who was now sitting on the edge of the bed tying his right shoelace. "Ta ta, big boy."

He nodded to her. Then behind the slamming door, she was gone.

***

They sang hymns for their supper, a supper that consisted of hard bread, soup, and coffee, all black.

They showered and were shown to their bunks, which were made up with clean white sheets and pillows. The room slept fifty men. Most of the bunks were occupied. Rayf and Cal sat on their own bunks, facing each other. Sitting right next to Cal, on his bunk, was Hobo Jack, a guy that befriended them. They watched Hobo Jack as he rolled three cigarettes, one for each man. He passed out the thin, uneven, white cylinders to the two waiting men and then set all three butts to smoking with a wooden match that he struck to life on the lower outside of his right jean-covered thigh.

They pulled in the Bull Durham smoke and relaxed. They were inside, taking a time out from the Wild West outside.

Hobo Jack told them all kinds of stories—stories that were meant to bolster their courage and self confidence. "Them's are the thangs ya kain't buy in no five and dime store ya know. A man all alone on the road has got ta be able to count on hisself."

He told them that he had traveled all over this great country and then some. Even up to Canada and down into old Mexico where he smoked much loco weed, a very wonderful and exhilarating experience to be sure. He just couldn't understand "... why such a little plant could be the cause of so much trouble with the lawmakers. Hell, it only gets you high, and in the morning you ain't even hung over. Sheet, you know our Constitution ga-run-tees our right to happiness, don't cha?"

"Right," said Cal, "it guarantees the right to life, liberty, and the pursuit of happiness."

"Boy's got hisself a brain there." Now he looked around the room as if he were going to tell them a big secret.

Rayf had the best view of Hobo Jack, since Jack was sitting on Cal's bunk. He thought, *Shit, he looks old, but young at the same time*. He was clean shaven and wore clothes that looked almost pressed. This hobo kept himself neat, trim, and fit. His black hair was cut short and slicked back, and his teeth, which were all there, had only the slightest trace of tobacco coloring on them.

When Hobo Jack caught Rayf giving him the once-over, he said, "Boys, I am a hobo by choice. This is the only life that suits me. See, when one lives the life that one truly chooses, then one is totally at home wherever one goes, whether it be on the inside of some Sally with a bunch of other road apples, like right now with y'all, or under a bridge all by your lonesome; you are always at home. And remember, home is where the heart is. Now I don't know about you boys, but mine," he said tapping his chest, "is right here." He broke out into a gale of laughter. The boys all fed and clean, laughed along with him. Then Hobo Jack leaned in, all three heads met in the middle of the aisle, and he whispered, "What say we step outside. Got somethin' I'd like to show y'all."

He knew the layout of the place and led them out a side door that took them into an adjacent parking lot. He jammed the door open with a stick. They were now beneath a wide expanse of Texas nighttime sky with millions of stars blinking away in the void overhead.

Hobo Jack looked the place over as a killer or a robber would. He nodded in the direction of an adjoining, faded, red brick building. And there laying on the ground on his left side, facing that old brick wall, was a long-haired American Indian. The brave was drunk and slapping his rear-end as though he were riding a pony across the endless plains of his dreams. Hobo Jack shrugged him off and, with squinty eye, pulled out of his shirt pocket a thick cigarette. He drew them in close, held up this fat joint between their three heads and said, "Here it is boys. Got me a little reefer. Care to imbibe?"

They nodded. Rayf looked back at the drunken Indian.

Hobo Jack lit up the joint sucked in a deep, lungful of smoke, and then put the smoking joint directly in between Rayf's gaze and the horseless horseman. Rayf focused on the joint, took hold of it, and breathed in deep before passing it on to Cal. From there, on it went from hand to hand with a regular rhythm that was only broken by the occasional need to sleeve-dry a wet lip here and there.

Hobo Jack said, "Hold in the smoke for as long as possible, and release it through the nostrils ... slowly. That'll help get ya even higher." They did like he said and, sure enough, they got high.

Cal was the first one to break out with the giggles. At first he thought it was because of this scene: three grown men in a vacant lot near a Sally, under the black San Antonio nighttime sky, holding down the sweet-tasting smoke of a marijuana cigarette. It was contagious. Rayf and Hobo Jack started into laughing, too.

The cool night was getting colder. It was time to retire.

The Indian rode on.

As they negotiated the concrete stairs that led up to the second floor dormitory, the world seemed friendlier—for them anyway.

Once in the dorm, Rayf and Cal felt as if all eyes were on them. They walked down the center of this long room between bunks on their right and left.

Back at their area, Cal burst out laughing. Rayf joined in almost telepathically. Hobo Jack just grinned and nodded at these two neophytes. He waited for the laughter to subside before asking, "Where you boys been?"

"We," said Rayf, wiping tears, "were at the Alamo today."

"So you went to see where big Jim Bowie and the boys bought the farm, eh?"

"Jim Bowie was at the Alamo?" said Rayf.

"Yep," said Hobo Jack, "Defending his one million acres of prime Texas real estate. He got real estate all right, six feet of it. Where y'all headin' tomorrow?"

"Dallas," said Cal.

"Why y'all goin' up to the Big D?"

"We're going to see where J.F.K. got killed," said Cal.

"You boys ghouls or somethin'?"

"No," said Cal. "It's history."

"I see," said Hobo Jack, now sitting on Cal's bunk facing the two. He looked around the room, as was his custom before speaking. They thought this was funny—Hobo Jack getting ready to share another one of his big secrets.

"Hey," said Hobo Jack in a harsh whisper, as he leaned in, "Wanna see sumthin?"

Rayf and Cal cracked up.

"Well?" said Hobo Jack. "Wanna?"

"Yeah," said Cal wiping away his tears, "Wha' cha got?"

Hobo Jack reached into his back pocket, pulled out a folded piece of paper, looked around the room once more, and then unfolded it.

"What's that?" said Rayf, fighting back a laugh.

He held out the paper in such a way that only they could see it.

"What is it?" said Cal, a little more sober.

"What's it look like?"

"A Wanted poster," said Cal, "... of ... of J.F.K.!"

"Ah know who it is," said Hobo Jack yanking it back and looking around the room; now in a whisper, "Look at it and be quiet. OK?"

"OK," said Cal, returning the whisper. He took the poster from Hobo Jack.

It showed President Kennedy as a wanted criminal, like the ones seen in the post office. Under J.F.K.'s full-face and profile photos were the charges. Cal started reading the charges just loud enough for Rayf to hear.

"WANTED FOR TREASON. This Man is wanted for treasonous activities against the United States:

1. Betraying the Constitution (which he swore to uphold): He is turning the sovereignty of the United States over to the communist-controlled United Nations. He is betraying our friends (Cuba, Katanga, Portugal) and befriending our enemies (Russia, Yugoslavia, Poland).

2. He has been WRONG on innumerable issues affecting the security of the United States (U.N.—Berlin wall—Missile ..."

"I guess he meant Missile there," said Cal.

"What?" said Rayf.

"He misspelled Missile."

"Go on, for crissakes," said Rayf.

"Hold your horses," said Cal. "Now where was I? Right: Missile removal—Cuba—Wheat deals—Test Ban Treaty, etc.)

3. He has been lax in enforcing Communist Regulation laws ..."

Cal stopped reading and looked at Hobo Jack in disbelief. Rayf took the poster from Cal and continued reading:

"4. He has given support and encouragement to the Communist-inspired racial riots.

5. He has illegally invaded a sovereign State with federal troops."

"He sure likes the word sovereign," said Rayf.

"Read," said Cal.

"Relax, man."

6. He has consistently ..."

"Spelled that one wrong, too," said Cal leaning over Rayf's shoulder.

"Stop interrupting, will ya? I lost my place. Where was I? Okay, here it is:

He has consistently appointed Anti-Christians to Federal office: Upholds the Supreme Court in its Anti-Christian rulings. Aliens and known communists abound in Federal offices.

7. He has been caught in fantastic LIES to the American People (including personal ones like his previous marriage ..."

"He spelled that one wrong, too. Right?" said Hobo Jack.

"Yeah," said Rayf. "But he got the last words right: '... and divorce)'."

Rayf handed the poster back to Hobo Jack and said quietly, "What's this all about?"

"Got me. I was passin' through Dallas about a week ago and saw a whole shit load a these plastered all over the place. So Ah took me one fer a souvenir."

"This some sort of a joke?" said Cal.

"Hell of a joke if it is. He's dead ain't he?" said Hobo Jack, licking a freshly made cigarette. "So, y'all goin' up ta Dallas, are ya?"

They didn't answer.

Hobo Jack lit up a cigarette stub, sucked in some smoke, and folded the Wanted poster into his back pocket.

After a long silence, Cal said, "Yeah. Yeah, we're goin' up ta Dallas."

Someone yelled, "Lights out!"

In an instant it was dark and all that could be seen was the glow of Hobo Jack's tailor-made. He took one last drag.

~ 16 ~

THE GAUNTLET

Five days had passed since they had first heard the news about J.F.K. The Florida Everglades were just a memory to them now as the Big D skyscape continued to grow on the plains before them.

Rayf, from the back seat of their present ride, watched the approaching Dallas skyline and thought back to the last conversation that they had had with Hobo Jack.

He had joined them for the early morning hymn and later in the dining hall for breakfast, which consisted of oatmeal, black coffee, toast, and orange juice. Two meals in a row; they were on a roll.

They told Hobo Jack that they had traveled over 2,500 miles. He said, "Hell, that ain't nothin' but a skip to a stepper." Then he asked them if they had ever heard of the Eastern philosophies.

Cal answered, "Yeah, we're from Jersey City."

The hobo enjoyed that joke very much.

"I'm talkin' about karma, man—ever heared of it?"

"No," said Cal between mouthfuls of oatmeal.

"It's kinda like, you git what you give. Dig?"

"Nope," said Rayf, swigging his orange juice.

"Like in order to get a plant to grow, you first gotta sow the seed, see?"

Rayf stopped eating and looked across to Hobo Jack sitting on the opposite side of this very long table that was filled with black, brown, white, yellow, red, young, old, healthy, and sick people. Their common bond: down on their luck. Rayf thought that he had just heard Hobo Jack say something, but he wasn't quite sure what. It was similar to hearing a mosquito buzzing around in the dark, even though you heard it, you still didn't know where it was or how big it was. But one thing you did know— you were going to get bit.

"It's like cause and effect," said Hobo Jack, gulping his coffee.

"You mean like one of Newton's laws?" said Cal.

"Now you got it, boy! It's like whatever you do, good or bad, has got to come back to ya. It's a universal law. Dig?"

Rayf finished his cereal and got up to get another cup of coffee; he would need this caffeine for that long road north.

The last thing he recalled Hobo Jack saying, and laughing at after breakfast, was, "Remember boys: All's well that ends well, and all ends. Well?!" And the first thing Rayf noticed about the Dallas skyline was that it sat right out there in the middle of nowhere and nothing. The land around it was dry, black, and barren.

The last ride in their odyssey so far was from a young mother. Two small boys bounced around in the shotgun seat like kernels of popcorn. Rayf and Cal were in the rear.

Rayf thought, *Maybe this woman has a few screws loose to actually pick us up.* True, they were showered and shaved, but to Rayf, Cal still looked pretty bad.

The housewife told them about the sadness that all of Dallas felt for the terrible crime that had been committed by "one right-wing madman" and that her beautiful "Athens of the alfalfa fields" would rise above this senseless crime and, in the end, overcome.

The children in the front seat took an immediate liking to Rayf, who tousled their hair and spoke kid-talk to them. Cal, on the other hand, stared solemnly out the window towards the flat plains that seemed to go on forever; he was truly under the spell of history. It was becoming, unbeknownst even to him, a sacred moment.

"You got kids?" said the lady to Rayf.

"No. I'm an uncle two times over, though."

"My boys' got an uncle."

"Yeah we do," said the five year old. "He's in the Army. Ain't that right, maw!"

"Yes he is darlin'."

"He's in Vi-et ... Nam. Ain't that how you say it, maw?"

"Yes it is, sweetie."

"Hey, quick, look at that cow," said Rayf.

The kernels looked out the closed window.

"That ain't no cow, silly," said the seven year old. "That's a steer. An' anyway, that one's a bull." Both kids giggled.

The driver lady smiled back to Rayf. He winked.

They continued on US 71 North.

Dallas, outside the windshield—like a dream—grew larger with each passing mile.

They were now inside the dream, driving down Main Street.

Rayf saw an old gray turreted courthouse on his left. And when they turned right onto Houston, she said, "This is the same exact route J.F.K. took just five short days ago."

She pointed across the triangle park plaza to the last building on the street and said, "That's the Texas School Book Depository."

There, on top of that old red brick building was a huge Hertz rent-a-car sign with a giant electric clock that read 4 p.m.

"Oswald was up on the sixth floor," she said.

Cal stretched his neck to get a better view.

She pulled up to the corner of Elm Street and stopped. Cal, in a daze, got out and walked in the direction of that building. Rayf thanked the woman. He hugged the two kids and said, "Hey, now don't you worry about your uncle. He can take care of himself."

The kids bounced from seat to ceiling.

She smiled graciously and then drove off down Elm. He stood there for a moment watching them go then turned to follow his friend.

Cal had crossed over Elm and was now approaching the grassy knoll in front of the School Book Depository when Rayf saw them. Cutting across Dealey Plaza not fifteen feet behind Cal was Ali Baba. Cal, staring up at the sixth floor window and thinking about his hero's tragic ending, did not see the other man stand up on the grassy knoll directly in front of him. It was Soapy. Cal was in a vise.

Before Rayf could warn him, Ali Baba had Cal's arm twisted up behind his back, and Soapy grabbed him under the other arm. He was taken without a fight.

Instinctively, Rayf looked around for an escape route. What should he do—fight or flee? Fight? With what? What if both of them were caught?

What then? He ran back up Houston and took a left onto Main. He stopped. Now, with back to building, he peeked around the corner.

Ali Baba yanked up on Cal's arm and said, "One wrong move and I blow you away right here jest like dey did ta J.F.K."

Cal obliged and kept walking towards the now infamous building and the large, black, rented Lincoln parked in front of it.

Ali Baba and Cal got into the back seat. Soapy was the driver. The Lincoln pulled away, and no one but Rayf was the wiser.

He leaned against the building staring blankly towards the old courthouse on the opposite side of the street.

He had to do something, but what? His mind went blank. And then a name flashed: Billy Wolf. He grabbed hold of that thread, and with it came the Seminole Indian's words: "You had better make up your minds boys, panthers or sheep, which one you be?"

He walked up Main Street past the crush of people and large buildings that reminded him of New York City—smaller, but taller than anything he had seen since Canal Street in New Orleans.

What he saw here was a city in mourning. People were going out of their way to be kind to one another, trying to ease the pain that the proud residents of this town felt; the sadness was tangible—he could feel it.

Walking towards him was a man wearing a sandwich board. He expected it to read: Eat At Tex's, but instead it read:

We are Virginians no longer.
We have now to live for America.
We had a loyalty; we have a loyalty;
Virginia knows us; she will know us forever.
But we are Americans once more and must not
Dispute about it.

It was signed: General Robert E. Lee.

Here are some words that need lots of circulation, thought Rayf as he continued alone up Main Street.

It was four-thirty before a plan started to form.

Safety pin, public phone booth.

***

He called long distance information and got the number he was looking for. The long distance operator connected him.

Two rings later, Angela picked up the phone. "Hello."

"You've got a collect call from Rayf. Will you accept?"

"No operator. I will not." She hung up.

Two minutes later the phone rang again. It rang five times before she picked it up.

"Hello."

"You've got a collect call from ..."

"Angela?" interrupted Rayf.

"Yes. I'll accept."

"Angela, this is Rayf."

"I know who it is. What do you want, Rayf?"

"What's happenin' with Cal?"

"What do you mean?"

"They got him."

"I know."

"Your father?"

"Yes. They phoned him about fifteen minutes ago."

"What're they gonna do with him?'

"What do you mean?"

"What are they gonna do with him?"

"They're going to take him back to Jersey City."

"And?"

"As far as I know, my dad is going to speak to him tomorrow."

"Where?"

"At his office."

"When?"

"Why all the questions?"

"What time?"

"Noon. Why?"

"Angela, how many people know why Cal is being chased?"

"Rayf, what is this all about?"

"Angela, how many people know?"

"Know what?"

"You know what."

After a pause, "Me and Cal?"

"That's it?" said Rayf.

After a very long pause, Angela said, "Only dad, me, and Cal. Why?"

"And I'm number four." There was a moment of silence. He spoke again,

"If you don't tell your father the truth, I will bring in ten guys from the corner who'll claim that it was their kid."

"You bastard."

"The truth."

"It is the truth," said a cocksure Angela.

"You had better be there tomorrow at eleven-thirty, tomorrow morning ..." said Rayf.

"And what if I don't show up, tough guy?"

With perfect timing he said, "I already told you."

"You wouldn't do that. I know you too well."

"You wanna try me?"

There was no answer.

Now he said, "I will be in Miranda's at eleven-thirty tomorrow morning with a whole crew of guys who are going to swear up and down that it is their kid if ..."

"You wouldn't do that. You know better."

"So, you're calling the bet."

No reply.

"Angela, your father is gonna have to kill half the neighborhood in order for you to have your kid." The silence on the other end was deafening. Now quietly, yet confidently, "Angela, do you hear me?"

After a sweating pause, Angela mumbled involuntarily half to herself, "Eleven-thirty?"

"That's what I said. Either you are in Miranda's at eleven-thir ..."

"Rayf!"

"Do you hear me?"

And now, through a sob, he heard her say, "Yes, I hear you." She hung up.

He was standing in Dallas with a dead phone in his right ear and not one cent to his name.

Then it came to him.

Once more he dialed long distance.

"Yel-low, Rag Doll. Jimmy here."

"Jimmy, this is Rayf."

"Rayf! How the fuck are ya?"

"I'm OK. I think. Look, Jimmy if you don't do this I'll understand, but ..."

"Try me."

"I know you told me to lose your number and all ..."

"Spit it out."

"The way I figure, I got ten days pay comin' to me. Now, you don't have to pay me after what happened. I understand. But I was wonderin' if ..."

Angela, meanwhile, wasted no time in calling La Madonna Del Lume Convent.

***

The 707 from Dallas Fort Worth International landed at Newark at eight a.m. Jimmy met Rayf at the terminal.

"Happy Thanksgiving," said Jimmy.

"Yeah, same to you," said Rayf.

They headed to short term parking.

"I'm just liftin' ya to your car. I don't wanna be around when the fireworks start."

"That makes two of us," said Rayf with vapored breath.

"You look different somehow," said Jimmy as they walked towards his '62 Mercury; a lot leaner maybe."

"Yeah, like about fifteen pounds leaner."

"I still think you're crazy for coming back," said Jimmy over the roof of his car.

"Jimmy, either a panther or lamb be. We all make the choice."

"One thing's for certain, though. You still talk crazy."

***

Back at the apartment, nothing had changed: greasy skillet and dirty dishes in the sink, bed unmade, windows open, bird bell still on the line,

He ran the hot water, took a shower, and shaved. He laid out his clothes and dressed in the tribal garb of the neighborhood.

Like a gray cloud, Rayf's Chevy floated towards downtown. On Newark Avenue, the Manhattan skyline came into view; he was home.

He parked the Chevy across from Miranda's, got out, and walked up to the corner to where the group of eternal hanger outers gathered forever.

"Hey, you guys," said Rayf, "coffee?" They didn't need a second invitation.

"It's about time you're buying," said Punky.

"The wanderer's back," said Dr. Benny. "Where's your pal?"

"Around," said Rayf.

"You got a smoke?" said Punky.

"Here," said Rayf, tossing him a Cigarillo.

"What's this shit," said Punky, flinging it into the gutter.

"Where you been?" said Chubby.

"Miami, New Orleans, Dallas."

"No shit?" said Anthony, fixing his hair. "Did you get to see where the president got killed?"

"Yup."

"With what money?" said Chubby.

"None of your business," said Rayf.

"I know where you got your money."

Rayf looked at the little weasel.

"Beaks called and told me to get the seventy-five he lent you in Viginia."

"Seventy-five!?"

"Yeah, he told me to put in a little collection fee for my troubles."

"Get it from Cal," said Rayf.

"Where is he?"

"If he was up your ass, you'd know."

Punky shrugged it off with a witty retort, "Fuck you."

"It's a miracle no one knocked you off out there," said Dr. Benny.

"They tried."

"Ya know," said Anthony, "you look better skinny."

"Thanks."

"Yeah, you look like you starved out there," said Chubby.

"I'm on a diet," said Rayf as he walked stone-faced towards Petey's place. The hanger outers followed.

Parked behind a truck and watching from across the street in her newly repaired powder blue Corvette, was Angela. Sitting in the bucket seat next to her, working a set of rosary beads to beat the band, was her Aunt, Sister Camille.

The crew walked into Miranda's. Rayf ordered seven coffees, one for himself, four for the followers, and two for a couple of guys already in there.

It was Soapy in the back room who first heard it. He jumped up and looked through the peephole.

"It's Rayf," said Soapy to Pete. Cal lifted his weary head.

"Get him in here," said the boss.

Rayf looked up at the Coca Cola wall clock. Soapy entered the room at exactly eleven twenty-five. He walked towards Rayf, stopped, and said very softly, "The man wants to see ya."

Soapy grabbed him by the arm.

He snapped away from Soapy's grasp. "I know the way."

"Easy does it, toughie," said Soapy for show.

Pete was behind his desk. Cal was tied to a chair over in the corner and sitting right next to him, with feet propped up on the card table, was Ali Baba. He waved a clenched fist at Rayf.

Soapy closed the door.

"Rayf," said Pete. "You, of all people; how can you hang out with a guy like this? For Christ sakes, you're heads and shoulders above him. As a matter of fact, you've got a head on your shoulders." Soapy and Ali Baba laughed. "You let me down, Rayf."

"Petey," said Rayf very casually. "I have something very important to say." Cal's eyes went from friend to foe.

"Speak."

"In private."

"This *is* private," said Petey with an all-encompassing sweep of his arm.

"This is very personal," said Rayf.

Soapy eyed Ali Baba. Ali never took his eyes off Rayf.

Capo Pietro weighed the moment before telling Soapy to frisk him. Soapy searched, then said, "He's clean boss."

"Good. Now you and the Babs wait out front until I call for you." The two thugs left the office, leaving Rayf, Cal, and Pete alone.

"Cal," said capo Pietro, "I am doubly disappointed in you. You who had everything going for yourself—knocking down four hundred a week. You had it made. Half of the kids on the corner'ed give their mothers for what you had. And you blew it."

"Petey, what are you gonna do with him?" said Rayf.

"Since when do you ask me questions?"

Rayf swallowed hard. He felt the stars above his head, he could smell the cedar smoke from the fire and, off in the distance, he could see the wild ponies on the prairie and hear the natural life and death struggle of the wild. He felt strong and knew the way.

"I believe you have the wrong man, Mister d'Alloro."

There was no visible change in capo Pietro's demeanor other than the flash of red which Rayf saw right there in his left eye.

"Do you realize what you're saying? The implication? The consequences?"

"Yes. That's why we needed to talk in private, sir."

The boss, stunned, started rubbing his smooth chin with his left hand. The clock over capo Pietro's head read eleven twenty-nine.

Pete squinted as he studied Rayf, who was in sharp contrast to the road-filthy Cal. "What do you have up your sleeve, Rayf?"

Just then, there came a very delicate knock on the alley door. Pete got up and looked through the peephole.

Cal gave Rayf an "are-you-out-of-your-fuckin' mind?" look.

Rayf shrugged back with a "hey, it's a shot, you got any better ideas?" look.

Pete opened the door. And there, framed in the doorway, stood Angela with her aunt, Sister Camille.

Cal was baffled.

"Camille?" said Pete. "What the hell are you doing here?"

"Watch your tongue, Peter."

"Excuse me Camille ... it's just that ..."

Sister Camille barged in with Angela in tow.

"Camille, what are you doing here with my daughter?"

"My niece," said Camille, closing the door.

She looked around at the three men inside, but showed no sign of disgust. Instead, she said, "Pietro, we need to speak of this family matter in privacy."

"You can speak here," said capo Pietro.

"We ... is you, your daughter, and I," said a woman accustomed to wielding a ruler.

Pete opened the coffee shop door.

Out there he saw the six hanger outers along with Soapy and Ali Baba, all of whom turned to look back at him. He looked at each and every face for what seemed to him an eternity.

A slight nod; Soapy and Ali Baba responded.

Ali Baba, the tough, sauntered in, but upon seeing the nun, made a very quick sign of the cross and bowed his head in respect. His look, if properly read, said: What the hell is going on in here?

Soapy, on the other hand, looked as if he had seen a ghost. His look said: Holy shit, I'm caught.

But all of their looks went unnoticed as Pete, with back to everyone, was walking to his desk.

"Soapy, Ali," said a very controlled Pete, "take these two into the alley and wait until I call for you."

"Right boss," said Ali Baba, grabbing Rayf's arm. Soapy took Cal's. Angela lowered her eyes as Cal and Soapy walked past.

***

It was November 28th; the blue moon was just two days away.

~ 17 ~

WEDDING DAZE

The sun shone on the church side of the street.

The rice was at the ready.

Somewhere off in the distance, over a car radio, the Beatles could be heard singing, "She loves you, yeah, yeah, yeah ..."

Wedding bells pealed. People in their Sunday best jockeyed for choice position. White Cadillac limousines were parked tight to the curb, and black-suited chauffeurs gathered in groups. Inside, an organ played "Here Comes the Bride."

It had taken only nine days for the festivities to commence.

Invitations that were not to be ignored at any cost were sent by phone. A vast crowd had gathered.

It was Saturday, December 7th. Only seventeen shopping days till Christmas; twenty-two years since Pearl Harbor; and, for Angela, her twentieth birthday and wedding day all rolled into one.

Two men across the street within the shadow of a dirty, black train trestle watched the proceedings.

A locomotive from somewhere in the direction of the Hudson River yanked a line of freight cars. The sound of steel-on-steel reverberated from the train tracks above.

Instinctively, Cal looked up towards the sound as he used to when sitting in his Holy Cross grammar school classroom across the street. Back then, he would look out that school window, trapped inside with some nun, while outside, on that thirty-foot-high granite bulwark across the street,

282

long lines of freight trains would roll past. Up on that wall—that looked to the kids like the Great Wall of China—boxcars, coal cars, tankers, and flatbeds would roll off to exotic lands. Cars by the names of Baltimore and Ohio, Pennsylvania, Southern Pacific, Rock Island Line, Erie Lackawana, Illinois Central, Santa Fe, Union Pacific, and The Rio Grande, would come and go. Cal, the trapped student, would remain.

Back then, he actually had enough imagination to transport himself across that street to share in a cup of coffee with the railroad guys on their break in their cozy little red caboose. But sometimes, even before he could put in his third spoonful of sugar, Sister Thomas would slap him back to reality with a heavy hand or a stinging ruler.

Cal turned his gaze from the dirty train trestle overhead to the gathering crowd in front of the church.

The organ played on.

He looked at the old granite church with its dirty, stained-glass windows and thought how close he had come to being the poor sucker in that monkey suit right now, walking his last mile. "There but for the balls of you go I," said Cal to Rayf standing next to him.

"You owe me one," said Rayf.

The mob across the street went wild as Angela emerged with raised veil; the baby within her womb moved with the noise. Next came Sister Camille, then her brother Pietro, his fiancé, his counselor, his soldiers and their wives, and last but not least came the groom.

The groom was in a daze, protecting himself from the rice and cheering throng with his one good arm. Angela, his glowing bride, grabbed hold of his slinged arm and, like a princess, waved to her subjects; the prince was in shock.

"I wonder who she'll name it after," whispered Cal.

"Probably your psychiatrist," said Rayf, as he pulled a white envelope from his back pocket.

Wha'd'ya got there?" said Cal.

"You're a nosy bastard. Know that?"

"What's in it?"

"It's a wedding favor from Petey," said Rayf, waving the envelope under Cal's nose.

Cal, trying to snatch the envelope from Rayf's hand said, "From Petey to you?"

"To us," said Rayf, pulling it away.

"Get outta here!? For us!? He gave us a gift? You gotta be kidding?" Wrestling for it he said. "What'd we get?"

"Knock it off," said Rayf, stuffing the envelope down into his crotch.

"Come on, man; what is it?" said Cal, backing off.

"We got us two one-way tickets to California."

"California!? Get out!? Really? That's great! One way!?"

"That's what they say."

Back at the church, the photographer continued snapping pictures of the newlyweds. Now he was posing the family, modeling and shoving them this way and that.

"Gimme my ticket," said Cal.

"Bullshit. I got 'em, I hold 'em," said Rayf.

"Let's get outta here before I start crying," said Cal.

Just as they were about to leave, Rayf said, "Wait up!"

"What's a matter, now?"

"Where's Ali Baba? I don't see him."

"Maybe he's too sensitive."

"How come he's not here?"

"How do I know? Maybe he wasn't invited."

"Wasn't invited!?" After a pause, "I don't know, maybe I'm just ... You're right. Forget about it. Let's go."

"When are those tickets for?"

"Six o'clock tonight."

"Six!? Hey man, I got a thousand things to tie up. I can't leave that fast."

"You do what you gotta do. It's your life."

"Shit," said Cal, as they walked towards Rayf's car.

Rayf had his car parked in the alley on the opposite side of the granite bulwark. The alley that once served as combination playground/schoolroom to these inner city kids was actually a one-lane dirt road that ran between the backyard sheds of decrepit houses and that granite railroad wall. In this alley, they would practice field and track skills like climbing up telephone poles onto the old ramshackle sheds and garages and jumping from roof to roof, or shinnying down clothesline poles into the backyards where they would then study agriculture by robbing a tomato or digging up a radish, as some tenants had gardens; most raised nothing but weeds. This is the alley where they studied sex education from Cowboy Sam, the old wino, who would trade refundable beer bottles for peeks at his girlfriend Maggie-the-Bum's tits. This is the alley where they learned the skills of math by shooting craps, or playing three-card ante or automotive repair, which also included courses on how to hot-wire cars. This alley, with backyards on one side and a thirty-foot-high granite wall on the other, served as a training ground for the streets. And right now, this thick granite wall was the only thing that separated Rayf's car from the church and the people across the street on the opposite side.

As they were just about to turn into the alley, Rayf grabbed Cal by the arm and pulled him back.

"Hold it!" said Rayf.

Now with their backs against the granite wall, Cal said, "What the hell's wrong now?"

Facing towards the other side of the street, Rayf said, "I found Ali Baba."

"Where?" said Cal in a whisper.

"He's messin' with my car."

They peeked around the corner just in time to see Ali Baba very gently closing the gray Chevy's hood.

"Wha' d'ya think he's doin'?" said Cal.

"Can't tell from here."

Job finished, Ali Baba hurried back down the opposite end of the alley towards Bushwick Street on the far side.

Rayf and Cal ran back up to the corner. The happy revelers were still milling around in front of the church when Ali Baba emerged at the Bushwick Street end of the block and crossed over to join the celebrants. He moved into position near capo Pietro, they conferred briefly, and he melted into the throng of well wishers.

"Wha'd'ya make of it?" said Cal.

"Let's go and see," said Rayf.

Rayf and Cal reached the primed-gray Chevy in fifteen seconds flat. Very gently, Rayf lifted up the hood and looked inside. There were six sticks of dynamite tied to the ignition switch.

"Man, we can't go in this bomb," said Rayf.

"Was that supposed to be a joke?" said Cal as he peered into the engine's well.

After a moment of cheek-biting thought, Rayf said, "We, my friend, are about to die."

"You're out of your fuckin' mind, man. I ain't dying. I'm too young to die."

Immediately Rayf went into action: he grabbed a broken bottle, climbed onto the nearest shed and proceeded to cut down the lowest clothesline.

"What the hell are you doin' up there, man?" said Cal in a hoarse whisper. Rayf didn't answer, but jumped down with the rope. At his car, he opened the gas tank and stuffed the clothesline into it.

"You're not gonna ..."

Rayf pulled out the gasoline-soaked clothesline, opened the hood, and tied one end of it to the six sticks of dynamite.

"Say goodbye, Cal."

The wedding party was posing, the photographer snapping; the bomb went off.

Angela jumped, "What was that?"

"Probably our one-gun salute," said Soapy, the not-so-slippery groom.

Ali Baba and the rest of the boys laughed; Pete turned his head to avoid the prying gaze of Sister Camille.

Now smoke could be seen coming up over the great, massive, granite Wall of China from the alley beyond.

One of the invited guests yelled, "Somebody call the fire department!"

***

Later that day at the site of the investigation, the police would find one singed envelope with two one-way airline tickets to California made out to the names of Tom Califano and Ray Falcone.

***

On the shoulder of the road, near the on ramp to the brand new New Jersey Turnpike extension, just a few blocks west of the Holland Tunnel and a notch above Hoboken stood two hitchhikers aiming thumbs south.

"Besides your life, you owe me a car, too."

"Bullshit. It was your idea to blow it up."

"Did you have a better plan?"

"Not at the time. But I would've come up with something."

"Yeah, maybe like this time stealing Petey's car, right? How much money you got?"

"Enough," said the other.

Just then a 1958 five-seater, hard-topped Studebaker Golden Hawk pulled over.

The strains of Bob Dylan singing "Don't Think Twice, It's All Right" were heard escaping from the eight-track within.

The young female driver leaned across the bucket seat and yelled out over the music, "Where you boys off to?"

"California," shouted Rayf.

"I'm going to Philadelphia. You could catch the Pennsylvania Turnpike there and take it out to Route 66, that'll take you right into L.A.," said the pretty, yellow-haired driver.

"Thanks," said Cal as he held the door open for Rayf to climb into the rear.

Rayf shook his head and said, "Chose ya, man."

Reluctantly, Cal balled up his right hand into a fist and put it behind his back. Rayf did likewise, and on the count of three they let fingers fly; Rayf called even, Cal odd. The fingers totaled four. A long-faced Cal climbed into the rear. Rayf took shotgun and closed the door.

The Studebaker peeled out and negotiated the long New Jersey Turnpike entrance ramp that rose steadily above downtown Jersey City. They drove through a dark plume of smoke rising from some one hundred feet below.

The smoke was hardly noticeable for the Jersey City smog.

***

The State of New Jersey resembles an American Indian chieftain looking westward. Were Chief Jersey actually alive then, Jersey City would be located near his limbic system, that region of the brain which controls the four F functions necessary to insure the well-being and continued survival of the species: fighting, feeding, fleeing, and sexual reproduction. The city of Camden, on the other hand, would be located nearer the region of Chief Jersey's heart.

Two hours later, the Studebaker Golden Hawk, with its passengers Rayf and Cal, blasted out of Camden, New Jersey, heading west into the sunset.

The driver lowered the volume and said to the two young guys, "Namaste."

THE END

www.ingramcontent.com/pod-product-compliance
Lightning Source LLC
Chambersburg PA
CBHW051245260626
47162CB00002B/621